# SOMEDAY, MAYBE

Also by Onyi Nwabineli

*Someday, Maybe*

To learn more about Onyi Nwabineli,
visit her website, onyi-nwabineli.com.

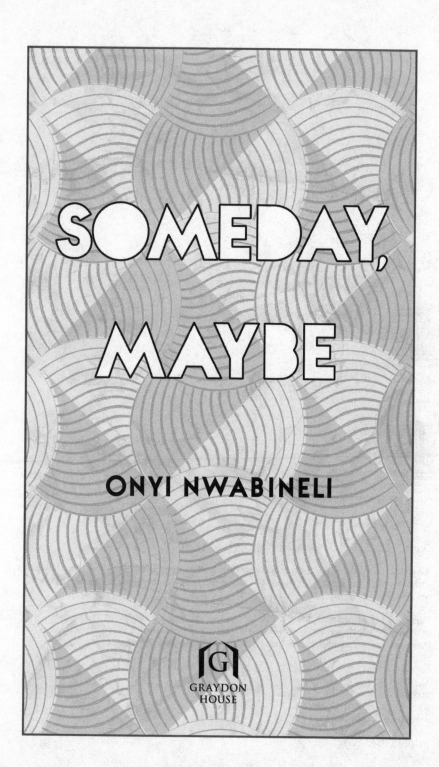

# SOMEDAY, MAYBE

## ONYI NWABINELI

GRAYDON
HOUSE

GRAYDON
HOUSE®

Recycling programs
for this product may
not exist in your area.

ISBN-13: 978-1-525-89980-5

Someday, Maybe

Graydon House
22 Adelaide St. West, 41st Floor
Toronto, Ontario M5H 4E3, Canada
www.GraydonHouseBooks.com
www.BookClubbish.com

Printed in U.S.A.

For my parents, the beginning.
For J, the end.

# SOMEDAY, MAYBE

# PROLOGUE

Around the time my husband was dying, I was chipping ice from the freezer in search of the ice cube tray wedged in the back. But only because I was taking a break from filling his voice mail with recriminations about his failure to communicate his whereabouts. The memory of this along with countless other things would weave together the tapestry of blame I laid upon myself in the days and weeks after his death.

Therefore, in the spirit of continued honesty, here are three things you should know about my husband:

1. He was the great love of my life despite his penchant for going incommunicado.

2. He was, as far as I and everyone else could tell, perfectly happy. Which is significant because…

3. On New Year's Eve, he killed himself.

And here is one thing you should know about me:

1. I found him.

Bonus fact: No. I am not okay.

# HOME

# 1

I read somewhere once that going through a breakup is like experiencing the death of a partner. They called it a "kind of bereavement." While there are certain similarities—the spontaneous tears, the despair, the need to press items of clothing to your face and inhale the lingering scent of your beloved—this sentiment is incorrect. Bullshit. Well-meaning, perhaps, but bullshit nonetheless. Of course death trumps breakups. Always. How could it not?

Death makes it impossible for you to demand a list of reasons for the demise of your relationship. Logging on to Instagram to stalk his profile reaps a hollow reward; there will be no updates, no new faces, no experiences lived without you. Your beloved is frozen in time. There are no relapses, unplanned nights of passion wreathed in nostalgia followed by bittersweet, awkward mornings where you navigate the putting on of clothes, suddenly aware your jeans are ripped, your underarms unshaven for the past three weeks.

But the worst thing about death, the thing that makes the comparison laughable, almost cruel, is there is no chance of reconciliation. With death there are no do-overs. No drunk-dialing snowballing into hour-long reminiscences that end in reunion—the kind of sheet-tangling makeup sex that makes you stop in your tracks when you are besieged by a flashback. This isn't something that can be forgiven with a kiss.

With death your suffering is permanent.

When someone you love dies, there's this period of disbelief—a time of dug-in heels, the refusal to process your new reality. A preamble to real Denial, which brings its falsehoods and proclamations of *It's not true* and *Not you, girl. Someone else.*

I spend the first two days after Quentin dies pacing the house, twitching curtains to watch the parade of visitors arriving only to be sent away and dodging the arms of my family, who, after the police finally ceased their questions, begin asking their own. "How could this happen, Eve?"

"Did he have a doctor, Eve?"

"But you saw him that day, no? How did he seem, Eve?" *Eve, Eve, Eve.* My own name becomes a curse. I have no answers for them.

Then, when I learn that there is to be a postmortem, the emotional duct tape keeping me together finally gives way. I take to my bed like a consumptive Victorian lady. And so here I am. I can no longer miss him like I have been, like there's an end in sight. I am no longer suspended in that terrible limbo. He is gone. The house is silent, his noises conspicuously absent. He is not coming back. The realization keeps hitting me, clubbing me over the head, pounding away at the back of my skull.

It would have been a lot easier to just break up with me. But Q was nothing if not thorough.

In the film *Run Lola Run*—one of Q's favorites and eventually one of mine—Lola, the red-haired heroine, sprints through the streets of Berlin in a bid to procure an obscene amount of money to save her hapless boyfriend, Manni. She runs because she has only twenty minutes to secure the cash. During her mad dash to save a man whom, frankly, she might have been better off leaving to perish, she bumps into strangers along the way. The best thing about this film and one of the reasons Q fell in love with it is that we, the viewer, are shown flash-forward sequences depicting the futures of those Lola meets. We are privy to the consequences of Lola's fleeting interactions with these people and they are often lovely or sad. It's a wonderful thing to watch and watch it we did, repeatedly, never tiring of Franka Potente's questionable late-90s fashion or the way we felt when the credits began to roll: spent, like we had done the running ourselves, but also sort of grateful.

I slip our well-worn copy of *Run Lola Run* into the DVD player (because Q insisted that DVDs could live alongside streaming services in perfect harmony) and watch it start to finish in a continuous loop. And I imagine a series of alternate futures for Q and myself; futures where he lived like he was supposed to. In my little scenes, there are the usual things most married couples imagine for themselves: trips and birthdays, house improvements and career advancements, but mostly I dream of simple things like calling in sick to work so we can spend the day in bed or having someone handle the spiders who act like they pay rent. It's a future full of moments like this I would sell skin to have back.

I focus on the back of Lola's head as she races around a corner and ignore my sister, Gloria, who stands beside my bed with a plate of food I won't eat.

"Eve," she says, "this has to be the sixth time you've watched this today, love." Her voice is gentle. A voice that has quelled a thousand toddler tantrums and stilled courtrooms across the country. She is right to use it here. My behavior is bizarre, and what people cannot understand, they fear, more so when five days prior, the person in question was able to dress herself and form coherent sentences.

I say nothing but reach under his pillow and drag out Q's sleep sweatshirt—a gray thing with frayed sleeves. My stomach bottoms out as soon as I pull it over my head. Wood and soap and the slightly acidic tang of photo-developing chemicals—his own scent. I curl into a ball, desperately pressing the sleeves to my nose, wishing I could conjure him back into existence, and when I start to cry, Gloria draws the duvet up and curls around me until I fall asleep.

To grieve is to frighten the people you love. My behavior seems to have scared my husband's name right out of my family's vocabulary. They treat me like a patient afflicted with a nameless disease. But patient or not, they do not leave me in peace.

"Please try," Gloria stage-whispers from my bedside. Two days have passed since I took to my bed and I have neither spoken nor moved. "Ma is constantly speaking in tongues. If you get out of bed, she'll stop."

My mother loves Jesus. Therefore, she does not get stressed; she gets holy. Straining, I can hear her milling about the kitchen uttering a stream of spiritual gibberish. She must be beside herself. I respond by wrapping Quentin's sweatshirt around my face. Gloria eventually disappears. But not for long. Since I ignore all the advice offered to me—to eat, wash, move—since this particular case of misery eschews company, and since Gloria pioneered Nigerian guile, she sends in my niece and nephew to hold my hands and stare at me with wide eyes until I am moved to sit up.

I drag my heavy limbs into the bathroom, where I spend half an hour in the shower, trying to sluice the cloying stench of loss and sadness from my skin. Using your own children as soldiers to fight your emotional battles is the type of tactic that will see Gloria rule over us all one day.

As I exit the bathroom, I hear my phone ringing and I can be forgiven, can't I, for thinking, just for a second, that it's him. My mind races for the familiar. I know Quentin is dead. But I fall into that gap between reality and memory. I forget about the police and the blood, and my husband's lips—lips I had kissed mere hours before—cold, blue and lifeless. The time I have spent sweating under our duvet evaporates. He is on his way home, swinging by Sainsbury's to pick up a cheesecake in lieu of dinner because he is a man and, as such, lacks the gene that produces common sense. Nobody tells you that irrational hope is a side effect of grief. And they should because it is dangerous.

I run into our bedroom, calling his name, voice made bright by the mad, delusional happiness rearing up inside me; felled when I reach my phone and see Aspen's name flashing on the screen. The mistake hardly warrants my reaction, which is to pause as I understand that it is not, in fact, my husband, but the person I would rather remove my fingernails than address, and then I scream for so long Dad calls in an emergency prescription of diazepam. These are the perks of having a doctor for a father. Hands on my shoulders and my wrists wrestle me from the floor to my bed. My towel slips. My scream turns to a howl.

It turns out you can only scream for so long until you extinguish your own voice. Mine burns itself out like a spent match. I turn my back on my family, who have congregated around my bed and are watching me with matching expressions of horror and helplessness. I am exhausted, but as always when I close my eyes, sleep dances out of reach.

When Dad returns, it is with two pills, which he presses into my palm. I let him hold my hand while I swallow them dry and I wait for darkness. When it comes, I step into it, gratefully blacking out as Gloria calls Dad from the room.

"She's going to have to speak to Aspen, eventually. She's his mother."

# 2

Tragedy. The great equalizer. My extended family have been informed. Far-flung cousins who, in the Before, filled my WhatsApp with sporadic pleas to cover school fees and requests for the latest Apple gadget but asked little of my general well-being are now offering obligatory condolences. Now I am the one to be pitied. My grandma, when I refuse to pick up the phone, insists that Ma carry her own to my bedside and press it to my face so she can utter exhortations in Igbo.

"Okay, Nnenne," I whisper back.

My phone flashes so often, I am treated to my own personal light show on the ceiling of my bedroom.

Here in the After, where my life is one excruciating open wound, bitterness has started to creep in and pills are my only relief. Ma, who never liked pills, who used to struggle through headaches and twisted ankles with nothing but a pained expression and a prayer on her lips, passed the aversion, along with her hips, to me. The aversion died with Q. Zopiclone provides the type of dreamless sleep I crave. It kills my thoughts and wipes out great chunks of time. The days start blurring together. The Eve of Before would have worried about her supply running low, but my GP, summoned by my parents to the House of Mourning, filled out a repeat prescription and disappeared, worried that my misery might cling to her coat.

Dad doles out my prescriptions, an assortment of antianxiety and sleep meds. He is head of neurosurgery, and because sickness does not stop for compassionate leave, he arrives at the house late, his jacket over his arm. He rations his energy and uses the last of it to check on me. Whenever he enters a room, I calm down, if only for a moment. It has always been this way with us—his proximity directly proportionate to my peace.

Tonight, he rubs my back while I gulp back my pills. I want to thank him for always waiting until I fall asleep before he leaves. I should tell him his presence is an emotional salve. The *shoulds* are already stacking up; this time will be rife with them, colored with remorse and vital things that remain unsaid. He hums until I can no longer hear him. Mercifully, I slip under.

My family keep everyone at bay. The news will have spread throughout the congregation of my parents' church. Prayer circles are being held to bring my plight before the Almighty. Dad and my brother, Nate, have stationed themselves by the front door, a duo of sentinels seeing off the pushier of the well-wishers, the ones who don't understand *She's not seeing anyone right now* and *Thank you so much, but she's not up to it.* I'm out of it most of the time while remaining oddly aware of a new sternness to Nate's voice, and the increasing force with which the door is shut.

Ma, a veteran handler of business, brings me meals I don't eat and tries to knead feeling back into my feet. On the days it's just the two of us, she sits and reads for hours, and without opening my eyes, I know she is peering at me over the top of her book or laptop, holding her breath while she waits for the confirmatory rise and fall of my chest. She has chosen to ignore my current dependence on prescription drugs and Googles the hell out of natural remedies for grief, and when she stumbles upon a cache of articles claiming that nuts are the juggernauts of serotonin, she aways to Holland & Barrett, and the next day, I can't take a piss without stumbling past a bowl containing walnuts, almonds or cashews. But I don't open my mouth for anything other than pills and bawling, and eventually she sends Gloria to try instead.

Gloria is worse.

She begins by trying to tempt me from my stupor with tales from the world of corporate law, salacious office gossip I would have eaten up pre-tragedy. When this fails, she segues seamlessly into emotional blackmail: "Your niece and nephew miss you, Eve. So do I. Say something. Ma and Dad don't know what to do." Her final attempt involves simply talking to me as if I am a responsive and eager participant in the conversation. She will have read this online somewhere— *regale the partner of the deceased with distracting and jovial anecdotes; make sure the partner of the deceased understands he or she is needed and loved.*

Gloria's intelligence, temerity and inability to tolerate bullshit have brought her all her successes in life: as a lawyer, as a wife and as a mother. Failing so consistently to bring a smile to my face must be a terrible blow to her ego. But grief destroys. A wrecking ball that crushes your ability to enjoy. She has, I reason when the guilt nibbles at me, a living husband and perfect kids. She will be fine. The jury is still out on my own chances.

Quentin is gone and this, his persistent absence, should be the worst thing about losing a spouse. But—treat of treats—I have the added bonus of a searing, unabating, viselike guilt, a result of failing to notice he was in danger of being lost. So I lean on medicinal support like a crutch. And because the world insists on continuing to turn even though your grief necessitates it pause, if only temporarily, eventually, inevitably and despite your best efforts at avoidance, Aspen finds a way in. She arrives on a night when the pain of lying in a half-occupied bed has become too much and I am roaming the house in darkness.

Quentin's ghost stalks me on these nights. I glimpse him disappearing around corners, hear his chuckle bouncing off the high ceilings. He refuses, however, to speak to me, which is rich considering how all this is his doing. I follow him past the second-floor hall window that looks down onto the street and see a car idling by the curb. It is two twenty-six in the morning, and despite Battersea's gentrification, another chunk of London being consumed by froufrou coffee shops and new builds, I know none of our neighbors owns a Bentley.

Aspen.

I have been ignoring her calls for days, but something compels me to go down to her. Maybe it is because she has never been here before and I want her to see that this house is real, a place her son loved. Maybe it is because her unanswered calls have brought her to my doorstep and I want to look at her face and see whether she, too, is drowning, undone by grief. Most likely it is because nobody is there to stop me.

Outside, my bare soles move silently against the pavement. The cold snakes its way inside my clothes and underneath my skin. Aspen rolls down the rear window as I approach. Her face is half in darkness. I examine her profile. But it isn't like I am in her presence enough to determine whether she has undergone any drastic transformation. I, on the other hand, look and feel like I have been turned inside out; the person I was no longer exists.

Aspen being Aspen does not let me speak. She does not even look at me. Her voice is tired but hard.

"You've been ignoring me," she says.

"I— Aspen, what are you doing here?" The cold has worked its way up from my feet and is wrapped around my ankles, anchoring me to the spot.

"Quentin was not a man who would just kill himself." Aspen has never been one for small talk.

And there it is. Confirmation I am not alone in the cruel, unannounced, unexplained bombshell of Quentin's death. There had been no signs for me and none, it seems, for Aspen either. She is as clueless as I am, as tortured as I will ever be, and I have no words for her.

Only then does she look at me. "Did he not leave a note?" And with those words, I fully appreciate her desperation. She has been driven from her bed, propelled to my door by a need to know if her story is different from mine. But even though we are bound together by the same wretched narrative, I can see her wrestling with herself. She will not beg, not even for this.

"There was no note, Aspen." She is about to contest, but I add, "I didn't get one either. He left nothing."

Her face closes. She turns from me and looks forward. "I will never forgive you, Eve. You have cost me my son."

She rolls up the window until I am staring back at my reflection. A moment later, her driver slips away from the curb and the car rolls off into the night.

For a long time afterward, I cannot get warm.

Quentin's best friend, Jackson, is the sole person aside from Aspen with whom Q maintained a relationship when he fled his former life of ballrooms and blue blood. Jack is a kind-hearted adrenaline junkie who sends us a Fortnum & Mason hamper every Christmas, and travels the world looking for new and weird ways he could possibly die. His Instagram page features him (usually shirtless) after he's hurled himself from the precipice of some mountain or some such foolishness, with a caption that reads something like *Sao Paulo: #FeelTheRush #Grateful #RiskTaker.*

It is because of Jackson's healthy disregard for life and death that I have given him the Aspen treatment and ignored all his calls since Q died. Irrational, I know, but by rights, he should be the one on a slab somewhere. What a terrible thing to think. But grief torches your capacity for both sympathy and empathy. I am nothing but a selfish collection of exposed nerve endings.

A memory of "that night" flares. Jackson roaring up in a fucking Bugatti of all things. Already delirious with panic and pain, all of it cutting through his New Year's drunkenness. He looked like a lost little boy.

I vow to answer his next call. And I do, knowing it is not a completely selfless act.

"Eve. Shit, I didn't think you were going to— I've been calling."

"Hi, Jack. I'm sorry. I just haven't been— It's been really hard. I'm sure you know."

"Listen, I want to come over. If you're up to it. I… I can't stay here. I keep thinking about him and that night and I—"

"Jack," I cut him off. "Did he leave you a note? He didn't leave me anything." It is hard to push words past the lump in my throat. Jackson is already crying.

"I'm so sorry, Eve. No, I didn't get anything. I looked everywhere, but there was nothing. I keep expecting something to turn up in the post or something. I promise you I didn't know he was… I should have seen it. I'm sorry. I'm sorry."

Another memory. Jackson stumbling from the car and falling to his knees even as I sat, numb and blood-soaked, with my legs hanging out the back of the police car.

I choke out an apology and hang up the phone, too weak to carry Jackson's guilt along with my own.

A week. My husband dies and seven days is all it takes for things to begin to shift. It manifests in the moods of the people around me. For outsiders, the atrocity is limited to knowing I am hurting. For them it ends there. And I can't blame them. They have their own lives and for them the nightmare is already over. They are able to return to normality. There is a door they can close. The sound of the doorbell no longer fills the house, the Tupperware containers are washed and returned to their owners. The calls from well-wishers dwindle and then stop, but my phone still rings endlessly. Aspen. I ignore it. Gloria's lamentations about my refusal to speak to Aspen become more pointed. So I ignore her, too.

I pinch my skin to distract from the sting of Aspen's incessant antipathy. I piece together a thousand rejoinders, arguments designed to beat her into submission. Q loved me. He married me. We were happy. These arguments crackle to life within me and fizzle out just as quickly. Q left me. *I* was happy. I was also blind. A marriage now characterized by my ignorance. She has something nuclear to add to her arsenal. I will never be allowed to put distance between Q's death and my guilt.

Husbands are not supposed to die in real life. Not when they are thirty-three years old and healthy; not when they leave behind a wife who is struggling to cope. The future is this huge, yawning black thing I can't see into. Before Q died, I could see our retirement house clearly—a *Grand Designs* concoction by the sea with rooms stuffed with books and photos. I could hear the waves. Now, when I try to set my mind forward, everything is blank. A mere fortnight ago, I was a woman with a husband who filled her world with shiny, pearlescent moments. I am now a woman with bloodstained jeans and hollow eyes, one who screams at her sister and frightens her mother and cries so hard it makes her choke. A woman being garroted by grief. A woman asking, *How did I get here? How the hell did this happen to me? Is this something I even deserve?*

# 3

You don't grow up the daughter of two high-achieving Nigerians without learning a few things about perseverance and the art of long-suffering. My parents packed up and shipped out from Benin and landed in London ready to live out their Igbo dreams and give us the best British life had to offer. This meant academy schooling. Gloria and I in the girls' chapter of St. Jude's and our brother, Nate, in the boys' down the road. You know the sort: pleated checked skirts, Latin lessons, stiff blazers and a coterie of rich white people who think they are better than you and laugh at your Jheri curl because you look like Lionel Richie as you trudge dejectedly through the polished halls. School life was a study in abject misery. I was one of ten Black kids at St. Jude's, a school of over eight hundred. Gloria was another. The others were in the years above me and we locked eyes as we passed one another in the halls, our expressions conveying our shared abhorrence at being shut up in such an establishment every day.

Our parents thought they were doing the right thing. Nigerian parents don't leave much room for failure. Your options as a Nigerian child are success or greater success. Mediocrity is to be cut out like a cancer, your pliable loin fruit molded into world-class surgeons and lawyers through discipline, a diet high in roughage and the best education a combination of government funding and extortionate school fees can buy.

I was already something of a shrinking violet, doing my best to remain anonymous and invisible, unlike Gloria, who commandeered the captainship of both the lacrosse and field hockey teams and braided her hair, meaning she did not leave smears of Afro Sheen on every surface she encountered. But St. Jude's made me fold into myself like an intricate piece of origami.

"It's like you *want* me to be miserable," I complained to Ma from the kitchen floor, where I had thrown myself after failing once again to convince her to pull me out of St. Jude's and allow me to attend the local comprehensive. Ma, who was waking up at 4:00 a.m. every day to hustle to a lab on the other side of London to analyze samples for her PhD thesis, eyed me in a way that made my blood freeze in my veins.

"First of all, am I your mate?" she asked. "Oya, pụa n'ebe à! I said get up! You don't lie on the floor in a uniform your dad and I paid for and tell me I want you to be miserable. What is making you miserable?"

The thing is you can't just *tell* African parents about your school troubles. Ma and Dad were breaking their backs to give us the best and to disparage St. Jude's would be to pour scorn on their efforts, to demonstrate your position as ungrateful offspring. They assumed St. Jude's to be free from the problems plaguing state schools. They were wrong—it only meant I got bullied by kids with tighter accents and double-barreled surnames. I also knew how these things worked. Parent-teacher meetings would be called and would do nothing but leave Dad grave and Ma shrill, readying herself to rain down the righteous fury of every indignant mother who has ever had to go to bat for her kids. So, I kept my mouth shut.

"Go and face your books and don't let me hear your mouth again this night." Ma would frown, but she'd still pat my Jheri curl as I trailed despondently out of the kitchen.

Gloria tried to teach me how to fight, but my attempts were pathetic in a way that infuriated her and exhausted me, so I spent my time either with my limited circle of friends or hiding out in the library with Ms. Collins, the fuck-free librarian who gave me books I was technically too young to read. Around the time I discovered books and computers were enough, puberty discovered me, bringing with it a pair of hips and a six-inch growth spurt to balance them out. Suddenly I had a pair of boobs nestling underneath my school shirt, a set that may not have been of Gloria proportions but still moved liberally enough for my sister to haul me before our mother and demand I be taken shopping for a reinforced bra.

"It's almost pornographic, Ma," she'd hissed, gesturing at my chest. *"Do something."*

It was unfair. It was more body than I knew what to do with. I was unused to the male gaze, comfortable in the shadows, sneaking through life unnoticed and unbothered. I had, like Gloria, discovered books on Black feminism, much to my sister's delight, who thought I ought to use my blossoming ass to torment boyfolk of all kinds.

"You should join the field hockey team," Gloria said at the behest of her coach, who had also clocked my new height and the thickening of my thighs.

"What? No." The thought of spectators watching my behind bouncing up and down on the hockey pitch was enough to push me toward cardiac arrest.

"It's fun. You get to hurt people without getting into any real trouble," Gloria said, excellently impersonating a psychopath.

"No."

"Marcus Raines has rugby training at the same time." This piqued my interest. Marcus Raines was the hazel-eyed object of adolescent female lust from ages eleven to seventeen. Gloria registered my interest with disgust. "I was kidding. Leave that boy alone," she warned as we waited outside the school gates for an aunty-but-not-really to swoop by with Nate and pick us up. But these, like so many of Gloria's sage words, fell from her lips onto my newly braided hair, rolled off and plopped into the dust by our feet as we climbed into the car.

In the end, the only thing that kept me from Marcus was my own shyness compounded with a crippling awkwardness I hid behind the autobiographies of great women Ms. Collins recommended.

The point is this: I was unprepared for Quentin when I met him at nineteen. I took a place at King's College to study English and digital media (I could do this without guilt as Gloria had dipped and twirled off to Oxford to study law) and combined my love of books with an aptitude for Adobe Creative Suite. Until Quentin, university for me could be summarized as a series of questionable outfits, evenings spent reading Dostoyevsky by lamplight (because I was an idiot who thought it romantic when what it was was the catalyst for my now diminished eyesight) and realizing I could stay out until four in the morning without any ramifications more serious than weathering the inevitable battle to stay awake during lectures. Limits were hazy and could be traversed with the right amount of gumption and liquid courage. I was still shy, still self-conscious of what I looked like from behind, but I had an expansive vocabulary and access to cheap shots at the student union. Anything seemed possible.

I had clumsy sex for the first time with a boy named Dane, who had large hands and pawed at my chest like he

was trying to commit the swell of my cleavage to memory.
I dated him half-heartedly because for me, wallflower ex-
traordinaire, nothing about sex was casual. I even grew fond
of the way he would arrive at my campus room every Friday and pretend to care as I cut his hair and told him about
my week. On campus I did as much reinvention as I could.
I wore butt-length braids, I swore a lot. I tried but failed to
become the hard drinker university students are expected to
be. I started bandying about the phrase *patriarchal stultification*
and befriended a group of radical feminists who signed me
up to a debate team.

I wasn't ready for Q. He was not someone that was supposed to happen to me.

On the day I met him, I left Dane sleeping in my room and
headed to Tesco for the obligatory replenishing of cheesecake
and cheap lasagna—my staples once the food Ma forced into
my arms whenever I visited home ran out.

That he approached me at all instantly made me curious.
The few boys brave enough to spit whatever lackluster approximation of game they thought they had were met with
laughter or a hail of verbal missiles from my friends. I was
an introverted girl, easily tongue-tied, but I imagine I came
across as standoffish and I intimidated the majority of boys,
cowed as they were by the sight of me striding across campus, braids swinging.

Quentin materialized at my side as I scrutinized the frozen dessert selection. I didn't notice him right away. I tossed a
New York–style cheesecake into my basket and moved along
and it was only then I realized he had been standing there
barely breathing and staring at me with an intensity I had
heretofore only associated with those on campus who had
discovered hard drugs.

I moved to fresh produce.

Moments later, there he was.

Look, I'll just say it. He was gorgeous. Not just gorgeous, beautiful. Almost painfully so. I dug deep for a scathing comment but was rendered speechless by his eyes—the color of an unsullied ocean, the kind you see in travel brochures advertising islands you have never heard of.

"Hi," he offered and matched the word with a hint of a smile so beatific it actually made me angry.

"You're following me," I snapped.

"I am," he agreed amiably.

"White men don't follow Black girls around supermarkets unless they suspect they're being robbed."

"Interesting theory."

He was familiar. Of course he was. People who look like Quentin looked don't roam the earth unnoticed. However, he was not a plainclothes security guard but a fellow student.

I sighed. "What do you want?"

"Um. Well, I was hoping you could help me choose the right kind of pepper for—"

I cut him off. "What makes you think I know anything about food shopping?" I indicated my basket. "Or is your assumption that because I'm a woman, I should know about groceries?" This was the person I was back then. That I hadn't once again been ostracized by my peers was nothing but God at work.

Q took great pains to assure me that wasn't it. "I'm going to attempt jollof rice and—"

"You what? You're making jollof? For what exactly?"

"My Visual Culture class is having a potluck and we have to choose a dish from someone else's—"

I could not stop interrupting him. Me, a person who went to school in a place that made me swallow my own voice. "So it's not only that I'm a woman but because you assume I can cook jollof?"

He scratched the back of his head and my heart hiccupped. "I think it's more because in your last debate, you said that just because you can make the best jollof rice this side of London doesn't mean you, under patriarchy, should be compelled to do so. I'm not compelling you to do so. Just so you know."

I had said that. In an impassioned diatribe to my debate teammates in a half-darkened lecture hall we had been fairly certain was occupied by no more than six people, most of whom had come to ogle Cynthia, our stunning ringleader.

I helped Q locate the Scotch bonnets.

He said he had "noticed" me on campus because he thought "my cheekbones would photograph well" and he wanted to be the one to take that photograph. I remember laughing at him even as I snatched glimpses of his ocean eyes. His game was a limping, struggling thing, but I liked the way he looked at my face, like it was the only thing he could see. We made a second circuit of the supermarket, and even though I hated how intrigued I was, I was riding the wave of lust he rode in on and now there was intrigue in my sails.

"So, you should let me," he said when we were outside.

"Let you what?"

"Take the photograph. Of you."

I searched his face for signs of bravado, but he was swinging his backpack onto his shoulders, looking more nervous than I felt. "Alright," I said.

I changed my mind the next day as I sat in my lecture and resolved to tell Quentin as soon as I saw him, which I did unexpectedly quickly. He was waiting for me outside my classroom when I was done.

"Hi," he said and handed me a biography of Judy Garland. He saw the expression on my face and he flushed, redness creeping up his neck and cartwheeling across his cheeks. "I...

I saw you had the biography of Billie Holiday in your bag yesterday, so I thought maybe you'd like this."

A boy. Bringing me books. Wanting to photograph me. It was too much.

"I do," I told him. "Shall we go?"

His off-campus student digs consisted of one long room with bare, paint-flecked floorboards and walls filled with Polaroids and prints of his own shots. Even then his talent was a wild animal refusing to be tamed, but his confidence was still tightly furled inside him. On the way over there, I'd battled with myself, trudging alongside him wondering what Gloria and Imani, my most feminist friend, would think of me. I didn't pull shit like this. And look, I get it. There's nothing "empowering" about capitulating to a dude with pretty eyes and a killer smile, and had Q's teeth been crooked or his skin acne-scarred, there is an excellent chance I would have sprayed him in the eyes with Tabasco sauce in Tesco and gone on my merry way. But beauty does something to us all. If a beautiful person demonstrates interest, it is as if we've been given a gift, and right now, I was the girl with all the damn gifts. I was shallow. But I was also nineteen.

"Look," I said to him as he unlocked his front door, "this doesn't seem..." I did not finish my sentence because he smiled a smile I felt on my skin and below my waistline. It was a wrap.

He sat me on a stool and took my photo, and afterward, he showed me my face on his computer screen and asked me if I wanted him to cook me something.

"The jollof?" I asked.

He blushed. "I thought I might make something different."

"So you actually cook?" I asked.

"For you, I cook," he replied.

Over inexpertly prepared pad thai eaten cross-legged on his floor, he talked his way into my life. I learned he was one of *those* Morrows, Britain's less ostentatious answer to the Rothschilds, and suddenly his expensive student housing made sense. He was studying photography and digital art. He wasn't flashy. His voice faltered more than once, like our conversation was an interview, an oral exam for admission into my world. It was like he dipped his hand past the buttons of my shirt and snatched out my heart. He never did give it back either. *You need chairs*, I told him. *I'll buy chairs*, he responded before gently curling his fingers against the back of my neck and kissing me. We talked some more. We kissed again. Eventually we fell asleep on the mound of body pillows he had the audacity to call a bed, and in the morning, I woke first and took the opportunity to commit his face to memory. Later, with my shoes tied and my glasses back on my face, I idled by the door, wretched. Was I simply a conquest? A box to be ticked? What came next? The thought of this being a onetime occurrence made me sick to my stomach. Q asked me to wait while he buttoned his shirt, and in the age it took him to cross the room, I tasted a hundred flavors of rejection.

Then he laced his fingers through mine.

Dane was apoplectic.

"The fuck you mean?" he thundered when I finally mustered the courage to tell him a few days later. "You're leaving me for some white boy?"

Quentin leaned languidly against the doorjamb and dared Dane with his eyes to do something. Dane considered it, but his pride more than his heart was bruised. I would be forgotten in a month, swapped for a girl who looked at him like he was the sun.

Like I said, it was unfair. Dane never stood a chance. Nor did I for that matter. Q and I. We fell in love without preamble. My premature cynicism about him began to erode almost immediately. Because Q seemed so sure about everything: that we would love each other forever, that we would get married, that this was it for him. I trusted him because he had given me no reason not to. We had sex for the first time on his body pillow bed and I got not one but two splinters in my behind, which he tweezed out as the late afternoon sun dropped behind the London skyline. For once, I was unconcerned with eyes on my body; I loved the way he looked at me, like I was too good to be true. The time we spent apart lessened by the week until my clothes were stacked in the corner of his room and his photographs lined the walls of mine. By week three, we were spending every night together. By week six, my friends, angry and baffled by my desertion, staged an intervention, which Q gatecrashed, bringing beignets and charming them all. Fucking beignets. That boy.

We would laugh as we'd fold ourselves around each other in my minuscule bed, ending up, no matter the position of the mercury, sweating after a night's sleep. He asked me to read to him a lot. So I read him *The Virgin Suicides* and he bought me biographies about the wives of famous men. He was artfully disheveled in that way the very wealthy often are. Although his efforts seemed a tad forced. The untucked shirt that his fingers strayed to tuck in before he remembered that was the entire point. Right from the beginning, he suffered infuriating lapses in sense that left me staring at my phone with mounting irritation, waiting for him to text, only for him to appear hours later, his face open and beaming. He was always thrilled to see me and his smile would falter; he could never understand my annoyance.

I didn't say a word about him to anyone at home. Not even Gloria.

By week twelve, there was a ring on my finger. I said yes without blinking. The night he proposed, we drank lukewarm wine straight out of the bottle and had giggly, fumbling sex in

a deserted train station on the outskirts of London. I wanted
to run away. Get married on a deserted beach somewhere ex-
otic where hibiscus grew and the sand would be white and
hot between my toes. I wanted to wear a sundress and wed
with my feet in water the color of Quentin's eyes. Mostly, I
wanted to escape so I wouldn't have to face my family and
tell them I was marrying the boy I had known for five minutes. And he wasn't even Igbo.

"Relax. You've known me at least seven," the bastard said,
because when it came to us, he somehow knew things would
work out. As I threatened to float away on a storm cloud of
worry, he grabbed my ankles and tugged me back down to
earth. "You'll regret it if you get married without your family there," he said.

He was right. Plus, he was fascinated by us. He was an only
child and I could see the envy in his eyes whenever I spoke
to Glo or Nate on the phone, the sad little smile on his face
when he heard me telling my parents I loved them. He wanted
to be part of something new, something warm. He wanted
more than weekly calls with a mother who treated his voca-
tion like a pipe dream, a silly display of youthful defiance. He
had so much love in him and had swiftly run out of places
to put it and have it reciprocated in a way that made sense to
him. So, because he graduated a year before me, we made a
deal that we'd get married the day after my own graduation.
And we did. In a "small" ceremony with two hundred guests
(listen, a normal Nigerian wedding has upward of five hundred; this was tiny by comparison). I remember Dad decked
out in his smart black-and-gold Isiagu, Nate winking at me
from his place beside Jackson. Ma managed to keep it together.
She was mentally listing all the friends and extended family members to whom she would have to explain—playing
out the exclamations of sympathy she would get from her
friends when they realized her girl was marrying the hand-

some oyinbo who had rushed her into marriage at the tender age of twenty-one.

"Are you worried," Q asked one evening, "about marrying me?"

"Damn right I am. Every feminist worth her salt outlines the perils of partnering with men and here I am. Risking it all because of lust. ọ bụ ihe ihere—that means *it's disgraceful,* by the way."

He laughed. "No, but seriously. Did you think you'd end up with someone like me?"

"Nah. Definitely not. And I know my parents didn't either. Dad has probably phoned his sisters back home and told them to call off the search for a prospective Chigozie or Nonso."

"It matters to them? That I'm not Nigerian?"

I kissed his face because there is no easy way to articulate what it means for your loved ones to worry that your person's ability to love you is limited by their inability to comprehend many of your lived experiences. "What matters is that I'm happy."

He caught my head in his hands and kissed me back. "We can start a YouTube channel."

"Interracial content? Swirl Tube? This is what it's come to?"

Q had the best time at our wedding. He loved the culture of it all, surrendered himself to Dad and Nate to be fitted out for his traditional wear for the native law and custom. He laughed the loudest, prostrated even though that is a Yoruba custom, and never once let the sound of Aspen's whispers and tutting wrinkle his mood. He took photos of me as I stood outside the church. I saw him arguing with Aspen at one point, but he didn't bring any trace of the fight back to our table. We spent a week in Hawaii, traipsing up and down the beach, locking ourselves in our hotel room and tasting salt and happiness.

My wedding dress was an ivory prom dress we found on sale at Debenhams, much to Ma's and Gloria's shock and dismay.

It still hangs in my wardrobe alongside his suit, a pair of unwearable memories, a reminder of what was, what could have been and, now, what never will be.

# 4

Today, Nate administers my sleeping pills, holding them out of my reach until I sit up.

"I don't want you to choke," he explains.

Nate was a surprise baby. After two pregnancies during which her ankles swelled to elephantine proportions, Ma decided two was enough. But four years later, Nate happened and was named after Dad. He careened into the world silent and blinking and he hasn't changed much. Our love for him has, since his birth, been paired with the knowledge that there are times when small acts of violence seem like our only recourse. As he dangles the pills above me, it is as if I have never felt this sentiment more acutely.

Nate understands that his burly presence and ineptitude when it comes to serious personal matters help nobody, so he has limited his role to assisting Dad in keeping visitors away from me and helping me to the bathroom. This, the temporary role of pharmacist, is an important one, and I appreciate his efforts but still threaten bodily harm if he doesn't hand over my pills. He drops them into my hand, passes me a glass of water and produces his iPad.

"You don't have to stay," I croak at him.

He eyes me levelly before replying. "Yeah. I do." He goes back to his iPad and I return to my pillow.

When I open my eyes again, Nate is on the phone. I can tell by the way his foot is tapping that he is speaking to Cleo, his girlfriend. She is a blisteringly beautiful PR officer who, for the duration of their year-long relationship, has been plotting when she can eject Nate's best friend, Everett, from the Walthamstow flat they share, and take his place. Nate is handling this by ignoring it. It is not that Nate doesn't love Cleo; it is that he doesn't love her enough to capitulate to cohabitation.

Cleo is unsure what to do with the uncomfortable fact that Quentin is dead. She phoned once to offer strained condolences and, duty done, now spends her time pretending she is not upset that Nate is spending so much time at my house. She is not a good actress.

"Sometime after seven," Nate says into his iPhone. "Nah, I don't, you know. Shampoo launch parties ain't exactly topping my list of priorities right now." He pauses. "Her husband is dead, Cle'. Perspective, yeah?" He ends the call and catches my eyes. "Sorry. Didn't know you were awake."

I roll onto my back and stare at the ceiling for a few seconds, waiting for the pain from his blunt yet accurate assessment of my situation to abate. "You should be happy you have someone to fight with."

"Yeah? How come you and Q didn't do it more, then?" He goes back to his iPad.

"Nate," I say.

"Yeah?"

"Get out."

"Why for?"

"I'm about to cry and we both know it'll be awkward for the both of us if you're here when it happens."

He begins to protest but thinks better of it. Before he leaves the room, he doubles back to the bed and scoops the top half of my body into a hug. He smells like Nate: Creed cologne and new leather with a hint of protein shake. I stay in his arms, limp as a rag doll, until he gently lays me down and leaves. I cry myself back to sleep.

When I wake up, Nate is back in the chair with his iPad.

"Nate?" I rasp from beneath the covers.

"Jesus, you scared the shit out of me."

"You should go see Cleo. She misses you."

"Why are you trying to get rid of me?"

I say nothing.

"You going to cry again?"

I say nothing.

"You okay?"

"No. I feel bad that you're here when you didn't do anything. You didn't kill him. Everything is still normal for you. Your life hasn't changed." It is not lost on me that this is the closest I have come to talking about Q since Aspen's visit.

Nate returns his gaze to his iPad. "You're my sister. Your life changes, my life changes," he says, and this time, I don't even have the chance to tell him to leave. He sets his iPad aside and sits on the edge of the bed. I feel the gentle weight of his hand on the back of my head. He doesn't say anything. But Nate rarely does.

When Nate was eleven, Gloria deduced that he was being bullied at school. It was the little things she, hypervigilant even then, picked up on—the torn shirts that were attributed to playing sports after school, a split lip explained away by good-natured roughhousing in the changing rooms after

PE, Nate's reluctance to expound on the list of friends he insisted he had. Gloria was no stranger to it. Before Glo was Glo, she had endured her fair share of adolescent spitefulness at the hands of her blonder, more popular peers and as a result she was wise to the bullshit. While our parents toiled away at their jobs and their studies, too busy and exhausted to think their son could be lying to them, Gloria was logging evidence and playing Sherlock Holmes; because Glo was now Glo, she made other people's business her own. I cried when she shared her observations with me. And Glo let me cry because she knew it was only a matter of time before my tears dried up and I became incensed—she needed that, needed us to be united in our anger.

"What are we going to do?" I demanded of her.

"*You're* going to keep your mouth shut, understand? Don't go grassing to Ma and Dad. You know what it's like."

I did. I stayed quiet but made it a priority to be a little nicer to my brother, pushing the last drumstick onto his plate at dinner and ironing his school shirts with mine. He would cut his eyes at me as he accepted the shirts back, but I would brush it off like it was nothing, like I was doing it out of boredom rather than a pressing need to let him know he was loved and not alone. "Don't make a big deal out of it, Junior," I'd say to him. He'd roll his eyes.

Gloria confronted him one evening after an oblivious aunty dropped him off after cricket practice. That was one thing you could say about Nate; he might have been getting his arse handed to him on a daily and painful basis, but he was damned if he wasn't going to soak up every last one of those private school perks, and a spot on the cricket team counted as a perk. Gloria asked him where the graze on his cheek had come from, and right in the middle of his story about somersaulting into a wicket, she cut him off.

"Stop it, Junior. We *know*."

"Know what?"

"C'mon, Nate, stop."

"I dunno what you…" He stopped. You couldn't argue with Gloria. Once she had you cornered, you knew to cut your losses and settle your tongue.

He dropped the act, stood there with his backpack hanging off one shoulder, looking smaller and more forlorn than I could ever remember seeing him. Back then he was sporting a not insignificant amount of baby fat and a face that was downright cherubic. I remember wanting to cry so badly I almost bit through my lip.

"Don't tell Ma and Dad," he said. His voice matched his demeanour: defeated.

Snitching wasn't Glo's style, so instead she made a point of trying to turn Nate into her personal loser-to-hero story. She taught him how to jab, bob and weave, told him not to hit below the belt lest he get tagged as a bitch. *You're not listening to me*, she would shout at him, and he'd screw up his face at her. *There's no point*, he'd reply with all the weary knowledge of a child routinely getting his behind kicked up and down the school halls. *There's only one of me.*

I would sneak into his room after Glo had stalked away in disgust and I would sit there while he cried furious, silent tears and we wouldn't say a word, but sometimes he'd let me hold his hand.

"You're making it worse!" I'd yell at Gloria when we were back in the confines of our bedroom. I'd wait until she was at her most vulnerable, when she had just unhooked her bra or when she was trying to tie her headscarf.

She looked at me like I was stupid, then let her arms drop to her sides. "They'll kill him if he doesn't fight back. That's what you want?" She didn't wait for my answer before turning her back on me. "He has to stand up for himself."

We'd fall asleep livid with each other.

By some twist of fate, Ma was home early the day Nate came barreling through the front door with the arm of his blazer torn clean off. Gloria and I had tried to keep her occupied, even suggesting a trip to Brixton Market, but this made her suspicious—she knew we'd rather shave our heads clean than go willingly to drag back boxes of yam and plantain. She dropped the tea towel she was using to pat the spinach leaves dry when she saw Nate's face. His cheek was a swollen pulp of rapidly bruising skin and his lip was split, but a look of triumph blazed through his injuries. He faltered a little when he saw Ma standing there, her expression darkening by the second, but even with industrial-grade bleach, you couldn't have wiped the smile off his face.

Ma wanted details. Names, dates of birth and physical fucking descriptions. Even as she was pressing alcohol-soaked cotton pads to Nate's mess of a face, she was formulating the type of revenge only an African mother can exact. Nate, on the other hand, had abandoned his capacity to be anything other than jubilant. He was excited in a way we had not seen him in a long time, twisting out of Ma's grip and calling for us in a voice three octaves higher than his usual pitch. It went like this: he had been in the middle of a particularly brutal ribbing from the usual suspects, was being called all manner of pussies and bitches and fat niggers, when, at long last, he arrived at his breaking point. Before he could consider the consequences, he was hammering his fist into the face of the nearest Tristan or Tarquin or Rupert.

"I dunno what happened!" Nate was squeaking from behind Ma's fingers. "They were hitting me, too, but I was hitting them back. All of them! And I won!"

Ma lowered her hands. "Nathaniel, you *won*? This is winning?" Her accent, as always, became more pronounced when she was agitated or upset.

You couldn't kill his vibe, though. He shook her off and

presented his grazed and bleeding knuckles like they were individual trophies. "I won," he said with an air of finality.

After Dad got home and marshaled Nate into the living room for a long discussion, a conversation of which Gloria and I heard nothing no matter how hard we strained, after a family dinner fraught with tension and with all eyes on Nate's eye, now swollen completely shut, and after we were sent to bed so our parents could ruminate on how much they didn't know about their own children, Nate crept into our bedroom and sat cross-legged on the floor.

"So?" Gloria asked.

"So nothing. No punishment," Nate explained cheerfully. He grinned at our incredulity. "*Serious.* Dad asked what was going to happen with the boys I fought."

"What is going to happen to the little pricks?" I asked.

Nate giggled at my curse. "Nothin'. They asked me to kick ball with them tomorrow and Christian asked me to come to his house on Saturday."

Gloria stood up, brushed down her pajamas and kissed Nate on the head. "They're racists, Nate. Don't befriend them. The patriarchy is alive and well. You beat the crap out of a boy, and he invites you to play sport with him. If this was our school, those bitches would ruin our credit and tell everyone we were pregnant."

"Patri...patriar..." Nate was confused.

"She means you won." I smiled at him and he beamed back.

The new Nate had friends vying for his attention and so he no longer needed me to squeeze his fingers at night so he could fall asleep. But he never forgot. We'd formed a new bond, which, years later, brought him to my door an hour before he met up with the "pengest girl in school" to "jam." Glo had already imparted her advice—don't place too much emphasis on her looks but also compliment her on the complexity of her mind, to not touch her without explicit consent—but he wanted me to tell him whether he ought to wear his Kickers or his trainers, if I thought she liked him, *liked* him. You know, the important stuff.

"Relax, Junior," I told him. "Maybe she won't notice you're a neek."

He gave me both a dead arm and a hug before he shut the front door.

Sometime later, Nate leads Bee into my bedroom. I chalk her presence up to a side effect of the pills and I stare right through her for a minute before closing my eyes and turning away. Nate kisses his teeth.

"Eve."

I roll over and she is still there, looking at me with doe eyes full of sadness. "Bee?"

"Didn't you tell her I was coming?" she asks Nate.

"You try telling her anything," he says.

Nate leaves for work and Bee kicks off her Pumas and climbs into bed with me. She lifts my head into her lap and tells me I have every right to be broken by this, gutted by it. And there are no sweeter words than those spoken by your best friend when you are in the thick of it, when you feel this pressure in your chest, like your lungs are meting out each breath only after careful consideration of how it will be used. Being consumed with missing Q means until now, I hadn't realized how much I missed her.

Bee rocks away the tension in my body and I fall asleep, my head still on her thighs. When I wake up, she has moved to the window, smoking one of the cigarettes she was meant to have given up months ago.

"Those things will kill you," I say.

"We all have to go sometime," she quips, catches herself and stubs out her cigarette in the bottom of the coffee mug she's holding. She moves back to the bed, tilts her head. "God, babe, you look like shit." Her voice is laced with tenderness.

I would like to admit to her that sometimes in the dead of night, I slip out of bed and into the living room, log on to my laptop and reread all the emails Q ever sent me. I want to own up to lingering on the one he sent me the day before our wedding, the one that reads *Promise me you won't regret this*, and I want to tell her that sometimes my guilt manifests itself physically in my throat and I start choking on it. I made him regret it, made him regret me. And as much as I loved him, that was not enough to keep him here.

But I say nothing. This is not what people want to hear from the bereaved.

She purses her lips at my silence and switches gears, lifting her dainty foot onto the bed and examining her pedicure. She is sun-kissed and beautiful, an inky-haired heartbreak. "I'm so sorry it's taken me this long to get here, babe. When I finally got Glo's texts, I had a nightmare changing my ticket. Then all flights were grounded for days. 'Inclement weather.' I ended up flying from Buenos Aires via Istanbul to get here sooner. I got in last night and came straight here." She is jet-lagged and shattered, but she is here. And without complaint. "Tell me what you need."

"I need someone to be as sad as I am."

"I hear you're not taking calls from the one person who is." She means Aspen and I'm not yet ready to cross that rickety, bitter-ass bridge.

"Have you been talking to Gloria?"

"Well, duh. You don't pick up the phone."

I am no longer capable of smiling, but if I were, I would do so now. "I don't want to talk to her."

"Gloria?"

"Snowdrift." This is the moniker Bee assigned to Aspen after having the misfortune of meeting her.

"Who do you want to talk to?" she asks.

I turn my head on the pillow and face her. "My best friend."

"I'm here."

I face the ceiling again. "He's gone."

Before she can answer, Ma knocks and steps into the room. She tucks Bee into a quick hug, something passing between them. "How are you, Belinda?" She will never refer to Bee as "Bee." I asked why once and she said, "Is the girl an insect?" Case closed.

"I'm great, thank you, Aunty," Bee replies, all manners and smiles. No doubt she was high and topless twenty hours ago, but now she is polishing her halo for my mother.

"You look lovely," Ma says. "Maybe you can convince Eve to eat a little something. I fried plantain."

"Don't do this, Ma. Don't rope Bee into your crusade for calories," I whine.

"You have to eat. Tell her she has to eat."

"You have to eat, babe," Bee says.

"Judas."

Ma strokes my forehead. "You need to eat something before you take your medication." She says it like I am popping an amoxicillin or two, fighting strep throat and not downing sedatives to escape the torturous reality of my life.

I struggle into a sitting position and Bee plumps the pillows behind me. Ma brings me a plate and they sit on either side of me, Ma with the plate in her lap, Bee with a glass of water in hers. I am spoon-fed like a toddler and I manage eight mouthfuls of rice and plantain before I declare myself full and, mercifully, the pills are dropped into my hand.

"You're not going anywhere, are you?" I murmur to Bee as I start to drift.

"No, she's not," Ma answers for her. "Belinda, come downstairs and take some tea."

I'm falling again, stepping over the edge into the soft, temporary oblivion of sleep. Before I land, I ask Bee, "Are you sad he's gone?" but I'm asleep before I hear her answer.

# 5

Before Quentin died, the worst of my dreams concerning him involved him coming to his senses, realizing he was a demigod to my mere mortal and abandoning me for someone worthy. Like Beyoncé. Or Aphrodite. Which is stupid and clichéd and ultimately a complete crock because, lo and behold, I *was* the catch and here I am still caught while he is busy being dead.

I dream differently now. Blood, tears, featherlight kisses, the sound of his voice asking me why I could not save him. Memories mingle with dreams and turn to nightmares.

"Eve." Bee sweeps my hair out of my face. "Babe. Shhhh, it's me. It's alright. It was only a dream."

The sweat pastes my clothes to my skin. My heart is beating so hard I feel it in my throat. I don't wipe the tears from my face for fear of seeing Q's blood on my fingertips. I focus on Bee's face until my heart rate slows. She sits on the bed. There is a half-buttered crumpet in her hand, and she's removed her wig. The braids underneath are at least two weeks old. An unlit cigarette dangles from her painted lips. She's a vision. *I* would look like I was coming off a seventy-two-hour methamphetamine binge. Bee looks like she's strolled out of the pages of a *Vogue* fashion editorial.

"Come down to the kitchen," she says and waves the crumpet. "I was making breakfast."

My shaky legs slow our progress, but at the kitchen table, Bee slides a plate of bacon in front of me while she butters another crumpet. I may puke, but it is progress. I accept a mug of peppermint tea.

"Want to tell me about your bad dream?" she asks.

I don't. But this is Bee and talking might distract her from all the food she has prepared that I am not going to eat, so I try to explain about the blood tears and, despite how excruciating the dream was, how euphoric I was to be in my husband's arms again for a moment. Bee bends over me and wraps her arms around my shoulders until I regain composure.

"Look, babe." Bee sits, extracts two rashers of bacon from the pile and pushes them toward me. "You need to talk to someone. I mean, I'm here for you always, but there are, y'know, people who deal with this sort of thing."

"With husbands that kill themselves out of the blue?" I hope she detects the derision in my tone.

"With bereavement." Apparently, she does not.

"You want me to seek professional help?" There is no masking how much the very idea appalls me.

"I'm just saying," she presses, "I'm guessing you don't want to pour out your innermost feelings to your parents. Or even Gloria. Although, God knows that woman believes she can lawyer you into happiness."

It's not like she is wrong. I have completely absconded from my responsibilities. There are arrangements to be made and a death certificate to collect. My voice mail is filled with messages from the police, who need to speak to me, from Aspen, who... No. I need to start handling things, but breathing is a chore. Surviving, a continued effort. Carrying on with life is unconscionable. I have taken up my new full-time position of Professional Mourner. There is no room for anything else. And, I want to remind her, to remind everyone, it has been just over a week.

I stare blankly at Bee but say nothing. She knows she's pushed me too far. She squeezes my hand and gives up on campaigning for my consumption of pork products.

I head back to bed while she washes the dishes.


Unlike the majority of English graduates, I was fortunate enough to score a job right out of university that actually had something to do with my degree. Sure, it was at *Circle*, the most pretentious magazine to ever grace the shelves of your neighborhood high-end specialty store, a magazine catering to people (most likely bearded or spouses of the bearded) intent on crafting lives so far removed from the evils of everything mainstream, they needed recipes for nettle and chia seed preserves and instructions on how to arrange freshly picked carrots on their rustic picnic tables. And sure, *Circle* was still new enough that everybody was almost certain it would fail, but it was a job that combined copywriting and design, so when I was offered the position of online curator, I enthusiastically accepted and sat stone-faced while Gloria asked, "What the hell kind of twee-ass job is that?"

My days were spent working on the *Circle* website, writing blog posts, editing photos of bunches of lavender artfully displayed in mason jars and creating digital illustrations of the magic of thrift-store shopping. I was so good at it that in a little over a year, I became senior online curator. Nate would greet me with "Alright, sis? What's new in the world of burlap fashion?" but this was a small price to pay for the hefty pay raise I received—all of us had underestimated how starved for boho-bijou bullshit the people of the world were.

Bee breezed into my life one overcast Wednesday morning. She brought with her the scent of expensive hair products and menthol cigarettes, and an aggressive indifference about being liked. So obviously, I liked her immediately. I looked down at my desk (rough-hewn oak that gave me splinters but was in line with *Circle*'s shabby eco-chic aesthetic), and when I looked up, there she was being led through the office by Barry, our VP of Creative (and incidentally, at the time, the stuffiest, most insufferable man to ever walk the earth, but he has since transitioned into a kaftan-wearing, hemp oil–dabbing imbecile). She wore six-inch heels, a fire-engine red pencil skirt, a stud in her nose and an expression that said, *You are all beneath me.*

"This," Barry said, his tone almost reverential, "is Belinda Contois, our new art director. Let's all make her feel welcome with a Circle Hug."

Bee looked at him as if he had suggested public self-flagellation. "Oh, we don't have to do that. It would only end badly for all of us," she said and quickly scanned the room. "Charmed." Her voice was dripping with sarcasm. She spotted me stifling laughter at my desk and winked. My fate was sealed. I was smitten.

At lunchtime, she materialized at my desk. She had swapped her heels for Doc Martens and now she was tiny. She wore the smirk I would come to know as semipermanent. "Eve, yeah?" she said. "Lunch?"

I agreed because when it comes to Bee, it may take you a while to realize it, but you have no choice. She showed up at my desk every lunchtime for almost a month before I took her attempts at friendship seriously and it was only as we sat in the *Circle* cafeteria, her poking at a salad "so rife with nuts, I may as well be in a men's locker room," that I finally cracked.

"Belinda. At the risk of sounding needy, why are you interested in me?"

She grinned and I swear the heavens opened and poured sunlight directly onto her wig of choice that week—a raven, chin-length bob. "You're asking what I see in you?"

Her translation of my question brought home how pathetic I sounded. I picked up my book and pretended to nonchalantly leaf through the pages. "Just a question," I squeaked.

"You look like you hate the same things I hate," she said. She was wearing violet eyeliner. "Everyone needs someone who hates the same things they hate."

"That's it?" I replied. "You think I might dislike the same things as you?"

"I said 'hate,'" she pointed out, pushing her salad away. "Plus, you seem to be playing hard to get. I like that in a friend. And call me 'Bee,' would you? 'Belinda' is my mum's way of punishing me for not being born a boy."

I considered her as she produced a cigarette. Smoking was prohibited under *Circle*'s Wellness Clause, but Bee had made it clear she was not one to waste time with anything as petty as rules. "You're kind of scary," I told her plainly.

When she stopped laughing and her smirk was back in place, she said, "That will fade."

She was right. Both about the terror fading and her capacity for identifying people who despised the same things she did. Our friendship was forged on nights out after work, deriding Barry and the *Circle* mission statement over battered calamari and cocktails. Our mutual disdain for strip lashes and eye shadow brought us closer. I learned that she was the product of overbearing yet loving Guyanese parents. I marveled at the way she did not seem to earn respect but collect it, unopposed from every person she encountered. I was slightly jealous of her in a way that only made me want to do better.

When I think of friendships, mine and Bee's is the prototype. Which is why when she finishes the dishes, comes back upstairs and says my name gently, I respond by lifting one corner of the duvet and letting her crawl in with me, friendship intact.

Day Nine.

Nate and Bee are leaning against the bedroom wall watching me watch the ceiling when Gloria enters. She touches fists with Nate and says, "Wha'gwan?" and Nate responds with a pained, "Don't ever do that again."

"All this time and you still haven't come to terms with how down I am, Nate."

Nate sighs. "Glo. You're not down. You're a mum."

Gloria tilts her head in my direction. "What's happening here, then?"

Bee produces a nail file, which she points at me. "We're trying to convince her to get up, but she wants to lie there and look at the ceiling."

"Do none of you people have jobs? How are you always here bothering me?" I say without looking at them.

"It's Saturday, innit?" Nate replies.

"And the word you're looking for is *loving*," says Glo. "How are we always here *loving* you?"

"At least let me run you a bath, babe," Bee tries. "It'll help."

"Yeah, because the smell in here ain't it." My brother, ever the paragon of tact.

"Nice. Very nice, Nate." Gloria pulls the curtains open and pushes up the window. The light assaults my eyes.

"For fuck's sake, Glo. Can you not?" I moan.

"Listen. You either take a bath or I fetch Ma and Dad and have them call Kenneth Copeland Ministries to cast the demons of uncleanliness out of you. Your choice." She stands with her hands on her hips. How is it that in thirty-six years of life, she is yet to lose an argument?

"FINE," I growl through gritted teeth. "I'll have a bath."

"Thank fuck for that," Nate mutters.

In the bathroom, Q's toothbrush is minding its own business next to mine in the turquoise glass on the sink. I remember us standing in Boots; he'd shown up late to meet me, as always, and was now taking an age to choose this simple item. I was growing ever impatient, needling the fuck out of him.

"It's a toothbrush, Q," I'd said. "This type of decision doesn't warrant the focus you're giving it."

"You're lucky I love you enough to chew your food for you when we're eighty and you're toothless." My annoyance fell from me almost immediately.

I close my eyes until the pain recedes.

Bee and Gloria lower me into the scented water. They first detangle, then massage bubbles into my afro, and Glo runs a loofah over my back. It feels like it is stripping away skin as it moves. Perhaps I should be more self-conscious about my appearance—there are bruises on my wrists, shadows of my own fingerprints left after clutching myself for days, trying and failing to keep myself from falling apart. I let my hands drop into the water. It would be so easy to slip beneath the surface and join Q, a recurring thought since he died.

There is a timeline to all this. I only have so long to work my way to wellness, to reach "better" before my support system fades to black as they tire of me, of my sorrow. The outpouring of love from my family and friends, it's like a weight. Everyone means well, but I'd like a second to break free from the pressure to recover. But grief does not operate in a silo; it sucks everything and everyone into a vortex and the only way to escape it if you are not directly affected is to distance yourself from it. I glance at Bee. I am not ready for her not to be here.

Bee tips water over my head. Glo lifts my hands and trims my fingernails. When they help me out, the bathwater is gray.

"That's disgusting," I say.

"Who are you telling?" Gloria mutters.

During the night, Quentin's smell disappeared from the sheets. No gentle waft of him when I rolled over, not even a trace of him when I buried my head into the pillows. I'd woken that morning with my heart thudding erratically in my chest. I had considered screaming, but to what end? It was my fault. Stewing in your own misery and sweat for days will, it turns out, erase the scent of your husband from your pillowcases. Back in the bedroom, Ma has wiped surfaces, changed the sheets and set a scented candle burning on the windowsill. She kisses my eyelids. I spy new shadows under her eyes put there, no doubt, by me. Guilt slices through me. "Feel better?" she asks.

"I feel better," I say as firmly as I am able. I can give her that. "Thanks, Ma." I stifle my comment about the new sheets—any hope I had of getting the Q smell back is now draining away with the remnants of soap suds. When I think that, like this, other details of what it meant to be Q—the way his voice sounded first thing in the morning, his "thinking" face, the left elbow of all his shirts worn away to transparency—will continue to diminish in even my memory, it is like I have forgotten how to breathe.

She smiles. "A hụrụ m̀ gì n'anya." A new thing: being told how loved I am, as if there is a chance I might forget.

While Glo rubs lotion into my shoulders and Bee rifles through my underwear drawer, I assess the hollows in my cheeks, my protruding clavicles, the emergence of a thigh gap. Would Q even recognize me?

"Come on, babe." Bee approaches me with a pair of underwear in her hands. Her face is a study in pity. "Let's get you dressed."

# 6

Quentin was a big believer in escape plans.

His first included leaving behind a grand old heap, the specter of a semi-famous father and an unbearable mother, swapping his world of galas and old money for a life less lavish. His second was more permanent. He knew everyone needs a plan B. I learned this from him.

Aspen calls and I am barely awake and too dazed to remember I no longer take calls. My phone shocks the last remnants of sleep from me, and before I know what I'm doing, I hit the green symbol on my iPhone and she's breathing into my ear with such venom, I physically recoil.

It needs to be said that Aspen is not a nice person. Because she thinks she has dibs on suffering, she will expose every morsel of tender flesh before sinking her fangs in. Her default tone of voice is "hiss." She is not pleased I have been avoiding her because Aspen is not to be avoided; she is to be revered and her needs are to be met above all. I thought the incoming interaction would center on the night of the Unexpected Visit, but here she is taking it upon herself to explain the ways in which she blames me for Q's death. I am lying here in my marital bed wearing my dead husband's pajamas listening to all the ways I gave him no other option than suicide.

"I have never encountered someone so selfish." She adds another layer of ice to her voice. It works for her. "Do you think," she asks in a display of irony so potent it burns, "you have the monopoly on pain?"

She is the most stylish of pots calling the most bedraggled of kettles black. "He was my son. You barely knew him and yet you can't summon the grace to see how I'm doing?"

Aspen concluding that our almost three years of courtship and ten years of marriage amount to "barely knowing" Quentin encapsulates her opinion of me with pinpoint accuracy. It is laughable. So, I laugh. Hard enough to drown out the sound of Aspen's voice. I end the call mid-tirade and toss my phone across the room. No more distractions. Melancholy requires concentration.

Summoned by the clatter, Gloria walks in and plucks my phone—with its newly smashed screen—from the floor.

"You look annoyed," she says unhelpfully.

She has come from the gym and is glistening with perspiration and health and vitality. She is the anti-me. It makes me want to punch her. Gloria, with her Lycra-clad legs and her sports bag, with her angelic children and her living husband, makes me want to scream. I hate her in the way only a person whose life has ground to halt while everyone else's continues can.

Gloria urges me to talk to her, but there is nothing I can say that would not horrify her. When she persists, I tell her to get out, and although she remains calm, I see it there, an infinitesimal flicker of hurt in her eyes. She leaves, closing the door behind her, leaving me with nothing to do but play back Aspen's words. However, my mother-in-law is losing her touch, saying nothing I have not already levied against myself. Even as I watched the vehicle carrying the person who used to be my husband drive away in the wee hours of January 1, I was already thinking about how I was now a woman who would need to convince people about the validity of Q's and my relationship. Of its steadfastness. I was now tasked with talking up the joy we experienced. The days passed and brought with them the overwhelming sense of failure.

What is love if it misses that which drags your husband beneath the surface, never to be rescued? How could it be possible that the same Q whom I convinced to start taking multivitamins and drinking two liters of water a day is the one who agreed to these health-prolonging measures and killed himself anyway? This was the man who reminded me about my smear test appointments. The one whom I would catch staring at me with ill-disguised affection as I wrestled my legs into tights in the morning. I knew everything about him. That his left knee clicked ceaselessly after an equestrian accident at age nine. That he hated all mushrooms with the exception of shiitake. That he was mildly allergic to strawberries but ate them anyway because he didn't believe he should be deprived of the joy of a sun-ripened fruit bursting against his tongue even if it meant itchy lips for a couple of hours afterward. But perhaps I did not know him at all. That thought sits there, immovable, formed the night he died. Maybe he loved me only to a point. A point that did not include the comfort of confiding in me. And that has to be my fault, doesn't it? At who else's feet am I to lay that particular blame? Aspen thinks she beat me to it, but how could she? She wasn't the one who slid in his blood. God, it *hurts*.

Aspen can't be alone in blaming me. My family have been careful to drop Q from their topics of conversation. Do they feel the same? Do they carry their blame behind buttoned lips? Does Jackson?

Aspen calls again. I ignore her.

★ ★ ★

Quentin and I bought the house a year after we got married. We had outgrown his studio flat, which, sweet as it was when the alternative was a house-share with six other students in various states of inebriation, had lost some of its appeal as newlyweds who want to bone in more than one room. We searched for a while, but by the fourteenth viewing, I was ready to start playing in oncoming traffic and Q was even considering asking Aspen if we could move into the Knightsbridge apartment.

One day we slammed out of a minuscule one bedroom and stalked down Lavender Hill, eventually becoming lost in a tangle of residential streets. Already aggravated by Q's lateness, which almost resulted in us missing the viewing in the first place, my exasperation was compounded by us losing our way. While I consulted Google Maps, Q sidled up to a "For Sale" sign and instantly fell in love. We viewed it on the same day, and even though I should have run at the first mention of "character," Q was busy lusting after the scarred walls, bowing floorboards and something he called "the excellent, almost prismatic light."

That night, he handed me a bowl of the tom yum soup we'd picked up on the way home and said, "Well?"

"What do you mean, 'Well?'"

"The house, Eve."

"What about the house, Quentin?"

He took my spoon out of my hand and leaned over to lick the chili residue from my lips.

"Stop it," I warned.

"We have to buy it. It's perfect for us."

"It's perfect for people who can afford a mortgage. Q, be serious. I've just started at *Circle*, and the way they are over there, the likelihood is I'll be fired for not caring enough about green juice or arrested for aggravated assault if someone asks me again if my knitwear is ethically sourced. You've just set up your business. We can't buy a house."

Beyond the wage gap and the "debt chat," wealth disparity was not a topic I envisioned ever having to address in a relationship. But because I didn't push Q on many things, because he was cagey about his upbringing and I understood that his boundaries were valid and worthy of respect, and because I had read enough to understand that being financially beholden to anyone was dangerous, this—the purchase of property—was something I needed to interrogate more.

"I know you hate talking about money, babe," I said to his back that night in bed. Darkness softened everything, gave you a softer place to land. I inched closer and pressed my lips to his spine. "But we can't discuss buying a house without talking about how exactly we'd afford it."

"I'm asking you to trust me on this one," he said. He was already tensing, the subject matter pulling him away from me.

I refused to concede. I kissed his shoulder. "And I'm asking you to trust me."

He turned to face me, night pushing in from all sides. "I do trust you. I'm just not that person anymore."

"Which person?"

"Quentin. Malcolm's son. Distance is all I have and I'd kind of like to keep it that way. So that's how we can afford the house."

"You've lost me, Q."

"The deposit. When he died, my dad left me two of his vintage cars. I'm selling them and using the money on the house."

We never spoke about Malcolm. I felt like I was wading into dark water or readying myself to step onto a tightrope. "I can't let you do that."

"Eve, I promise you I have no emotional attachment to them." He rolled onto his back.

Perhaps I should have stopped there. There is no salvation in worrying old wounds and he, my Q, was a patchwork of timeworn injuries. Still, I persevered. "But—"

"You know one time he forgot me in his members' club while he drove one of those cars to take some woman he was seeing to the opera?" His laughter was mirthless and it settled on my skin and made me shiver. "When he finally remembered, he tried to act like I was the inconvenience. I told my mum. Funny, he could only grasp betrayal when he reckoned he was on the receiving end."

Under the duvet, my hand found his. "Okay. So your dad was a bit of a prick."

This time when he laughed, it thawed us both. He pulled me to him. "Let me do this. Let me spend the money on us."

"You're definitely not him, Q." He was so close that I could feel his pulse against mine. "We can find a place that's, I dunno, easier? One I can actually help buy. We don't need to buy that house."

We bought the house. Or more accurately, he bought the house because he presented me with a sheaf of financial spreadsheets outlining how post-deposit, a mortgage and associated homeowner costs were not out of our reach. Even with my *Circle* salary and his takings from QM Photography. I gave in. He loved the place, and I loved him. It would have been fruitless to fight him.

On move-in day, I was struck with such a severe case of buyer's remorse that I thought I might faint. The mortgage had been secured and the scales had fallen from my eyes. The house became this huge, ugly and massively expensive mistake. Q, on the other hand, was gamboling about the place and turning to me with shining eyes, saying things like "Shall I carry you over the threshold?" when what I wanted was to be carried back in time so I could talk Eve of the Past into holding on to common sense. He dashed through the rooms using phrases like *board and batten* and *structural integrity*. I stayed in the entrance hall and thought about the best time to call my parents and ask if I could move back in with them. Q found me there minutes later.

"What's the matter?" he asked.

"You spent so much money on this place," I choked out. "We have to live here. We— Oh God, oh God, I think I'm going to pass out."

He caught me as I started to tilt too much to the right. "Eve, breathe." He stroked my face. "Take a few deep breaths. That's it." He lowered himself gingerly to the filthy floor and guided me into his lap. "It's all going to be alright."

"It is not!" I half shouted and collapsed against his chest, weak with hysteria. "You sold your dad's cars. You sold them! Oh God, I'm going to vomit."

"You are not going to vomit." His voice was calm. He was radiating tranquility. "And I was always going to find a way to use those cars to make me happy. What makes me happy?"

I stuck out my lower lip like a kid serving time on the naughty step. "I do."

"And who loves you?"

"My dad."

"Alright, but who else?"

"My mum."

Pause. "Who else?"

"My sister."

"Eve."

"Fine. You do."

"That's right. I do. Once I'm done with this place, you won't recognize it."

I pressed closer to him. "Was Aspen pissed?"

"She wasn't happy. I wish I gave a fuck."

"If I wasn't scared of falling through the floorboards or

catching a staph infection, you could give one right here in this hallway."

He scratched the skin on the back of my neck and smiled at me. "Life is made for risks."

I'll say.

The house was a risk in the same way those Velcro walls bored people like to throw themselves against are. Sure, there's a chance you might misstep, fail to pick up enough momentum and drop like a stone, but if it all comes off, you'll stick, and your life is that bit more enriched. Q stuck. In the evenings, he pored over books on electrical maintenance and how to make the most of reclaimed wood. On Saturday mornings he would, much to my chagrin, wake me up and coax me to home improvement stores, where we would wander the aisles, he explaining the pros of recessed lighting and I struggling to care. He roped Ma into helping him pick out tiles and appliances. He threw himself into that house because he was on a quest to secure my happiness. It was one of the things I could never wrap my head around. He was never content with "okay." He was in search of a luminescent joy. I thought he had found it. I was wrong.

# 7

Because I, for fear of judgment, kept Quentin a secret until well after we were engaged, and because when I did finally bring him to meet my parents, he made more than one faux pas (including nervously making a joke about what turned out to be Ma's favorite celebrity pastor), my family took it upon themselves to investigate the good-looking white boy leading their precious Eve astray.

"Since when do you do things like this?" Gloria phoned to demand.

"Since when is this your business?" I, with all the defensiveness of someone in the wrong, retorted.

"Since when do I care what's technically my business or not?" Gloria shot back. She then went on to ask if I had slept with Q, and when I questioned if she thought I would remain chaste forever, she said, "Some of us are forgetting that we previously loosened the chastity belt for Dane."

I hung up on her.

Undeterred, Gloria took matters into her own hands, scouring the internet to find out what she could, and a few days later she called me back. "You are engaged to the son of Malcolm Morrow."

"And?"

"You are engaged to a person whose family basically own Sussex."

"I wouldn't say they ow—"

"'Quentin Morrow,'" Gloria cut me off, reading from Wikipedia, "'is the only son of Malcolm Morrow and Aspen Bowes-Morrow, whose combined assets make them the thirtieth wealthiest family in the United Kingdom.' Eve, you are engaged to semi-royalty. And he's billboard, underwear-model fine, too."

"How do you know the last part?" I asked.

"I found him on Facebook."

This is what Gloria did. She refused to rest until she had answers, and having located Q's social media presence, she was e-stalking him with an unsettling fervor.

"No wonder you've lost your mind," she said.

I wanted to protest, but she had a point. Truth be told, I was somewhat jealous of my sister. She had done everything "right." She married Alex, a dashing Igbo student she met on the third day of law school and whom she held at arm's length for a few months while she finished dating Charlie, a man who insisted on calling her "Glorious." Alex was introduced to our parents two months after he and Gloria started dating. A year later, he flouted Gloria's feminist proclivities and went to ask Dad for permission to marry her. They were married in all the pomp and circumstance a Nigerian wedding dictates. I had not so much ignored the conventional way of doing things as doused it in gasoline and set it alight.

"I love him," I said quietly into the phone. I wanted her to love him, too, because I knew Gloria's bad side extended three-quarters of the way around her and took real work to escape once you were there.

We sat there on the phone and we both stared at Quentin's Facebook page, lingering on his profile photo, a shot of him staring at something in the distance, the beginnings of a smile staking its claim on his face. A shot that made my heart twang every time I saw it.

I am staring at the same photo when, less than two weeks after he dies, I deactivate Q's Facebook profile. It is such a trivial thing, paltry as hell, but it is the only decision I have made in weeks. Despite my prolificacy when it came to furnishing *Circle* with all its online needs, I was inept when it came to maintaining my own online presence. My Twitter was a barren wasteland, I possessed an Instagram account only because Q made it clear it was my marital duty as a photographer's wife to "double tap" each and every one of his posts, and Snapchat overwhelmed me.

Facebook was different. Facebook was something he sweet-talked me into joining back in the day before I decided social media would be responsible for the demise of real human interaction.

"Why do I have to do this?" I'd asked him.

"Because I want to change my relationship status to 'Married to Eve Ezenwa-Morrow,'" he'd replied without looking up from his *British Journal of Photography*.

"This is not a reason," I'd mumbled, but by that afternoon, natch, there was my Facebook page and there was his new relationship status.

Now I have to be reminded that this thing still exists. I am downstairs—look, Ma, progress!—slouched on the living room sofa with Bee beside me listening to our work colleague Jamie talk about my husband's death.

"It's so awful, y'know?" Jamie says, as if he is the one with the dead spouse and I am the person trying to grasp what it means to have a blowtorch taken to your happiness. He raises his hand to his face in a show of affected sorrow. Jamie is only in my house because he came to bring Bee some sign-off sheets so she could work from my side. He is not supposed to have opinions. And fucking yet. "Your Facebook wall is flooded."

"My what?" I say dumbly, and Jamie sniffs, nods and reaches forward to touch my knee. I stare at his black-painted fingernails until he removes them from my person. Suddenly, I remember I am a person with a Facebook wall. A person who had a life Before.

While Bee sees to her sign-offs and talks shop with Jamie, I wipe the dust from my MacBook—a birthday present from Q, who refused to take me seriously while I clung to my aging HP—boot it up and start scrolling through messages of condolence. Messages left because this is the done thing, the unspoken online social convention for when calamity befalls someone else. Jamie is right. There are hundreds of messages from people telling me they are sorry, *they can't imagine*, doing the other done thing, which is to take someone else's tragedy and somehow make it about yourself. I deactivate my account without a second thought and log on to Q's. Apparently, he is still "Married to Eve Ezenwa-Morrow" and he is still founder and CEO of QM Photography. Apparently, nothing has changed for Q except that he is dead.

I scroll through the messages on his page, each one a needle to my heart. Where was—I squint—Meredith Wheeler-Grayson when my husband was plotting a suicide I knew nothing about? What exactly does Thomas Shepperton know about the ways in which Q lit up lives? How is it so many people I have never met before are crawling out of the woodwork and making this heartbreak theirs? My finger hovers over the track pad. I deactivate his profile and return to bed.

The Ezenwa children, headed by our fearless leader, Gloria, are a unit. Therefore, just as was the case with Nate and his bullying, after I finally revealed my engagement to Quentin and the shock waves had finished reverberating through the family, it made sense that Gloria arrived on campus with Nate in tow ready to stage an intervention.

"Glo? Nate? What the hell? What are you doing here?" I asked upon opening my door and finding my siblings before me.

"Get your coat," Glo said, and although I was due to meet Q, there was something in her tone that told me this was no time to be obstinate. I tugged on my denim jacket and followed her.

She took us to the Southbank location of Strada, an Italian chain heavy on the aesthetics, an Instagrammer's dream. "Order what you want," she told us, and while Nate whooped with excitement, I scanned the menu. Every time I dared raise my eyes, Glo was appraising me, her expression designed to be neutral. Even then it was clear she was going to make a formidable lawyer. Everything we would be was still in sight but not quite yet in reach, at least not for all of us. Not yet.

We ate hand-stretched pizza and Gloria permitted Nate half a glass of wine, which he hated but pretended to tolerate because he was fifteen and balancing the teenage shame of being seen with his sisters with the personal joy of being with his sisters. I ordered panna cotta for dessert and only as my spoon split the creamy expanse of the surface did Gloria stop circling her point and land on it, more lightly than she had ever done before. I learned this about my sister as we grew up—that she could hold a thought in her head as delicately as glass and there it would remain until she determined that enough time had passed for her to properly tackle it.

"Eve," she said, "this thing with you and Quentin. It's a little fast, no? Chèlụ nwantị ntị, hmm? You *can* wait, can't you? What's the rush?"

My spoon slipped from my fingers and dropped noiselessly to the tablecloth. "I—"

"Before you lose your shit," Nate said, scrutinizing the dregs of his wineglass, "look at it from our point of view."

"And what is your point of view?" Nate was correct, I was quick-tempered when it came to Q because they were right to have questions. I should have been happy that they cared enough to ask.

"Well. He seems nice enough, but we don't know him," Glo began.

"And it's been what? A couple of weeks? You don't know him either," Nate added.

"It's been more than a couple of weeks," I mumbled.

Gloria waited until a passing waiter refilled her water glass. "He's your first boyfriend, Eve. You guys are babies. What's wrong with dating around a little first?"

"Okay, relax," said Nate. "You're telling her to be a sl—"

"Finish that sentence, Nathaniel, and I will throw you into the Thames. All I'm saying, Eve, is that you don't have to jump into anything. We have a few more choices these days."

"Firstly, Q isn't my first boyfriend," I protested. "You're forgetting Dane."

"Who the hell is Dane? There was a Dane?" I know that it pained Nate, male as he is, to think of either of his sisters as autonomous humans with libidos.

Glo chose to ignore our brother. "Sexual liberation is a thing. I don't want you to feel like you have to tie yourself to the first guy that shows real interest. I can give you a book by—"

Nate jumped to his feet, his face twisted with repulsion. "I'm going to the toilet, man. I can't believe you lot are chatting about sex. You're my sisters. You shouldn't even know what that is." He departed quickly.

Glo and I looked at each other and the tension cracked, then fell away. Gloria's face, already striking, took on a luminosity when she laughed. I would never tire of looking at my sister. She was always radiant. "You get what we're saying? Tell me you get it?" Gloria reached for my hand, which I gave her.

After lunch, we dropped Nate home, but Glo insisted on returning to campus with me. That night, she handed me a tub of coconut oil and I braided her hair while we channel-surfed on the tiny TV Dad had brought to my room on the day they all helped me move in. I painted my sister's nails and we browsed plastic surgeon reviews because this was the time Glo had convinced herself she needed a breast reduction. When she crawled into bed with me, she tucked the covers under my chin like she did when we were kids.

"I'm worried," Glo confessed. "That's why I'm saying all this."

"You've met him! Surely you of all people can see he's harmless." We lay facing each other, our knees pulled up and touching.

"He's a sweetie," she admitted. "From what I've seen, he's a gem. But nobody can deny the power dynamics at play here."

"Power dynamics? Glo, he's a twenty-one-year-old photography student."

"He's also a Morrow. Yeah, I know, he's renounced his past. But really? Eve, use your head and chè echìchè. Please," she repeated her request. "Just think. You said his mum's a nightmare."

What she was saying was justified; it warranted consideration. But stubbornness is a Nigerian trait cultivated in the red earth of our home. And here it was nurtured by my youth and the potency of dopamine. "I love him, Glo," I said. "I don't want to have to kiss a hundred frogs. I've already found my prince."

"That is so gross and such a cliché," she said, and we

laughed again. She reached up and secured the knot of my headscarf. "I want you to be sure. Are you sure?"

"I am," I told my sister. "I really am."

I wander my own house, standing in the center of rooms where we once argued, made up, planned, fell apart and pieced each other back together again. I scrape away the scab keeping my memories in and let myself bleed. I binge on the memory of Quentin. I immerse myself in it and let myself drift, weightless. I end up outside, in the back garden that, along with the light, sold the house to us. I sit cross-legged on the dewy grass and let the January cold seep through my pajama bottoms. I start to shiver and am nearing frozen when Nate finds me. He stares at me for a second, panic trying to break my brother's ceaseless cool. He tucks his iPad under his arm and shoves his hands in his pockets to ward off the cold.

"Do I need to get Dad?" he asks.

I start laughing, new truths leaving me manic. I am a widow. A *widow*. It is so comical, so damn farcical—I can't stop laughing. Nate eyes me in the way you would expect someone to eye a person who after weeks of being mired in woe suddenly starts cracking up at nothing.

"Nah," I wheeze. "It's… I'm a widow. How funny is that?"

My brother contemplates the suit he is wearing before sitting beside me on the grass. He searches my face. "Yeah. Hilarious?"

"I… I'm a widow because…my husband killed himself." I stop laughing.

"It's fucked-up," Nate says.

It is bloody ludicrous. I'm not married anymore? What is that? What does that even mean? I try to reason with myself. The whole world did not stop because mine did. I do not say any of this to Nate.

"It is."

"Let's go inside, yeah?" Nate helps me to my feet, and we head back into the house.

After that, I am not left alone for quite some time.

Jackson visits. He has come to try his hand at grief management. His version involves impressing on me how much Quentin loved me.

"Damn it, Eve," he says to me, now he has emerged from whichever version of hell he has been occupying, "he loved you so much. I knew him all his life and he was never as happy as he was when he was with you. You were his everything." He has tousled hair and bloodshot eyes. He speaks in a voice that has been annihilated by pain.

"It's sort of nice to see someone who looks as terrible as I do," I say to him. I have no filter now. It's refreshing.

"Scotch. And lack of sleep," he admits.

I nod in solidarity.

"You understand what I'm saying, though?" Jackson reaches for my hand. "He adored you."

People think saying things like this is supposed to help me. It does not. It is abhorrent to me that Jackson should be sitting here staring at me when Q is dead. Yet he deserves a companion in mourning, and while I can't fulfill that role, I can rewrap his gift of reassurance and give it back.

"He loved you, too. You know that, right? *Brother from another mother* were his exact words—cringey as it is." I lean forward to offer him the last of my pocket Kleenex, which he accepts, grateful even in the midst of his breakdown. A wave of nausea washes over me. "Excuse me, Jack," I say, rising to my feet. "I'm going to go throw up now." Because this is something else that happens when you miss your husband so much you could puke—you actually do. By the time I return to the living room, Jackson is on his feet and looking rather peaky himself. He pulls me into a one-armed hug, mutters something about not being a stranger and leaves.

Dad is at work and I am pill-less for the afternoon, so I find my bottle of Kraken black spiced rum (a gift from Nate). I drink to achieve the same numbness the pills afford me, but I don't quite manage to get there. I give up only when my stomach revolts, and for the second time today, I find myself paying homage to the cold porcelain of the toilet bowl.

I leave the half-empty bottle of rum on the living room floor and drag myself up the stairs and back to bed to sleep off the hangover I already feel coming.

I forgot how draining hangovers are. I wake briefly to ask Dad to close the curtains, but a few hours later, nausea drives me to the bathroom, and while there, I develop a violent aversion to our bedroom and move downstairs to the sofa, where Ma is answering texts on her mobile. I shuffle into the living room and she is immediately on her feet.

"You don't have to get up, Ma," I say to her. Since Q died, she has given over her entire life to caring for her widowed daughter, something I don't imagine anyone, relative or otherwise, would enjoy. I want her to forget my sadness for a moment, to just be Ma.

"You're okay?" she asks, still on her feet.

"I'm physically sound," I answer because of course I am not okay and we both know it.

Ma picks up the pile of papers next to her and drops them on the side table, clearing space for me. Ma is a consultant endocrinologist. She does lucrative locum work so that she has time to write her book on reproductive endocrinology and deliver lectures on the subject. I have no idea how she doesn't wither with shame and disappointment whenever she looks at me. I understand nothing of her work but am proud nonetheless, and nod with a rictus grin whenever one of our play aunties or uncles ask me, "So you enjoyed your mum's paper on squamous cell carcinoma of the thyroid in last month's medical journal?"

I lower myself onto the sofa beside Ma and put my head in her lap. She commences scratching my scalp with her free hand and it's as comforting now as it was when I was small. I relax for the few seconds it takes for Ma to ask me how it is Aspen came to have her phone number after almost a decade of pointed silence.

"She's been calling you?" I ask, tension creeping back into my temples.

"She is very angry. She is going through a lot, but she— ọ na-akparị ka madu." Calling Aspen rude is Ma's way of declaring war. Aspen might as well have walked into Ma's kitchen unannounced and spit in her ogbono soup. "I told her not to phone me again."

"I'm sorry." Because it's my fault, isn't it, that Aspen's wrath now stretches to my parents.

"Don't worry." Ma presses her hand against my neck, gauges my temperature. "Hmm." She turns on Food Network and we watch Guy Fieri like we used to, Ma providing a running commentary on all the ways he baffles her. "Why won't he wear shoes? Why is his hair this color? Why does he always put his fingers in people's food? He is always shouting. Why?" And it is almost like old times except Quentin is dead and my stomach is a knot of anxiety and rage as I think about what Aspen could have said to my mother.

Dad arrives as he does without ceremony, humming as he enters the room, and for the briefest moment, my world has not gone up in flames and he is here, dropping in after a day at work.

"Evie-Nnadi," he says to me but chooses not to complete his sentence. There is no need to ask how I am feeling; it is etched into the fabric of my person. He sits on the other end of the sofa, lifts my legs and tugs my slouching socks up my calves. Then he speaks. "I know this is difficult. But in time, it will slowly start to be less difficult. Ànyị nò ebe à, do you hear? We will always be here." Everything I love about my father—his measured manner, his essence of calm, his persistent optimism—is encompassed in this simple gesture and statement. As a neurosurgeon, he has dedicated his life to putting people's heads back together. Yet he knows better than to try and fix whatever is going on in mine.

# 8

The list of grievances against Aspen, were I petty enough to compile one, would be long enough to paper the walls of the rooms in her mansion. I didn't stumble upon my intolerance of her like one comes across a stray puppy and chooses to hold on to it. She led me there and made it clear she was happy to inhabit the House that Hate Built.

I met her for the first time about a year after Q and I became Eve and Quentin. Thanks to Google, I felt like I already knew a fair deal about Aspen Bowes-Morrow and was not too stressed about meeting her in person. I knew she came from a long line of moneyed Boweses and had been married to Malcolm Morrow (also from money) and that she, like so many other Wives of the Rich, spent her time holding charitable auctions so she could single-handedly save all the orphans in Africa or whatever.

Google also told me that Q's father had had two messy extramarital affairs and that Aspen had stood by him while the media feasted on the corpse of their previously highly respected marriage. I read about the car accident that had claimed Malcolm's life when Q was twelve and let my jaw drop when I learned there had been speculation about Aspen's involvement as she along with Q had inherited all of his assets.

I also learned that Q had no desire to talk about this Jerry Springer–worthy mess.

"It was the worst time of my life and extremely hard on my mother, so we don't talk about it," he told me. Q, who had done his best to escape the trappings of his upbringing, had not yet mastered the act of not repressing difficult memories.

It was enough for me. Aspen sounded like she wasn't doing too shabbily following the death of her husband and seemed to have transitioned seamlessly into her new calling as martyr. She had, up until that point, shown exactly zero interest in meeting me, so I assumed she would be one of those satellite mothers-in-law who only appear for the most important events. I was so beyond wrong it's almost funny. Almost.

She showed up unannounced at Q's flat one afternoon and it was only by the mercy of God we happened to be clothed and engaging in an activity that was not the making of the beast with two backs. Through the window, we saw her as she stepped out of a chauffeur-driven Mercedes and then she inflicted her presence on us as we chopped spring onions for the stir-fry we were making. I had never seen Quentin so shocked.

As he stammered out a greeting, Aspen's gaze settled on me. "You are always otherwise occupied, so I thought I would visit. Is this why?" This. I was a "this."

Q persuaded her to meet us in a couple of hours for afternoon tea at the Landmark. I put on a navy, knee-length skirt, scraped my braids into a bun and scrubbed off my red lipstick. Q looked at me and sighed.

"You do not have to be Jackie O for my mother's benefit."

"Have you met your mother?" was all I could say in response.

At the hotel, Aspen proffered each cheek for her son to kiss.

Her ash-blond hair was pulled back gently and two delicate yet sizable diamonds glittered in her earlobes.

"Mum," Q said, "you look wonderful. This is Eve, my fiancée."

Aspen glowed at the touch of her son's lips to her cheeks. "It's this new diet Alana has me on. So many leafy greens I'm surprised I'm not sprouting roots myself." She was cooing. She was cooing at her twenty-one-year-old son. She turned to me and immediately stopped. "Hello, Eve. Do sit."

Meeting the parents is always fraught with anxiety and the will-they-like-me pressure that turns previously intelligent, articulate people into gibbering introverts. I was already an introvert and I expected this. I made an effort (hence the skirt) and all I wanted in return was to be treated with a modicum of respect. Which, on the face of it, I was. Aspen was never overtly rude (that came later). She asked me questions ("What do your parents do, dear? Doctors! How sweet!") and she never once came out and said, "You are so far below what I want for my son that I would sooner lacerate my own face with the broken shards of this tea saucer than accept this," but her disdain was there; bubbling quietly underneath the surface of everything she said to me, it was there. After a while, she angled herself away from me and spoke exclusively to Q, and while part of me was fine with that, relieved even, the part of me raised by parents who equated bad manners with necrophilia and atheism flared up and I had to restrain myself from tipping £55 per person tea and sandwiches over Aspen's head. Occasionally, she would shoot me a brief look, asserting her dominance, her superiority. I could do nothing but imagine pouring battery acid onto her feet. She did not mention the engagement once.

At one point I excused myself to the bathroom, and when I returned, Aspen turned to me and said, "Did you find the facilities, dear? You were gone so long I thought someone had mistaken you for the help and dragged you off into the kitchen or something! Your outfit *does* blend in." I refrained from asking if anyone had ever mistaken her for Satan, and back in Q's flat, we argued about his reticence.

"She didn't mean it that way," Q insisted when I pointed out the obvious.

"Oh, is it? Learned racial sensitivity from her hordes of Black friends, did she?" I pulled the pins from my braids and the bun collapsed around my shoulders. "What do you reckon she meant, then?"

He opened his mouth, then closed it.

"Oh my God, Q, borrow her credit card and buy yourself a clue."

Again, we had acknowledged the elephant in the relationship. In time, I would harness my patience and try to explain to Q that being a Black woman meant having to skate across a lifetime of eggshells or be painted unduly "angry" or "aggressive" even on days like that day, when anger and aggression were warranted. Being with Q meant making peace with never being completely understood no matter how valiant the effort, with battling the impulse to run or scream when the expression on his face asked the question he was too wise or too scared to voice: *Is it really a race thing?*

Q brought us together on three further occasions over the next few months, each meeting taking place in a venue of Aspen's choosing. I was the embodiment of saccharine at each one. She used the opportunities to not so subtly trash me ("What an *interesting* jacket, Eve. Where did you say you found it?") and I'd come home exhausted from the effort of not asking her if any muscles in her face still moved of their own accord.

Things never improved from that point on.

I want it known that I tried. She didn't deserve it, but I bit back every retort to her barbs. I continued to dress like Gov-

erness Maria every time I was around her. I did the things a
soon-to-be daughter-in-law was supposed to, and with each
time I was sent to Aspen's voice mail or told she was "unavailable" to take my call, more tumbleweed blew across the rapidly emptying reserves of my patience. When, after months
of silence, Q and I were sent for to "discuss wedding plans,"
I was immediately suspicious.

"Why are you being this way?" Q asked me, and I listed
the reasons as I paced the floorboards of his flat.

1. There were no real details to work out. Ours was
   going to be a wedding devoid of any real pageantry.
   I had fought my own mother, my sister and a host
   of incredulous relatives on this and had come up
   bloodied but triumphant.

2. If Aspen was so desperate to discuss details, this
   could be done over the phone and, at a push, via
   Skype. There was no reason to dedicate an entire
   day to driving out to West Wealthshire or Money-
   on-the-Vale or wherever it was she lived to talk
   about things over which she had no control.

3. Aspen and I didn't see eye to eye, so her motives
   in summoning us had to be filed under "ulterior."

And still I went because Q said, "I am all she has," which
was a lie, because when we arrived, I realized she also had
a stately home with manicured gardens, lime-washed walls,
several porticoes and a powder-blue Aston Martin sitting on
the gravel of the expansive driveway.

I sat on a chaise in Aspen's drawing room and accepted the
white wine I was offered, giddy at not being openly shunned.
I stupidly hoped this might be the turning point, that Aspen
would harken back to the days before Malcolm's parents de-

termined she was of good enough breeding to become a Morrow. I hoped she would cut me a fucking break. I thought she might remember what it was like to nibble the corner of a tomato tart and explain in falsely buoyant tones that yes, pink roses *did* sound delightful, but the decision about the flowers had been made weeks ago. Most of all, I hoped she might see that I made her son happy and, given the amount of tragedy the family had endured, that this would be enough. It wasn't.

After a bathroom break, I returned to find a blonde sitting in my vacated seat. She wore a tan skirt, a sleeveless cream blouse and—get this—a cardigan draped across her shoulders, its sleeves tied loosely around her neck. She looked like she tumbled from a copy of *Country Homes & Interiors* magazine. When she produced a slender, engraved case from her clutch and tapped a cigarette on its lid before slipping it into a holder, I began to look around for the cameras. She was introduced as Madeline Brook, a family friend who was "an absolute triumph when it comes to wedding planning." She called Quentin "Quinny" and stroked his arm with a territorial affection that made me want to strangle her with her own knitwear.

I sat. I drank my wine. I did not finish my tomato tart. I watched as my fiancé made conversation with this perfectly plucked and coiffed person, the type of person Aspen had no doubt been dreaming her son would marry until I came along and scuppered her plans. It was a little surreal. But the message was clear, and as my eyes met hers over the rim of my wineglass, Aspen smiled. The smile spoke volumes and was probably the one she used before she drained the blood from her prey.

I felt oddly calm in that moment. Convincing yourself that a person despises you is easy, and a lot of the time you will be wrong, but there was something like relief in how right I was about Aspen's feelings about me. It was there in her eyes and

in the way she invited me into her home for the sole purpose
of humiliating me. It was there in every comment made by
Madeline, who found it amazing I had plans to enter employment after the wedding and who "would be hard-pressed to
leave whatever room Quinny was in even for a second. If *I*
were marrying him of course."

"If only! I might have had a look-in if you were Quentin's
fiancée—wishful thinking!" Aspen met my eye and waited a
beat too long before adding the laughter meant to convince
us all she was joking.

I smiled back.

Then I left.

I wanted badly to channel Gloria, who, too, would have
risen to her feet but not before leaning forward to curse them,
these two giggling women, in highly enunciated Igbo: *Wishful thinking? Wishful thinking gbụkwa g'ebe ahụ.*

There was some commotion as I made my way out through
the grand entrance hall. I recall the sound of Q's voice, hard
as steel and polished by years of elocution lessons, informing
his mother that "This was low, Aspen. Even for you," and I
would use that memory as a source of joy for years to come.
Out on the gravel driveway, he enveloped me in his arms,
trying to comfort me, but I was fine.

"Your mother hates me," I told him without emotion, and
this time he did not try to argue.

We heard nothing more from Aspen until a few days before the wedding when she phoned Q to make both amends
and arrangements. To me, she said nothing. I rolled over in
my bed and thought about what my life would look like after
the wedding, when there was nothing Aspen could do to tear
us apart. I hoped she would mellow, see her way to if not cel-
ebrating, then at least accepting my place in Quentin's life.
If nothing else, I wanted us to be allies in making Q happy.

But her dislike of me colored every interaction we had, and after a while, I gave up being civil and chose to be mute instead, communicating everything I had to say by carefully constructed, impassive facial expressions she struggled and failed to decipher. Q's relationship with Aspen was, for the most part, undamaged and unchanged. They spoke several times a week. Every year, he helped her choose the twelve-foot Christmas tree for the Great Hall. Once a month, he talked her out of sending her driver and instead booked a train ticket to go and see her, the air in the days before this sojourn always a little heavier with things unsaid. He would kiss my face before he left and extend a milquetoast invitation we both knew was more about propping up my disintegrating pride than anything else. We pretended that it was mere coincidence that my busiest workloads always happened to coincide with his trips. The front door would close, I would exhale and begin to count the hours until he was mine again.

I don't say any of this to defend myself. Or perhaps I do. The consensus is that when someone beloved by all dies, those closest to that person are supposed to band together and parse out the grief so it doesn't succeed in destroying anyone. The little energy I have is being used solely to ignore Aspen and this is puzzling to some and downright brutal to most, so maybe I do have to justify myself. Yet as I stare at her name flashing up on my shattered phone in the dark, I remember Madeline and that tiny smile she gave me, and I decline the call with a swipe of my finger.

# 9

If I was a different sort of person, the type to find value in even the most devastating circumstances, I might say that your husband killing himself and having to remain upright while your world collapses around you is a great metaphor for how loss shapes you. I may allude to how the damage rearranges itself to allow or even compel moving forward—the putting of one foot in front of the other. I am not that person. Your husband dying should rightly be your rock bottom, the worst thing that ever happens to you. But then you have to formally identify his body. The body you held in your blood-encrusted hands while you pleaded with emergency services on the worst night of your life. Because why not? Why should there be any respite in this?

The house is full. It is Saturday and because circumstance has made me the temporary nucleus of the family, everyone is here. Downstairs in the kitchen, Nate is manning the grill. He has a tray of bacon crisping beneath the glow of the orange filament. Cleo is hovering at his side. Dad is brewing coffee. Ma is bleaching surfaces. Alex and Gloria are imploring their children to be still. Bee is nowhere to be seen. All noise ceases for half a second when I enter the room and I see myself through their eyes—demented hair, dressed in a hodgepodge of Quentin's clothing, unwashed and sleepy. I wave my hands in an approximation of a greeting and they carry on about their business. I slump into a chair and Dad puts a mug of peppermint tea in front of me. I twist my lips into what I hope is a smile but, judging from the troubled expression on his face, has clearly fallen short of the mark. It's nice being amid bustle but not being pressed upon from all sides. Everyone recognizes my confusing state of never wanting to be alone but also not wanting to engage with anyone around me. They all know this except Cleo, who is shuffling in my direction, a determined smile on her face.

"Hi, Eve," she says. She bends, chokes me with her Miss Dior and gives me an awkward hug. We've never been particularly close, but she's trying, so it is only right that I make an attempt at kindness.

I pat her back. "Hey, Cleo. How are you?"

"Oh, you know! Busy with work, forever chasing this one." She motions to Nate, who, spatula in hand, is watching us warily.

"Chased him over here, did you?" I am being cruel. Cleo is lovely in a doggedly efficient way. The problem is I have lost the capacity for empathy. My social graces have withered away to nothing.

She continues to smile. Her skin is poreless. "He's never free these days!" she says before remembering the reason she now has to share Nate's time. "You look good, Evie. Really...slim."

"Christ," Nate mutters.

Cleo is indignant. "What? She does look slim."

"Because she doesn't eat anymore. She's depressed," Nate says.

I slip out while they argue and take my tea into the empty

living room. I sink into the sofa and fix my gaze on the fire-place. After a while I become aware that I am not alone. My nephew, Benjamin, is standing at the arm of the sofa watching me with curiosity. Ben is four ("Almost five, Aunty Eeeeeve!") but is small for his age. Gloria is awaiting the first of his growth spurts with trepidation—she loves her baby as he is. What Ben lacks in height, he makes up for in cuteness. And precocity.

I wonder how I must appear to him. Gloria, a realist in every other area of life, fails to paint her children with the same pragmatic brush. She is convinced her offspring will be the key to my salvation and has been foisting Ben and his older sister, Elechi (Ellie for short), on me at every opportunity. However, since realizing the depths of my gloom, Glo has quietly allowed them to relinquish the responsibility of "cheering up Aunty Eve," and I have seen them less. The sight of my intrepid nephew in his Batman shirt is therefore a welcome one. He climbs up onto the sofa.

"Are you sick?" Ben asks. He is the only person I know who can hug you with his eyes.

I am not sure how to answer him. There are times when Q's absence is so debilitating I feel like a hospital is the best place for me. But mostly, I am tired. "No, I'm not sick."

He does not look like he believes me. "Where's Uncle Q?"

"He's…not here anymore," I say carefully.

"Because he's dead." Ben knows enough to sound som-ber. "He died."

"Yes. He died. He's not coming back." My voice wobbles and Ben pats my leg like I am a puppy.

"That's sad. My pet rabbit died, and I was sad then, too. Uncle Q was better than Rocket."

A tear sneaks out from under my eyelid and rolls down my face. "Yeah. Uncle Q was the best."

"Mum says you'll feel better soon. But you've been sad for a million hundred years." Ben. Lover of hyperbole.

I put an arm around Ben and pull him to me. "Maybe not a million *hundred* years. But yeah, I am pretty sad."

"Will you be happy next week?"

This is what people are waiting for. But it's not that simple. This is not something you get over. Two weeks, six months, ten years from now, Q will still be dead, and I will still be a widow being dashed against the rocks of husbandless pain. It doesn't get better; it just doesn't get any worse.

This might go over a four-(almost-five!)-year-old's head, so I give Ben's hand a squeeze and say, "I hope so."

Pleased with this response, he gets up onto his knees, throws his arms about my neck and administers a somewhat saliva-heavy kiss to my cheek. He exits the living room at the same time Bee lets herself into the house. She heads straight for the kitchen and says, "Have you told her yet?" in a voice loud enough for me to hear, a voice met with a maelstrom of protest at her volume.

Not one minute later, a procession of adults file into the living room. My niece and nephew are not present; they have no doubt been dispatched to some far-flung corner of the house.

I survey my family standing before me. Cleo is so tense I fear she might snap in half.

"Take a breath, Cleo. You look like you're about to pass out," I say. She claps her hands to her cheeks.

Nate's eyes narrow. "What's wrong?"

"There's nothing wrong," Gloria replies. But is that…is Gloria sweating?

I sigh. "Is there something you guys need to tell me?"

Dad steps forward. He sits next to me and straightens his trousers. "Inspector Morgan called, nke m. Do you remember him?"

I freeze. What I remember is a blur of uniforms and too

many hands hauling me to my feet. I remember a series of questions and eyes heavy with accusation and pity. All of this is a smear on my memory. I don't remember an Inspector Morgan. Not specifically. Not now.

"He's the one in charge of Quentin's...case." Dad treads carefully. "He called to say that the coroner is finished with Quentin's...with the postmortem, and they're ready to release him."

*Release.* It sounds so accusatory, so guilt laden. Like Q is coming home from a prison term or a war camp. It has been two weeks. I assumed, perhaps idiotically, that this, like so many other things, had been handled. "But..." I start.

"There was some..." Dad pauses. "There was a delay. Some issues with paperwork and then, uh, Quentin's mother requested a private postmortem. Of course, it was denied in the end."

This is not fresh news. I imagine my family would have discussed this development at length, thrashing out the best, most delicate way to break it to me. My husband, even in death, engaged in a tug-of-war with his mother. And I, completely ignorant.

Dad takes my hand. "There's no reason for you to do this alone. We'll come with you." I remember Ma telling me that before anything else, she fell in love with Dad's tenderness.

I don't understand what he is trying to say to me. Do what alone? Then the horrendous truth clicks into place. "They want me to go to the morgue?"

"It will be quick," Ma interjects. "We won't leave you alone for a second."

"It will be difficult," Dad says.

"It won't be," I reply, "because I'm not doing it. Excuse me." I stand up.

"Eve. Come on." Gloria has stepped forward. I'm in no mood for this.

"Gloria. I am going to use the toilet. This will happen whether or not you let me go."

She releases me.

Of course I do it. Of course I do. The only alternative is to allow Aspen to take matters into her own hands, and frankly, I would sooner barrel-roll into untreated sewage than speak to her. Besides, as petrifying as the prospect is, it means being reunited with Quentin.

Morgues are strange places. Dad tries to explain this to me on the drive over. He tries to explain that they are upsetting by their very nature, and that if I am uncomfortable at any time, I should take a break. I hear him, but I'm not listening. I am too busy worrying I will encounter open chest cavities and gruesome disfigurements. On my way to see Q, the only person with whom I want to discuss the potential freakery of a morgue is Q himself. How meta. Or something. The process in my case, I am told, is backward. A postmortem was ordered by the coroner, something someone of my lowly standing would not have had the power to dispute. Apparently, a CLO, or "coroners liaison officer," has written to me on numerous occasions, has left messages that have gone ignored. Another acronym made flesh. Who knew death could be so educational? It is she, this unknown person who impressed upon my parents the likelihood of regret should I not take the opportunity to slip through the closing window provided to me to view my husband before he is forever lost to the coldness of a cemetery.

When we arrive and I have summoned the courage to exit the car, Ma and Dad flank me and together we walk into the cold, dimly lit viewing room. It is also deathly quiet. Deathly. Ha. Inspector Morgan and who I assume to be the liaison officer stand side by side, a somber and slightly intimidating duo. Beyond them, through the semi-tinted glass, is Q.

He is not sporting a tag on his toe like cinema told me to expect, but there is a pallid tinge to his skin. I turn away and take a deep breath because for one terrible second, I think I am about to throw up everything I have ever eaten plus a few vital organs to boot. I focus on the Glade plug-in at ankle-height. A half-hearted attempt at masking the smell of chemicals and death that has infiltrated even the viewing room.

I force myself to look. My husband is long and lean and sculpted. His personality is luminous interspersed with sardonic flashes I love. He has an artist's fingers that know exactly where to go to leave me a postorgasmic mess. What he is not is a collection of appendages, a lifeless shell. Except now that is exactly what he is. I press my fingers against the glass, my breath clouds the window and obscures Q's face. Ma prays in tongues under her breath. I wipe the condensation from the window.

"Hello, you," I whisper through the glass. "It'd be great if you could wake up now. Promise I won't be angry." He remains dead.

"Can I go in there?" I ask. "I just… He'll be cold." Behind me, Ma's prayers intensify.

Inspector Morgan is no stranger to the scene before him, and as if reciting from a mental dossier, he tells me in a soft voice that protocol forbids it. "I can only imagine how difficult this must be for you."

I gaze at Q. He is so near and yet a world away. I only want to trace his cheekbones the way I did when he was climbing to the surface of sleep. To be kept from him is a cruelty for which I had not prepared. Inspector Morgan shifts. He is sensitive enough not to look at the time, but he scratches the skin around his watch. I drag my eyes away from my husband. "Do I have to sign something?" I ask.

"Yes," he replies. "We also have a release form, which will allow us to return Mr. Morrow's belongings to you."

"Belongings?" I parrot.

"The, erm…the paraphernalia your husband had on his person at the time of his death."

My parents lift me into a chair before I even notice I have sunk to the floor. Inspector Morgan watches, his lips a thin line. Is this what life will be? Wilting at the merest hint of stress? How then to tackle a wardrobe full of clothes I can't yet look at? An office of intricacies that made him, him? I sit in my chair and let the grown-ups handle this ludicrous business.

"It's not a problem, Mr. and Mrs. Ezenwa." Inspector Morgan is consoling now. "Your daughter's reaction is not uncommon. We just need her signature on a few forms, and we can wrap up here."

Dad casts a doubtful glance in my direction. I focus my attention to the ceiling and begin counting the square tiles.

"Do you need a glass of water?" The CLO materializes beside me. She is a mousy thing with huge eyes, a bluntly cut fringe that obscures her eyebrows and a fetching cardigan in pale green. She does not appear old enough to be dealing with the business of death. "Was that a no on the water?"

"Oh. I guess. No, thanks. Not unless you spike it with rum."

She smiles at that. A little smile. It lasts for half a second. "Sorry, we don't serve alcohol here."

"No. It was a joke." Ma has wiped my fingerprints from the glass of the observation window. She is watching Q. I lower my eyes to the carpet.

"Your husband is very handsome," the CLO says, and I don't know why but this helps. "Excellent bone structure. The forms. If you're unable to sign them, they'll have to call another relative. The closest living one apart from yourself would be his mother, right?"

"God forbid."

"Ah. Problems with the in-laws?"

"The in-law is the problem."

"Then I would sign the forms if I were you." Inspector Morgan coughs and the CLO pats me on the shoulder and says no more.

I join Ma at the window. An escaped lock of hair tickles Q's ear and I recall the last discussion we had about his next haircut. He could be sleeping. He could wake up and end this hell.

"Please," I whisper to him.

Nothing.

I turn to Inspector Morgan. "What do I need to sign?"

After the sun has set and I'm back home, I close the bedroom door and turn my attention to the clear plastic bag of Q's things I was given. There was a sticky moment where I was so overcome by the reality of never seeing him again that I refused to leave the viewing room and had to be talked down by Dad and the CLO. I wept the entire journey home while Ma massaged my knee and said, "I know, I know," in a low voice that provided no comfort.

Inside the bag is Q's mobile phone, his wallet and his wedding ring, all of which have been wiped clean. His clothes, Inspector Morgan explained to me kindly, could not be returned.

"But what happened to them?" I asked tearfully.

He shifted uncomfortably. "They were destroyed."

It was at this point Dad had to strong-arm me into the car. He could see something troubling in my eyes.

Before I even reach into the bag, I am gasping. These were the things Q had with him when he took his last breath, when what he should have had was me. Thankful as I am for his wallet, each of these items is a reminder that in the end I couldn't save him. That he didn't want to be saved. I open his wallet and cast aside the crumpled tens and shake out the collection of loose change. I finger the snapshots he kept in the photo holder—us smiling and carefree on our wedding day, me lost in sleep, us grinning and dripping after spending a windswept day on Peel Beach on the Isle of Man. A trio of memories providing a microcosmic glimpse at what was and is no more.

I thread Q's wedding ring onto a necklace and secure the chain around my neck. It lies against my heart, which, considering how wrecked it is, is fitting. Even after charging, Q's phone refuses to switch on; it is dead, forever silenced like its owner.

He was shooting a series on UK beaches for a travel magazine and thus had spent the previous six weeks gallivanting to the far reaches of this island, calling me from tiny B and B rooms in Devon, Norfolk and the Outer Hebrides. This was around the time the photography world was starting to really take notice of Q, his talent made even more exciting both because of its quiet insistence and Q's complicated and curious past. At first there was an element of romance to it— I'd watch his face distort on FaceTime as the signal dipped and we would joke about how all the proprietors must have banded together to decorate their establishments in the same aggressive florals. We were star-crossed lovers hamstrung by geography and the fickleness of technology. Q tired first. Surprising since he was living the dream. But following a few failed attempts at video calling from Pembrokeshire, I opened my eyes the following morning and there he was after traveling through the night to make it back to me.

"I'm taking you with me on my next assignment. Isle of Man. It's only for a couple of days, but we can extend and do my birthday there?"

On the longest days of shooting, he ordered breakfast to arrive at the door long after he'd left but just as I was waking up. He'd return exhausted but elated, pushing his face into mine while I screamed with laughter and yelled at him to shower the sand out of his hair. I'd massage the knots out of his shoulders and draw the curtains so he could sleep for an hour before dinner. Q shot as many of the Isle's beaches as he could manage, and on the day he went to Peel, he wrapped me up in his windbreaker and carried me piggyback style to the edge of the waves, the spray drenching us both, our laughter lost in the wind.

"God, I love it here," he told me on the way back to the hotel.

"I love you here," I replied.

"More than London me?"

"London you can be a bit of a dick."

He reached under my windbreaker and tickled me until I threatened violence. "I'm happy enough that I could die, you know," he said.

"Yeah, don't do that. Dramatic ass. Why ruin the holiday by dying? Men are so inconsiderate."

He laughed. "When I do die," he said, "I want to go out like a Viking."

"What, you want to be slain in battle or die from hypothermia or some form of gangrene?"

"No," he said, "I want to be put on a burning Viking ship and floated out to sea. Like a king."

"I see. Chances are I'd have to fold you into a pedalo and send you out into the middle of the Serpentine. How does that sound?"

We laughed about it because we never stopped to think that one day death would find us and render cutesy conversations about Norse burials moot because I would be so incapacitated by sadness that it is all I can do to pick up the phone and beg clergymen to allow me to bury my husband.

# 10

During the time I spent hiding from the world and shunning my responsibilities in favor of hibernation, the earth has continued to turn, lives have continued to be lived and plenty, it seems, have also come to an end. I can't locate anywhere with an opening for Quentin's funeral. I can be accommodated, I am told, but not now. With a Google results page open on my MacBook, I plead with officiants, priests and pastors who offer me their sincere apologies but beseech me to please understand. Their hands are tied. Their schedules full.

Bee finds me facedown on the bed. "No luck?"

"None. The world is conspiring to stop me from burying my husband. This is life's way of reminding me I suck at it."

"You're doing fine, babe."

"I need this to not be so hard. I promised everyone I could do this." And it's true. I've batted back offers of help to arrange Q's funeral and dug in my heels. I have been seized by an almost violent need to do it alone. Yet here I am, already falling at the first hurdle. There is a casket to secure, floral arrangements to choose. There is a plot to procure, invitations to address, notifications to be made, and my failure is a portent of what is to come—how hopeless I will be without him. "You know of anywhere in London that sells Viking ships?"

Bee raises an eyebrow. "Yeah, I'd say you're shit out of luck with that one, babe. But the freaks at work are *all* about helping you with the funeral process."

I lift my head. "You're joking."

"No word of a lie. Esme wants you to consider a pagan funeral."

"A what?"

"You'd buy a wicker casket and wrap Quentin in grape leaves or something and cremate him in the woods. Incense would be involved."

"She wants me to give my husband a hipster burial. Would I be expected to hang a dream catcher over his grave? Nothing says nonconformist like a hearty dose of cultural appropriation. I can't go back there," I say.

"'Course you can." Bee moves to the window and lights a cigarette. "You know you don't have to do this to yourself, right? You can phone Nosferatu and have her pull some strings."

I bristle. I know the kind of strings Aspen would pull, can already feel them around my neck. "I don't need Aspen. I can handle this. I need to handle this." This may not necessarily be true, but that is by the by. I might drown in this, the minutiae of planning, but I will do so knowing that in the end, I proved how deeply I loved Q. My motivations may not be the purest—I understand they are colored by the looming figure of Aspen and her disapproval—but they are also valid. I will prove to Aspen and to everyone else that I was a good wife. That I *am* a good wife. Chief Widow. An Aspen-branded funeral would be heavy on the calla lilies. My family and I would be invited only under duress and there would be terse correspondence about even that: *The dress code is listed in the invitation. Will your sister insist on bringing her children?*

The literature the police give you after they have scraped your loved one off a two-lane highway or informed you that your dear one is now dearly departed offers a bunch of weak advice about "transitioning" and bracing yourself for the post-numbness onslaught of pain. Like pain hasn't shadowed me nonstop since Q died; like I don't walk around feeling as if someone picked up an industrial-sized ice cream scoop and scraped out my insides. I ignore the advice but highlight the list of provided numbers you are supposed to call for assistance with arrangements. I am about to make the first call of the day when my phone flashes to life.

It's Aspen.

Nosferatu is unrelenting. "Hello, Aspen."

She wastes no time. "Eve, I have left you at least fifteen messages. Did you not think it proper to tell me they had released my son's body?" Her tone, as always, makes me want to correct my posture and dive headfirst out of a window.

"I've been busy," I say without warmth. Over by the window, Bee makes a face.

Aspen tells me there is a "proper way" to deal with these things. She details my myriad insufficiencies. She is cruel in a way that makes me step outside of my own body and witness the look on my face when she once again reminds me that I was inept at keeping him happy enough to remain alive, thus making it clear she should be allowed to take the reins and provide him with a fitting send-off. All I can think about is how on my wedding day, she refused to kiss my cheek, hand hovering above my arm so it looked like she was touching me—a show for the photos. She says something about the family plot, and I find my voice.

"Aspen, I don't possess the words to express how much that is not going to happen."

Bee stares at me.

"No... No... I don't care. You're shouting, Aspen... No... I don't... I— Aspen, I am handling everything. There's nothing you need to do. You have my address. Feel free to send a wreath." I cut off the call and shove my phone underneath a pillow, simultaneously tipping the landline phone off its cradle with an outstretched finger. It is a petty victory, I know, and the guilt grown from the seed of knowing the less than perfect impetus behind my obsession, the desperation to prove myself as primo wife, is something I choose to tend. The hardship of planning is one I willingly step into, hoping that the result will be worth the pain, that perhaps some of the questions people carry in their eyes when they look at me will be answered.

From her place by the window, Bee asks, "Shall I get out the Yellow Pages?"

I compartmentalize. I try to stub out my desolation for the time being. It is harder to crash and burn when folks are not expecting it of you. I've always been obstinate that way, working myself into knots rather than admitting I could use a little help. I boss up, though, and do what I swore to Aspen that I would. The thought of setting foot outside of the house again sends me into paroxysms of panic, but hell, she Bentley-d her way over here to demand a nonexistent note. I'll have to deal.

"Let me come with you," Ma begs, but I tell her no, tell her to go home and rest, that I will call her the second I'm in over my head. She reluctantly agrees and I keep to myself that I started being in over my head right around the time I found Quentin lifeless in his studio.

I visit funeral directors and leaf through pages of catalogs expounding the virtues of oak versus mahogany, and at one point I ask a balding man named Frederick why he thinks an extra thousand spent on a deluxe model means I love my

husband more than if I plumped for the perhaps-not-deluxe-
but-still-perfectly-adequate-considering-it-will-never-be-
seen-again model. Words fail him and I calmly hand him
back his catalog and walk out, stopping to lean against the
front of the building until the world stops spinning. Until I
can move without fainting. I call Ma and she picks me up and
brings me home. Too tired to make it up the stairs, I sit on
the sofa and stare into the fireplace, and I keep staring until
inspiration comes at five in the morning.

When we first moved into the house, our central heating welcomed us by refusing to work. It took all of two days
of wearing multiple layers and fighting frostbite in my own
bedroom for me to be over it. Q suggested we use the fireplace and I remember asking him through chattering teeth
what part of me looked competent enough to build a fire.
He did it himself because he was smart enough to know he
could use newspaper as kindling. He ended up with a faceful
of soot, and as he blinked at me through the dust, my mood
lifted enough for me to laugh. I wiped smudges of dirt from
underneath his eyes and he bought a bag of marshmallows,
which we toasted over the flames. We huddled in front of
the fire for the rest of the night, me eventually falling asleep
in his arms, and the next day, he shelled out an eye-watering
sum on an emergency plumber to fix the boiler so I wouldn't
have to go to bed cold again. It took us almost a year to finish the surplus of leftover marshmallows, and every time I felt
one melt against my tongue, I remembered that night: the
soot, the crackling flames, Q's icy fingers inching underneath
my two jumpers and three T-shirts. That was Q. Performer
of small yet profound gestures. Refuser of haircuts. Singer of
Bon Jovi songs without irony. Inventor of ingenious ways to
make up after a fight. Like the time we rowed after moving
in and I, frustrated with myself for not being able to articulate the ways in which he was wrong and a complete idiot,

broke down into the kind of tears you hate yourself for. The kind you cry because you're so angry and no other reaction is forthcoming. Q handed me a pen and paper, which I prepared to fling at his head. *Write down whatever it is you want to say*, he said. *I'll do the same.* We did, and by the end, I had forgiven him, but that didn't stop him from gathering up our pages and tossing them into the same fireplace. It was a display in corny symbolism, but it worked. We watched the papers curl and evaporate with any residual rage. He bought me roti, and afterward, we had the kind of makeup sex that left me listing to the left for the next couple of days.

Therefore, because my husband was a man who did things like this, who knew me so well he could gauge my reaction sometimes before it bubbled into being, I pick up the phone as soon as it is late enough to do so and I call the balding funeral director and ask him whether or not his coffin supplier is open to custom orders.

"What kind of thing are you looking for?" he asks.

"I'd like a simple structure," I reply. "It should be shaped like a Viking longboat."

# 11

If anyone finds it weird that I pay for a casket-sized replica of a Viking ship for my husband to be cremated in, they wisely keep it to themselves. Ma checks me for fever but says nothing. Aspen, who knows nothing of my acquiescence to this one element of my husband's eccentricity, remains vocal about her exclusion. So vocal, in fact, she threatens legal action if I "refuse to dispense with this ridiculous charade."

I call my sister.

"She can't sue you," Gloria tells me. "Not for refusing to let her seize control of funeral arrangements. Perhaps she could in America, but we're not too big on the whole 'emotional distress' thing over here. Besides, one could argue you're experiencing an equal amount of distress right now."

"You're right, one could argue that. One should. Can I sue her for causing *me* emotional distress?"

"Unfortunately not," Gloria says. "Harassment, maybe. Are you okay?"

The question, which I am asked multiple times every day, does nothing but prick another hole in my already delicate composure. I feel less okay as the days insist on going by. "You mean apart from the whole finding-my-husband-dead thing?"

She pauses. "Yes. Apart from that."

I sigh. I have learned that "fine" is the only acceptable response. Nobody really wants to be landed with the responsibility of negotiating any other reply. "Thanks for doing the lawyer thing, Glo."

"My pleasure. Putting any type of smackdown on Aspen, litigious or otherwise, brings me nothing but joy."

The Viking casket is constructed at enormous cost and I arrange for a cremation and funeral service and, by a profound miracle, both are held with little incident. A milky sun hangs in a sky the color of tears. Aspen attends, draped in Stella McCartney, and as she did on my wedding day, she vibrates with rage the entire time. Her anger threatens to erupt and drench us all, hitting me the hardest and staining. I take a single pill before leaving the house, but it's like the fluoxetine seeps from my pores as soon as I step into the church courtyard, its calming effect rendered useless. I have pulled this together. I have checked boxes, made phone calls and fixated on crafting Quentin's farewell. Now it is here and even a pill can't dull the ache. Would he be proud? Undoubtedly. Is he still gone? Irrevocably.

I don't look at Aspen directly. I watch her heels hit the ground and shift my gaze to my own uninspiring ballet flats, the ones with the leather flower on the toe, and I wonder whether I should have put more effort into my ensemble. I weep through Jackson's eulogy. In my hands, I hold a lovingly and painstakingly prepared speech. It outlines the joy Q brought to my life and only briefly touches on the pain I feel now he's gone. It's a speech laden with happy memories. It includes a beautiful quote. It is a good speech. And it is curtailed because I cannot rein in my emotions long enough to give it in full. Nate and Dad catch me when my knees give way. Aspen leaves before I am fully upright.

I return home with Quentin in a tasteful white urn and everyone returns to their lives. I go back to bed and things tick along as they have been—me refusing to engage with the world and everyone else wishing I would. I reinstate my long-standing staring contest with the ceiling and Ma reinstates her shifts of hovering. It would be a comforting return to what appears to be the new definition of normal if it wasn't so tragic.

People think because you have cried in their presence, they have witnessed real grief. They are content to sit across from you, hand you Kleenex and cluck sympathetically while you dab at the tears and lower your eyes in meek appreciation of their company. They make you food and phone you once, maybe twice, and consider their jobs done, their sympathy meters drained. They would much rather you walk with your head held high, shoulders back, a silent decree that *Yes, I am mourning, but feast your eyes on the dignity I maintain*. People are not prepared or simply don't want to see the reality of it: the jutting cheekbones and bloodshot eyes—the result of night after night spent crying until your corneas burn. People don't want to witness your slight, wretched figure hunched over the toilet retching bile and saliva when what little food you managed to ingest has run out. They don't want to see plates being hurled at the wall and sometime later find an incoherent, inert figure lying among the debris. Better to make tea and pat knees and act like this is a nasty case of flu rather than an all-encompassing torture that refuses to fade. Grief is not neat. Pain is not dignified. Both are ugly, visceral things. They rip holes through you and burst forth when they see fit. They are constant, controlling companions, and if they don't destroy you or your relationships with others, they certainly go a long way to damaging you, disfiguring you internally and altering your existence so much so that when you are lucid enough to look at yourself, at your life, you are astounded (and often disgusted) by what you find staring back at you.

There is nothing eloquent about my grief. It scares people. I slouch into a room and nobody knows how to react. I will take silent uneasiness over unsolicited advice any day, one more *everything happens for a reason* might push me over the line into homicidal.

# 12

Nate is a person whose genitalia might be on fire—actual flames licking at his crotch—and his reaction would, at most, stretch to a slight creasing of his brow to denote inconvenience. Once when he was twelve years old, he arrived back at the house with his chin split open after flying over the handlebars of his bike. His shirt was drenched in blood and the flesh was open right down to the white meat, and even as Ma screamed and Dad began bundling him into the car so they could race to A&E, Nate remained baffled as to why everyone was freaking out. He just wanted to eat a grilled cheese sandwich and watch *ThunderCats*. He was almost insulted people cared so much.

I walk downstairs and find him in my living room in jogging bottoms eating a bowl of Coco Pops and browsing sports channels. I shriek in alarm. I shriek in alarm and he barely acknowledges me before shoveling another spoonful into his mouth.

"You scared me! What are you doing here? Is it the weekend again?"

"It's a Saturday," he says.

"Oh, okay." I turn to leave before I realize something is awry. "Why are you here on a Saturday morning eating cereal in your jogging bottoms?"

"I slept here last night."

"Nate, why aren't you at your girlfriend's house? Or why isn't she here with you telling me I look slim?"

He appears extremely burdened by this conversation, but I press on.

"What happened?"

"Nothing. Cleo's pissed because I lost my job and now we can't go to Portugal like we were planning."

"You lost your job?" Nate is a business analyst. Surprisingly, despite being so laid-back he should rightly be in a coma, he is terrific at what he does.

"It's a recession." His indifference is awe-inspiring.

"What are you going to do?"

"Find another one. Listen, do you have any toaster waffles?"

"Toaster— Nate, your job! Do Ma and Dad know?"

"They have bigger shit to worry about."

"Like what exactly?"

He looks at me like I am the simplest of yokels. "Like you."

He makes us toaster waffles and we watch lacrosse because it is the only thing on, and inevitably, he eats my waffles as well as his. I stop asking him why he is hiding out in my house and he makes sure the words *How are you doing?* never pass his lips. It is easy to be in the company of my brother. There is little pretense going on here. He knows I am miserable in the extreme and I know he is perhaps marginally concerned by his newfound joblessness.

An hour passes and only when he has acquired more food does he decide to speak.

"So. It's been, like...a month now?"

"Nate, we don't have to do this."

"Are you sick of people being around all the time?"

"Nobody's around now. Only you." Even as I say this, it dawns on me that my support system is tiring of me. Things have not quite returned to how they were before the memorial. On any other Saturday morning, the place would be full, but now it is just my brother, whom I suspect is only here to hide from his girlfriend and Everett's comments about his girlfriend. Even Bee is absent. My family have spent too long maneuvering around my emotional state; it is no surprise they need a break from me.

"They'll be here in a bit," Nate says.

"Tell them they don't have to."

He frowns. "But we do have to. We're your family."

"You people just want me to be happy again."

This time, Nate lowers his plate so he can dedicate all his attention to staring me down. "And you don't?"

The answer is no. I don't want to be happy. There is no happy. I am content to wallow in this cesspit for all eternity because it is like poking at a mouth ulcer with the tip of your tongue—inadvisable, painful, but addictive. What I choose to say to my little brother instead: "Someday. Maybe."

Nobody tells you how the first time you laugh after a major bereavement will destroy you. You may not have even registered that you don't laugh anymore—another point on the itemized list of things grief steals from you.

When you do laugh, you will freeze and your blood will run a little colder and it will dawn on you that this simple act, an act you performed routinely in the Before, seems alien to you. Then you will stop almost immediately because why the hell should you be laughing when your husband is dead. Laughter should no longer exist.

Bee makes a joke about Barry, something innocuous about his fashion sense, but I laugh and startle myself back into si-

lence. Bee offers me her wineglass. I drain it. We turn our attention back to the rom-com on TV. A postcoital scene plays
out on screen. The actress swings her legs out from under the
duvet and stands at the side of the bed, sheets wrapped tightly
to protect her modesty. She reminds her partner that she is a
person, not an assortment of body parts. There's real pain in
her face—maybe she tapped into a memory of an ex to bring
the scene to life. I am overcome with remorse. I excuse myself to the kitchen and grip the edge of the sink so hard the
skin on my knuckles threatens to split.

It's strange because Quentin and I spent most of our time
laughing. Once he had acclimatized to my brand of humor
(slightly dark, dry, steeped in cynicism) and I'd made peace
with his (corny, almost infantile; fart jokes and the like), we
laughed our way through more than a decade together. We
developed inside jokes like every couple does. Q's laugh was
a rambunctious animal you ought to but can't bring yourself
to control. I was obsessed with it. I will never again get to
hear him unleash his laugh all over the house. He is the thief
of my joy, but to laugh feels like a betrayal.

The next day, I find one of Q's shirts underneath the sofa—
a throwback to the days spent doing unspeakable things to
each other in every conceivable place, promising that we
would never become one of those dour, sexless married couples—and, after an hour of wailing, have fallen asleep when
the sound of my phone infiltrates my nap. I assume it is Aspen,
who, since the funeral, has graduated from voice mails to ven-
omous text messages. But it is Nate, and he wants something.

"You want to come over tonight?" he asks because apparently greetings are passé.

"Wh-what?" I mumble through the dispersing fog of sleep.

"I'll cook something, yeah?"

Nate last invited me over to his flat because Cleo had

thrown herself a birthday party there and we were all required
to attend and lend him moral support while he entertained
her friends and work colleagues. He does not generally extend
invitations into his personal space unless there is something
in it for him. Apparently, my little brother is big on boundaries. I wake up a little more. "You'll...cook?"

I imagine Nate frowning in exasperation. "Listen, will
you just come over? Do you want me to come pick you up?"

Nate's boundaries extend to his car, a Mercedes, which he
treats like a rare and priceless jewel, refers to (without irony, I
might add) as Black Sapphire, and prevents the likes of family
from entering unless he is under duress. "You— Um, alright."

"See you in a bit."

On arrival at his flat, we are greeted by the sight of Everett, standing in the hallway in his boxers examining a stain on
the collar of a shirt I assume he has recently removed. At six
foot five and with more than a passing resemblance to Idris
Elba, Everett is what most people would call "arresting" and
what Bee used to call "the Emperor of Optical and Genital
Stimulation" during the two weeks she allowed him to date
her before growing restless. Bee's rejection is responsible for
the broken hearts of the women Everett sought out to dull
the sting of losing the affection of one Belinda Contois.

Everett has been Nate's best friend since they were fourteen, and since his growth spurt, "flirtatious" has been his
default setting. To disgust my brother, the two of us would
put on an act of biding time before we could run away and
live a life of wanton debauchery together. Q found it hilarious. I can't think about it without being overcome by nausea.

"Mate," Nate says through clenched teeth, "put some
clothes on."

When he sees me, Everett grins, then sees I am dragging
around my misfortune like a child being hauled along a supermarket floor after being denied access to the confection-

ery aisle, and his face morphs into an expression of contrition. "Alright, Eve?" he says.

"Oh, yeah," I say, "I'm great."

"Don't you have a thing tonight?" Nate, in a spectacular display of subtlety, asks.

"Yeah. Is there a stain on this shirt?" Everett thrusts his shirt toward Nate and my brother almost steps forward to examine it but catches himself at the last second.

*"Fam."*

"Ah, yeah, okay. My bad. Good to see you, Eve, yeah?" Everett leans down from his lofty height, all solid, sinewy heft, and moves to kiss my cheek and I back into my brother in an attempt at avoiding his lips.

"That was a bit much, wasn't it?" Nate says of my reaction when Everett has returned to his bedroom.

"I—" I start to explain that the thought of another man touching me makes me want to eject my intestines from my mouth. "Sorry," I say instead.

Nate has done some cursory tidying in preparation for my arrival. The kitchen sink is empty, the bathroom smells of something piney and the living room sofa is no longer a catalog of Everett's limb indentations. He has roasted a chicken. And by roasted, I mean he has purchased a roasted chicken from Waitrose and roasted it *more* because Dad taught us at a young age never to trust chicken that has been cooked by white people. My brother offers me a plate, and I recognize whatever has inspired this display of effort, it is important. "What's going on, Nate?"

He takes a mouthful of food before answering. "I like spending time with you."

"Oh God, has someone else died?" I start shaking, and before either of us knows what is happening, I am crying into my plate of untouched poultry. Nate's fork freezes en route to his mouth and the food he was in the process of chewing takes an unscheduled detour. When Everett appears again on his way out, he walks in on me sobbing while Nate, now choking on his food, coughs and splutters in helpless terror.

"Christ." He bounds over to clap Nate on the back. "What the hell?"

"It's fine. It's cool," Nate reassures him when he has regained the power of speech. "Go on your date."

"I can stay." Everett might be emotionally unavailable, and might have an aversion to doing laundry, but he is at his core a good and decent human being.

"You don't need to stay. Don't stay." Nate takes a sip of water. The front door closes. "Stop crying. Nobody's died." He frowns. "I say I like spending time with you, and you burst into tears and assume someone's kicked the bucket. Nice."

I stare at him. "So what is it, then?"

He throws a newspaper on the table and points to a highlighted article. "It says here that *Circle* is one of the best places to work in Europe. It's number nineteen on the list."

"Are you shitting me?" I peer at the article, but sure enough, there is the list and there is *Circle* sitting at number nineteen. Bee has not mentioned it, but this is likely because she doesn't give anything even adjacent to a fuck. "Wow."

"Yeah. So. I thought. Maybe. You'd like. Ask. If…"

"Spit it out, Nate."

Nate looks like he wants either to hide under the table or pick it up and smash it over my head. "Would you mind asking Bee to see if she could get me an interview?"

"At *Circle*?" My incredulity is so palpable I could wear it as this season's newest accessory.

"I realize I might not have been all that complimentary about it."

"You have ripped the piss out of me at every opportunity since I started there," I remind him.

He carries on as if I have not spoken. "And there's a chance I haven't been too nice about your colleagues."

"You've called them 'pretentious gits,' 'holistic neckbeards,' 'hemp-wearing pussies' and many other colorful things. All of them except Bee."

"You never disagreed," he points out.

"Well, no, because it's true. But now you want to work there?"

"Beggars can't be choosers."

"You're hardly a beggar, Nate. You've been out of work for five minutes. You'd hate it there."

"Yeah, but my bank account wouldn't have a problem with it. And they have this benefits package most companies don't even consider. Ma and Dad like the idea."

"Oh, please, what the hell would you do with a monthly subsidized colonic? You've told Ma and Dad?"

"Dad was the one who told me about the article."

This is not easy for Nate. He has always had his career locked down. He has never had to ask. He believes in working for things. Nepotism has been known to churn his stomach. "Does *Circle* even believe in business analysts?" I twist my napkin. "And how come you didn't ask me to get you an interview?"

"Either of you—all I need is a meeting with your boss. I'll do the rest," he says. "Also, you've been going through some shit lately and I didn't want to make you go to work before you were ready."

My little brother, the Beater of Bullies. "I'll call Bee."

Once she manages to stop laughing, Bee makes one call and gets Nate a 10:00 a.m. meeting with Barry the next day. She may mock *Circle* and its try-hard aesthetic, but when it comes to her job, Bee is a formidable force of nature. Being indispensable means Barry would suck the dirt from her shoes if it means keeping her on staff. When Bee asks his assistant, Maya, to clear an hour from his diary so she can bring in some new talent, Maya knows better than to ask too many questions.

Too tired to do anything but clutch Quentin's wedding ring and maintain the fetal position in our bed, I listen to Bee advise Nate on what to wear—they both arrived at the house at the crack of dawn this morning to "prep."

"The navy suit—no tie," Bee instructs. "Better yet, you have anything made of sackcloth?"

Nate buttons his shirt and surveys himself in the mirror. "What do you think, Eve?"

Without lifting my head, I give the thumbs-up. "You'll slay," I mutter. My enthusiasm has wilted like a parched peace lily. Which is unfair because for once, Nate is nervous. Even I can see past my apathy to recognize it. He and Bee stare at me. "You don't want to be late," I tell them.

"It's only eight thirty-five. We've got time. Do you need anything?" Bee asks.

I need them to stay with me. I need to be held for a while. And in the absence of either of those things, I need to go with them.

I sit up. "I'm coming with you."

"You sure about that?" Nate stares pointedly at my unruly hair and the crust in the corners of my eyes. He does not want me to show up at the office and scupper his chances of employment. It is an understandable fear.

"If you could give me, like, twenty minutes," I say. I stand, am helped to the bathroom. Bee insists on sitting on the toilet seat while I shower and brush my teeth. She multitasks her concern for me, informing Barry of my imminent arrival and interview prep for my brother. Were my heart not already a dead thing, it would explode.

Twenty-five minutes later, we are trundling toward *Circle*'s offices in Nate's car. The original plan was for him and Bee to tube it in, but since I have inflicted myself upon them, Nate has deigned to play chauffeur—I may be showered and degrees more presentable than before, but neither Nate nor Bee trusts me to navigate the remnants of rush hour on the Underground.

If I hold myself still in the back of my brother's car and stare up at the brick face of *Circle*'s headquarters, I can nearly fool myself into believing I am the Eve of Before. The one with a husband to kiss before making her way to work. The one who passed through these same glass doors and took the stairs to the second floor where a torture device of a desk was waiting complete with a twenty-four-inch iMac. The one who drank salted caramel lattes from Starbucks even while her colleagues drank chicory coffee and kale smoothie shots from the canteen. It seems so incredible, that I was a woman who put on eyeliner and went to work like everyone else. That woman is gone.

"You okay?" Nate asks when we've stepped out of the lift and are standing in front of the second set of glass doors leading to the Creative Domain floor (the names in this place; good Christ).

"You can still back out," I say, and neither of us is sure if I am talking to him or myself.

"No, he fucking can't," Bee chimes in. "He's going to go in there, get himself a job and join me in this hipster hell. Right, Natey?"

Nate demonstrates his most devastating half smile. "Right."

"Excellent. Shall we?"

My desk is exactly as I left it before Christmas. Nothing has been touched. A clutch of holly leaves that have seen better days nestles beside my drawing tablet. I sweep them into the bin and sit. Within seconds of stepping through those doors, I was bombarded with salutations and the wary questions of people who are terrified of your tragedy rubbing off and infecting their own lives. As Bee led Nate away, I saw him shoot me a concerned glance over his shoulder. When Royce, one of the junior curators and a guy who wholeheartedly buys into *Circle*'s vision, laid a hand on my arm and asked who was in charge of monitoring my "out-of-grief rebirth," I knew it was time to seek a moment of solitude. My desk was as good as it gets. It's not like I'm invisible here, but ever since I was hired, I've flouted *Circle*'s "Open Arm Desk" initiative by clamping headphones over my afro and working hard on an expression that says, *No, thank you, not today.* Colleagues tend to give my desk a wide berth and I have always been thankful for it. The distance is now caused by fear. The blackness of catastrophe might mar the pristine expanses of lives otherwise undamaged by anything as tawdry as suicide. I have been here ten minutes and am already seeing the questions in people's eyes: *How is she even doing this? What could have been so wrong with her that her husband had to kill himself?*

I power up my computer and access the password-protected folder housing a treasure trove of Q's emails, inaccessible from my personal laptop, missives he'd fired off from his phone during long days of shooting. A combination of everyday observations, emails handling the practicalities of married life (*Do we have eggs? Also, the window cleaner is due tomorrow— 7:00 p.m.*) and the kind of filth that probably had my name in red on IT's watch list. I dive into those emails and soak myself in nostalgia, willingly setting myself alight. At least this is of my doing; at least I have some semblance of control instead of being back at the house, where I am routinely ambushed by something as innocent as a sock hiding down the back of a radiator. Knowing the only thing here capable of wrecking me is locked up in this password-protected folder brings some relief. The thought of heading back to the house, where the life I could have had haunts me with almost as much fervor as the life I lost, is so sickening that when Nate and Barry appear at my desk beaming and Barry says, "Your brother is extremely persuasive, Eve. We're going to welcome him to the *Circle* family." I get to my feet and reply, "That's awesome, Barry. You can welcome me, too, because I'll be back on Monday."

# 13

Crying in public only ever becomes the heroines of the big screen. They make sadness look beautiful. The reality of it is, to escape the memories suffusing what was meant to be the "Forever House" of you and your husband—now deceased— you go to Waitrose even though you and your husband— now deceased—never shopped there because you considered it bourgeois and one thing you weren't was bourgeois even though the mother of your husband—now deceased—won't lower herself to shop among commoners. You walk through the aisles of Waitrose thinking, *This isn't so bad. I might be able to do this.* But while you are being so bold as to think that maybe you can make it through a trip to buy bread, you come across a shelf holding jars of olives, and before you know it, you're thinking back to the hundreds of times your husband— now deceased—tried to talk you into liking martinis. How he'd put on a show in the kitchen of what was supposed to be your "Forever House," using a cocktail shaker and a stupidly expensive chilled martini glass. He did this on at least five separate occasions, but every single time, you got bored and ended up feeding each other olives and drinking vermouth straight from the bottle. Suddenly, everything in this Waitrose is a reminder of everything you have lost. The woman in the blue coat walking by with her shopping cart reminds you of your husband—so very deceased—gliding through the aisles like he was a kid. The man in the freezer aisle scrutinizing a tub of Ben & Jerry's reminds you of the way your husband would yell, "Nipping out to Sainsbury's," and return half an hour later with nothing but ice cream. And yeah, like you'd expect, it is too much and you drop your goddamned jar of olives and people stop what they are doing to eyeball your meltdown and feel silently superior, grateful their lives aren't so miserable that they have been reduced to causing a scene in Waitrose on a Saturday evening.

Despite Quentin's belief in plan Bs, there was never one for us. We were doing all the things we were meant to do. We fell in love, we got married, we bought a house. We went on holiday. We cooked and cleaned and worked. We fit. It was only ever supposed to end one way—us growing old and wizened together, surrounded by his photographs and my books. Instead, all I got was blood-soaked jeans, blue lips and what I can only presume will be a lifetime of guilt. It's making me crazy. I say this to Bee when she shows up on Sunday afternoon, the day before I am due back at the office. She curls next to me on the sofa. She looks small and beautiful, but underneath her makeup, I see she's tired. She catches me staring.

"I look like shit, I know. Blame Barry. He's incapable of approving a layout unless I'm there babysitting him. What the hell did he do before I got there?"

"He has you working weekends and you're here?" Guilt flares in my belly. "Bee. Go home and sleep."

"I'll sleep here. Besides, I thought you might need a pep talk before you come back tomorrow. You know there's no pressure, right? Barry isn't going to replace you."

"I need to be back."

Bee shrugs noncommittally and her eyes sweep the room. They land on the birthday card I found earlier in the day. It was the last birthday card Quentin gave me. Thirteen days before he died. I was so upset when I found it, I put my fist through the fishbowl that houses my tangled collection of jewelry and had to lie to Ma and Dad when they rushed in to see what had happened. "It slipped," I'd said. Dad bandaged my hand and we said nothing else about it.

"What's that?" Bee asks.

"Birthday card from Q. He wrote that line from *The Bluest Eye*, the one that says, *You your best thing*. It's my favorite book. He added, *You my best thing, too*."

Bee nods to the mantel, where the card sits next to Q in his urn. "And you're just going to...y'know...keep it up there?"

"What?"

She shifts into a sitting position. "It's... I dunno, Eve, it doesn't seem healthy, keeping all this stuff around. This place is like a shrine."

"I can't actually win with you. I'm still too sad to come back to work, but I'm also healed enough to wipe every trace of Q from the house?" The bass in my voice only surfaces when I am angry. I inherited it from Dad.

Bee has never been one to walk away from an uncomfortable situation, not when she thinks she's right. "Look, babe, I get it, okay? I understand that you're in hell right now, but at some point, you're going to have to start trying to move past this."

"And in your opinion that point has arrived?"

"I know you can't just flick a switch or something—"

"It's funny," I say, talking over her, the bitterness surging inside me, fueled by weeks of looking into the eyes of my loved ones and seeing the naked longing, the impatience for me to get "better." "You keep saying you get it. But how exactly would you get it when your one serious relationship was with a guy who turned out to be married?"

They say you're meant to say fucked-up things when you're grieving—all the pain you're feeling comes out as shots you throw at others, knowing they will forgive you because they have no choice. But you are not prepared when it happens. Bee's face sets, and while part of me wants to reach out and cram the words back down my throat, the other heartless part of me that was born when Q died gives one of those villain laughs. You know the ones: *muahahahahaha.*

"Alright," she says. "You're right. I don't know how it feels to have someone I love commit suicide. I don't get it, so I'll ignore that low fucking blow, but I'll tell you this, babe—he's not coming back." She halts for a nanosecond while I flinch but then continues. "He's not coming back, so there's no point starving yourself to death or downing pills and booze or leaving everything exactly as it was when he was alive. It won't help."

She closes her eyes for a second, exhales and leaves the room. The scent of her perfume along with her words hang in the air. She's right and the fact that she is right makes me want to rip her face off. I press my knuckles into the wooden surface of the side table until this new pain replaces, at least temporarily, the enduring bite of Q's absence.

# WORK

# 14

So here's how things lie almost six weeks after I found my husband's body:

1. Because I can't control my tongue, my best friend is barely speaking to me, and were it not for the fact that my husband is dead, she would be well within her rights never to do so again.

2. I am back at *Circle*, and thanks to all the sleep I didn't get last night, I am sporting the kind of bloodshot eyes and dark circles that cause me to recoil at my reflection.

3. My brother, in his charcoal suit and pastel shirt, is also at *Circle* and is charming the "pretentious gits" with his acumen and aloofness.

4. I had 3,175 emails when I logged on this morning, and in lieu of doing any real work, I am making my

way through them and becoming more and more depressed by the second.

5. As fucking things up goes, I seem to be on something of a roll.

Nate insisted he drive me in this morning, rolled up in his car and paced in the downstairs hallway, irritating the shit out of me until I came down, half-dressed and looking like hell.

"I have nobody to impress," I said to him when he cut his eyes at my wrinkled jeans and oversize scarf. And honestly, I thought I didn't. But part of being back at work means having to act, to play the woman who isn't teetering on the knife-edge of breakdown, to pretend everything's hunky-dory, like I don't snatch the voices out of the mouths of my colleagues as soon as I step into a room, like I don't notice that they're all loitering, waiting to see whether I'm going to go off the deep end and crumple into a wailing heap, like I don't know they're all discussing me. That's suicide for you. Had Q met his end in a manner these people could parse—an illness with a face, a pink charity logo and an ad campaign—perhaps they might be able to maintain eye contact. Maybe even extend the sympathy I was so worried about receiving when I got here. I can't help being angry on Q's behalf.

The effort of maintaining my poker face is exhausting. By 11:00 a.m., I'm spent. I make my way to the kitchen and pour myself a coffee, which I am stirring absentmindedly when Bee walks in. There is a moment when she considers walking out, I see it, but she isn't spoiling for a fight.

"That bad, is it?" she says.

"Hmm?"

"You're willingly drinking chicory coffee."

I look at the mug in my hand and set it on the counter. "I didn't drink it."

When it comes to apologies, Bee and I were never the ones

to make a protracted deal out of it. She tests my waters and I test hers, and as long as they are lukewarm, we know that somewhere down the line, we will make it back up to hot. Right now, we are lukewarm and that's good enough; I'm glad she isn't gunning for a showdown because she'd knock me out right now, verbally or otherwise.

"They're planning a Circle Hug at lunchtime. Consider this your heads-up."

I am about to thank her when Nate walks in. "Hi," Bee and I chime simultaneously. "How's it going?" I add.

Nate shakes his head in response. Spying the steaming mug beside me, he scoops it up and takes a sip before I can warn him. The resulting arc of coffee into the sink reduces Bee to tears of amusement. "What the fuck is this?"

"Chicory coffee." I slip the mug from his grasp and pour the remainder down the drain. "There's a Starbucks on the corner. Not having a great first day? I swear everyone loves you."

"'Course they love me. I'm charismatic. But you people wouldn't know a business requirements document if it punched you in the face."

"We people? Aren't you the one that wanted to work here?" Bee straightens Nate's lapels as she speaks.

"Good thing this is a fixed-term contract. Long-term here? I don't have bail money." Nate shakes out his limbs and does a few neck rolls like he's about to step into a boxing ring. He pauses at the door and turns to me. "You okay?"

"They're planning a Circle Hug at lunchtime. You don't have a cyanide pill to spare, do you?"

"Drink the coffee—should have the same effect. I'll ring you when I'm leaving, yeah?"

I nod and he exits. Bee plucks an invisible piece of lint from her sleeve and pushes off from the counter. "My office is open if you need to escape. I'd give it until quarter to, then make a run for it."

★ ★ ★

By creeping into Bee's office and hiding in her coat-cum-stationery closet when Barry puts his head around the door to ask if she's seen me, I escape the Circle Hug. I do not, however, escape the impromptu "catch-up" with Barry and the digital guru (hand on heart, that's her fucking job title). They tag team me at the end of the day when I am waiting for Nate to finish admonishing the team for failing to develop an app. Aurora (honest to God, that is her name) and Barry invite me into the Zen Zone (please don't get me started) and the loaded silence is enough to tell me whatever's about to go down required a near-empty office and the added safety of a private meeting room.

"Eve," breathes Aurora. She is the type of woman who wears artisan perfume and wants you to believe she uses only organic products when in fact she is a loyal customer of both Space NK and Jo Malone and splices clothes from Free People with clothes from Pucci all for random and often disastrous effect. She sits in front of me with a folder pressed against her chest, wearing an all-magenta ensemble that is having quite the effect on my corneas. "It's *so* good to have you back, darling heart. We've missed you." When Aurora promoted me, she got it into her head that we were going to become tight, and when this didn't happen and I got tight with Bee instead, she hid her hurt feelings with hyperbolic sweetness—pet names, *touching*, frighteningly large grins—interspersed with sullen moods. She seizes one of my hands and squeezes it. "We truly have. We're so, so happy you're here."

"Rory's right," Barry agrees. "It hasn't been the same without you. It's great to see how you've dived right back in."

I think about the barrenness of my day and keep my mouth shut. Something is coming and I don't want to make things worse by speaking. I fix my gaze on Aurora. She is a pen clicker, a toe tapper and a shoulder wiggler—she shimmies her shoulders every now and again as if she is trying to free herself from the confines of her violently colored clothes.

"We want you to know we—that's all of us—are here for you. Completely. We have a holistic grief healer on speed dial waiting for your call." Barry smiles at me, unaware I would rather bodysurf the ninth circle of hell than consult such a person. "We're a family here and we wanted to reiterate that. Nothing's changed. Not one bit."

When we were kids, Ma sat us down and explained to us clearly the difference between Nigerians and White Folk. "We talk about our problems within the family," she explained. "Most oyinbos will talk to anybody that will listen." Years later, here's Ma's wisdom once again battering me about the head with its accuracy.

"Thanks, but that's totally unnecessary." I need to nip this here shit right in the bud. "I'm fine."

"You're consulting your own counselor?" Aurora flutters her eyelashes at me.

"Let's go with that," I say.

"Brilliant. So important. I am glad to hear you say you're fine, Eve. You know we value your contribution here at *Circle* and we also believe there is more than one way to work through difficult times." Barry pauses and exchanges a meaningful glance with Aurora before continuing. "Which is why we'd like you to channel your emotions into something that could help others."

I wait, and yes, it gets much, much worse.

They told me they want me to write a new series of blog posts entitled "Chronicle of a Transformation: Wife to Widow" in which I narrate the stages of my grief and offer advice to *Circle*'s readers about how to navigate the muddy waters of mourning. Barry and Aurora sat salivating at the thought of all the wealthy and bereft stumbling across my series, consuming what amounts to trauma porn and forking over thousands for the sponsored products the marketing team will tack to the bottom of each post. Aurora was so excited that the shimmying increased to the point that I anticipated dislocation. Awards and special snowflake acclaim were *Circle*'s bread and butter, and I wondered, as I sat mutely, whether the lack of shame was something employees of this place cultivate over time, or whether it was innate to these people.

At the time, I was too shocked, too dumbfounded to react accordingly (severing their heads neatly), but now I am at home, breathless with anger. It is the same impotent, irrational fury that results from stubbing your toe on a door frame or accidentally spilling coffee over yourself. You are livid, but the anger is misplaced—there's nowhere for it to go. Rationally I know Barry and Aurora are only doing their jobs and, in their own twisted way, believe they are helping me, profiting from my pain only as a by-product of aiding me through the horror of losing Q. But God help me, I want to gut them like deer.

The next day, I find myself staring at a blank page on my computer screen. There are words, of course, but what part of "Of course I had no idea he was going to do it—do you think he frequently left pools of blood all over the house that I simply mopped up?" do Circlers want to read? Bee ad-libbed her shared fury as I lamented, a sign that I am forgiven for my outburst, but Nate says the blog series is a good idea. He is convinced that done well, it could boost traffic to the *Circle* website exponentially and is already babbling about trying to make it a crossover series—get it in the print copies, too; he's chatting about a special edition bound volume of posts I have yet to write.

"No, Nate," I tell him. We are in the canteen and Nate is poking through the heap of tangerine spinach salad he's had to settle for (he is so busy that he doesn't have the time to leave the building to search for meat).

"Why not? It might help to, y'know, talk about it?"

"What are you, Sigmund Freud?" We are a hair's breadth away from the subject I have sidestepped for weeks. "It's gross. I'm not talking about Q to *Circle*'s readership. They don't deserve him."

"See, part of me thinks you want to. You would have said no."

"I'm saying it now."

"To me. You know where Barry and Rory are. Go tell it to them."

"You're calling her Rory?"

"She asked me to."

"Bye, Nate."

Back at my desk, I bite a pill in half and swallow it dry, and under the pretext of work, I dive into Q's email folder. Ten minutes later, I take the other half of the pill, and twenty minutes after that, I take another two pills, which is why, an hour later, I am foggy-headed, thick-fingered and back in front of Barry trying to explain my current state. There is talk of coping and expectations, then Bee and Nate are hustling me into the back of an Uber. I may be buzzed, but their judgment is strong enough that I feel it through the film of the narcotics.

"What are you doing, babe?" Bee says softly, and it is like she is speaking from a great height. She puts her hand on mine, but when I try to squeeze her fingers, I can't quite manage it.

"Falling apart," I mutter before falling asleep.

# 15

At the end of my first week back at work, my family call a war council designed to tackle the problem I have become. When she arrived, the first thing Gloria tried to do was braid my hair and it took all my limited strength to get her to leave me alone. She picked up her jar of coconut oil and left the room, and I felt triumphant for the six minutes it took me to realize she was sent in to disarm me so the rest of them could voice their quartet of "concerns":

1. That although they agree with the premise of me returning to work, I seem ill-equipped to handle the "constraints of office life" (this is Dad's euphemism, used to describe my failure to wear anything but Q's Picasso T-shirt and a pair of his jeans since I went back. It could also refer to the fact that makeup is now an alien concept to me, and the sight of my hair causes children to cry in alarm);

2. That my return to work is failing to demonstrate any upswing in my mood or recovery and has in-

stead resulted in my being sent home for admin-
istering sedatives at my desk, and my being given
a written warning for the use of expletives in an
email to the newest member of the *Circle* family
when he innocently asked whether or not my husband would be joining us for *Circle* Couples Camp
(evidently, "No, because he's fucking dead" is not
an appropriate response);

3. That the aforementioned behavior is putting Nate
   in a difficult position as a new employee and my
   brother;

4. That all of this necessitates the need for drastic action—they are cutting me off. No more happy pills
   for Eve.

Dad frowns when he explains this to me. His is a simple
existence. He loves God, his family and his work, and is de-
voted to all three. When something moves in and threatens to
disrupt any of the points in this perfectly constructed triangle,
he takes it seriously. Right now, I am the threat, and I am
also his daughter, and this makes for not only shaky ground
but unstable walls and a rickety ceiling, too. He is struggling.

"Evie," he says gravely, "is there anything we can do?"

I want to convince him that in the grand scheme of things
these weeks of erratic behavior are nothing to fret over. Except to do this would mean that at some point, Q would
become less dead. Since this is not the case, since his death
will continue to stretch out before me, a hazardous, depress-
ing road pockmarked with ditches and potholes, I am going
to carry on troubling my family until they either tire of me
completely or something equally tragic happens to one of
my siblings so the effort can be concentrated there instead.
Neither of these prospects is appealing. In my lap, my phone
rings. I ignore Aspen's call.

"I'm fine," I lie. "I'm just getting used to things again."

"There's getting used to things and then there's this." Gloria has little time for people screwing up at work. You are there to do a job, and if you are incapable of doing it, move the hell aside and let someone else have a crack at it—this is one of many chapters on Life by Gloria Ezenwa-Okorie.

Ma steps in. "It's a new job for your brother. He's trying to make a good impression there, build a good reputation."

"And in the process of destroying my own, I'm tarnishing his. I get it." I am annoyed because at a time like this, tears are all I have.

"That's not what Mum meant," Dad tries. He looks so perplexed that spontaneous combustion is not entirely out of the question. "She—"

"No, it's fine." I cut him off. I never cut my dad off. "Nate is the new boy and I need to get it together so people at work don't assume mental instability runs in the family." I am being petulant. They're coming from a good place. They don't want to see me ruin all the hard work I have poured into my inflated job title at *Circle*. But I feel like they are ganging up on me, like I should be forgiven my irresponsible behavior because that at least is something I can—and choose not to—control.

"Sis." Nate stands up. He is perturbed in the same way Dad is. When they stand beside each other, he is Dad without the glasses and the wrinkled brow.

"It won't happen again." My voice betrays me by cracking. A jutting lower lip wouldn't be out of place in this performance. "I— Will you— I'm going to bed," I announce to the four of them. My shame will not permit me to ask Dad for the pill he won't give me. I jam a pillow over my head so I don't have to hear them discussing how badly that just went. Later, I will ask myself if they knew even then just how much worse it was going to get.

★ ★ ★

It turns out that as a newly made widow of the worst kind, you can take prescription drugs at your desk, curse at your colleagues and even post a blog illustrating your mourning with a detailed digital drawing of a heart (anatomically correct, naturally) having an anvil dropped on it, which quickly has to be removed from the website and damage control undertaken with alacrity. You can do all these things, but when your boss asks you to perhaps concentrate more on "your words" and in the fug brought about by insomnia and mild withdrawal, you title your next blog post "The Happiest Cocktail" and detail the mix of benzos and barbiturates you would recommend to make it through a grief-laden day, *this* is the line in the sand. Who knew this would be the proverbial straw that broke the *Circle*'s back? I am fired the next day. Or rather, I am given the choice to accept a substantial severance package, sign a confidentiality agreement and walk away quietly or else be fired. Barry does not even have the nerve to do it himself; he gets Tom from HR to send an email asking me to come to his office, and when I don't reply, Tom himself appears at my desk shortly before lunchtime.

"Alright, Eve?" Tom and I are somewhat acquainted through the times he has walked new curators up to my desk and introduced them. He always says things like "I'll leave you in the capable hands of Eve here" and "Eve is the senior curator here, she's very smart" and he smiles from behind his glasses, putting everyone at ease. I used to think this was something they teach you when working toward your HR qualification—the friendly smile: two-thirds teeth, one-third eyes.

"Hi, Tom," I say without looking at him. I am staring dejectedly at my screen and have been for the past hour.

"I'm guessing you didn't get my email. Shall we go to my office?"

I shrug and follow him. Tom has a framed *Les Misérables* poster on the wall of his office. He has a small collection of Star Wars bobbleheads on his desk. He has a fern. And he gets straight to the point.

"Management feels your time at *Circle* has come to an end."

I hold myself still, expecting first the shock and the subsequent hurt and humiliation to kick in at any moment. Nothing comes. I suppose after you have lost your husband, the loss of your job at the world's most ridiculous magazine pales in comparison. "You don't have to sugarcoat it, Tom," I tell him. "Was it the heart thing?"

"More the encouraging drug abuse thing," Tom says. "Barry was as close to pissed off as I've seen him. We all know he's far too rich to experience any real anger."

I shrug again. "So, they want me gone."

"They'll miss you. Rory cried."

"She did?"

"Yup. Said she was dreading trying to find someone to take your place. She's responsible for how much they're offering you in severance."

"They feel guilty."

"It's not every day they have to sack someone whose…who is going through such a tough time. It doesn't exactly align with the magazine's core values." He slides some documents across the desk to me. "Your choices are outlined here. Like I said, the severance is substantial enough to tide you over for a while."

I flick dispassionately through the papers and offer Tom a wry smile. They are offering £1,000 for every year I have been at *Circle* plus a few thousand on top of that. Stacks upon stacks to assuage guilt. I let my job slip through my fingers and don't so much as lift one to put up a fight. I sign what I need to and Tom salutes me sadly before I walk back to my desk, too exhausted to care about the stares I am attracting.

I reach for Q's jacket, and out of nowhere, Bee is there helping me into it.

"They didn't tell me," she says. "I only found out now."

"Don't go making any grand gestures on my behalf, Bee." She has it too good here and I don't want to see her throw it away out of a misplaced sense of loyalty.

"I love you," she says quietly.

"Ditto." I try to smile, but my face muscles have fallen asleep. I peek over the top of Bee's head and see Nate approaching. I have never noticed until now that my little brother strides. It suits him. "Hi, Nate."

"Is it true?"

"Don't worry about it. They gave me money."

"Do you want me to… I can do something."

"Just don't turn into one of them. I never want to see a single chia seed pass your lips. See you at home, yeah?"

I don't even look back as I walk out of *Circle* for the last time.

# 16

Before the house and before the studio, there was a version of Quentin so riddled with self-doubt that I had to download the Calm app onto his phone and sit with him through half an hour of meditation every evening just so he could fall asleep. We were still in his uni flat, much to my parents' chagrin, but after we celebrated my being hired at *Circle*, I used part of my first paycheck to spring for a real bed, so at least my splinter days had drastically decreased. We were kids still subsisting on takeaway and the food Ma sent home with us after a visit, but we were also grown, feeling our way through the business of adulting, giddy with the knowledge that our sex life was now *marital*.

The microcosmic fame Q enjoyed on campus did not translate in the real world. His work on the university publicity team capturing student life in as enticing a manner as possible for the prospectus did not stretch to impress commissioning editors. That his were the photos people gravitated toward during his class showcases meant nothing. The recommendation letters written by his proud instructors went unheeded

by those whose desks they landed on. I watched as the limited confidence he'd built during those three years dwindled,
eroded by rejection after rejection for jobs, for internships,
for anything other than the most paltry of freelance assign-
ments—photographing different kinds of gravel for garden
centers or product shots for new varieties of nut milk.

"What do you think, babe?" he'd ask me wearily. "You
think I captured the essence of the polar white chippings?"

I was introduced to a unique and novel helplessness watching the keeper of my heart be demoralized in this way. I was
clueless about the world of photography and knew nothing
of the barriers that lay between Q and the success he was
searching for. I also knew that whatever the issues, it would
take only the revelation of Q's lineage for them to dissolve.
I never dared suggest it. Instead, I ran us baths and massaged
his scalp as I gently asked him whether or not there was an
alternate path for him. Surely, he of the backup plans had one
for this. But he didn't.

"I can't really fail, Eve," he whispered. "My mother is...
Well, failure in this field is expected of me. I have to figure
out how to make it work."

I did not own a magazine or newspaper. I had zero influ-
ential contacts. I could not tell you the difference between a
fish-eye and a macro lens. But what I was, was the daughter
of two brilliant Nigerians who taught me how to make bitter leaf into ofe onugbu, and I was also a new wife who knew
we couldn't survive on a single salary, not when simply stepping outside in London was a cash loss. I couldn't burden Q
with my worries. So I became the proverbial cheerleader. I
had Q's gravel and almond milk shots blown up and framed,
and hung them on the dingy walls of the flat, watching his
bafflement melt into incredulous glee when he got home and
realized what I had done. I talked him up to my cousin Ndidi,
who hired him as her wedding photographer. I observed the

uptick in his self-assurance as the bookings rolled in on the back of that event—Nigerian word of mouth proving more powerful than any portfolio. And when Q cautiously raised the idea of perhaps going out on his own, properly this time, I read the uncertainty in his eyes, the desperation to not only make me proud but to prove Aspen wrong. I spent five sleepless nights creeping out of bed and hunching over my laptop in the farthest corner of the flat, designing his logo, business cards and website, which I presented to him as he reheated Ma's okra soup.

"Eve, what did you do?" He ran his fingers over the embossed cards (£17 extra) and set the bowl down on the counter.

"It's not a big deal, babe. You're a businessman, so you need business stuff. It's not every client who's gonna be happy to do contracts and book you over WhatsApp— Q, are you crying?"

He turned away and addressed the wall. "Nah. Nope. Must be the onions in your mum's food."

I wrapped my arms around him from behind and rested my cheek on his back. His skin warmed my face even through his shirt.

He took a breath. "I love you. And I won't let you down."

"Better not. I require both shoe and bag as a token of your gratitude."

On the night of his first group exhibition, an achievement gained after photographing the vow renewal of the gallery owner, I held his trembling hand in the taxi and promised him it would be fine. The words spilled from my lips and I hoped that I would not be made a liar by the end of the evening.

"I don't think I can do this," he said as we pulled up outside of the gallery. "I feel like a fraud."

"My mother didn't tie wrapper to celebrate a fraud."

"What?"

"Look outside."

I had called a family meeting a week earlier and explained

how much their attendance would mean to Q, that his was no longer a dream deferred, and because they loved me and therefore him by extension, there they stood at the entrance.

Q got out of the car and Ma held his face in her hands and said, "My dear, Eve says people have come to look at your photos. Won't you comb your hair?"

None of us understood Q's affinity for this medium of art. Not really. It was like he came into the world already understanding that he would need to develop a voice that could be heard through pictures. Over a period of one year, he surreptitiously captured candids of our family: me sleeping on the sofa with an infant Ellie curled into my side; Nate's face a firework of joy as he and Dad laugh for some unknown reason on the deck of a rented family cabin; Gloria and I sandwiching Ma in a hug when she accepted her International Excellence in Endocrinology award. The photos were beautiful and still hang in my parents' house, and no matter how many times we visited, he would stop and look at them again. I knew to leave him in front of the pictures for a moment until the wistfulness worked its way through his body once more and emerged in a hug for Ma and Dad, purged of bitterness.

Even as his star began to rise, I knew there were still nights he locked himself in the bathroom to have his own private freak-outs. He considered his budding career precarious—a house of cards waiting to be toppled by the softest breeze.

Later and inevitably, adulting lost its gloss. I was all about business so Q could be all about his art. I would, when he called me to look at his latest work, give it a glance but not what he really wanted, which was the chance to bond over what came from the deepest part of him, to understand what he couldn't say in words but through pictures. I remained proud and assumed he knew it.

"You're doing it," I told him one day as he chewed his bottom lip and pored over his latest portrait commission.

"Not yet," he replied. He caught my hand as I moved toward the door. "But whatever I am doing is because of you."

He won his first prize a year later.

When Jackson texts a few days later to find out how I am doing, I inform him of my firing, and a few hours later, he arrives at the house carrying a picnic basket filled with assorted bottles of champagne. It is the first time I have left my room all week.

"I don't really want to talk, Jack," I tell him when I spy longing in the new lines on his face. "Let's just drink." And he agrees because you don't deny the request of your best friend's widow.

The next morning, I peel my tongue from the roof of my mouth and shut my eyes against the weak winter sun. Downstairs, Jackson remains on the sofa, and coward that I am, I back away from the sound of his sobs, the wretched curl of his shaking shoulders as he struggles to harness his grief. I have reached the upstairs landing when I hear Bee let herself into the house and make the same discovery.

"Jackson? What the shit is all this?" I do not hear his reply, but Bee's displeasure carries up to me, clear as a bell. "There are four empty bottles in here. You got her drunk? Look, I know...no, I know...just...clean up and go home, okay?"

I creep back under my covers and the guilt churns my already roiling stomach and rises to my throat. I feign sleep when Bee reties my headscarf, and by the time my hangover passes, Jackson and the bottles are nowhere to be seen.

"Here's the thing," Gloria says to me, "you're going to have to talk to her sooner or later."

I, on Gloria and Alex's trendy L-shaped sofa, train my eyes on their equally trendy glass orb chandelier and reply, "Then let it be later. Much later."

I am here at Gloria's behest. As a lawyer, she has thrown herself in the firing line when it comes to dealing with Aspen and her litany of complaints regarding my inability to conduct myself toward her with the respect she feels she deserves. Aspen's lawyers have been in touch with Gloria. As have the insurance brokers, police and countless other bureaucrats. This is the business of death and my sister is standing in the gap for me.

Alex and Gloria live in Hampstead in a house that wouldn't look amiss in the pages of The White Company's catalog. It is a gorgeous space to inhabit and there aren't too many Q-colored memories lurking in the corners waiting to jump me. One does live above the fireplace in the living room—a giant monochrome photograph of Ellie and Ben taken by Q. An anniversary gift thought up by me and orchestrated by the two of us on an afternoon we'd been asked to babysit. We bribed my niece and nephew with a trip to the cinema, and after the showing, they grinned against the chosen backdrop in Q's studio. I still remember the way Q bumped fists with Ben and knelt by Ellie so she could choose which shots she liked best. In the photograph, Ellie is missing a front tooth and Ben's dimples almost swallow his cheeks whole. I miss them.

"Eve, I'm happy to do this for you, but could you at least pretend to care?" Gloria thrusts a wad of papers under my nose. "They finished their investigation and they've signed off on the trust payout." Glo swallows audibly. "You should look."

When Quentin was born, his parents enjoyed him for all of five minutes before calling the lawyers in to put the finishing touches on the trust they set up for him when they learned an heir was in the making. It's something Q mentioned to me about a year after we got married, when out of nowhere, papers arrived at our house detailing that he was now in possession of an amount of money that made my stomach lining itch. With Q gone and my being the beneficiary in his will, this money is apparently now mine—a fact that has driven Aspen to distraction according to Glo, who reassures me my mother-in-law does not have a legal leg to stand on.

I had forgotten all about it, but now on Gloria's sofa, under the unmoving eyes of Ellie and Ben, this fact and all its implications hitches up its skirt and sits firmly on my chest. Q really isn't coming back. A group of people I have never met have raked over the coals of his extinguished life and found his death acceptable.

"I can't breathe."

"Oh, Eve." Gloria puts a hand on my head.

"I don't want it," I gasp.

"You say that now, but—"

"I mean it, Glo. I don't want the money."

My sister is far too practical to listen to me. She tucks the papers in a folder and fixes me with the look she reserves for obstinate clients and her children. "This money is going into one of your accounts, Eve. Which one is up to you—but it's going into an account. Spend it or leave it to accrue interest, but this is a thing that's going to happen."

"Q didn't take it when he was alive. He didn't want it and I don't want it either." I lock eyes with Glo, but she is unmoved.

"I don't care what you want right now."

"Money won't make me any better, Glo. Money gained explicitly because my husband killed himself will only make me worse."

"Eve. You have to think about security. You're done at *Circle* and that severance money won't last forever. You won't have to rush back to work before you're ready."

"I said I don't want it, Glo."

"Like I said—" Gloria places the folder on the coffee table "—you don't have to spend it. Choose an account and sign the papers and make you go stop vexing me, abeg. Let me do work for other people who are grateful to me for depriving my kids of my time to help them."

A long moment of silence follows.

"What?" Gloria says. "You know the pidgin makes an appearance when I'm annoyed."

"Okay, *Ma*."

"Just..." She takes a breath. "Just sign the papers."

I'm dragged back, for a second, to St. Jude's and my cheek against Gloria's blazer as she instructed me in the corner of the courtyard to hide my anguish from my aggressors, a cluster of girls who looked like they could have stepped from a shampoo ad, yet who had, in a singular act of violence, torn two braids from my scalp. I was eleven. They were watching. Gloria's command seemed impossible. The tears were almost there, crowding the edges of my eyes. Gloria's hand on my back, her face close to mine: *Don't. Bite your lip and clench your jaw.* She spoke from experience. She crossed the courtyard to deliver a promise of retaliatory violence should I be touched again, her slang mingling with pidgin to sound strange in this place where kids rolled out of the womb with nine months of elocution under their tongues. The words jostled against each other, but the sentiment was clear.

This is what Gloria does. She protects. She makes the choice to be the bad guy so the rest of us don't have to. It is a role she stepped into readily and which, somewhere along the way, I started to take for granted. It is the role she is playing even now.

I wipe my face with my sleeve and sign the papers. A week from now, more money than I know what to do with will be sitting in an account I have no plans of touching.

I hang around long enough for Tess the nanny to collect Ellie and Ben from school and for Alex to come home. I watch surreptitiously as he leans into my sister and, for a second, focuses all his attention on her. His eyes soften, he lifts his hands to either side of her face and he kisses her. It hasn't gone unnoticed that since Q died, Alex, never one for overt displays of genuine affection (he prefers wolfish grins and inappropriate comments), has made it a point to dip into his well of sincerity and demonstrate to Glo that he is as besotted with her as the day they met. More so. These days, you can't miss the way his shoulders relax whenever Glo enters a room and the way he seeks her out and wraps them both in a temporary bubble of marital bliss whenever he returns home from work, just for a second, until he administers his kisses. I would be appreciative if jealousy wasn't burning holes through my lungs.

My phone rings, but I send Aspen to voice mail.

I escape upstairs and into my niece's room. She is in her pajamas and enjoying her permitted twenty minutes of iPad time before bed.

"Hello, Snicker," I say and sit on the end of her bed.

"Hi, Aunty Eve. I still have thirteen minutes." She brandishes the iPad at me to emphasize her point.

"Right. No. I'm not here to stop you from… I came to say hello."

Ellie frowns. She has inherited a deep-seated mistrust of most things from her mother. "Hello." It takes a few seconds, but she continues to play on the iPad, winding down her thirteen minutes and stopping the precise second they are over.

"You can have another five minutes," I tell her conspiratorially. "I won't tell your mum."

"I've had twenty minutes. It's time for bed." Ellie delivers this news with the solemnity and derision only a child with the moral high ground can.

"Well, alright. Good night, Angelface." I kiss her cheek and tug the covers up around her chin.

"You can stay for a bit if you want." Her face tells me she is quite aware of her benevolence.

"Thanks." I slip under the covers beside her like I used to before devastation turned me into an empty shell of a person. I hold her, waiting for her breathing to slow. She smells of fruit and talcum powder and all the sweet things children smell like before they are ruined by age and pessimism. Before life finds them and disappoints them time and time again.

"Are you crying?" she asks through the dark.

I had not noticed, but it seems I am. Into her hair. "Sorry."

"You're always sad now," Ellie says. She doesn't sound put out or exasperated; she is simply making an observation.

"Sorry," I repeat.

"I know why. It's because Uncle Quentin died."

"That would be it, yes," I confirm.

"What a waste."

From the mouth of babes.

# 17

Today begins with the severance money arriving in my bank account in all its shameful, abundant glory—a stark and unnecessary reminder of my inability to keep either my husband or my job—and ends in hospital. Nate wants to meet for lunch. I want to get drunk. Bee wants to bike around Hyde Park like a person with an actual life. Because of the ongoing tug-of-war between keeping me "happy" and refusing to indulge my destructive whims, we compromise by meeting at my place, where we order in lunch. Mexican food (that I don't eat) accompanied by sangria that Bee makes. While Nate and Bee eat and exchange office anecdotes, I drink my sangria. I suspect it is more ginger ale and fruit than wine, but if Nate and Bee remain distracted by their conversation, there is a good chance I can drink their share and set myself up with a nice buzz. After my third glass, I feel sober (disappointing) and Bee is making noises about riding through Clapham Common because it is one of those rare days in a London winter where the sun has roused itself so as to be ferociously present in a sky the color of hope. So I bundle up in Q's green hoodie, the one he wore on the Saturdays we did nothing but schlep around the house, meandering in and out of naps, watching film after film and eating things we'd regret later, and the three of us go to the park after all, where there are new banks of Boris Bikes ready for us to ride.

I am not sure how it happens, but I have been on the bike no longer than five minutes when the sangria suddenly asserts itself in my bloodstream and my head fills with cotton wool. I am not drunk—three glasses of diluted sangria will not do this to you—but I am also not sober. I open my mouth to call out to my brother, who is ahead of Bee, flouting all his social rules by engaging in such a sugary activity, and my bike, like a belligerent mule, twists and slips out from under me. I feel like I fall in slow motion, but soon enough the ground rips through my jeans and into my skin and my head makes contact with the curb, and before I black out for the few seconds I do, I hear Bee screaming and Nate shouting and the gasps of passersby who now have a story to tell their friends when they meet them later for drinks.

This mishap is how I find out I am pregnant.
Pregnant.

I roll the word over my tongue and around my mouth like a boiled sweet, and even though it has been a good three hours since I found out, it is still foreign and strange, and brings my mind to a screeching halt when it dares to wander off to other things. Like a series of electric shocks.

The fall led to hysterical phone calls made first to emergency services and my parents and finally to Gloria, who managed to put aside her displeasure at "always being the last to know when something goes down" and race to the hospital. I tried to dissuade Nate and Bee from calling an ambulance, but they kept bandying about words like *concussion* and *cerebral hemorrhage* and *you were out cold for thirty seconds, Eve,* so I lay still on the path where I fell, with my head in Bee's lap, and watched Nate with his phone pressed to his ear.

At the hospital, I am examined by one of Dad's colleagues and friends, a doctor with graying hair who, after some prodding and poking and examining my abdomen in the ultrasound room, frowns at me and says, "The paramedics didn't say anything about you being pregnant." And after he says this, everything slows around me and his voice dissolves into white noise and my head is filled with neon letters spelling out *PREGNANT* in loud indisputable capitals.

Things happen quickly after that. My mother, at my behest, is called into the ultrasound room and works through her shock in record time before turning her attention to me and the grainy *thing* displayed on the screen. As the news filters out of this little room and reaches my dad, my siblings and Bee, there are more doctors and talk of amniocentesis, along with a battery of tests to find out the damage I have inflicted on—and saying this makes me want to pass out— my unborn child by descending into madness, by forgetting then refusing to eat properly, by binge drinking and my daily ingestion of sedatives and antianxiety medication. All the while, my skinned knees sting, my head and ribs throb and my ankle screams every time I move it, and all this physical pain is penance for giving myself over so entirely to the emotional pain of losing Q; so much so I have failed to notice that I am with child. With his child. Gloria and Bee ask rapid-fire questions: How could I not know? Did I not realize my period had absconded? Were there no other symptoms? The answers should be clear: *Because my husband killed himself. No, because I was stressed because my husband killed himself. Yes, I threw up a lot, but I thought that was either because of the grief or because of the alcohol I drank to dull the pain caused by the fact that my husband killed himself.*

They talk, but their words drift above my head like so many

clouds. What else, after all, is there to think about other than the biting humiliation of having your capacity to parent called into question before the child has even been born. *After all,* says a voice in my head that sounds a lot like Aspen, *you failed as a wife. What chance do you have as a mother?*

In all the literature that exists separately about suicide and pregnancy, it appears nobody thought to include a chapter or two on what to do when your husband kills himself and, weeks later, you discover you are carrying his child. This is not how it is supposed to happen. Babies are supposed to provoke something a little more potent than indifference. Which is what I feel in all its nothingness.

I am back in my bed the next day with my ankle propped up on a stack of pillows, and when Bee asks me how I am feeling, I admit to this ambivalence. This is the first time anyone has actually asked me the question and I surprise even myself with the answer.

"What do you mean you don't know?" Bee is folding my laundry.

"Exactly that. I don't know how I feel about it. This time yesterday, I wasn't pregnant. Now I am. It's a lot."

"Chances are you were pregnant yesterday, too."

"You're choosing now to be literal?"

She throws down a fitted sheet—the hamartia of all laundry folding. "Babe, it's not just a baby. It's *Quentin's* baby."

"I'm aware of that." Suddenly, Q's name has found its way back into the mouths of those around me.

"I thought you'd be happier."

"Sorry to disappoint you."

She picks up my laundry basket and leaves the room. It appears that silently accepting this pregnancy as fact isn't going to be good enough. I'm supposed to be happy. A baby. A final link to Quentin. Ma will be wanting to gather us for a prayer of thanksgiving. But to think about nursery colors is to freak out.

The truth is I feel exactly the same as I did yesterday before I found out: still raw inside, like my internal organs and—oh, fuck it—my soul have been dragged over broken glass. I don't feel any closer to Q. The only difference from before is that now I have the external bruises to match. I turn onto my side. My ankle throbs in protest and I wince. Another thing I know—relapsing is no longer a possibility for me. *Me*, the girl who hid in the school library. No more drinking, no more pills—sleeping, anxiety, pain or otherwise—and I'm surprised when this realization, over anything else, brings tears to my eyes.

It was one of those days where the seams holding together the fragile fabric of familial routine ruptured. Gloria was anchored to her desk, burning the midnight oil, Alex was visiting his brother who had recently decamped to the Netherlands and Tess the nanny had called in sick. The family flexed to fill the gap and Ellie and Ben ended up with us. I called Quentin, garbling apologies even before he picked up but which he brushed away.

"Eve, relax. You're at work, right? I'll pick them up."

"You sure?"

"I love hanging out with those tiny people."

It wasn't a lie. Ellie and Ben revealed a tenderness in Q he reserved solely for them. Even after the rest of us briefly tired of Ben's persistent curiosity, of Ellie's little-girl perfectionist phase, Q would always unfold another layer of patience and wrap them in it. They loved him back—their tall, slightly weird uncle Q.

Thirty minutes past pickup time and he remained unreachable. The nursery calling first Gloria, then Alex, who swam to the surface of his legal high and called me. By the time

Q arrived home that evening, eyes wide with fear, we were halfway through a dinner of sweet potato fries.

"Eve. I—" he started, but the kids were already hurtling toward him, their shrieks of joy drowning out my curt "don't."

We made it through half of Disney's *Inside Out* before eyelids began to droop and little mouths grew slack with sleep. Ellie, our keeper of rules, was pajamaed and snoozing within minutes, her one request being that I held her hand until she was "sleeping sleeping" as only then would the shield against monsters be fully activated. Q, on Ben duty, read one story and then another, the little one buoyed by the second wind that sometimes comes with the change from day clothes into night ones.

"Okay, Trouble," I heard Q say, "one more and that's it. Say deal."

"Deal!" Ben squeaked. He arranged himself into a more comfortable position in his uncle's lap.

Three hours later, I was texting Gloria while Q picked up some Calpol. The fever had sprung from nowhere and Ben was already burning, sobbing miserably into my chest, his tiny body trembling. "We'll handle it," I reassured my sister. "Get some rest and I'll update you in a bit." He wouldn't settle and refused to be put down. I carried him through the house singing Igbo nursery rhymes while he whimpered, and after my arms grew weak, Q took over. I watched, exhausted, as he walked laps around the first floor, his hand on the back of Ben's head; and in the end when he appeared at our bedroom door with bloodshot eyes, I nodded. He brought Ben into our bed, and within minutes, the kid was out.

"You okay?" I asked. I reached over the sleeping child and ran my hand through Q's hair.

"Worn the fuck out," he said and checked that his curse was not registered by our gate-crasher. "I'm sorry. I messed up."

"You're so good with them. With him."

"It's different when you know you can give them back at some point, right?" We smiled at each other. "But I hate seeing him sick. He's so little."

"Ben should stay home tomorrow. I'll try and sort it out with work. Glo's got enough on her plate."

Q reached for one of the cool flannels I'd brought up and dabbed it gently against Ben's brow and neck. "So do you. It's cool. I'll watch him tomorrow."

"Yeah?"

"Yeah."

Sleep tugged at me, but Q's voice stole into my last seconds of wakefulness.

"Do you...do you reckon we could do this? Like for real?" he said.

I don't remember how I answered.

When we spoke about it at all, Q and I discussed the subject of children the same way people discuss that trip to Fiji they will take. *Someday.* Maybe. We assumed someday was a reality for us, like our lives had no room for something as unlikely as disaster. We were the fools who think they are immune to becoming their parents. We thought our interests would always lie in fascinating things like film noir, dark rum and sex in new and exciting places. We built collections. For me, it was decades-old books and the biographies of famous women and their lovers. For Q, it was not the ubiquitous assortment of vintage cameras favored by would-be photographers from Kansas to Kabul; rather it was vintage photographs—originals foraged from auctions, house clearances, markets and the internet. He wanted the real thing, fragile and flaking in his own hands. There were times I wished he'd develop the same tireless devotion he had for old photos for things that might benefit me, like learning how not to shrink my clothes in the dryer or cleaning the kitchen counters after he'd sawed through a baguette.

I had my books, and he had his photos, and we would banter with each other about whose collection would mean the most to the hypothetical kids we might have. Someday. Maybe.

"We live in the twenty-first century, Eve," he'd say, waving a photo in a sage manner. "Our children won't care about any books they can't read on their iPad 19s or their Kindles. Photographs are timeless."

"Yeah, nah," I'd reply. "The stories these books tell mean something. Photos fade. *These* stories are timeless."

"Photographs tell a thousand stories without wasting a single word." It was one of the more profound things he'd said and it shut me up until he ruined it by adding, "And when our kids find daddy's boxes of old photos, you think they'll give a fuck about old books with half the pages falling out?"

"You're selling our kids short."

"I'm not, though. Little Edgar will have a good eye like his dad."

"It's not my son you'll call Edgar."

"Laramie? Ulysses? Topaz?"

"Stop."

And now? Now *someday* is today and maybe is still maybe, but there is an infinity spreading out in front of me; one where Topaz truly could exist and have her father's good eye and could love old books, and this infinity is terrifying in a way that makes me question whether I want it at all.

# 18

I am woken by the ache in my ribs. There is no reminder of pain as poignant as the physical manifestation of it over the place your heart resides.

On the windowsill is an arrangement of blooms brought over by Jackson, who appeared only after a number of his calls went unanswered and Bee finally explained about the accident and assured him that I am still in the land of the living. I had not seen him since our evening of bubbles and shame. His subsequent visit, I understood, was equally about confirming that I was in fact still alive and reminding Bee he was a person capable of tact and sobriety. Jackson is another recipient of Bee's fleeting interest. There was a single date, many moons ago, which ended with Bee slamming into my house and asking Quentin how he turned out so normal while his best friend became a caricature. Jackson handed me the flowers even as Bee arched an eyebrow and asked in a syrupy tone, "No bubbly today?"

"I guess it wouldn't be appropriate given the pregnancy," I offered, wanting to rescue him after my previous spineless retreat, and if I am honest, wanting to test whether his reaction would be the thing to jump-start me out of my ambivalence.

Alas, Jackson's surprise and glee did not do enough to either warm the cockles of Bee's heart or inspire joy in mine. After that, I wanted him gone. His happiness only served to further highlight my indifference. Bee ushered him to the door, transferred his flowers to a vase and brought them back to my room, kissing her teeth.

"That boy needs to learn that sex and binge drinking, fun as they are, can't cure everything."

My ribs throb again and I shout for Ma. She comes quickly, phone in one hand, dishcloth in the other, eyebrows knitted together. Ma has always been afflicted with the inability to stop Doing Things. She is in perpetual motion, dominating endocrinology departments, cleaning or cooking, saving some wayward, parentless member of the church. Everything has taken a back seat so she can dedicate her time to me, the most forlorn of her children. She is of old Igbo stock. A woman raised to always look her best lest someone important or a visitor with a tendency toward judgment and/or gossip show up unannounced. Ma has temporarily sacrificed this lesson in order to focus on me and so today's ensemble has been hastily put together from whatever was closest: one of Dad's jumpers, beanie stolen from Nate, jogging bottoms rescued from God knows where. She tilts my chin up and assesses my split lip.

"Everything hurts," I whine. There is nothing more unbecoming or indeed pathetic than a thirty-two-year-old pouting at her mother. Yet here we are.

"I'm sorry," Ma says, and there is so much in these words. She is sorry she cannot give me anything to take the edge off my pain. She is sorry my husband is dead. She is sorry I am now preparing to traverse parenthood without a copilot. She is probably sorry that of all the men in all the world, I had to meet and fall in love with Quentin Christian Malcolm Morrow, but she does not say any of this because it is verboten; all she can do is repeat her commiserations. "Do you have Deep Heat? Let me rub some on your ankle."

She rolls up her sleeves and massages the ointment into my ankle, and because when you are beholden to your family, at the mercy of their patience and good nature, and because you understand that you have not been the easiest person of late, you acquiesce to otherwise inconvenient activities like attending the sixtieth birthday party of an old family friend.

Deep Heat applied and invitation accepted, Ma is satisfied. "You need to eat." *For the baby* hangs unsaid in the space between us. "I made okra soup, ayamase, yam, rice, plantain, moin moin, stockfish—"

"You made moin moin?"

"I'll bring you some. You need to eat before you take your vitamins." Prenatal vitamins, a new set of pills I'd rather avoid. Ma leaves before I can protest.

The party is for Aunty Bisola, who is only an aunty in the African sense of the word where every woman older than you is an aunty. Her husband has hired a hall. We are to dress accordingly. Nigerian hall parties are an institution. Matching shoes and bags, the finest outfits delivered at the last minute by overworked and quarrelsome tailors you swear you will never use again but to which you return because their work is unparalleled. Crates of malt. A buffet table ruthlessly manned by an ensemble of aunties who smack your hands when you reach for more chicken than you are entitled to. I haven't been to one in so long, I forgot the effort that goes into making yourself presentable enough to attend. Ma and Gloria put me into our traditional wear—the blouse and two wrappers worn by Igbo women for centuries, but in a modern style. Gloria is now wrestling with the crowning glory, the ichafu, which has no desire to stay atop my head without the administration of what is surely seven thousand pins.

"Hey! Kpachara anya, will you?" I protest as Glo stabs another pin into the head tie that rises from my head like a majestic and irate peacock.

"Your head has shrunk along with everything else on you," Glo informs me. "I can't wait until you start gaining baby weight. You're not even a bobblehead. You're a pea head. A pinhead."

"I don't have to wear this," I point out.

"And ruin the effect of the outfit?" Ma secures the wrappers at my waist with her sixth safety pin. "You look beautiful."

Dad enters the room. "Ladies," he says and smiles the smile that has been unintentionally cleaving the hearts of women in twain since he learned how to do it. "You are all gorgeous. We're going to be late."

Ma steps to him and straightens his shirt on his shoulders. Glo and I stand back and survey what thirty-nine years of marriage looks like and my stomach contracts. "Did you put the puff puff in the car?" Ma asks.

Dad smiles at Ma and she smiles back, and although he doesn't answer her question (because of course he's forgotten, the tray sits on the kitchen counter unwrapped and rapidly cooling), they have stepped into a temporary but perfect moment of happiness, untarnished by newly widowed daughters and the weight of all the things that haven't happened but have the potential to destroy. "We should go."

Nigerian parties, while they are awash with vibrant people, culinary miracles and the occasional money dance, are also breeding grounds for the type of petty competitiveness of which only people who have known each other for many, many years are capable.

Here in this hall festooned with balloons, banners and ribbons, the uncles palm bottles of malt and shovel forkfuls of rice. The aunties pull each other into perfumed hugs and trade stories. It isn't long before the stories turn into verbal contests of whose children are the most successful, who has the most grandchildren (as if this is somehow a personal achievement), of whose dish has been scraped clean the quickest. There is talk of which family is undergoing the most amount of misfortune and/or disappointment. Aunty Esther's son is currently going through a divorce (we never trusted that woman, you could always see the tracks on her weave), Aunty Vida's second daughter has been unemployed for the past six months and has been forced to apply for benefits, Aunty Tokunbo's youngest daughter's engagement has crumbled to nothing as the fiancé disappeared to Jos with over £10,000. When Ma steps into the circle, these tales are tucked away; there is nothing as awful as a dead son-in-law, especially when the cause of death is suicide. Ma has effortlessly taken the gold in the Sadness Olympics. These women express their joy at my presence and their shock at my appearance. When Dad appears with a plate of food for Ma, I take the opportunity to limp away. As I do, my parents begin the grand retelling of my accident.

I settle beneath a balloon arch and prop my ankle up on a chair. Ben brings me Fanta in a glass bottle and Nate soon joins me below the balloons. He's eating suya and the smell of the meat turns my stomach.

"Africans are nosy as hell," Nate says.

"You never come to these things. They're excited to see you."

"Yeah, well. I can't stay long." I raise an eyebrow at him. "Cleo."

"How's *that* going?" I have neither seen nor heard anything of Cleo since the morning of the Toaster Waffles.

"She's happy about the job. Still Cleo, though."

I think of Cleo in her tailored clothes and perfect makeup and I reach out and punch Nate in the leg.

"Mate," Nate says, "what's your problem?"

"She loves you. You're this annoying and she still wants to be with you." I am thinking, of course, of Q and how it truly is a waste of not only his life but of mine because my capacity for loving Q had not reached fruition; there were still un-mined depths to it I am never going to be able to explore, and it's not Nate's fault, but sometimes he is so chalant-deficient and it is frustrating in a way I am only able to express through mild violence. "You should be nicer to her. To Cleo."

Nate looks at me for a long time but stays quiet. Perhaps a little more emotion than planned bled out from my repri-mand. We pass a few minutes watching the room.

"I'm going to get you some food," Nate says finally. "Eat-ing for two and that." A few pairs of young, thirsty eyes fol-low his progress to the buffet table.

My phone buzzes. A text from Jackson. And because Q's death has exposed the tenuity of the control I have over my life, because I have subconsciously become accustomed to hav-ing the painful pleasure of mourning repeatedly stripped from me in order to manage some other pressing emotion, because bad news sticks to me like burrs to an antelope, I barely reg-ister what he is telling me before my phone begins to ring. There was something about him having fucked up, about let-ting something slip. About Aspen. And I try to scroll, but in doing so, I answer the call, and in doing so, I answer Aspen.

"Eve."

"Aspen. Hi."

"I hear congratulations are in order," she says. No pream-ble with this one. She aims for and always finds the jugular.

Remnants of naivety allow me to believe for a second that she is congratulating me for something else. Perhaps she has learned that I am newly jobless after my name was quietly wiped from *Circle*'s "Our Family" page on the website and in the magazine. I already know I am fooling myself. Aspen does not know what *Circle* is. She has never known how I make a living.

"Congratulations?" I echo.

"I want to be clear that I will not allow you to keep my grandchild from me. Do you hear me?" And part of me almost wants to commend her on her ability to voice the fear I have been resolutely ignoring since the day in the hospital. She, if nothing else, has a unique ability to bring to light that which I have so desperately been chasing through shadows.

"Who told you?" But the answer lives in a text message that will reappear when this call is over.

She continues to speak, but I do not. Because what is there to be said?

# AWAY

# 19

Jackson picks me up and drives me home because I ask him to. Because I want him to absorb the gravity of betrayal in close proximity to its recipient. There are moments that, when you look back on the showreel of your life, will be cemented in your memory, indelible. Jackson's expression through the window as I approach his car will now occupy space alongside Gloria's nod to Alex as they were joined in holy matrimony, and the first night Quentin and I spent in our bedroom. Jack's gaze falls away. If he were able to concertina himself into nothingness, he would seize the opportunity. We drive in the sort of silence that I can liken only to the softness of a drizzle you ignore until too late, you realize that you are drenched.

In the house, he follows me up the stairs and stands in the doorway of my—and Q's—bedroom, watching me being pulled under by panic. His eyes follow my movements, his chest rising and falling in time with my own ragged breathing.

"Eve," he asks, "what are you doing?"

I can't locate all the pins of my ichafu. Ma and Gloria had done a better job than I originally thought. Sweat begins to trickle into my eyes and yet the ichafu will not shift. My fingers, which were carefully searching, probing the pleats and valleys of the material, now begin a frantic hunt for the pins. I try yanking it from my head.

"I can't… I can't breathe." I double over, gasping, my heart in a vise grip.

"Hey. *Hey.* Eve, it's okay." Jackson hesitates only momentarily before clasping both my wrists in his hands. He holds them until I can once again stand upright, and only then does he start plucking pins from my ichafu. His fingers roam over my scalp; I shiver beneath his touch. "You're alright." He eases the ichafu from my head and lays it on the bed.

When he turns back to me, I slap him. "How the fuck could you do this? How could you tell her?"

"Eve—" his eyes are bright with remorse "—it was an accident."

"An accident."

"I was so happy for you when you told me. This—it's… Quentin's child…and you've been going through so much, you know? I just… It was a good thing. To me. It was a good thing to me. And whenever I'd go to Aspen's, she's just there, y'know? Angry and upset and it just came out. I didn't— Shit, Eve. I didn't think."

"You've been seeing Aspen?"

Jackson cried at Q's and my wedding. Even before the alcohol started flowing. I caught him wiping tears roughly with a separate handkerchief, careful not to tamper with his pocket square. The joy caused the corners of his eyes to crease even as his lip trembled. I loved him fiercely in that moment. The tears he presents to me now have a different quality and I can feel the blood pulsing through me, causing my fingertips to throb.

"She's Quent's mum. Sure, I see her. Eve, I—"

"I need you to get out."

"Eve. Look—"

"Get. Out."

Once Jackson leaves, it is not long before my family arrive. Nate surveys the scene—the crumpled ichafu, the floor littered with pins, his sister wild-eyed and wild-haired in a rapidly disintegrating outfit. He would have seen Jackson's stricken face on his way out. My fury, an untamable thing, surges and drives him toward the door, but Ma steps around him.

"Eve? Ò gị nī zị?" *What is it this time?* She has been waiting, fretful of the next hiccup, and here it is. "How can you just leave the party without telling anybody? We were looking for you. Your phone you cannot answer?"

My phone, forgotten in the folds of the duvet where I dropped it on arrival, has no doubt been collecting the worries of my family. "I'm sorry. Aspen called. She knows I'm pregnant and I had to get out of there. Jackson told her."

"Jackson? Lovely boy, but—" Ma kisses her teeth. "You can't let a man drive you to madness." And though she omits the word *again*, all of us hear it.

"Ma. Didn't you hear what I said? Aspen knows I'm pregnant."

"And so?" Glo slips her ichafu off her head. No wrenching of pins for her because why should Gloria have to struggle for anything? "So what if she knows? It's not like she can do anything about it."

But she can. Why is it that none of them can see that? The pregnancy is untouchable, perhaps, but a child is not. Even now, Aspen's voice reverberates in the part of my mind I can't suppress. *You couldn't look after my son, so what makes you think you are equipped to raise his child?* To reject this is to pretend that I have not spent almost three months asking myself what kind of wife I was to have seen nothing? To have not even recognized that this sort of pain existed in him, never

mind trying to understand it? Have I not, since I looked at
that ultrasound screen, been wondering what kind of life I
could provide for a child when the reality is that I failed to
keep their father on this earth? The words do not become
less true because they come from Lucifer. The pill simply becomes all the more bitter.

"I... I don't think I can do this. I'm not cut out for it."

"For what? Eve, slow down and talk to us." Dad moves
toward me, but to be touched at this moment would be my
undoing. I step back.

"Motherhood!" The word escapes me in something that
resembles a yelp.

Nate shakes his head. "C'mon, Eve, don't talk nonsense.
What do you mean?"

How can you explain to people who have not whispered
desperate pleas to their husband's lifeless body what it feels like
to carry the weight of new potential disaster? What words do
you string together to convey the would-be devastation you
may cause to a person dependent on you for everything? I
would already be in deficit. It wouldn't be fair. I never reached
the point in our relationship where the love I felt for Quentin
began to dull. My rose-tinted glasses were permanent. Dan-
gerously so. But love, it appears, was not enough to keep him
alive. And this is not something I can risk inflicting on his
child. It is not something I can live through a second time.

"Let's be real, I would make a terrible mother," I tell my
family and wait for the roars of protest to subside before I
continue. "On my own. I would make a terrible mum on
my own. If Q was here, it would be different. God, it would
be so different."

"So, what? You want to get rid? An abortion?" Glo's expression darkens.

"Chelukwa! My daughter? Tufiakwa!" Ma is shrill. Her

Christianity, maternal instinct and Nigerian-ness converging to strike down the very utterance of a termination.

Dad clears his throat. "Alright, enough. Ekwuzina." His tone would be enough, even without the direct request, to silence us. We do as he says and stop talking. Outside, the sky is dark. "Different how, Eve?"

"I just don't think I want to do this without him. He would have made things okay. I wouldn't feel like…like I'm about to trip and fall into some kind of bottomless crevasse. He would have fixed it all. This fear, Aspen, all of it." I reach for my discarded ichafu and begin toying with its edges, my gaze so focused on the colors of the material that my vision begins to blur.

"Evie, sweetheart." Dad eases the ichafu out of my fingers. He takes my hand. "Try and be reasonable. Quentin was a good man, a loving one. But he was human, same as you."

"Dad's right," Nate puts in.

"Okay," I say, letting my hand drop from Dad's. "What does that mean?"

"It means Quentin wasn't perfect," Glo explains. Her voice steady but low. She holds my gaze.

"And what the hell does that mean?" The blood rushes to my face. My heart rate increases to a gallop for the second time this evening. The room quiets for a moment and the air fizzes with the specific rancor of harsh truths struggling to remain unspoken.

"Q would have done his best," Nate begins, "but it's not like he was Iron Man. He would have made mistakes, too."

Quentin's ashes are downstairs. He sits unassuming on the living room mantelpiece while my family, a family he often called his own, impress upon me his capacity for failure. And tonight, after experiencing the great and terrible loss of a secret with which I am still coming to grips, after realizing that my trust cannot, in fact, be given to as many people as I imagined, this is disgusting to me.

"Can you all go? Just go." I scowl to hide the undulation in my voice. Their pity engulfs me, and this, above all, leads me to the reaction that my family will later label as "irrational." I turn away.

"Eve," they all say at once, in various octaves and with varying degrees of exasperation. I opt not to mangle my thoughts further by voicing them. I tell them to leave a second time and there is further protest—Dad beseeching me in Igbo to put thought into what I am saying, Ma scandalized at being spoken to in such a manner. Like the hum of a plane engine as you are carried to your destination, Nate's sighs are constant. A pointless cacophony. I will not turn. Stubbornness roots me to the spot. When this memory returns to me, I will remember focusing on the right upper corner of the photo frame on my bedside table while shouting that they will not disrespect my husband in his own house. I will feel Gloria's hand on my shoulder and shiver at the memory of the force with which I shake it off.

"I am so sick of everyone thinking I should be over this already." I am, inexplicably, out of breath.

"Nobody thinks that," she says.

"Liar."

"We're not lying. But you're screaming at us and trying to kick us out when…"

"When what?"

"Never mind."

"No. When what, Glo? Your mouth has never had a problem running. Don't start now."

All the bluster goes out of her; she deflates like a forgotten pool toy. "Come on, Eve."

"Glo. Stop." Nate's voice is more like Dad's than I have

ever heard it. The look that passes between them tells me this conversation is not new to them.

"No, Junior. How long are we meant to let this go on?" Glo turns back to me. "He didn't even leave a note. He couldn't leave you a fucking note. *What is that?*" And what she's really asking is *How can you miss someone who did this to you?*

We do not swear in front of our parents, so Ma's gasp is expected, but my silence is the loudest. It drowns out all else. My expression, one I wish I could bottle, is enough to make them all flee. In the hours it takes for me to stop shaking, I digest this revelation—I have been so worried about being seen as a bad wife that it never occurred to me that it was he, my Q, that others would judge.

# 20

These are the ingredients for escape: some form of trauma; in this case, a dead husband, and his living mother's anger. The collapse of your safety net; the loss of a job you are not sure you enjoyed but provided you with a place to go when your house wrapped its fingers around your throat. Sprinkle in a broken heart and pair with the discovery of a pregnancy you neither planned for nor discovered until you were well into your new codependent relationship with rum and pills.

That I needed to leave was imperative. That it had to be immediate was somewhat hampered by the banalities that accompany the planning of travel. I chose Los Angeles for two reasons. The first because it is a city Aspen would abhor. A land of green smoothies, of shiny, happy people. Aspen, I am sure, would be more comfortable strolling the streets of hell. The second reason was shallow and simple: sunshine. California does not subscribe to seasons and so even in March, it delivers the kind of blue skies and balmy temperatures the UK can't stop shivering long enough to fathom. The thousands of miles separating me from Aspen was paramount and

the sunshine would be the icing on this new cake of irre-
sponsibility. Leaving was supposed to be easy. A few clicks
on Airbnb and Kayak, the typing of debit card expiry dates,
an updated visa, and I was meant to disappear. I am, however, with child and it should have come as no surprise that
travel insurance companies are not exactly fighting to cover
a pregnant woman who is running away to the land of no
free health care.

I gazed at the screen of my MacBook and watched as the
palm trees on which I pinned my hopes drifted farther and
farther out of reach. Then I crept beneath the duvet, my
clothes a colorful puddle on the floor, and, realizing that I was
shaking, tucked my hands under each elbow and held myself
together. I turned my phone over when Jackson began to text.

The next time my phone buzzed, it shook me from the
type of sleep to which your body has not yet fully committed. Aspen or Jackson? Which shovel of shit would I prefer to
heave over the fence at that precise moment? A breeze tickled the toe that had found its way out from underneath the
duvet. My phone buzzed again, and my breath caught in my
throat when I saw Quentin's name on the screen. The mere
sight of his name and the pain spread through my body like
black ink through water. A reminder, and rightly so because
such things were long gone from my mind, the mind of a
wife with a husband to prod.

March 4: Quentin's photography retreat—remind him to pack
extra cam batteries

He had burst into the house a few months earlier, wrapped
his arms around me even as I grumbled about how we ought
to perhaps get him tested for the strain of foolishness that
made him remove his clothes and leave them *beside* the laundry basket as opposed to inside it. He had teased the irritation

from me with lips against my face and I had felt him smiling against my skin. They wanted him for a retreat; one where they would showcase some of his work and have him speak to eager amateurs about his craft. It was all he ever wanted, and it would be held on the Isle of Man, that tiny jewel in the Irish Sea where we had once spent a few halcyon days for his birthday. His excitement was infectious, and I tapped the reminder into my iPhone even as he capered around the kitchen.

It is apt, I think, for him to come to me like this in the wee hours and solve the dilemma of my escape; his kindness reaching me from wherever he is. A kindness I have not yet become accustomed to missing.

A cardigan of Quentin's, with snatches of his scent caught in the folds. Three head wraps hastily scrunched into balls. Underwear, initially forgotten, then purchased in duty free. My MacBook tucked beneath a small stack of shirts. Thick socks initially bought for Q to wear on this trip he would now never take. I made a list in my mind and didn't notice half of it moonwalk right on out even as I booked my flight to the Isle and then, after memories had taken their fists to me, found the hotel—the Sefton—we stayed in way back when and wrote a special request: *Room 111, please. It would mean so much to me and my husband.* I deleted the "and my husband" before I hit Send. I packed my little case and wrote a long message to Bee explaining how I needed to be gone for a while, to not exist in London for a time. To my family, I said nothing. Then I had Jackson drive me to City Airport, his guilt and unhappiness clambering into the back seat because I refused to sit up front.

"Eve," he'd said, his eyes starting to water again, "what's happening?" And to look at him was to feel like the worst person in the world because he lost his best friend, someone he had known and loved longer than I had, and I had not paused in my own selfish mourning to even consider him. I averted my eyes as I muttered my thanks. Let Aspen comfort him.

We experienced turbulence as we descended into Balla-salla and I wouldn't have noticed the plane being tossed about like a dry leaf had my seatmate not pressed a Kleenex into my hand. I froze outside the hotel, the wind yanking my afro from where I had tucked it into the scarf around my neck, re-membering the day Q and I arrived here years ago, his fingers at the nape of my neck. That day, we had arrived to a sky that had been single-minded in its blueness, had faced a sea that lay opposite the hotel like a sheet of antique glass. Tonight, the wind dragged the clouds across the sky and the waves shook their white heads as they crashed through the darkness.

I froze again at the check-in desk, the smile dropping from the lips of the clerk as she repeated my room number and failed not to stare at my bruises and busted lip.

"Room 111, Ms. Morrow. Ms. Morrow? Room 111, is that not what you requested?"

"Ezenwa-Morrow."

I forgot my case in the lobby and was called back to re-trieve it. Walking through the leafy atrium, I remembered how giddy Q and I were when we'd seen it for the first time. He had looped an arm around me, pulled me in for a kiss, our PDA offending the other guests, our oblivious cocksure-ness still years away from being obliterated.

I froze for the third time outside the door of Room 111. Quentin had dropped the key card on our journey up from the lobby. He had patted himself down, dropping his week-end bag so he could search his pockets thoroughly. I blew a sigh through pursed lips, but it was a half-hearted annoyance, a lazy one that failed to take root. Not even when he went back for a new card and left me digging the toes of my train-ers into the carpet outside the room. Now I glanced down, half expecting to see the well I made in the pile. Inside, I left the light off and crossed to the window. It was there that the adrenaline that carried me out of London sputtered and died, and my legs gave way. I climbed into the bed fully clothed—could it really be the very same one or had they changed it?—and cried myself into the kind of sleep only my full bladder could penetrate. I slept through calls from Bee, from Nate and Glo, from my frantic parents, from an unknown number (Aspen, I assume), even from Jackson and Alex.

I've slept through breakfast and it is only as I sit on the toilet, eyes still trained on the waves, that I take stock of my situation. I am thirty-two years old. My husband is dead. I am roughly eleven weeks pregnant with a child I am not yet certain I want, whom I may or may not have irreparably damaged with my unintentional negligence, I am unemployed and I am alone. There is at least one bank account fat with the literal proceeds of my husband's death that I never wish to even look at, never mind touch. My lip still throbs, my ribs still ache. But. *But.* Aspen does not know where I am. I cling to this like a life buoy in a hurricane.

I wash my hands and curl into the mattress, Jackson's betrayal casting long shadows on the walls. Being awake is vastly overrated. My body aches in protest, and a light film of perspiration settles on my brow. My fingers curl and uncurl, missing the almost imperceptible weight of a sleeping pill in my palm. This is a hotel, and a nice one, too, so there will be a minibar, and at the bottom of six or seven of those teeny bottles, there will be the temporary void into which I sorely wish to dive. Alas. No more. My hand strays to my stomach. Still flat. But now the center of everything.

Quentin held me in this room. He idly traced imaginary patterns on the skin of my inner thigh as we licked the molten cheese of a pizza from our lips and watched *Pretty Woman* on TV. He grumpily demanded I turn off the light when I flicked it on so I could stumble to the bathroom. He stroked me into a trembling, pleading mess. He promised me forever and had not only broken the promise but taken precautions to guarantee I wouldn't notice he was leading me into oncoming traffic. Death is the great purifier. I was always convinced I would die before Q. So convinced that I made him promise that when I did, he would never romanticize me, that he would be honest about how he hated how I slept through multiple alarms, how I held grudges like they were precious, how I didn't always remember that I had left my period panties soaking in the bathroom sink. He laughed his starter-pistol laugh and he swore he would. Then he left me anyway.

I use a pillow to muffle my screams.

# 21

It takes them three days to acclimatize, but housekeeping now understands that arriving at my door before nine forty-five in the morning is fruitless at best and inadvisable at worst. The first day, I heard a light knock just after 8:30 a.m. and froze, thinking it was either Ma with an armful of prenatal vitamins or Aspen with a mouthful of reprimands. From my position in bed—facedown, smearing the pillowcases with catarrh—I heard the door open and the tentative "Hello? Housekeeping," which, of course, I did not answer. What followed was the shuffling of feet, a gasp and a "So sorry, miss. We can come back later. Stick a DND on your door next time so we don't disturb you."

Then I was alone again.

I forgot the Do Not Disturb again, so the following morning, the same treacle-voiced maid entered my room, tiptoed toward the bed and then beat a hasty retreat when I opened one eye to find her staring at me and the fading bruises on my face.

The third day, I slept until hunger beat me into wakefulness, my stomach twisting in on itself. I splashed cold water on my face, removed the DND from my door handle and made my way to the hotel's Harris Restaurant, where breakfast is served.

The first day Quentin and I ate here, he left me at the table because he was drawn to the windows, which splashed light across the room, spattering the table linen and glinting off the silverware. The restaurant faces the bay and Q drank in the panoramic views. He'd brought his camera with him, couldn't help but snap a few shots and then a few more. By the time he returned to the table, his eggs were cold, and I was annoyed. When he leaned over to kiss me, he knocked over my teacup and we watched in dismay as the tablecloth absorbed his clumsiness.

"Sorry, baby," he said, "I'll get you another one." My annoyance crumbled to dust as I watched him turn on the smile that could outdo the sun. That smile had peeled my jeans from my body, put my heart in a chokehold. That smile brought us a new tablecloth and a pot of Lapsang souchong. He pushed the pot to the side before he tried to kiss me again. I remember feeling the happiness knotting my insides like macramé. I caught his bottom lip between my teeth. The tutting of the other diners was a metronome to our canoodling, and just when we were on the verge of being scolded, Q would flash his grin around the room and scowls would drop from faces.

These days there is no scowl-erasing grin. There is no charming the waitstaff. There is no Q. I haunt the hotel like a wandering specter. I hiccup into my tea (English breakfast; there is no Lapsang souchong for me this time). Diners shift uncomfortably in the tufted seats the moment they see me. My misery enters rooms before I do, pulls out chairs for me to sit in. I catch sight of myself in the atrium fountain and bark out a laugh so abrupt, it pierces the air like gunfire. The discomfort of fellow guests provides me with a sick sort of satisfaction. It is the most power I have had in months—I pull smiles out of orbit, extinguish joy simply by existing. Aspen would be proud. I prolong my visits to Harris Restaurant and take Q's place at the windows. I stand there for so long that there is a film on my fried eggs when I slope back to my seat. I eat everything on my plate because arriving here has made me ravenous and Ma isn't here to witness it. But I eat and still feel hollow. I watch an older couple in the corner. She is a slip of a thing with a cloud of soft white hair. She wears equally soft cashmere twinsets in pastels that she couples with a thin necklace and beige chinos. He was once grand. I see it in the way he carries himself, as if he is being watched by more important eyes than mine. He hovers over her, allows her to straighten his lapels. In the coming days, I will note how he always pours her tea for her. One day he presents her with a book, on another, a silk scarf. He keeps her glasses in an inside pocket and gently cleans them before handing them to her. There is tenderness in every look they exchange.

This was how Q and I were meant to spend our twilight years. I told him that when his hair faded from gold to snow that I would love him just the same, a silver fox with a camera in his hand. By then he would be speaking fluent Igbo because I would have spent our life together teaching him. He should have been around to clean my glasses and bring me books. I should get to watch him grow old. Instead, I get nothing.

When the nausea comes, I upend my water glass in my haste to escape. The lady in cashmere presses her hand to her mouth as I stumble out; our eyes meet for less than a second.

Back in my room, the maid, whose name I have learned, via a name badge, is Henrietta, has worked her magic. The air smells faintly of grapefruit-scented cleaning products, and in what could be a gesture of sympathy or one of frustration at my coating the bed linen with snot, she has put an extra tissue box on my bedside table. I open the door of the mini-

bar and drink in the sight of those bottles. I can almost taste
the heat of the Jack Daniel's hitting the back of my throat. I
shut the door and climb into bed.

There is only so long a person can ignore her Nigerian
family and each day I wake up and clear notifications from
my phone screen is another day closer to Ma rupturing the
limits of her patience and shaking down every inhabitant of
this earth until she finds me. The thought of her storming
the hotel and explaining to the beleaguered reception staff
that "God will deal with you" brings the weakest of smiles
to my face. I tap through Jackson's texts, deleting them as
I go. They are all the same flavor: please, I'm sorry, are you
okay? And his guilt is not something I can carry right now;
not along with my own.

I still can't face my parents, and the thought of speaking to
Gloria makes me want to tear my ears from my head and flush
them down the toilet, so I opt for Nate. He calls when I have
relocated from the bed to the chair by the window. The sea is
restless, like a child fighting sleep, tossing this way and that.

"What the fuck," he says by way of greeting, "are you
doing?" His voice is soft.

"Hi, Nate," I sniffle.

"You know that it's only me and Bee stopping Ma coming to get you?"

"Yeah, I know, I— Wait. What do you mean 'coming to
get me'? You know where I am?" If they know, then Aspen
can't be all that far behind. Visions of her storming into Room
111 bloom in my head like fireworks.

"Eve, you've had the same email password since you were
twelve. It took Glo three seconds to hack into your Gmail.
She knew where you were before you landed."

It is so brilliantly and uniquely Gloria that I almost laugh, even as my face burns with embarrassment. My hiding place unearthed before I ever entered it. "Oh."

"Why did you just piss off? Why didn't you say anything?"

"Because I was fuming. And you wouldn't have let me go."

"Nah. Well, yeah. But only because you're knocked up and that. We want you to be okay."

"I know."

"And?"

"And what?"

"Christ—are you okay?"

I have no answer.

"How's your face?" Nate asks. "Ma wants photo evidence that you're alive, so it's probably better if you don't still look like you got rushed."

"I look like I got rushed by three people now instead of five. Progress?"

"You still on that abortion stuff?"

"Nate, don't start."

"Nah. I'm starting. You can tell me. You know you can tell me."

I do know that. But there is nothing to tell. I remain in limbo, understanding little, feeling even less when it comes to this kid. So I tell my brother that instead.

Nate's silence is not a sign of reproach; he is considering my words. "You know when you're coming home yet?"

"I just got here, Nate. How's *Circle*?"

"It's fucking weird. You're not there, so me and Bee have lunch and just talk about how fucking weird it is that you ain't around. I work late most days."

"Taskmasters, yeah? I didn't know Barry had it in him to go all dictator on the fresh meat."

"Hmm. Yeah, it's more that I don't really like going to yours anymore. Ma is always there cleaning like you'll pop up any second."

I think of Ma scrubbing my house, her face brightening at the sound of the front door opening, only for her to be crestfallen when she sees that yet again, it isn't me. My words don't quite make it past the lump in my throat.

"It's just…it was one thing to be round there with Q gone, but now you're both…" Nate leaves the sentence suspended between us.

"I just need some time," I manage.

"How much time?"

"I don't know yet."

"Text me every day," he says before he hangs up.

It has been sixty-one days since Q died.

I drop my phone onto the duvet. My eyes are dry.

Our conversation comes back to me throughout the day. In the shower when I am finally rinsing London from my hair; jumping out from my case as I rummage for a shirt to pull over the fading purple-yellow splotches on my ribs; springing from the fountain in the atrium, where, needing a change of scenery, I have come for my customary afternoon pity session. As an African kid, you live your life at times skating perilously on the edge of your parents' disappointment. Their love is a fierce and sometimes frightening animal that you sometimes convince yourself you could do without. They have carried the burdens of their own parents and have fought battles the likes of which we, the offspring, cannot begin to comprehend, and we, the offspring, have complained and disappointed them a thousand times anyway. Q died and Ma and Dad accepted my self-inflicted infantilization without complaint. It is because of them that I have been able to choose grief above all else. I have rewarded them by becoming the valedictorian of Avoidance and Poor Choices. Ma is in my house praying in tongues and laundering every item of clothing she can find. Dad is there, too, because where his wife is, he will not be far behind. They await a daughter who has resolved to re-main on this island, cherry-picking the kindling she will use to set herself ablaze.

Quentin's photography retreat has a theme, one he ex-plained at length when I was struggling to meet a couple of work deadlines as well as plan Glo's birthday with her two deeply irritating best friends. FRACTURED: A Composi-tion of Portions is taking place in Port Erin and I have al-ready missed the first day. Another side effect of grief is the unconscious misplacement of time.

Uber does not exist on the Isle of Man. The app tells me this (rather gleefully) when I open it on my phone for a fare check. Port Erin is on the other side of the island and Google informs me (also rather gleefully) that it would take me four hours and thirty-five minutes to reach on foot. I sit on the bed, bite my lip and toy with Q's wedding ring where it still hangs around my neck. I am still in this position when Hen-rietta arrives to clean the room, and it is only then that I re-alize I have missed breakfast. Misplacement of time.

"There was no DND," she says, almost angrily. "I'll come back."

"No, it's fine. It's my fault. I lost track of time."

"I'll be out of your hair in two ticks." She disappears into the bathroom. Ten minutes later, she's back.

"Is something wrong?"

"Well, I kind of need you to move, chicken. So I can do your sheets."

"Oh, right. Sorry." I move to the window. Sliding Q's ring down each of my fingers is bringing none of its usual comfort.

"Here." Her voice is gentle as she places the extra box of tissues on the side table next to the chair. A woman whose bruised face is perpetually moist—what must she think of me? "You okay? You're not sick or anything, are you?"

Sure I am. Sick of Quentin being dead. Sick of waking up
every day and thinking about him being dead. Sick of waking up every day, period. "I don't know how to get to Port
Erin," I say.

"Is that all? There's a concierge, love." She tips her head
to look at me. "You can just ring down and ask for a taxi.
They'll let you know when it gets here."

"Right. Of course. Thank you." Since I can't meet her eyes,
I focus on the patterns my tears have made on my jeans, dark
constellations drifting across denim.

While I am pulling myself together in the bathroom, Hugo
the concierge leaves a message informing me that my taxi has
arrived. I am wearing clean clothes, my hair parted neatly and
packed into two puffs at the side of my head, and if I am to
meet my demise under the island sky, my mother will ensure
these facts are typed in bold in my obituary. I exit the hotel
for the first time since my arrival and try to ignore the collective sigh that hits my back as the doors close behind me.

Port Erin sits at the foot of the Isle of Man. It is a bay created by gouging a pocket of land from the flesh of the island's ankle. It is a place Q and I never visited together, but
he will, of course, be there; pieces of him have been curated
and are currently displayed somewhere called The Falcon's
Nest. There are magnificent sunsets to be seen over Port Erin
Bay and Bradda Head, Samuel, my taxi driver, informs me,
if I feel like hiking up there. Samuel has the constitution of
a man whose diet consists of strong liquor and six kinds of
meat, but he offers me this nugget of information, then leaves
me to my thoughts, only occasionally glancing at me in the
rearview mirror. Samuel and I, we understand each other.

He deposits me outside of The Falcon's Nest, a white rendered hotel overlooking the bay, and it is as if he detects my
hopelessness because he also presses his card into my palm

before I walk away, and tells me to give him a call when I'm ready to head back.

"'Samuel Baladyne,'" I read. It is written in an unfortunate choice of font that Bee would reject with a sneer.

"Aye, the wife had those made up for me. Told me I needed to get with the times."

"It's a lovely card, Samuel."

He shifts, twists his cap in his giant hands and slaps it back on his head. "Aye, well. You ring that number when you're ready."

There is a moment after I have confirmed that I paid my £175 registration fee and have been directed to the conservatory at the side of the hotel, when I have the program in my hands and I see Q's name and picture on the front of the glossy paper, that I believe with all that is left within me that if I take another step forward, I will die. It is an inexplicable bolt of clarity that strikes me from nowhere. Move and die. It is the one thing I am sure of. And after months of drowning in the uncertainty that comes with the loss of a spouse and attempting to exist in a world without them, it gives me a split second of twisted reassurance. Then the feeling is gone, and my trainers are moving soundlessly to the back row of the conservatory, and I am in a seat blinking at blown-up photographs taken by my husband. By my Q.

There are close-ups of abandoned buildings, a crumbling aqueduct invaded by vines that wrap it like a living funeral shroud, and there, displayed along one wall, are a series of eight by ten shots taken of a path weaving through an industrial estate and ending in a wooded area, each photograph depicting less and less concrete and more foliage. Q gradually increased the saturation, so the series begins monochrome and ends in a riot of greenery. His work is beautiful in its simplicity, yet striking, and I drink it in, wishing not for the last time that I had heaped more praise on his head, doused him and his work with the sort of banal yet heartfelt adoration that he deserved when he was alive. I should have prolonged my cheerleading, should have made his successes mine, too. Give people their flowers when they are here to appreciate them, they say. How much of a part did I play in extinguishing his light? Could I have been the one who, after the initial delight, neglected to care for those flowers, missing them wilting, glossing over the drooping heads until it was too late? The program slips from my hand and lands with a rustle at my feet.

"This series resonates particularly with me," a woman with an extraordinary take on head wear is saying to the coordinator. She motions first with the feather on her hat and then with her hand to the eight by ten series. "Quentin's despair is evident in these pictures."

The coordinator, a woman the program told me is named Darla King, nods and touches the necklace at her throat. "Would anyone else like to speak to that?"

A young man whose shirt has never been in the same postcode as an iron corrects his slouching position and clears his throat. "Well, it was like we were saying yesterday, isn't it? Quentin's particular skill was his mastery of composition. Everything about every piece is a showcase in that art. Since that was his niche, it makes sense that his state of mind would shine through."

"One could say that about any talented photog, though," another girl chimes in. She uncrosses then recrosses her legs before she continues. She can't be older than twenty-one. Her eyes flit from face to photo to face. "Quentin's work is different. Yeah, his composition was flawless, but there's something else. Remember that article in *BJP* where he said that he can walk for up to eight hours until he finds what he is looking to capture?"

I remember that article. The *British Journal of Photography* had run a short interview with Q after he won an award for a shot of an inferno that chewed up an old theater in central London. He had been so nervous before that interview that I'd left work early to talk him down.

"Almost like he doesn't seek out what he thinks could be popular but allows his mood to dictate what he captures," Feather Hat concludes. "It's almost effortless with him."

"Wouldn't quite call eight hours of walking effortless," someone else puts in, and a ripple of quiet chuckles moves through the group.

"And this?" Darla stands aside and gestures to a photograph I had not noticed. A self-portrait. In it, Q is wearing the linen shirt I bought him to attend a dinner at Aspen's, a dinner to which I was not invited and about which we fought furiously until he said he wouldn't go if it meant I wouldn't be angry with him, and which I told him he'd better carry his behind to, because his mother hated me enough and this was not about to be another item on the list of transgressions she had no doubt started compiling when she first clapped eyes on my braids and my navy skirt all those years earlier. He is backlit so most of his face is in shadow, but one eye stares from behind an overgrown sweep of that hair I loved so much. His hands lie in his lap, upturned and idle. The photo is titled *Sundown*. "It was taken about nine months before Quentin took his own life and was the key piece he was coming here to discuss." Darla turns back to the group.

"I think he was spiraling by that point," Feather Hat says, and her statement is met with a chorus of agreement.

There lives within all humans an inherent arrogance. An oftentimes misplaced confidence and assuredness that we are in control of every occurrence in our lives. I told myself that coming to this retreat would bring me closer to Q and take me farther from his mother. That looking upon his work in this new environment would pacify me. I did not allow for any other outcome. We all do this. Tell ourselves the sort of easily digestible lies we know will not stick in our throats when we swallow them. The truth is I seek, even now, absolution. A clarity I can slip into my pocket and remove to appease myself when the guilt threatens to overwhelm me. I came here to understand what took him from me and to hope the answer would not be staring back at me in the mirror. What I did not bargain for was to listen to strangers draw what could be more accurate conclusions of my husband's state of mind than I was ever able.

"It's his eyes. Or eye. He just looks so bleak." My face twists involuntarily when the young girl wipes a tear from her face. "He must have been going through so much. The pain is right there."

"I agree, Emma," someone else says, but I almost don't hear over the blood pounding in my ears. "Like Margaret was saying about the *Concrete Clearing* series, I think we can see him decompensating. He chose these works to present for a reason."

"I cried for, like, three days when I heard he killed himself," Emma says. "I still cry...obviously. Suicide is so violent, don't you think? And I just keep wondering what pushed him over the edge and whether his family did anything to, like, stop him."

"His family could have been the reason."

"Exactly. You know his dad died when he was a child."

"Yes, but I'm talking about his family *today*. He was married, right? Do you think his wife knew he was depressed? I feel like it's so obvious in what we're seeing here that something wasn't right."

It is one thing to hear the sound of my husband's name in the mouths of strangers—like nails on the battered chalkboard of my heart. But it is something else to have your marriage dissected before your very eyes as you sit incognito in the back of a retreat where you have come to try and understand why he is gone.

"Yes, he was married," someone says. The someone is me, but my voice sounds as if it has been siphoned from the mouth of another person. "To me. He was married to me. I didn't know. I didn— There was no… You can't sit here and just chat shit about me and my family and blame us when you didn't know him. None of you actually knew him." At some point, I have risen to my feet and the program is under my left shoe, and my hands have balled into fists. They gawk at me, Emma the Fangirl, and Margaret with her feather hat, and Darla, who, really, is responsible for this travesty, because why shouldn't they? A possibly unstable, previously silent interloper with one afro puff coming loose is shouting at them in the conservatory of The Falcon's Nest while gulls cry and arch across the lapis lazuli sky outside.

I pick my way down to the beach. One can't exactly stick around for the refreshments after insulting a group of photography enthusiasts; what kind of conversation can you make over paper cups of pink lemonade and elderflower cordial after such an outburst? It is March, and while the sun has hoisted itself high, the cold still snaps at my fingers, which I tuck first into the sleeves of Q's jumper and then into my coat pockets. Were I starring in a film, this would be poetic. A panoramic sweep of the bay before homing in on my tear-streaked face as I walk along the beach and fill my socks with sand.

I'm not a complete dickhead. I know I am backsliding, relapsing on fresh, uncut pain because eziokwu na'elu ilu: the truth is bitter. There *was* hopelessness in *Concrete Clearing*. He *did* look bleak in *Sundown*. And I hadn't seen it. And while it is bad to miss that the love of your life is drowning, it is infinitely worse for the love of your life to be drowning and not trusting you enough to share that with you. Was he expecting me to examine the intricacies of his work and draw out his pain like a single silver thread when words would have sufficed? This man you read to, lived with, who bought your tampons, for whom you purchased hemorrhoid cream, who knew everything about you and about whom you knew everything. Except this. Except *this*. I think I deserved better. And to feel that fans different flames of guilt that have burned inside me since he died.

Samuel picks me up as the sun is starting to hide behind Bradda Head, after the hours spent on the windswept beach have frozen the skin on my face. He looks at me and places his newspaper on the floor of his car so I don't have to remove my shoes before entering. He cranks the heating high without being asked. I sit in the back of Samuel's car and I think about how there was the Quentin who belonged to me and the Quentin who belonged to others—his work sparking something inside of them in a way I am jealous to have never completely understood. There were versions of him I never paused to contemplate. My family was right and I can see now it was their rightness along with Aspen that brought me here. I also think about how underneath the pain and the disbelief is that unmistakable hint of relief that this person I loved more than life will never get the opportunity to tire of me and find the someone better they deserved. Gone are the untold number of chances to disappoint. I always expected Q to leave me. I just didn't know he would leave everyone else at the same time.

# 22

I cannot get warm. Sweep one of those *Forensic Files* thermal imaging cameras over my previous movements, and you will see the heat begin to leave my body somewhere along Port Erin Bay, slowly leaking away in the back of Samuel's taxi, the last of it smeared across the handrail in the hotel elevator, which I gripped to keep myself upright. I shiver beneath the blankets I heap on the bed, even the extra one they keep in all hotel wardrobes—you know the one: beige, vaguely scratchy. I layer first my own clothes and then Quentin's, burrito myself inside the duvet, but my limbs quake persistently. *Please*, I whisper to the empty room, *please stop*. I spend an entire day like this, venturing out only once to the restaurant to drink cup after cup of scalding raspberry tea, the curiosity of the other guests traipsing behind me.

The second day, I crank up the thermostat, step into the shower and inch the temperature dial farther and farther into the red until the water threatens to blister my skin. I count the tiles until my sobbing subsides—1,132. Q's absence is like a maze of trip wire over which I continuously stumble, bringing whatever resolve I have managed to build crashing down. Henrietta discovers me shaking on the bathroom floor. Her eyes take in the goose pimples blossoming on my thighs and then wander back to the door. I have no doubt she is not being paid enough to deal with the likes of me. I close my eyes after she leaves, but seconds later, they are open again.

Henrietta eases one of the bathrobes over my shoulders. "You forgot the DND again," she says. "Shall we try and get you up, then, chicken?" My knees knock together as she helps me to my feet, my underwear and my shame pooled around my ankles. The room spins and her grip tightens. "Easy now. I can feel the heat coming off you, love. Here, hold on to the sink for one sec and let me phone down for some ibuprofen."

She is almost to the door when I remember. "I can't. I'm pregnant."

"You what?"

"I'm—"

She pinches the bridge of her nose between her fingers. "I heard." I know the look of a woman who is wrestling with herself, observing the safety barrier of common sense and choosing to duck beneath it. Henrietta gathers the bottom of the robe in her hands that are cracked and reddened by cleaning products, bends, and examines my inner thighs.

"Hey! What are you—"

"I come in here and you're on the floor. You're burning up. You can hardly stand. Then you go and tell me you're pregnant. Don't get all precious with me now, love. I've just seen your nipples, and I dunno about you, but I need this job and letting you miscarry on the bathroom floor is a one-way ticket to unemployment for me." She peers at my legs again. "There's no blood."

"No blood," I repeat dumbly.

Henrietta helps me back to the bed. She is tucking the cov-

ers around me before she catches herself and steps back. "I…
Look, is there someone you can phone? A doctor maybe?"

"For what?"

"For what? For your baby, that's for what. What is all this?
Drugs?"

Henrietta has already spent too long here and has thus become yet another victim of the cyclone that is my grief. She
deserves to be released. "It's not drugs." At least not anymore. "I'm okay. I caught a chill on the beach and probably
just need to sweat it out."

"I don't mind getting in touch with someone if you like."
Henrietta tweaks the corner of the bedspread—force of habit.
"Your phone has been buzzing like a mad thing over there.
Someone called Snowdrift?"

"Yeah, I— Don't worry. I'm good. Really. I'm fine. I'll
sleep it off."

There are many things I do not know in this world, but
I know that it does not take twelve minutes to fold a towel
and replace a caddy of industrial-strength toilet cleaner back
onto a housekeeping trolley. I continue to sweep into people's
lives, a disheveled whirlwind of discord. I squeeze my eyes
closed until I hear the door shut and the muted trundling of
Henrietta's trolley as it moves on down the hall.

Q could not have known the true gravity of his desertion; the breadth and depth of his death. A seismic shift that
continues to touch the lives of people who had nothing to
do with him, with whom he was never intrinsically linked.
When he knocked me up and then disappeared in the worst
way, the way unable to be undone by child support and a court
summons, he couldn't have known everything he was leaving behind and how far the ripples of his absence would fan.
Even I was not to know. But when Henrietta was lecturing
me about the possibility of miscarriage, my heart and stomach
both contracted in a way that alluded to the end of my am-

bivalence about this pregnancy. I left these feelings there on the bathroom floor along with my black boy shorts and my dignity. Fitting Q into the shape of a father is something I had hoped, when we spoke about it, to do together. It's what you do, isn't it, even if you are not yet wholly sold on the idea of children. You envision your other half as they are and paint over this image with sleepless nights, color it with colic, Vesuvius nappies, the constant threat of danger. Would Q have been the sort of father who laid a hand on my hip at 3:00 a.m. and told me he'd soothe our squalling kid? Would he have strapped a BabyBjörn to his chest and carried our offspring on his photo excursions? What are the lessons he would have taught? What are the examples he would have set? Would the baby have been enough to make him decide to stay?

When I eventually open my eyes again, my body is still, but the sheets are damp and a cool folded face towel slips from my forehead onto the pillow. The curtains are open, and the moon has elbowed its way through the cloud cover and is hanging over the sea, a glowing toenail. On the bedside table is a thermos with a yellow Post-it attached to the lid.

*Butternut squash soup. It has some blended cashews in, so I hope you're not allergic. Temp has gone down, and I'll be back to sort the sheets out tomorrow. —Hx*

"Why the Isle of Man?" Bee says, and I hear her fingers still over her keyboard.

I have become the person who, after prolonged silence, phones only to drop the informational equivalent of napalm. It is Bee's turn today, and because Gloria and Nate have chosen to inform her that I am in fact safe, well and on an island, I figure it's only right I fill in any blanks. It's early and I picture her sitting in her office when she should still be at home, shoes kicked off, toes brushing the floor as she swivels in her chair. Working because I am not there for her to watch. I know that she along with my brother have been running interference on my behalf. She deserves this call.

"Q was meant to speak at this photography retreat here. I decided to come anyway. And there's no Aspen here." Morning arrived bringing with it sunshine, which catapults itself through the windows. If I were the type of person to describe light as "incandescent," this would be one of the occasions I would do so. Since Quentin was that person and since he is now no longer a person, I flip the pillow and wait for Bee to respond.

Bee processes information in silence. Before I knew her properly, it was disconcerting to be in a room or on the phone with her, presenting your ideas or offering up the workings of your mind as fodder to be analyzed, listening to nothing but your thudding heart and concluding that her muteness was a sign of disdain, a wordless damning.

Now I wait her out and eventually she speaks. "The second reason is valid." Bee pauses. "You get that we're worried, right? We miss you. I know what you said in your text, but every family fights. You've heard the screaming matches I get into with my mum."

"This was different. And like I said, there's also Aspen."

"Snowdrift technically isn't our problem, babe. She's a nightmare. It's like she's made it her mission to rid the world of happiness. She phones me at work, y'know?"

"Are you fucking joking?"

"Wish I was. She freaked out Corrine and made her cry." Corrine is Bee's PA. A sweet, mousy girl who, like most people, is totally unequipped to deal with Aspen. "Now Corrine just patches her through, and I can't even get mad because who *wants* to speak to Aspen?"

"I'm so sorry," I say. Because Bee is right. Aspen should be nobody's problem but my own, but once again I have left my personal troops to battle the dragon in my place. In the pit of my stomach, there it is again, the impotent rage, bitter as it surges to the back of my throat—were he here, none of us would have to war with Aspen, but Q did not so much abandon his duty as ship it off to the rest of us without a return address. I hate him for this, and the hatred mingles with the love, and I choke on it.

"When are you coming home?" Bee asks the question I no longer know how to answer.

"I… I don't know."

"'Course you know, babe. When's the retreat thing over?"

I use the baby, unborn and unable to protest, as an emotional shield. "The time away is really helping with the pregnancy. I'm resting a lot and eating. I'm actually eating now."

A sigh. The sound of stiletto gels against a Mac keyboard. My best friend is swallowing her words. "You're fine for money?" she asks after another stretch of fact-digesting quiet.

I remind her about my severance, which proves an effective segue into the latest adventures of Barry and Aurora, and not one for prolonged goodbyes, Bee tells me she loves me and rings off, leaving me to watch the light skitter across the duvet and disappear under the bed.

I have never been good at meeting people. I am not what one would call charismatic and am the poster child for introverts, preferring books over conversation. No surprise then that my social circle is small. Until Q killed himself, it wasn't something I had to dedicate too much time thinking about. When I was young, Ma and Dad would occasionally make attempts to usher me out of my shyness, "casually" mentioning the church-organized Nigerian teen amusement park trip on evenings I spent in my bedroom and to which I would respond, "I was told I had to face my books," which resulted in a curt mechie ọnụ—an instruction to shut up—and the sort of stare that can pick you up and move you across a room. How-ever, there is nothing like having a chunk of that finite social circle annihilated in one fell swoop to make you reckon with loneliness. When someone you love dies, you are supposed to turn to your best friend for comfort. When your best friend happens to be your husband and his cause of death stains a pair of jeans your mother has almost certainly destroyed to stop you from screaming whenever you see them, you ques-tion whether you can trust any of the relationships you have left not to be ripped out from under you.

In the aftermath of Q's suicide, I found myself squinting at my parents, my siblings, at Bee, trying in vain to peer beyond their skulls and into their minds, seeing if I could pinpoint the exact moment they would leave me so I could fortify my-self against the impending pain. I oscillated between pushing them away with my erratic, selfish behavior and clinging to them, guilting them into staying by my side. And when the flavor of their support was not palatable to me, I cut and run. When grief shatters you and leaves you to try and put your-self back together again, it can be no surprise that some parts are accidentally omitted.

I leave Henrietta's washed and dried thermos beside the TV. From it, I have eaten butternut squash soup, beef stew and, astonishingly, scrambled eggs. Each time, I thanked her profusely and she responded only by taking my temperature and, yesterday, nodding once when the thermometer came back with a reading she deemed acceptable. She has the day off, another maid named Sophia informs me this morning as she sprays white vinegar on the mirrors in my room, but I wonder, briefly, if she has finally had enough, if her kindness, like that of so many others, has reached its expiry date. I do not ask Sophia. She avoids all eye contact and leaves without saying goodbye.

Bee texts to ask how I am. I reply with a photo of the beach where I have chosen to walk this morning, my first foray into the open since falling ill. I am wearing enough layers to at least make the cold give pause before attempting to enter my chest for a second time. Bee responds with a sole *x*. Bee has always been someone who can convey the most without uttering a single word. Her texts are, on the surface, those of a best friend who cares about my well-being, but I know her well enough to read the unsaid, the untyped *How long will this last?* Making this island my home has taken on an appeal underpinned by necessity. Before I slip my phone back into my pocket, I take another photo of the sea and kick a clump of seaweed at my feet. I'm no professional, but I liked to snap my own photos when Q was alive. I would savor the way he would sidle up behind me, gently tilt my phone upward or to the right, his chin or cheek pressed against my face while he helped me frame the shot. Most of the time he wouldn't even speak, simply dropping a kiss into my hair to signify that the shot was all lined up. That was his way: teaching without teaching.

The first time we came to this beach, he chased me across the sand until he tripped and face-planted, leaving a print of his body that he photographed before the waves erased it. There is a framed shot of me in the house, sitting on the rocks, my hair in waist-length braids the breeze flicked about me. It is a candid, his very favorite of me. We left the beach and moved to the promenade, stopping to play games at the old arcade and eat soft-serve ice cream sold to us by a pink-cheeked man who asked if he could touch my hair, and I, high on love and the smell of sea salt, had allowed him even as Q frowned in his direction and muttered that it wasn't cool. There is still soft serve when I return this time, but the proprietor is now a bored girl with blue eyeliner who asks twice whether I actually want a cone. It is chilly, after all, but is she not open? Are her wares not for sale? She jams a chocolate flake into the half-strawberry, half-vanilla concoction and hands it over. She does not ask to touch my hair.

At the end of the promenade, the last remaining wall of Summerland—the island's once premier leisure center— stands, a ballast to keep the cliff from spilling into the streets of Douglas. When we were here before, Q listened raptly as our tour guide spoke about the fire of '73, which ripped the old leisure center to pieces and claimed the lives of fifty people. It had been rebuilt and the adjoining aquadrome saved, but it was ultimately demolished in 2006, one wall left behind to preserve the cliffside. By the time I reach the ruins, I have long since given up on the ice cream and need to pause to close my eyes against the memory of my husband trying in vain to make that wall interesting to me. A particular gift of Q's was the ability to make desolation appear beautiful. *Effortless* was the word they used at the retreat. As if it was woven into his DNA along with his inability to dress like a functioning member of society. I imagine bringing our kid to this relic and mustering the same enthusiasm Q would have had, the same excitement brought about by mixed ice cream and a wide stretch of unencumbered sand. I imagine this and understand that I would have been the parent who walked a few steps behind, watching with the small smile that comes with knowing that you cannot be everything for a child but that the gaps you leave are filled by their other, maybe better parent. It is a reassurance I will never have.

Hunger wrenches me from my reverie. Port Jack Chippy sits as it always has, on the lip of Onchan, overlooking the sea. The first time Quentin and I came here, we shared a huge portion of vinegar-soaked chips and sat outside so we could watch the ferries arriving.

"I can't get over how gorgeous it is here," Q said. "Places like this exist and we live in London."

"What's wrong with London now?" I'd flicked a chip at him, and he'd grinned.

"Nothing. But you're telling me you wouldn't trade the Northern Line for this?" Salmon streaked across the sky. I could hear the breath escaping my lungs in a way London never allowed. The quiet was almost unnerving.

"Quentin, I will never trade London for anything."

But I was wrong. It makes no sense that I feel closer to Q here than I do even in the bed we shared for years, but perhaps the simplicity of the memories here have something to do with it. Remembering can be tiresome work. Not all memories weigh the same.

Inside, the simple wooden tables and chairs are unchanged. They have been wiped clean and the air is scented with oil, frying fish and salt. The cod is flaky and hot, the batter crisp. I sit by the window and play like the seat opposite is occupied not by my husband but by my child. My child who could inherit my dodgy eyesight and my small ears. I picture tugging the jumper of a school uniform over a miniature afro, lacing tiny shoes, hoisting a sleepy toddler higher on my hip and pointing to the ferries. Without Q, there will be no buffer. The opportunities to fail are doubled. There is no counter, nobody to offset the anger and the sadness and the "But Mum said!" I will bear the burden of this baby's happiness alone. And it seems almost impossible.

This time I wait for Samuel outside the hotel. As we pull away, he asks me what I have been up to, but when I mention my visit to Summerland, his jaw tightens almost imperceptibly, so I ask after his wife instead.

"Aye," Samuel says, "she's grand."

We leave it there for the duration of the trip. But before I exit his taxi, I pause, my hand on the handle of the car door.

"I'm sorry if you lost someone. In the fire, I mean. I know how much— Anyway. I'm sorry."

Samuel nods once. "Cold again today. You bundle up."

I have timed my arrival at The Falcon's Nest so that I may have some time alone with my husband's work. I am also hoping to extend an apology to Darla King. When she envisioned this retreat, dedicating time, effort and possibly some of her own funds, success to her looked like sold-out bookings, bonding over art, perhaps a few photo ops with the guest of honor. She was not counting on that guest of honor killing himself or his wife materializing and berating the attendees like a harridan. It is the least I can do to coat my sorry in shame and offer it to her. However, my plan is thwarted by the receptionist, who informs me that Darla is not yet down and thus the space is not yet open. She points me to the beige armchair in the corner and tells me I am welcome to wait.

"But—" the word sounds like it is being squeezed in a vise grip "—but I have to... I need to get in there."

"And you will," I am told brightly. "In about an hour or so."

"I... You don't understand..."

"It's alright, Stephanie," Darla says. She has appeared like an angel draped in the finest Marks & Spencer has to offer. "I was just heading in. Would you like to join me, Mrs. Morrow?"

"Ezenwa-Morrow." A reflex that has outlived Quentin.

"Yes. Shall we?"

New photographs. I have seen some of these—the trio of monochrome shots Q took of a set of young twins as they cycled through different moods. Q photographed them in a way that makes it near impossible to identify them, zooming in on facial features, capturing the stamp of a small foot, the hunch of an angry miniature back. The parents, I remember him saying, were grateful that he thought of this, that he built in safety and anonymity where they had failed to consider the implications of their children immortalized, their images gawked at by strangers. Then there is the series shot outside an A&E unit. These I had never seen. These he had never tried to show me.

"You have to know we—none of us—meant any harm," Darla says, abruptly bringing me back to The Falcon's Nest. "Your husband was a rare and unique talent. We all admired him and his work greatly."

"No, I... I came here to apologize. I shouldn't have... It's just that hearing about Quentin... His death was... I'm sorry I spoiled the day."

"*Spoiled* is a strong word. You certainly made things much more interesting." Darla smiles. She has no reason to be gracious, and yet... "I can imagine for someone who knew Quentin intimately this whole thing comes across as a bit, well, creepy?"

"You never think of your husband as having fans, you know?" I turn back to the A&E photos. "It's weird hearing people talk about him like that. About me like that."

"Celebrity is a strange thing, a bizarre phenomenon."

Celebrity? I frown. Q was the man who learned how to inexpertly part my hair and oil my scalp. He was the guy who couldn't grasp that a person was meant to wipe the bathroom mirror after accidentally splattering it with toothpaste. He was the guy who hung my personal moon, but outside of me, outside of our lives, his star was rising, and other people were taking notice. "I wonder how he'd feel about that."

"You think he would have been uncomfortable?"

Q was aware, like all extremely attractive people are, of his beauty. There was no way he couldn't be. It was all most people who met him talked about and responded to. And for that reason, he hated it. He worried that the sole mark he would leave on the world would be a beautiful one that lacked substance. He wanted to be more than the rich pretty boy and he spent time running from the life that made him what he was. I dismissed these fears a lot of the time because we all like to think that the very beautiful are not qualified to speak on the hardships of life. I was more concerned, as the partners of the very beautiful often are, that somewhere along the line, mistakes were made and the day would arrive when the love that you have received in error would finally be removed from you and given to someone more deserving. Q pretzeled himself convincing me he was here to stay, but I never really believed him. In the end, I guess I was right. The mother of all hollow victories. I stand here in a glass-walled hotel-restaurant-turned-gallery in Port Erin, speaking to someone who understood the power of my husband's work. Here is his mark, immortalized, and yes, it is beautiful, but it is more than that. *Babe, you made it*, I say in my head. I wipe my eyes with my sleeve.

"I don't think he would have believed it," I tell Darla. "Anytime I gave him a compliment, it's like he would squirrel it away so he could enjoy it later. I wish he got to see this. I wish he got his later."

Darla gestures to the set we are looking at. "Something about this speaks to you?"

The A&E series depicts the illuminated doors of the unit. In the first one, a man stands outside the doors, both hands covering his face, his fingers lifting his graying hair into spikes. Without seeing his expression, his anguish is clear. Q captured his rumpled clothes, the glint of tears between his fingers. Another of the shots shows a woman sitting in a wheelchair. A newborn nestles in a car seat on the floor at her side, but her eyes are closed, her mouth a taut line. Yet another photo and the bench outside the doors is occupied by a young woman in scrubs. Her head rests against the back of the bench. The angle of her body is severe; this is not someone enjoying a leisurely few minutes' break.

"There's no joy in any of these." As I say the words, I realize how true they are. I don't ask Darla if she knows when the photographs were taken. As his wife, I should have known. As his wife, his work should have topped my priority list. I should have been his biggest fan. Instead, I am outdone by a girl named Emma, a girl he never even met. Had I *seen* these, had I looked upon *Sundown*, I might have glimpsed a pattern—the gradual darkening of his spirit, shadows thrown across his light. I might have been able to save him.

His work may have been effortless as more than one person had said, and there is no parallel I can draw between the ease that comes with the expression of art and the utterance of words, but I think I deserve to have been given the chance to hear those words. Without trivializing the struggle he must have felt to speak them, it was me. And I earned the opportunity to help him. But he refused to give it to me. When I shut my eyes, I feel it there, under this new sensation in my chest, jockeying for position with the guilt. *Anger.*

# 23

My appetite goes into hibernation on the journey back to Douglas, the island's capital, and so at first, I blame hunger for my sudden departure from sleep. My stomach is, after all, cramping, wondering why it was furnished only with guilt and not an afternoon meal. Or an evening one for that matter. However, when I open my eyes and the recessed lighting comes back into focus, I realize that the gentle vibration of my phone underneath my wrist is the true thief of sleep. Gloria. A series of missed calls.

"Glo?" I croak. I have not spoken to my sister since I arrived here, but she has been with me nonetheless; her comment about Quentin's lack of a note living in my head rent free. And newfound anger aside, I still can't help but defend him.

"I know you don't care if you fuck up your own life at this point, but do you have to drag us down with you? Can you spare a thought for anyone but yourself? Your parents for instance?"

She is hissing. Gloria is not a person who hisses. Dread crawls up my spine and makes a nest for itself in my hair. "Glo, what happened?"

"Did Quentin leave you a note for Aspen?"

Gloria is so busy chastising me that she does not even hear my blood turning to ice in my veins. "What? No. No! Glo, you know there was no note. Not for me. Not for her. Not for anyone." And I can't resist adding, "You said it yourself. I can't tell her any more times."

"Are you sure?" It's a ridiculous question. Q devastated me in new and special ways by not explaining himself. I have sobbed the same into Gloria's bosom at numerous points since he died. Besides which, lying to Glo cannot be done. She is Achilles; the truth, Hector.

"You're asking me whether or not I'm *lying* about my dead husband leaving me a suicide note? Are you on crack?"

"Are *you*? You think you can just disappear, and Aspen will go gentle into that good night? She is accusing Ma and Dad of concealing a goodbye note from Quentin and you of kidnapping her unborn grandchild. Like that makes any sense. Like Ma and Dad would even have a clue about your husband and his reasons." I recoil at the way she says *husband*, like it is a swear word, a curse.

"She what? Aspen did what?"

"Oh, you heard. You ever think running off might push her over the edge? She's ready to hog-tie you, throw you in the back of her Aston Martin and keep you in her basement while she feeds you your own fingers. And failing that, she is threatening to try and have you declared incompetent the moment you step foot back in London. Do you know what that would mean? For you? For that baby you're growing?"

My throat closes around my words.

"Eve? *Uchenna?*" She uses my Igbo name.

"She...she'd try to take my baby?" But I know she would. She said as much.

"We're pleading ignorance over here, Eve, but you need to

come home. You have to help us handle this. I am but one lawyer and she's got loads."

"Why didn't Ma and Dad say anything?"

"Because you don't answer your phone!" I hear Gloria hurl something across the room. "And like always, they want to protect you. You have to come home. Now."

"Now that Aspen has the scent of blood? Mate, you're having a laugh."

Gloria explodes over the phone, studs the walls of her office with shrapnel and sends some over the Irish Sea for good measure. "ENOUGH! I am not fighting this anymore. Not without you here. Book a flight. Now." She hangs up and I wait for my lungs to refill.

Mine was never a foolproof plan. Like an antique one finds at the back of a store, it seemed adequate. Only on bringing it home and examining it closely do you then see the nicks and scratches, the damage that cannot be undone with wood filler and the right stain. On the table by the window, my MacBook is still open. If I wake it up, the screen will still be on Rightmove and the numbers of estate agents will still be scrawled across the hotel's stationery. There were three places I wanted to view in the coming days. I will never see them. Gloria did not sound understanding. She was not my beleaguered yet lovable big sister. She was apoplectic and I find myself at the root of her anger. I am, as my mother has always said, the architect of my own misery, but now I have branched out and am responsible for that of my family.

Aspen has always been someone I managed to separate from my family. *She doesn't like me*, I told my parents after our first meeting, and after Ma told me not to be stupid ("*What? ị nà-àkakwū akakwù!*") and Dad told me that simply couldn't be true ("*My daughter? Enweghị ike!*"), their incredulousness soon gave way to quiet bewilderment when I was repeatedly proved right. "*ọ nà-ayì alā. Onye nzuzu,*" Ma muttered to herself as she pounded yam in the kitchen. "It's my daughter she doesn't like? Abeg, leave her there." Then it simply became something we Did Not Talk About. She was the unmentioned phantom at birthdays and Christmases. Ma, too proud an Igbo woman to attempt friendship, but still too Christian to "leave her there" completely, relegated Aspen to the bottom of her prayer list and asked God to touch her and instill a contrite spirit within her. God, obviously, had more important things to do. I find the thought of Aspen accosting my parents with legalese and emotional blackmail so abhorrent, I rush from my bed to the bathroom, making it to the toilet just in time, my anger spilling from my gut and into the porcelain.

Here on the Isle, Aspen's wrath does not have the same effect. Her numbers are now blocked, and when her pride pushes her to use private ones, those ring out. Because it must travel farther, her fury loses power. And Glo is wrong, it *has* worked. For me, it has worked. London is now the place where Quentin died, the place where my footsteps are ordered in part by his mother. I could still call those estate agents, still find a house that looks out on the sea. I could live there, growing bigger, painting walls, putting together nursery furniture, and Aspen would rage against those I left behind. I would be the dealer of the bad hand. The Eve of Before could not have lived with that, but the Eve of Before died along with Q.

I take a breath and tell Siri to call Ma.

She answers after half a ring, and I wait for her to stop screaming before I offer sheepish greetings. "Where are you?" she shouts.

So Glo has not told. Divulging my location could mean there is a good chance Ma would be on the next flight out, making enemies of airport security. My mother is a scientist capable of brilliance and she is also a woman who cannot grasp that scissors are not allowed in hand luggage. Still, I opt for the truth. "The Isle of Man."

"WHAT IS IN THE ISLE OF MAN?" She increases her lamentations by a decibel or two so I fully comprehend the ways in which I have upset the apple cart.

It is more about what or who is not here. "How are you?" I ask, trying to steer her away from the cliff edge of hysteria.

"How am I?" she asks if I have lost my mind. "ọ bụ onye ara? You disappear without a trace and you are asking how I am? I— Talk to your dad."

"Eve," Dad says. He is calmer but working to hide the strain in his voice.

"It's hardly disappearing 'without a trace,'" I mutter.

"Eve," Dad repeats, "we should have spoken about this before you left."

"REMIND HER SHE IS PREGNANT."

"Your mother—"

"AND THAT THERE IS NOBODY TO LOOK AFTER HER!" It is an affront to Ma as a mother that I am elsewhere choosing not to be cared for.

"Please try to understand our concern," Dad presses on once Ma's yelling subsides.

"I know. I'm sorry. I need a break, a holiday." I say nothing of Aspen.

"Did you take your Bible?" Ma is back on the line.

"I have the Bible app on my phone."

Ma's breathing begins to return to normal.

"When are you coming home?" Dad asks. I picture them huddling together, straining to hear my voice through the same mobile. My parents always forget speakerphone exists in times of high stress.

"I'm not sure. In a couple of weeks. Probably," I lie.

"WEEKS?"

"Let us pray." Dad covers me in the metaphorical blood of

Jesus, and when he is finished, Ma takes over and engages in some spiritual warfare, banishing any would-be perpetrators of harm to the pits of hell.

I tell them I love them. I ask them to please understand. I promise I will phone them. They try to but do not understand and the strings forever binding parents to their children are pulled taut in this moment.

"We love you, too," Dad says. "Phone your sister. She is upset."

Henrietta is vacuuming. "Feet," she shouts at me, and I lift my legs so she can run the Hoover over the spot where they rested.

The curtains are open. It is raining today, and the sky's face has closed in on itself. My iMessage is full of unopened texts from Gloria. I did not think there would come a time I would hide alerts from my own sister, but this year is the gift that keeps on giving.

"Oi," Henrietta says, and when I look at her again, she is holding up three tiny bottles. "New shampoo options— lavender chamomile, honeysuckle rose or jasmine aloe? You want one of each?"

"Huh? Sure. Yeah. Thanks, Henrietta."

"Can you fake excitement, chicken? This is the highlight of my workday."

"Sorry." I close my MacBook and count the checks in the pair of Q's socks I am wearing.

"No offence, love, but you're the saddest person I've ever met. Granted I don't usually speak to guests, but I at least get a smile out of them now and then. Especially when there's new shampoo. Hey, it was a joke…sort of." Henrietta whips a tissue from the box she has just replaced and hands it to me. "All these tears. Where did all your happy go?"

Where indeed? I dry my face. I must cut a wretched figure. "I'm sorry. Things are just so fucked-up and I think I have to go home. Back to London."

"Yeah. I'd probably cry if I had to go back there." Henrietta meets my eye and grins.

I chuckle into the Kleenex.

"Home can't be that bad, can it?" Henrietta deposits the shampoo in the bathroom and begins wiping down surfaces with her lemon-scented industrial furniture polish.

"It's complicated."

"More complicated than being here on your own with a baby on the way?" She sees my face. "Sorry, chicken, I don't mean nothing by it."

"No, you're right. I guess maybe I thought I could do this by myself. Here."

"The guy who gave you that rock not around anymore?" She nods at my engagement ring.

I shake my head.

"Well, maybe you can do it alone. Night feeds and baby puke and that thing where they poo so hard it ends up in their hair. And then there's the colic and weird rashes and not being able to shower or sleep until they sleep. While finding a house and a job and doing the food shop when your ankles are swollen to three times their normal size." She pauses in her polishing to fix me with a look.

"I get it. I'd be useless."

"You wouldn't be. But nobody does it alone unless they really have to."

A few weeks ago, I was unable to make it to the bathroom without assistance. I fell asleep each night to the sound of Ma's prayers. I opened my eyes to Nate or Bee. On the days I needed it, I was held without being held. And on the days I needed it, I was held together by arms stronger than my own. Quentin is supposed to be my balance, but without him, my loved ones have stepped in to catch me. My loneliness is more pronounced here, a flawless sort of pain. Perhaps it is what I deserve, but where I fail, I will need that same net to catch this child. I think about the gentle peppering of gray on Dad's head as he ties the laces of my kid's shoes, his voice made softer as he explains the Igbo words for grandma and grandpa. I see Ma pinching pounded yam into infant-size mouthfuls, Nate awkwardly nestling a baby's head in the crook of his elbow just like he did with Ellie and Ben. I imagine lamenting to my sister about the ways I am getting it wrong. I pick up my phone and text Bee: I'm coming home x.

I book my flight home, giving myself two days. I repack my scant collection of clothes and toiletries. I erase the property listings from my browsing history. I tuck both Samuel's card and the brochure from the retreat underneath one of Q's T-shirts. I order the fanciest hand cream I can find for Henrietta and pay for next-day delivery. I tuck £100 in notes into an envelope and scribble her name on the front.

My phone wakes me from an uncomfortable sleep full of dreams I don't remember. It's Bee and her voice squeezes its way past the noise around her and into my ear. It takes a moment for me to register what she's saying. Something, something *here*, something, something *don't know*.

"Whatchu say, Bee?" I yawn into the phone.

"I said I'm here and I don't know where you're at. Fuck it's cold."

"Whatchu mean?" The noise in the background of the call surges again. I shout into the semidarkness of the room, trying to make myself heard over the chaos. "Bee? Bee? What do you mean you're here? You're where?"

"Babe? Can you hear me? Eve?"

"Bee, what's going on? Where are you?"

"I'm at this bitty-arse airport and there are no cabs."

"You what?"

"The Isle of Man, babe. I got your text, innit. Then Gloria called and, well, you know the rest. What's the name of your hotel again? Looks like I'll have to walk, but I'll get there eventually."

"You're *here*? As in on the Isle of Man?"

"I swear that's what I just said."

I am on my feet and rifling through my newly packed case. I give Bee Samuel's number and tell her I'm at the Sefton. I repeat it twice as Bee's signal dips and drops.

"Great. Give me, like, ten minutes. I'll call you back."

Ten minutes stretch into twenty, then thirty, and just as I become frantic, the phone rings. Not my mobile, but the room phone.

"Eve, babe, would you be a doll and come down to reception? The check-in commandant won't give me your room number and I don't want to be walking around here yelling your name. It's like *Get Out* in here. Yeah, yeah, she's coming. I'll be waiting, babe."

I am already shaking when the lift doors open, and I spot Bee brushing down her coral jeans and tugging at her cropped hoodie. She is wearing oversize sunglasses and a new wig, a burst of copper curls on her head. She sees me and points in my direction, hoisting her blue Mulberry weekender onto her shoulder. When she whips off her shades and folds me into a hug, I note that despite her own tears and an early morning flight, her mascara is intact. Back in my room, she drinks in my island life, silent as she digests it, then she drops onto the bed and stretches.

"Gloria didn't think you'd buy a ticket," she says. "Even after I showed her your text. She was going to drag you back home herself, so I told her I'd come and get you. When do we fly back?"

"Tomorrow." I take in the strip of stomach peeking out

above the waistband of Bee's jeans. At ease in every space she inhabits, she pops the top button of her jeans.

"That soon, yeah? Okay, better book my ticket, then." Bee fiddles with her nose ring, then yawns. I hand her my Mac-Book and she does the needful. "Food. Tell me I can at least get a full English in this place?"

I take her to the dining room, and I smile because I am here to terrorize my fellow boarders for the last time. Bee orders her full English, winking at the waiter as he notes her egg preferences. She stretches again, produces a tube of Pat McGrath lipstick and uses the back of a spoon to apply it in two seamless swoops. I have always envied the ease with which Bee moves through the world, as if the other inhabitants of earth are either slight inconveniences or simply not there. Every eye is on us and she has yet to register the attention she has commanded. When she does, she turns to me in bewilderment.

"Everyone in here is looking at you like you're about to start snorting coke off the napkins, babe. It's been like this the whole time? You want me to start knocking heads together?"

I shrug. "Nothing about me right now screams 'normal.'"

"Well, yeah. But they could at least pretend not to notice? Jesus." She spears a sausage, locks eyes with the husband of the closest staring couple and slides it slowly into her mouth. The poor dude chokes and splutters into his mug of coffee. It is not every day you encounter a petite bombshell simulating fellatio on a breakfast item. His wife tosses a napkin at him and shoots Bee a look that would cow anyone else with even a single fuck to give.

I can already feel my body thawing. This is the Bee effect. I lean across the table and kiss her face.

Back in the room, Bee tugs off her shoes and scrutinizes her pedicure. She digs through her bag and hands me two parcels, explaining that they had been waiting for me at reception and were handed to her only after I arrived to con-firm she belonged to me. "Getting post sent here? You really didn't want to come back, did you?" She is a ball of energy, gazing out of the window one second, jumping on the bed the next. She strips, leaving a trail of her clothes on the floor as she makes her way to the bathroom. She shouts that I should keep her company while she showers, so I perch on the closed toilet seat and do no talking, instead listening to her as she fills me in on work and how Nate continues to excel at *Circle*. I reach through the steam and hand her a towel when she is done. Bee lotions, pulls on a T-shirt and collapses on the bed. She is asleep in seconds, energy depleted, my own per-sonal supernova. I retrieve the DND from the chest of draw-ers and hang it up for the first time in days.

We eat an early dinner at Port Jack Chippy and, on our way back to the hotel, buy ice cream from the same girl, whose expression says, *There are two of you?* Before going back inside, Bee makes us cross the road and watch the sunset, her tongue leaving rivets in the swirl of the soft serve.

"Okay, so I sort of get it," she says, watching the sun punch the sky with an orange fist.

"Get what?"

"Why you thought about staying here. It's got this chill quality. London could never." She deftly tucks an escaped curl back under her beanie. "It's like all my synapses have smoked weed or something."

"Yeah. Here doesn't have you guys, though."

"Are you saying you missed us?" Bee dabs a small dollop of ice cream on the end of my nose, but when I laugh, it al-most hurts.

"How can you even ask? Of course I did."

Bee looks at me. It is the same sort of look she gave me

back at *Circle* when she was trying to figure me out, as if she is trying to see past my face and into my soul. "Hmm."

"What?"

She crunches the last of her cone and slips her arm through mine. "Let's go back in, yeah? My nipples are trying to break through all these layers."

Inside, Bee takes another shower, and we sit up in bed flicking through TV channels, settling on nothing.

"Babe," Bee says, "you should phone your brother."

My stomach tightens. "Is he alright? Did something happen?"

"Nate's fine. When is he ever not fine? But he misses you. And he's pissed."

"At me?"

"No, not at you, diva. Did Gloria tell you that Aspen went to your parents' house to pull that stunt about the note?" She lets this piece of information sit between us, soaking up my anger like a chunk of tofu in a bowl of marinade.

"She went to their house?"

"She's a witch on a mission. You staying here was never going to work. You get that, right?"

Since Q's death, my life has become a series of events dictated by others and almost exclusively categorized as "Can't." You can't starve yourself, Eve. You can't choose not to bathe, Eve. You can't be sad forever, Eve. You can't just up and leave, Eve. I have become a puppet, jerked and guided by the hands and sentiments of others. I was unaware of my resentment until this moment.

"No, I don't get it. I could have made it work," I say now, frustration pinging like gravel on asphalt.

"Could you? Because Aspen would have found you. You know that. You act like she can't board a plane. She might not even have to. Her righteous indignation is powerful enough to propel her around the world. Twice."

"I would have found a way," I shoot back. "Why the hell would I willingly go back to a woman who stalks my parents?"

"Well, ideally you wouldn't have to deal with her. Snowdrift is scary, but she's not insurmountable."

"I don't want to talk about this. I'm done." I kill the lights and turn away from Bee. But my grief is cyclical, so an hour later, I am hunched in the chair by the window, my face pressed against my hitched-up knees. I am still there when Bee picks her way through the darkness of the room and crouches before me.

"You're not alone, babe." Her voice is a caress, and when she tucks me back into bed, she acts as the big spoon even though she is eight inches shorter than I am. I fall asleep with the scent of her jasmine body lotion on my skin.

"So, it's true?" Henrietta says to me the next morning when I find her down the corridor cleaning another guest's room. There is a second where I feel betrayed, because I stupidly forgot that she is there not solely for my benefit. "You're off home?"

"Yeah. We actually have to get a move on." Bee is already in the lobby waiting for Samuel, and if I leave her alone for too long, there is no telling the sort of havoc she will cause.

"Right," Henrietta says. She is holding a stack of face towels.

"Right," I echo. "Look, I— You've been so... I couldn't have..."

Henrietta laughs and pulls me into a brisk hug. "You're alright, chicken. You'll do fine." I thrust the hand cream and envelope of tip money into her hands and watch her face travel through several emotions. "I had planned on pestering Kev for this cream for my birthday." She dabs her face with one of the face towels. "Go on, love. Don't get stuck here." I make my way to the end of the corridor and turn back. She waves and disappears into a guest's room.

Bee is turning her sunglasses over in her hands when I make it down to the lobby. "Oh, thank God," she breathes when she sees me. "Babe, please. Let's go."

Still, I pause outside the hotel, taking in the facade until she squeezes my hand and leads me to Samuel's waiting taxi.

"You gals off to the airport, then?" he asks, and when we reply in the affirmative, he gives a nod and with that my time at the Sefton comes to an unceremonious end.

Bee takes a work call while we wait to board. I remember my second unopened package and peel back the brown paper. Inside is an eight by ten photo. A half-open door. I recognize it immediately. It's our bedroom door. Beyond that, the window that did nothing to keep heat in or cold out until Q finally caved and had the panes and caulking replaced without damaging its character. Sun streams through and illuminates one foot hanging off the end of a bed, our bed. The foot belongs to me. *She.* This is the title of the photograph. I never knew he took this. There is a note with the photo, which I read once, twice, three times.

*A lot of his art focused on the derelict, the underside of the human condition. But a lot of it centered depictions of pure delight and of beauty. Your husband was more than adept at capturing it all. —Darla*

I can't stop looking at it. My hands shake, my eyes mist and my foot becomes a smudge. But I can't look away.

"What's that?" Bee is back beside me, shades pushed to the top of her head, peering at the photo in my hands.

"Q took it," I sniff. "I guess they showcased it at the retreat, but I didn't see it. The organizer sent this over."

"That's you?"

"Yeah. I had no idea this picture existed."

Bee exhales slowly. "This retreat. Did it help?"

"Help?"

"Like, do you feel more connected to Q or whatever?"

She doesn't need to know that I missed most of the retreat and all I've gained is a tenacious anger for my husband that I am struggling to reconcile with the guilt. "I just feel lost," I say, and a sob escapes before I can swallow it. "I miss him so much."

Bee rubs the spot between my shoulder blades. "Of course you do. But—"

"But what?"

"Nothing. Forget it. Look, we're boarding."

"Nah, what were you going to say?"

Bee sighs, ruffles her curls. "It's just… I always thought he was selfish in the way most men are, y'know? Like, he was a man, so he was born with that deficiency they have where they'll have their heads up their own arses at least *some* of the time. Then I clocked that maybe his selfish gene was a bit more pronounced. I dunno, maybe it was inflamed or something. You loved him and you were happy. But *this*? Babe, I hate him for this. He couldn't at least let you know it wasn't your fault?"

We are called to board and I walk ahead of Bee, my back conveying what my words can't. I hold Q's photo against my chest. This time when the plane is flung by turbulence, I sit on my hands and look away from my best friend's when they reach out for me.

# HOME AGAIN

# 24

"Do you want me to apologize?" Bee says hours later, when we have disembarked, paid too much for a car ride home in silence and are finally standing outside my house.

I am shivering inside my coat, have been since landing back in London and not because it is cold. I don't look at her. Because it is one thing for part of me to hate my dead husband, but it is entirely another for my family and my best friend to hate him, too. Like a patriot chastising a foreigner for criticizing his country, it should be me and me alone able to condemn Quentin's shortcomings. He left me, not them. I am justified. They should face their fronts because aside from this unborn kid who frightens me, they are all I have, and I can't afford to start hating them as well.

"No," I say to Bee. "You said what you said. And you meant it."

"Okay, so you're not speaking to me?"

"I'm not sure what you want me to say, Bee."

Bee's version of vulnerability is the lowering of flashing eyes, the tucking of stray wig curls behind her ear with barely shaking fingers. You need to know her to see it. You must have earned the right before she unlocks that door and allows you to place one foot inside. Even then, because you know her, you can recognize the tug-of-war, the tiny death she dies when her guard is temporarily down. "I don't want you to be pissed at me." She's so small and her voice is heavy with fatigue. She is worried about me. She dropped everything to bring me home. I tighten my scarf around my neck.

"But I am," I tell her. "I am pissed at you."

"Why?"

"I'm allowed to have feelings about you hating my husband, Bee. That is something I am entitled to." My voice cracks. "I don't want you all to hate him. He must have been so fucking sad. But he loved me, Bee. He really did."

I notice the shadows under Bee's eyes. Delicate bruises. Sleepless nights woven into her beauty. Because of me. "I know he did, babe. I'm sorry. I'm an overprotective cow. It's just that we all love you, too. And now it's you that's so fucking sad. So sad you ran away." She pulls me in for a hug.

"I left because of Aspen."

"I can't say anything else." She pats down her pockets and finds her cigarettes. "You don't want me to say anything else. So I'll just tell you again, I love you. I hate seeing you hurt."

"I used to be happy."

"You were. But you were also hurt before he died, babe. Because Aspen's always been a total bitch and Q always let her." She picks up her Mulberry, taps her phone.

Before I have time to react to this grenade, the front door opens and Ma, clad in Nate's peacoat, rushes out. "Eve-Nnadi!" She squeezes my arms, my face, brushes my afro back from my head. Her eyes search mine. I feel myself unraveling slowly in her presence. "ọ nọ ebe a!" she calls over her shoulder into the house.

"Ma. Hi." My voice is lost inside my scarf, but Ma squeezes my arms again and then looks over my shoulder.

"Belinda. You are not coming inside? I cooked."

"Not today, Aunty. Got some work I need to finish up. I'll call you guys." She walks off down the street before Ma can drag her inside. Ma drags me inside instead.

A lot can change in seventeen days, but my family looks broadly the same. If you did not know them, you would take in the scene inside my kitchen and think nothing of it. My dad, holding an unopened bottle of Supermalt, which he does not relinquish even as he hugs me; my brother, spooning jollof onto a plate from the pot on the stove; Gloria, in leggings and her reading glasses, casting aside the work she is doing. And Ma, peeling my coat and scarf from my body, pushing me toward the table, placing a plate in front of me. You might not notice the effort in the smiles or the relief in Dad's voice when he says grace and thanks God for my safe return. You could very well miss Nate's insistence that he sit closest to the door, I guess so he can tackle me if the need arises, or how Gloria continuously flicks her eyes from me to her food and back again. Lines in foreheads are a little deeper. Bags under eyes, just that bit heavier.

I swallow a mouthful of plantain and place my fork on the table. "I wish you'd all stop looking at me like I'm going to do a runner."

"Well, are you?" asks Nate.

"Ehn? Stop it, Junior," Dad says.

"Nate actually has a point. For once," Gloria says. We have not spoken since the phone call about the note, and her body may be in my kitchen, but her heart is far from here.

"Eve has had her holiday now. You feel refreshed, is that not right, darling?" Dad smiles and sips his Supermalt.

"How lovely for her," Gloria mutters.

"What's your problem, Glo?" I face my sister, who meets my eye, unflinching.

"When do you plan on giving your mother-in-law a buzz?" Gloria asks.

"Glo, she just got back. She hasn't even taken a pi—used the toilet in her own house yet." Nate uses a spoon to eat his rice. He will never change, and this small act of normalcy is comforting to me.

"Yes, let's all go easy on Eve. None of us even *know* Aspen, but sure, let's all protect Eve like we've been doing while she's been hitting the spa and *resting*." Glo pushes away her plate.

"That's what you think I've been doing? You have no idea, Glo, so why don't you just—"

"I actually don't care. You should have been here! That's the point!"

"Kà ọ dị nọòfụ!" Ma commands. "My children will not fight like dogs as long as I am alive. You think I labored for fourteen hours, Chimerika, for you to sit here and shout like you have lost your senses?" She uses Glo's Igbo name and re-inforces it with good old-fashioned Nigerian guilt-tripping, which means she is not far from snatching the three of us up like she did when we were knee-height.

"Can we just get through dinner? Glo, pass the chicken," Nate says.

Gloria does so, then stands. "I'm not hungry. I'm going home."

"Gloria, biko. Sit down. Finish your food. We will talk later." The line that has appeared in Dad's forehead is so deep I could pan for gold.

"Sorry, Dad." Gloria rounds the table and kisses his cheek. "Ma, everything was delicious. I just can't be here right now."

Dad follows Glo out to the hallway. I can't hear what is being said, but once the front door shuts and Dad returns to the table, every appetite bar Nate's has disintegrated. Only the sound of my brother scraping his plate can be heard. Eventually Dad clears his throat.

"Your sister has a full day tomorrow and she wants to see the little ones before they sleep."

"It's okay, Dad. Glo hates me right now. She's in good company. The best even."

"Nobody hates anybody in this family. What kind of language is this?" Ma collects the aluminum foil from its home and wraps the remains of Gloria's meal before returning to her seat with a sigh.

"You know what Glo's like." Nate leans back. "She'll get over it."

"Right. But you guys agree with her. Low-key, you think she's right." The brief silence that meets my statement is all the confirmation I need. "I think I should go and take a shower."

I cry the tears of the persecuted, then cry because the knowledge of being looked upon like a damsel in distress is painful and embarrassing and completely my doing. When I emerge from the bathroom, Ma is in my bedroom emptying my case and separating the clothes into piles ready for washing.

"I know you must be feeling better," she says.

I perch on the edge of my bed in my towel. I need to stand, locate a pair of clean underwear and put them on. My legs refuse to move.

"You need to sleep. Let me go and put these in the washing machine."

"Ma, you don't have to wash my clothes. I can do it. Tomorrow. I'll do it tomorrow."

"The Bible says 'Weeping may endure for a night, but joy cometh in the morning.' Did you read your Bible while you were away?"

"Probably not as much as I should have. I don't want you to feel like you have to look after me all the time. I'm grown." I stare at my feet against these familiar floorboards.

"You are still my child. But, Eve?" She waits until I look at her. "Don't disappear like that again. You are pregnant. You *are* pregnant, Uchenna?" Eyes damp, she holds herself still, not daring to breathe until she has my answer.

The gentleness with which Ma brings us back to the scene in this room that drove me from them, the prevention of a termination she has undoubtedly been bringing to God in prayer, is as good a sign of her love as any she has shown before. "I'm still pregnant, Ma," I say.

She squeezes my hand tightly before she picks up my clothes.

I want to ask her how Aspen's antics have affected her. Whether she and Dad have lost sleep. If they have been frightened. What toll my absence has taken on them. Instead, I hold my tongue and we, mother and daughter, look at each other until Ma breaks eye contact and leaves me to get dressed in peace.

In the darkness of my bedroom, I listen to Ma and Dad preparing to sleep in the guest room next to mine. There was never a question they would spend my first night back in London not under their own roof but mine, and now they believe I am sleeping (Dad quietly opened my bedroom door and left it ajar), they talk as married couples do before retiring for the evening. A few short months ago, I was one half of a married couple. I know how it goes. I can't hear everything, but I am transported back to my childhood and listening to the low rumble of Dad's voice as he first sang while he changed and then spoke to Ma.

"She is back now, Nkechi," I hear Dad say. "Let us try and move forward."

Move forward. What does that look like for me? I turn onto my side. My phone is silent for the first time in weeks. No frantic messages from Glo. No missed calls from Nate and Bee. No emotional blackmail from Ma. Only the cool blackness of a screen devoid of notifications. Under my pillow is *She*, Q's photograph. I stared at it for so long tonight that *Sundown* fell temporarily from my mind. Quentin was the man who, when I stupidly sprained my ankle walking down the stairs at Charing Cross station, hoisted me onto his back and carried me home. He was the man who, whenever Bee and I went out to dinner, always called ahead and ordered a bottle of bubbly for us. He knew the birthdays of every single member of my family. He started to learn Igbo so he could speak the language of our heritage, and he beamed with pride every time Dad slapped him on the shoulder and said, "Well done, young man," after he'd made it through a stilted, shaky conversation. He let me tuck my cold feet between his calves every night without complaint. He was also the man who left the room every time his mother called in case some of her acrimony escaped from the phone. He was the man who split his Christmas every year between the two of us. He didn't leave either of us a note. My husband was comprised of layers and his loss is exposing me to those I had never really considered before it was too late.

# 25

Drawn curtains, birdsong, prenatal vitamins on my tongue followed by the coldness of the bathroom tiles against my knees because the vitamins make me hurl. Staring at *She* until my eyes can no longer focus. No sea, no atrium fountain, no Henrietta. A week or so of this, my newest normal, and Nate stops coming directly to the house after work to make sure I have not fled again. Ma permits herself a night in her own bed. Dad's phone calls during the day decrease in number. Bee's texts are noncommittal but consistent. Work is frantic, she tells me, she's pulling all-nighters because of other people's incompetence. Gloria phones everyone but me. I hear her voice echo through the house once. She does not come upstairs. Aspen has a new number, and my voice mail count rises.

We are, all of us, performing the dance of the contrite, skirting around that which drove me from London. It makes no difference. When your effort is concentrated on not talking about a thing, the effort itself becomes another thing. I wear my family's opinion of Quentin around my neck.

The days are marked by the movement of shadows and the diminishing light in the eyes of my family. My sadness, it appears, should have been left on the Isle of Man. The expected momentum does not materialize. I have outdone myself again. Nobody tells you that to grieve is to shoulder the expectations of others. The requirement is that you mourn in silence, cloak yourself in dignity and make others comfortable. I do not know how. Therefore I grieve out loud.

I spend more time in the bathroom than is necessary, examining my changing body in the mirror—a body that, alongside my family, has decided that my wallowing days will not be permitted to continue.

Ma and Dad are waiting in my bedroom when I return from a forty-minute bathroom excursion.

"Come and sit down, Eve," Dad says, and he shifts to make room for me between them. I go and I sit because it is Dad, and he asks for so little in this life that any request he does make elicits an involuntary response of obedience. He picks up one of my hands and tucks it into his own. I am five again and Dad is helping me shop for my school uniform because Ma is neck-deep in her PhD thesis and school begins in a week. "You are in pain," he says.

"Dad. Please. You don't have to—"

He squeezes my hand, gently pinches the soft pad of my thumb. "You are in pain and it is time for you to try and find a way out of that pain. Remember when you were small, and you learned how to handle the bad dreams you had at night?"

"I think I had to. You guys were sick of me coming into your room in the middle of the night and flinging myself on the bed."

"I think," Dad says, "you were sick of it as well. You learned to manage your fear. Do you remember what Matthew 5:4 says? It says, 'Blessed are they that mourn; for they shall be

comforted.' I think, darling, that you are having trouble finding that comfort."

"I don't..." I choke down the lump in my throat. "I don't
feel very blessed right now."

"It's okay not to see it for a time. Anyị hụrụ gị n'anya,"
he reminds me. "Part of that love is telling you that it is time
for you to seek help. There are some wonderful counselors
your mum knows who—"

I lift my head from his shoulder. "Since when do you believe in counseling?"

I remember the advice shouted by sweating pastors from
the pulpit on Sunday mornings: *Pray. Whatever it is you are
facing, God is the answer. Your salvation does not lie in the words of
men.* It is how we were raised. When Ma and Dad received
a letter from the Home Office questioning their right to remain in the UK, they fasted for seven days. When Uncle
Osinachi developed a mass on the side of his neck he refused
to get checked out, Dad summoned a prayer circle so prolific
the house smelled of Old Spice and Dax for weeks afterward.
Our house was filled with the pleas of the pious as they be-
seeched God to remove the mass, and if not that, then Uncle's
stubbornness. I can't recall having brought a problem to my
parents and that same problem not being added to the inter-
cession during nightly prayers. To hear them now advocating for me to take my issues outside of us and outside of God
turns my mouth so dry, tumbleweed drifts across my tongue.
*Look at you, Q, changing the staunch opinions of my parents. Who
would have thought?*

"You continue to stare at your photograph of a foot," Ma
adds, pulling *She* from under my pillow. "I can't understand
it. And you don't want to talk to us. You don't want to eat
again. You and your sister are at odds. You don't even want
to watch Guy Fiery. What Quentin did was terrible. You are

right to mourn, but shebi you also have to live? You have stopped living."

Crawling under my bed would not be an appropriate response. So I mumble, "It's Guy *Fieri*," and wonder whether I am the only person on earth who has ever felt caked in a shame so thick you feel you must chisel your way out.

"Just tell us," Dad says now, "who you would prefer to see. We will do the rest." He picks up a small pile of pamphlets at his side and places them in my lap. Ma takes my face in her hands and kisses my forehead. Dad squeezes my shoulders, and then they are gone, and the room is quiet.

So of course, I do nothing. Because inaction is all I know now. Because I can list the activities I would rather undertake than to sit across from someone and speak about my *feelings*. Those things include substituting tampons for lemons, dunking freshly torn hangnails in vinegar, removing my own spleen with a spoon, stubbing my toe on the corner of the bed sixty times a day for the rest of my life and listening to all the voice mails Aspen has left on my phone. Because people can't just decide I need professional help and expect me to fall in line. I stay in bed, and yes, I continue to stare at my photograph of a foot and Gloria thaws her cold shoulder long enough to phone and ask me why I am ignoring our parents' advice.

"Up until three seconds ago, they, a neurosurgeon and endocrinologist, I might add, believed in 'praying through it.' Why is this different?" I ask my sister.

"How is that working out for you?" she asks me and hangs up.

I don't expect anyone to get it. What I feel is loneliness. An immense, girthy, encompassing loneliness that started gestating on the Isle of Man and has now unfurled its wings. Every day is like waking up and realizing your arm has wandered off during the night. You start a million conversations before reality slaps you. You throw up your prenatal vitamins and wish his hands were caressing your back. Nobody understands, so in my opinion, you get to look at your photograph and opt out of bathing.

That is until your grandmother calls and says, "Eve. Ozugo," then repeats the last word for emphasis. "Ozugo." It's enough.

Chinyere Ezenwa pioneered a new form of braiding, established a chain of high-end hair salons in Nnewi, became a skilled midwife and, because apparently she was still bored, bore six children whom she raised with her husband, Ochudo. One of those six children was Nathaniel Nwachukwu Ezenwa, who just so happens to be my dad. Grandma Chinyere is my sole living grandparent. She still lives in the house her husband built for her and their children and her letters to us kids arrive twice yearly on blue airmail paper, despite Aunty Grace teaching her how to use email and buying her an iPhone so we can FaceTime or WhatsApp call her and watch her brow crease under the mango trees in her garden.

My memories of my grandmother involve peeling plantains for frying in the kitchen of her house when Ma and Dad took us back to Nnewi to remind us our roots were not planted in UK soil. She had house girls to help her but trusted nobody to fry her plantain. She showed me how to slit the peel down the side and the perfect angle at which to slice. She sang in a low voice and let me sip palm wine from her glass. I envied my cousins who lived close to her and were able to congregate in the house regularly. Who received her head pats and exclamations of thanks whenever they brought her gifts or stopped by simply to absorb some of the peace that flowed from her, and which she passed down to Dad. I felt removed from her in England, read her letters tens of times over and kept them all. *Read your books*, she instructed me, *and make something of your life*. She was sleeping her way through malaria for Glo's wedding, but for mine, she boarded a flight with three of my aunties and watched from pride of place as I married Quentin.

"Does he treat you well?" she asked me.

"He does, Nnenne," I answered, and she nodded once and smiled.

"He's handsome. But not like your grandpa."

Grandpa Ochudo died long before I was a twinkle in Dad's eye. I never got to build memories of him, but I do have photographs of Dad standing rigid at the funeral. As the eldest son, his responsibility was to give his strength to others. He could only break down in the moments when those leaning on him found another temporary place to rest. He was not much more than a kid himself, his father's light snuffed out all too soon. Grandma Chinyere knows what it is to flatten your palm against the coolness of sheets your beloved can no longer occupy. She knows what it means to watch your future turn to dust. She gets it.

When she says "ozugo," her voice traveling to me from the sitting room in her house in Nnewi, I sit up in my bed and I listen to her. If a voice can age, my grandmother's does not. It is as clear as the times she called us inside from the compound.

"Your father says you no longer get out of bed."

"I'm just very sad."

"Sadness is not a reason to stop living, my dear."

"I don't know what else to do."

"You rise up. It does not mean you have stopped loving him. Your boy, he was polite and I believe he loved you. But, child, is it in this bed you will spend the rest of your life?"

"Maybe?"

"You miss him. You will always miss him." Her voice wavers for half a second. "But your life is never completely your own when you have people who love you. I think you know it." With these words she reminds me that you never stop being a parent, not really, not when your grown, successful son confides in you about his daughter who has given up. My grandmother is making this call as much for Dad as she is for me.

"I will send your mother dried bitter leaf. When it arrives, you will do the video phone call and I will teach you the best way to make bitter leaf soup. It will make you and your baby strong. And, child?"

"Yes, Nnenne?"

"You pray *and* you listen to your parents."

"Yes, Nnenne."

"They all sound like quacks to me," I tell Nate and Bee after we have spent an hour leafing through the profiles of the counselors. It is like a perverse form of blind dating where the chosen one wins the pleasure of mopping up the emotional vomit I will spill onto the floor of their office.

"You're being picky. At least two of them sound decent, and if Ma of all people is endorsing them, then they're all decent." Nate hands me the profile of one Kalisa Ferrante, BACP accredited.

"This is not a counselor. This is a *Game of Thrones* character."

My brother tuts and rolls his eyes.

"Okay, but, babe, you have to choose *someone*," Bee reminds me from her position on my bedroom floor, because I still have not "risen up," am still staying in bed pretty much all day. Baby steps. "If you don't like any of the people your mum picked out, then let's get online and find someone you actually like." When I phoned Bee and asked her to help me choose my purveyor of psychological help, any lingering unease was forgotten. She arrived within the hour.

"All of you are just desperate to get me into treatment, yeah? You're gagging for it."

"I know why you don't want to go, you know," Nate says.

I turn to face him. "Is that right, Confucius?"

"Well, yeah, it makes sense. You're scared. You go and talk to someone and what if they say, 'Yeah, you're fucked-up, no wonder Q killed himself'? You don't wanna hear that. Who would want to hear that? But that's not going to happen because it's not your fucking fault."

The silence in the room is broken only by Bee joining me on the bed so we can stare at Nate in mute unison.

"What?" he asks. "Whatever, man. I read." He stalks out of the room, leaving Bee and me to look at each other, mouths still agape.

"He reads," she says eventually.

"Evidently." I shuffle the papers and sigh. "I'm not vibing with anyone here."

"Maybe you need to speak to them first? Like the talking stage, but for mental health."

"The entire relationship would be talking. You reckon Aspen would be up for this?"

"Snowdrift? With a counselor? When she can just log on to the dark web and order the souls of six orphans to replenish her spirit?"

"She's self-medicating by threatening me and all the people I love."

Bee squeezes my knee through the duvet. "Come on, babe, let's Google."

In the end, I reject all of Ma's suggestions and agree to attend group therapy far enough away from my stomping ground that I will remain anonymous. The last thing I need is to be accosted by a neighbor when my skin has been stripped back and my emotional nerve endings are exposed. Ma and

Dad accept this news and try their best to conceal their relief, and Glo sends me a thumbs-up emoji and nothing else. The night before I am due at Hammersmith community center, I hyperventilate so badly that my breathing is still mildly labored when Ma opens my curtains in the morning. She smiles a smile so hopeful that my plans to beg off shrivel and die before they can be voiced. During the journey there, I turn over Nate's words in my head. It is one thing to have Aspen blame me for Q's death, to have spent all this time indoctrinating me into her cult of culpability, but it is entirely another to have someone objective sit for a matter of moments and confirm her assessment of me and of the life Q and I built together. I have no defense, not really. Q didn't leave me something tangible I could brandish as vindication. How far could his love truly have stretched if it did not extend to opening the door to his pain and letting me wade into it with him?

The community center's corridors smell of Glade plug-ins, disinfectant and aging magazines. There are bulletin boards advertising five-a-side football, an art fair, a double room for £975 a month inclusive of bills. I loiter down the hall from Recreational Room One, which someone has renamed "The Peach Room." They have attempted to cover the old nameplate on the door with an oversize sticker of the fruit.

The Peach Room cannot be accused of false advertisement. All the walls are painted an aggressive color and the standard-issue beige carpet causes enough static to raise the hair on my arms. Plastic chairs (also peach) are arranged in a circle, most occupied by a motley crew of what I can only assume are the bereaved. I could simply walk out, go and buy a Turkish platter from the place down the street I passed on my way here, then return to my bed and to *She*. Instead, I think of my grandmother, slide into a chair and wait. Our leader is a woman called Barb. She's over six feet tall, has ombré locs, a bosom that rivals even Gloria's, and tells those of us who are new that she is a French Canadian who moved to London because of love.

"If you are wondering whether I lost that love, the answer is yes," Barb says. "But only to someone called Samantha." She winks at us and folds her beringed fingers in her lap.

The format is simple. Barb will sit back and allow us to speak. She does not have too many rules here. If we remain respectful to others and kindly offer trigger warnings before launching into anything particularly traumatic, we can spew as much hurt in this room as we are comfortable with. Longtime attendees have no problem doing this, but those of us who are still coming to terms with sitting in the Peach Room, still acclimatizing to the gravity of our attendance, do not say much at all. Loss is our only shared connection, and a miserable one at that. The people here have lost parents, friends, lovers and children in a variety of ways, all of which have marred lives they are now attempting to live. I hunker down in my chair.

"I feel like it won't ever get better," the woman with the red hair is saying. She is twisting a handkerchief around her palm. "Every day I wake up and it's worse. Aren't you supposed to start getting better at some point? I'm sick of hurting. I want to be better."

I listen to this poor redheaded woman talk about what it's like to wake up every day after losing her three-year-old son to leukemia. She describes it perfectly: the desolation, the agony, the manic hope he will run into a room and make her whole again. I start to shake inside my coat. She is not alone. Others here have lost loved ones to cancer, to accidents, to old age. But I am alone in losing my person to suicide. If Q had to be taken from me, why couldn't something other than himself be the cause? Part of the cruelty of suicide, the reason it is still such a taboo, is the unanswered questions it leaves behind: What would it have taken to keep him here? What possibly could I have done better? What is so wrong with me that I wasn't worth living for?

"Beth, you're not sick. You don't need to describe grief like it's an illness." Barb speaks with an accented authority. "You have a right to your feelings, and they have a right to be felt. Time dictates you'll hurt less eventually because that's what time does, but one of the big problems with mourning and with loss is that people think they need to skip it and get right back to normality, like their emotions aren't important and aren't part of the road to 'better.'"

Beth is crying. "I still hear him at night. He used to babble away to himself in his room even after we put him to bed. I know he's not there, but I still lie in the dark struggling to hear what he's saying. Mark gets so angry. He says I need to stop doing this to myself."

Perhaps it is the sound of Beth crying, small, strangled sobs that erupt from her. Perhaps it is the thought of her lying in the darkness of her bedroom listening to her tiny son who is no longer there while "Mark" seethes beside her. Perhaps it is knowing that when quiet descends in my house, I also strain to hear Q's voice, but it has now been replaced with the sound of his mother's calls or my parents' whispers. Or perhaps it is knowing that I am growing a human who will no doubt require me to speak more openly than I am expected to here, who will ask questions to which I have no answers. Staying in the Peach Room suddenly becomes intolerable. I wait until Beth finishes speaking, but when someone called Abel starts explaining in painstakingly slow language how when his girlfriend died in a car crash, he sat in the same spot where the road curved and her car careened into a tree for six days straight, about how sometimes he still sneaks away under the pretense of a supermarket visit or a walk, to sit there silently because it's the only way he can feel close to her, I rise and, in my haste to be as far away from here as possible, knock over

the plastic cups of orange squash on the snack table. I expect
Barb to try and stop me, but she is busy calming down the
others who are gasping at my departure—drama in group!
My feet carry me past the bulletin boards and back outside.
My heart carries me back to Battersea.

"You know," my grandmother says to me later, after I have
tied a bow around my lies and presented them to my family,
"your daddy was prepared to die that day as well."

She has called me from her garden, and because I can't
speak to anyone else, I am grateful for her face on my phone
against the backdrop of red clay and green leaves. And now
she is telling me about burying her husband. "How come?"

"Igbo custom says the widow must cut her hair, and not
just cut but shave it—we call it kpàcha isi. The other women
came here to tell me. But your father, he would not allow it.
I had to remind him that for Ochudo, I would do whatever
was asked. It was he, your father, who told me that Ochudo
had made him promise to stop anyone from taking my hair."
She speaks deliberately, pausing briefly when she speaks the
name of her husband, an acknowledgment of that which still
aches even all these years later.

I think of my dad, still a boy, channeling his grief into defending his mother. "Did you do it?" I ask now.

"I told them 'onye m bù n'obì àrapụgo m wèlụ naba,' that
my sweetheart left me and died. I was ready to do all that was
asked of me. But this is how he always thought of me. He secured my dignity before he was gone. I didn't cut my hair."
My tears are not silent enough and my grandma makes small
shushing noises on the phone, at once soothing and sad. "I
know it's not the same, nke m. You must try."

I join Ma in the kitchen, where she is rolling out pastry for
meat pies. "Will you eat?" she asks, and I nod.

"If I can help."

Ma points with floury fingers to where the pot of mince, Scotch bonnet peppers, carrots and potatoes is sitting on the stove. I collect it and we begin: her cutting the dough into circles, and I spooning a dollop of the mixture into the center. Ma hums worship songs while we work, the soundtrack of my childhood before dead husbands and precarious pregnancies. I watch how she deftly folds then forks the pastry, how she hands me the egg wash while she checks the oven temperature. Everything my mother does is suffused with love. I stand and wrap my arms around her from behind, dwarfing her.

"Ah! Eve, careful now, you want to push me inside the oven?" She laughs and turns to face me, returns my embrace and reaches up to wipe a spot of flour from my cheek. "This support group helped, usom."

I hug her again; I do not want to have to voice any more deception. Not now. "I spoke to Grandma today."

"Yes. Mama worries about you. She's sent the bitter leaf."

"She told me about when Grandpa died. When they told her to cut her hair."

Ma begins wiping down the kitchen table. "There are many things about our customs I love, but that is not one of them. My mother shaved her head when Papa died. None of us could have talked her out of it." She washes her hands and touches my cheek, her fingers still warm from the water. "I worried," she says, "that you would find this out and cut your hair when Quentin died."

I can imagine it, too. Nothing would encapsulate my pain more than the ritualistic hacking of my hair.

Ma's voice is thick. "I'm glad you did not do it. I don't think he would have liked that." It is the first time she has mentioned him since the night I left London.

# 26

We broke up once. Quentin and me. I never told anyone. It came out of nowhere, a couple of months into our relationship, the proverbial blindside. One moment we were talking about our future, the next he was telling me he couldn't see me again.

I went from stunned to distraught in record time, breaking down right there on the floor of my room, shedding my dignity as readily as I had shed my Fela T-shirt hours earlier. I wept. Openly. I asked him why and all the while he stood there, his face impassive before frowning and offering me an unsatisfactory "I made a mistake." He was gone before I could compose myself long enough to demand a better answer.

Everyone knows you're supposed to go to pieces after your first love—first *real* love—ends. And overachiever that I am, I excelled in the art of Falling Apart, and look at me now. Years later and still defending my title. Despair had never welcomed an inhabitant so dedicated to its cause as me. I excused myself from lectures so I could sit in the bathroom for ten minutes at a time, my fist stuffed into my mouth so nobody would hear my sniveling. I avoided Ma's calls. I was a disgrace to myself as a woman and a feminist. When I was hit with a triumvirate of viruses that nearly brought Ma to campus, I considered it punishment for allowing myself to shed that many tears over a boy.

It started out with plain old influenza and quickly spiraled into a chest infection, and because clearly my misery was not yet complete, a case of strep throat arrived to finish the job. I lay in my bed coughing up globs of viscous, greeny-yellow mucus and shivering through a fever of thirty-eight degrees. I missed lecture after seminar. Eventually, I had to dispatch my friend Marie to the campus pharmacy to collect my antibiotics, which I eagerly awaited, praying that with the drugs, I would find some relief. Waiting was hard work and I fell asleep in a pool of my own sweat, waking several hours later to find Quentin sitting by my bedside, the bag of drugs in his lap. He was wringing out a washcloth into a bowl of water, and while I worked through the mental gymnastics necessary to ascertain that he was not in fact a tactile hallucination, he laid the cloth over my head and brought a glass of water to my lips.

We said nothing for a long time, but eventually, despite my weakened state, I couldn't hold back any longer.

"Why are you here?" I croaked with all the vehemence a wronged woman afflicted with three sicknesses can muster.

"I... I made a mistake," he replied, his brow creasing.

"Yes, we've covered that part already."

"No, I— The mistake was leaving. I don't know what I... I'm sorry."

"I'm too sick for this. Who said I want you here?"

"Nobody." He looked as miserable as I felt. "Do you want me to go?"

I lied and told him I did and, drained by the encounter, fell back asleep almost instantly. When I woke again, he was back.

"I brought you some soup," he said.

And that, it seemed, was that. Q camped out on the floor of my room. He pressed my antibiotics on me. He made rice pudding, and when I couldn't manage that, he bought more soup and spoon-fed me. He tapped out my dictated text messages to my parents, and he brought me lecture notes collected from friends, which he wrote out longhand for me to use when I recovered.

After ten days, my symptoms began to abate, and I could sit up in bed and start reading Grossmith's *Diary of a Nobody* because the threat of falling behind on uni work was now real. Essay deadlines loomed, and because our work was set at the beginning of the term, nothing short of Ebola could excuse you from submitting papers on time. It became clear three pages in that the likelihood of finishing the book and constructing a cogent, analytical response in time was slim to none. I panicked, and returning from lunch, Q found me in the fetal position murmuring incoherently about the two thousand and five hundred words due in seventy-two hours.

"Eve." He had more soup. "What's wrong?"

"I'm supposed to get a first," I said.

"Yes…" He approached with caution, unsure what exactly was unfolding.

"Then the flu…strep…the phlegm…"

"You think you're not going to get a first—" he placed the soup on my desk "—because you got sick. In first year. Where you need only forty percent to pass?" He did not understand the cold terror of not being the best you can be as has been hammered into you by your African parents. He began unwinding his scarf from his neck and only then did he register my distress. "Oh shit. Hey." He sat next to me and gathered my still-limp body to his chest. "Your first is not lost."

I sniffled into his jumper.

"Look, here," he said after a time. He held a wad of tissue to my nose. "Blow."

I did, and when he went to dispose of my mucus, I pulled myself together. "I have an essay due in three days."

"Yeah. George Grossmith, right?"

"How did you know?"

He rummaged around in his backpack and produced a copy of the book, which he handed to me. "I'm no English student," he said, "but with the help of a second-year and some notes from your friends, I managed to highlight and annotate some stuff." He handed me a slim folder of notes. "It should help you get started. I hope. Your lecturer refused to give you an extension. I tried."

And yes, I should have made him work harder; I should have spurned him altogether or, failing that, insisted he list the reasons for his abrupt change of heart. But I was so grateful he was back, demonstrating both his penitence and his love for me by stepping into the role of caregiver. I was floored he had flirted his way into basically writing my essay for me. I felt relieved that I would wake up and he would be there, watching me carefully from under the sweep of hair on his forehead, like I might disappear or change my mind and eject him from both my room and my life. I was pathetic. Gloria would crucify me. So, I said nothing. I clutched the notes and felt my control over my feelings for him wither to nothing, and like a wild horse awaiting the best moment to clear the fence and bolt, they broke free and trampled me underfoot.

Although I never forgot the day Q broke up with me or the desolate weeks that followed, I tied my tongue in knots and did not ask the questions I had about why he did it, what he was doing while I was scream-weeping and worrying that the pain might eat through my stomach lining. I wanted to know, but I couldn't ask because to ask was to risk losing him again—something I was certain I couldn't endure a second time. I waited for him to bring it up, but he never did. Instead, he took to looking at me like I was a bird poised to take flight if he made any sudden moves. At night, he held me like I might evaporate in his arms.

Now, because I have no other answers, because Q ducked out of my life as effortlessly as he did back then, this time with added permanence, I cling to things like this, blow them up into Signs That I Missed and Things I Should Have Known. Because I don't have the privilege of asking, of closure, I turn my husband from a guy who likely thought he was in over his head at age twenty to a man who was plotting even then how he would take a machete to my heart and leave me bloodied and broken in his wake.

Aspen has her lawyer leave a voice mail asking that I respond to a letter confirming my whereabouts. The letter in question is sitting unopened by my bedside, where it has been since it arrived three days after my return from the Isle of Man. I, master of evasion, have ignored its existence. The voice of Henry Huntington, QC, marches into my ear. The facts are these: Aspen, through human sacrifice, voodoo or, more likely, handsomely paid investigators, found out that I absconded to the Isle. She then sent forth a series of dispatches (be it in human, demon or written form; Henry is not clear about this, which is a shame as I am certain he is being paid handsomely to terrify me thoroughly) to the Sefton, which arrived shortly after my departure. Temporarily thwarted, my presence is now being "requested," but that cannot happen until my location has been confirmed. Aspen wishes to "discuss" the return of some property she has decided I am keeping from her. Henry is polite in the manner of a lion gingerly pawing at its prey before the death strike. I first open then read the contents of the letter noting that she has temporarily given up on her unborn grandchild and is concentrating on material possessions for the time being. I hide it in my underwear drawer underneath a pile of thongs that will never again see my glutes. I am sliding the drawer closed when Nate phones.

"You ready?" he asks, and I can hear the buzz of *Circle* behind him, can almost smell the artisanal wax melts they use against all safety advice.

"Ready for what?"

"…It's your group thing today, yeah? How you getting there?"

And it takes me a moment to understand what he's talking about because my brain has done that compartmentalizing thing it now does so well. I gave my family a tailored and truncated report after the first session, allowed them to believe I had placed my foot on the first rung and was about to start my ascent to healing. I didn't tell them I'd bolted or that once outside, I had to walk around for an hour until my panic attack abated. They think I will be back in Hammersmith today when the very thought makes me want to dunk my head into ice water.

"Oh," I say to Nate. "About that. I'm not going."

"You're sick or something?"

"Nah."

"So then what do you mean you're not going?"

"It's just not for me, Nate."

"It's just not for you? Are you joking?"

"I tried, okay?"

"Like fuck you did." Nate has never hung up on me. But there is a first time for everything, and the first time is often the worst.

Everyone's flavor of chastisement is different. Bee's is bittersweet. She calls not too long after Nate, having no doubt been informed of my stubbornness. She peppers our brief conversation with "but, babe" and "are you sure?" Her voice never rises but is shot through with sadness. Ma, invigilating a hall of medical students, breaks away to ask if she has heard correctly. "M naike gwụrụ," she sighs into the phone. She *is* tired. Of me. Of my unwillingness. Dad asks why and receives my answers with mute acceptance. He knows his child. "You have made up your mind," he tells me before being called away by his beeper. Gloria chooses an in-person reprimand. It strikes me as she marches into my bedroom that I have missed her. That despite my commitment to widowhood, there has still been space, however small, for my sister. She wears a blazer and pencil skirt combo, and a scowl, but I want to reach for her; my arms tingle as I press them into my sides.

"Ellie and Ben are in the car," she says by way of greeting. "I don't have long."

"Can I see them?"

Gloria pulls her earrings from her lobes and unclasps her hair. "No, you can't see them. Are you mad?"

I stand up and take a step toward her. "Glo, I know you're angry, but—"

"Don't." She steps away from me. "You will not see my children until you get yourself together and go back to that support group. You missed today's? Fine. It meets weekly, right? You'll be there next week."

These are the babies whose little heads I held, whose nappies I changed while Gloria snatched an hour of sleep. They are the kids to whom I have read stories, dropped at school, loved in the fierce but slightly removed ways aunts do. They are also the children I have neglected, frightened and forgotten over and over since Quentin's death became my reason for living. Grief may tamper with your own memory, but Gloria's remains intact, and she is a mother before she is anything else.

"I miss them," I say feebly.

I see it, a crack in her armor, which she immediately repairs. "You don't get to miss them. You get to go back to your support group and get better." I stare at the black mark her heel leaves on the floor long after she is gone.

A life without family. Had I not contemplated this when
I was eating soup made by Henrietta and looking at cottages
to rent on the Isle of Man? I knew then that the fissures that
were created when I walked into Q's blood would only grow
bigger, would turn into yawning crevices I may not ever be
able to traverse nor repair. I came home in part because I knew
I was too weak and too much of a coward to face motherhood alone, that eventually Aspen's need for revenge would
be the battering ram that leveled the defenses my family had
mounted on my behalf, and I would be required to deal with
her myself. Yet since returning, all I have done is reject their
love and shun the care they run themselves ragged to provide
for me. I retrieve *She* from its new hiding place, smooth the
edges back and close my eyes, desperately trying to transport
myself back to a time where I could lie in bed asleep, comforted by the knowledge that I would wake up to a husband
who loved me so much he was moved to capture moments of
mundanity and turn them into something beautiful.

When Q and I moved into our house, I had a big blowout
fight with Aspen over a wingback chair. The chair was hers,
purchased during one of her bouts of redecorating. It didn't
fit with her "vision" for the coral bedroom, and because rich
women with nothing else to do but spend money on pointless remodeling don't simply return pieces of superfluous furniture, she tried to foist it on us. Q didn't see the big deal.

"We don't have to use it," he appealed to me. "Let's just
stick it somewhere we don't have to look at it."

My issue wasn't that it was he who had jettisoned previous
attempts at introducing anything that could have been even
vaguely described as chintz into this same house, nor was it
that the chair was particularly ugly. It was more that Aspen
was between us again. Like an extra appendage one must either undergo lengthy and painful surgery to remove or else lug

around, she was flexing her power, asserting herself and the position in Q's life to which she still felt entitled. I wanted him to defend me, but he didn't, and because I wanted to scream at him but refused to give her the satisfaction, I screamed at her instead. She had never set foot inside the house her son had made his home. But here she was, insisting this chair find a place there. Three days after the fight, I sold the chair on eBay for £1,500 and she found out because witches tend to have flying monkeys who report back. She phoned me and we fought some more in that roundabout way where zero ground is gained. Before she hung up, she lowered her voice and she told me I needed to understand that Quentin was part of her, which meant that any child he produced would also be part of her, and everything that went before and came after paled in comparison to the fear I felt when I heard those words until I found the part of her dead by his own hand, found out I was pregnant and realized that the prophecy was being fulfilled.

You're not supposed to say it because babies are supposed to be a representation of everything good and pure and perfect, but now over one hundred days after Q died, the thought of meeting this person who could possess certain traits Aspen pioneered is making it difficult to look past the dread and find elation. I want to be happy because this tiny human is the last tolerable biological link to my husband. Before, I would have had the luxury to argue over the ridiculous waste of spending money on miniature Nikes. Now I must contemplate mental illness, a mother-in-law whose hatred of me could replace fossil fuels as an energy source and whether I am capable of being a single mum. Gone are the pastel-colored dreams of gently rocking an infant while Q watched over us, eyes suffused with love; now I face the prospect of having to explain the circumstances of his or her father's death to our kid.

This is what sucks about him being gone. Because I am sometimes still so angry at him. And if I feel this way, aren't my family's sentiments justified? Don't they also have a right to be furious? I am so heated he put me in this position, giving me the unenviable role of Bearer of The Worst News. I'm angry he's not here for me to hate because hating someone who isn't around takes up a lot of energy with none of the reward of witnessing how your hatred is affecting that person. You're not supposed to speak ill of the dead. I should be canonizing my husband because of all the good things he did and he was, but there's nothing like an untimely and deliberate death and the discovery of a pregnancy to hasten the falling of the scales from your eyes. Only because he never knew he had one am I managing to deal with the fact that he abandoned his child. And yes, suicide is something you can't explain; it is this gross, unwieldy thing people run from until they lose their footing and are dragged under, I understand this, and yet heleftmeheleftmeheleftmehowcouldheleaveme is the soundtrack of my life these days and now it is separating me from my niece and nephew.

"Lying in bed twenty-three hours a day is not taking care of herself, Ma. And if she's not going back to support group, this is probably the next best thing." Gloria's voice is tight, her tone almost pleading. *Don't ruin this*, she is telling our mother without using the words.

The rest of the conversation is lost to me, but the next morning, when Ma sets my vitamins down on the prenatal pamphlets I have been ignoring, she hands me my laptop without a word, and a little later, Gloria FaceTimes and passes the phone to Ellie and Ben. After the call, I commit the new details of their faces to memory: Ben's missing tooth, Ellie's crosshatch braids.

"Cleo has been ringing off my phone," Nate informs me when he calls a few days later. We have struggled through a few minutes of small talk while he worked up the courage to get to the crux of the matter.

"Is that not normal for Cleo?"

A pause. "Calls are meant to stop when you break up."

"The fuck? You broke up? When?" I sit up.

"While you were away. And before you try and cuss me for not telling you, you had enough on your pregnant plate. I was waiting for the right time."

I digest this. "You okay?" I ask my little brother.

"Just need to get out of the house for a bit, to be honest."

"Everett not helping?"

"If he tells me again to get on Tinder and fuck my way out of this, I'm going to end up on the six o'clock news. Nah. I was just going to go for a drive. Come with me."

"What about work?"

"I'm off today. I'll pick you up. We can get some lunch or something."

Nate does not mention our last conversation about support group, not even when I slide into his passenger seat and he pats the top of my head in the patronizing yet endearing way he can get away with because he is my brother and affection has never been his strong suit. I bat his hand away, but I am smiling. For the first time in weeks, I am smiling. I smile when he turns on Al Green in the car. I smile when he points to the Pick 'n' Mix in the center console. I even smile at the way he navigates traffic, littering the air with hushed f-bombs, offering his critiques of his fellow drivers: *Who let this joker on the road? Fam, we're all merging. Don't be a dickhead all your life.* My smile falters when Nate glides into the borough of Hammersmith and Fulham, and by the time he pulls up outside of the community center, it has been abandoned in the footwell, and I am trying the door, which he locks with a flick of his thumb. Like I'm a child.

"Not funny, Junior. Let me out." The air in my lungs is already turning to glue. I try the door again and slam my fist against the glass.

"Don't mash up my car," Nate says.

"Nate, open the fucking door! How…how could you do this?" I scrabble at the lock, knowing it will not give. I am transported to the night when Quentin died and then to the night of my family's "intervention," when it felt like phantom hands were twisting me in two. My breath fogs up Nate's windows. I grip the door handle as if I am drowning.

"Eve, stop. Stop it." My brother reaches across and grabs my wrists, and when I try to fight him off, he squeezes them until I stop thrashing. I notice only later that he applies just enough pressure to calm me down but leave no marks. "Breathe. Like this, yeah? Breathe."

"Why did you bring me here?" He releases one of my wrists so I can wipe my face. "I told you lot I wasn't going back. I said I would get a job."

"Because that worked so well last time? I'm not even asking," Nate says. "Lemme do a Gloria and tell you. Go in there and get better."

"Why can't any of you respect my decisions?" I wrench my other wrist free and hammer against his dashboard.

Nate responds by smashing his own hands against the steering wheel, shocking me into silence. "Because maybe I'm tired of you not taking this seriously! It's one thing to down Mount Gay and pills and mope all day when it's just you to think about. But you're going to be someone's mum! You have to get a fucking grip and you have to do it fast."

"What does going to some shitty support group have to do with—"

"Do you know that Black women are five times more likely to die during pregnancy and childbirth? Do you? Why do you think I was practically up Glo's arse when she was pregnant with Ellie and Ben? And do you know what stress can do to pregnancy? And to your health in general?"

He has not lied. Nate featured heavily in both Gloria's

pregnancies. Ferrying her to appointments when Alex could not. Insisting that he be present if banished to the waiting room for both our niece's and nephew's births. He had hovered around Gloria. Bringing her smoothies, casually asking if and what she'd eaten. We put it down to the excitement of becoming an uncle once and then again. And it was. An excitement mingled with fear and built on a foundation of love.

"What if I go in there with you and sit with you through the thing? Will you go then?"

"Junior, I didn't know you were so—"

"You're just giving up and I don't get it. It's scary to watch you. You don't care about anything anymore. It's like you don't give a shit. And we're trying to give a shit for you, but we can't. You have to try. You have to." He isn't looking at me, his eyes are trained on the bus that is slowing farther down the road, but I see the glisten of potential tears, and I turn away to give him his privacy.

"I'm sorry, Nate." An ineffectual and useless response, but all I have to offer.

"Q would have known what to do," he says sadly, and my heart breaks for my brother, for the things he has also lost, for the second brother he found in Quentin and for the loss of that bond that he has had to mourn alone.

"Don't give him too much. It's his fault we're here," I remind Nate, and when he looks at me, I give him a watery smile. "He was always a drama queen."

"The man didn't believe in doing things by halves. He was always excited about everything. Alex and I corned him for it all the time, but honestly? That was the best thing about him."

"You think so? You didn't find him too intense?" Q was Nate's polar opposite. I sometimes wondered, in the beginning, if his eagerness offended Nate, he of the split chin.

"Like, there was this one time that I didn't know what to do for Valentine's Day. You know how Cleo gets. And he showed me how to make this photo collage thing. I was just going to take her to Nobu. Cleo cried for, like, a week when I gave it to her. She loved it."

I had no idea. I close my eyes and imagine my husband and my brother laughing over Nate's weak attempts at romance, Q pointing out how to choose photographs that would highlight Cleo's beauty and emphasize the sentiment behind the occasion. "I didn't know he did that."

"Who knows if he even liked me," Nate says. "He was probably just doing it to make you happy."

"Don't be stupid. Of course he liked you. I just said I had no clue he did that. Come on, Nate. Outside of Jackson, you and Alex were the brothers Q wished he had. He was so grateful for you." It's true. In the car outside the restaurant we would enter so Quentin could meet Nate and Gloria for the first time, he gripped my fingers so hard, I had to pinch him to get him to release them. *So what if they hate you?* I had tried to joke. *I'll love you forever.* He had turned to me, his face ashen. *Don't say that, babe. You think they could hate me?*

"I miss him," Nate says and brings me back to this car, parked outside a different location I don't want to enter.

"Join the club." I tap the back of my brother's head—the standard response to his head patting.

"Did you know you're sort of showing?"

I follow my brother's eyes down to my burgeoning bump, so small it could easily be mistaken for period bloat or a larger than average lunch. But it is there, beneath my shirt, a reminder. "Okay, Nate," I tell him, "I'll go in."

I both keep and break my promise to Nate. I go in and stare down the Peach Room sitting at the end of the corridor. Thirty steps and I would be inside, a cup of lukewarm lemonade in my hand, my emotional innards splayed in front of strangers who have already shed their shyness, their fear of judgment. I walk the first fifteen steps before my courage slips from the sticking place. To my right through an open door, adults dust off chairs and sit at easels. When I am asked by a smiling man if I am here for the life drawing class, I nod once and step inside.

# 27

Henry Huntington, QC, my second least favorite pen pal, writes to inform me that he, on behalf of one Mrs. Aspen Lydia Bowes-Morrow, intends to sue for the return of certain personal property. I am, Henry tells me, in unlawful possession of the following:

1. 1 (one) vintage solid sterling silver Tiffany & Co. rattle. Engraved. Inscription reads: Quentin

2. 1 (one) Rembrandt reprint: *Woman Bathing Her Feet at a Brook* (1880), in antique gold frame

3. 2 (two) antique Italian marble end tables (1921)

4. 1 (one) vintage Hermès silk scarf. Gold and black

5. 1 (one) radiant cut diamond ring

6. 1 (one) pair sapphire-and-diamond three-claw drop earrings

7. 1 (one) vintage Oscar de la Renta silk print em-
   broidered coat

Henry helpfully reminds me that his letter serves as official
notice, and that I have fourteen days to turn over the property. He also adds that failure to comply will lead to further
legal action, which may include the payment of his exorbitant
fee. And, darling that he is, he provides the total value of the
property, a figure that makes my toes curl so hard I almost
puncture my own feet.

"Do you have these things?" Gloria asks, brandishing the
letter at me like the weapon it was intended to be. She taps
her foot while she waits for me to finish hyperventilating.

I gesture to my Zara cardigan and pajama bottoms. "Do I
look like a person who would know what to do with a vintage Oscar de la Renta jacket?"

"And you're sure Quentin doesn't have them hidden somewhere?"

"Q would never—" I force myself to say the words "—defy
his mother. Is she accusing me of stealing?"

"She's throwing her weight around because she basically
wants to gain access to your house and, as a result, access to
you. She would be brilliant if she weren't diabolical."

"Glo, where the hell am I supposed to get that kind of
money? Oh God, will I have to sell the house? Am I going
to have to move in with Ma and Dad?"

"Calm down, Eve, you will not have to sell the house. You
have the trust money, remember? But that doesn't mean you
have to pay her off. You don't have any of the items in question, so it's not like you can turn them over even if you wanted
to. Aspen will have to prove that they are in your possession.
She's a crafty mare, this one." Gloria scans the letter again.

"Why do you sound impressed?"

"I am having a small fangirl moment, forgive me. Henry
Huntington is something of a legal legend."

"My life is on fire and you have a hard-on for the person who struck the match. Classy."

"Technically," Gloria says, "it's your mother-in-law who struck the match. And nobody has a hard-on for anyone. I just can't believe I'll be responding to *the* Henry Huntington."

"You're drooling. You're practically offing pant and you haven't even met him. Have shame!"

"I have to get back." Gloria tucks her copy of the letter into her Aspinal document case. "Try not to freak out. And have a final look just to make sure there isn't a Tiffany rattle stuffed into one of Quentin's camera bags." She pauses at the door to look at me, and for a second, I feel the years melt away. For a second, she is not the woman whose trust I have squandered, but the girl who threatened my bullies in St. Jude's courtyard.

"Have you made a doctor's appointment yet?" she asks me, her voice neutral.

I touch my bud of a stomach. "No, I—"

Gloria's eyes drop to my hand. "What is that?"

"What is what?"

"That. On your hand."

"It's my engagement ring, Glo. You've seen it approximately three million times. Why are you—"

"That is, if I am not mistaken, a radiant cut diamond ring."

My gaze drops to my hand. At the ring Q placed there. Never once in our ten years of marriage did he care to mention that this was Aspen's ring. Another thing I deserved to know. Forsaking all others. Is that not what we fucking said?

"I... Wow. *Wow*." I breathe. "He gave me Aspen's ring."

"So you do have the bloody ring? You—" She catches herself, inhales deeply. "Fine. Return it. It will go some way to warding her off."

"I'm not giving her my ring, Glo. She can actually go to hell. Q gave me this ring!" I brace myself for my sister's rage.

This is, after all, an outrageous response to a problem easily solved, but she appears calm.

"It appears it wasn't his to give," Glo says. "Start saying your goodbyes to that ring, Eve." It is not a request.

I watch her go, the sound of her heels fading as she clips down the stairs. Gloria's lack of anger has left me wrong-footed. She has reduced this tactic to a sly endeavor to enter the house, but Aspen wants my ring. The ring Q slid onto my finger that evening in my room when he'd consumed enough wine to loose himself from the confines of his own nerves. His prepared speech forgotten in a rush of emotion, words tangled up and discarded in his desperation to be accepted. The ring signifies the start of a life legitimized by the binds of legality, but it also highlights that rare gift you are given when you not only find your person but when that person loves who you are and not what they wish you to be. We were kids. Foolhardy and overconfident. But we made it. Until we didn't. Or more accurately, he didn't. And the memories wrapped up into this single diamond are more precious than the stone itself. Relinquishing it would begin to chip away at what Aspen always considered the crumbling facade of our relationship; it's a viper strike as is everything Aspen does. I tuck my ringed hand into my sleeve. She is doing it, making good on her promise to relegate me to a footnote in Q's life.

# 28

Hiding from Barb and the denizens of the Peach Room has become vital to my continued attendance at the community center. The life drawing class—a class that Xavier, the chisel-cheeked teacher and object of collective lust for those who can still experience such, has explained will include still life as well as nakedness—starts at exactly the same time as support group. This means I arrive early and hide in the toilets like the pathetic excuse for a human I am until I feel it is safe enough to run to the Pistachio Room, where Xavier and his jawline are holding court. Support group was free. Life Drawing meets twice a week, costs me £20 a session, and after stumbling into the room that first day, I transferred enough for six weeks and slunk to the back to observe. Twenty pounds is a small price to pay to avoid looking my brother in the eye and explaining to him that I am even worse of a person than he initially imagined. The fee seems to go some way to providing the class with basic materials: easels, a small variety of pencils, paints, charcoals, a sparsely populated refreshments table, and keeping Xavier in heavy fisherman knit jumpers and shea butter to apply to his unblemished olive skin.

The Eve of Before would have loved this. Q was always pushing me to indulge my creative side more. When I said I liked painting, he visited a specialty art store and maxed out a credit card buying me equipment and supplies I'd never even heard of. Alas, the Eve of Now balances a pencil across her index finger and averts her eye from her blank A3 sketch pad. The important thing is that I am here. Ten minutes into the class, a woman joins me in the back row. Her wavy dark hair is piled up on top of her head and she is scowling as she drops her bag on the floor and swaps the blank A3 pad on the easel for one that has the beginnings of her latest piece. There is the gentle curve of a hip, the slope of an extended neck. She doesn't look at me as she gets situated, but after another ten minutes, she speaks.

"You gonna actually draw something?" She still isn't looking at me, is concentrating on sketching a foot, but there is nobody else back here, and if there were, that person would be indulging in the activity they paid money to do.

"Um."

"Or you just gonna sit there with that pencil on your finger?"

I bristle. "That a problem for you?"

"Just want to know if I'm in a class with a weirdo. You in here so you can look at naked folk? We already had three of those. Xavier will toss your ass out. I'll help."

"Gross. Perverts come to this class?"

"Are you one of them?" She turns her head slightly, pierces me with one eye.

"What? No. I'm no pervert."

"You sure, lady? I moved from up front because Ryan won't stop breathing through his mouth, but I'll go right back up there if I'm swapping mouth breathers for deviants."

"I'm not a deviant," I say in what I hope is a firm and re-assuring tone.

She nods and turns her attention back to her drawing. A few minutes later, her voice reaches me again. "So?"

"So?"

"Drawing. You gonna do it?"

"Is there a problem if I don't?"

"I just figure you can do nothing at home. And for free." She pops in a pair of earbuds and ends the conversation as abruptly as she started it.

Bruised by her brusqueness as I am, I can't deny that she has a point. Like so many other things, my hobbies died when Q did. There will never again be a time I feel the warmth of his breath against my neck as he peers at my work over my shoulder. He will never again bring me tea and kick back as I paint, reading or working, our silence a comfortable one. He will never get to see whether his child chooses to pick up a camera, a brush or both. The pencil rolls off my finger and hits the floor.

I pick it up and start to draw.

Through gritted teeth, Gloria points out once again that the easiest way to solve the issue would be to phone Aspen, explain to her that I am willing to return the ring, tell her that she already knows I have nothing else from her list and ask her to call off her henchmen.

"And deprive you of the opportunity to liaise with '*the* Henry Huntington'?" I mimic her voice.

I can hear her tapping her pen against her desk on the other end of the phone. A Montblanc gifted to her last year by her firm when she became one of the youngest partners. It is a while before she speaks again. "You know, Eve, I'm trying here. You can send her the ring and end all this. She wants blood, but we all want peace. And we deserve it. At some point, you're going to have to swallow the selfishness and think about someone other than yourself, understood?"

"You love this stuff, though," I remind her. "This is your bread and butter."

"Oh, you're paying me? Perhaps if I start charging, you'll return that ring." I have reached the eye in the storm of her anger. She knows I will not be moved. "I'll draft a response and send it over."

"I love you, Glo."

Another moment of silence. "Yeah," she says and hangs up.

Bee, who is watching *Diners, Drive-Ins and Dives* and ordering new bundles online, glances over at me. "Everything all good?"

"Gloria is going to write a response to the heirloom letter."

"Gloria to the rescue. She's bloody Superwoman, that one." Bee points to Guy Fieri on the TV screen. "You reckon I'd still get asked on dates if I just got that hairstyle? Three hundred and seventy pounds for these bundles and that doesn't even factor in the cost of the lace or paying the wig maker."

"Hey, Guy Fieri is a king among men, and I won't stand for him to be disparaged. And since when do you care about dates?"

"Nobody's disparaging your king, babe. Who needs to date when I have you?" Bee shimmies over to me on the sofa and rests her head on my shoulder. She pulls the hem of my shirt, grinning when she sees the soft slope of my stomach. "I can't believe you're going to be a mum. Remember when *Circle* did that 'Mamahood' special edition?"

"And we pissed ourselves laughing at the organic birthing shawl they were trying to sell people for £1,450? Yes, I remember."

"Now you need your own birthing shawl." Feeling me tense, Bee kisses my cheek. "You okay?"

I hold my hand up and watch my ring catch the light. "I can't believe he didn't tell me this was hers."

"Does it make that much of a difference?"

"Only because he never told me. Why didn't he tell me, Bee?"

Bee takes my hand, twists the ring gently around my finger. "I dunno, babe. Maybe he was scared he'd lose you? You guys can't have known everything about each other."

"I thought we did. Everything important anyway." The secrets Q kept eventually took him from me, from everyone.

Bee rocks me in her arms and smooths my hair away from my face. "Maybe you'd feel a little better if you gave it back. Then Aspen wouldn't have this over you." Her hug keeps me still. "Just a thought."

# 29

"You decided to join us." Xavier beams at me and the outline I am working on. Our model, Sylvie, stretches like a cat in a spot of sunlight and I sketch the gentle swell of her stomach and her thighs. "This is very good." I can feel the jealousy of the others in the room. I have not come here to be a teacher's pet.

"Thanks," I deadpan. Xavier moves away, on to someone who will bask in the attention he gives them.

My wavy-haired row mate stifles a snort. Our eyes meet for a second before she turns and smiles at her easel. It surprises me that the only approval I crave is hers. For two weeks now, we have met here in the back row of Life Drawing and I find some measure of calm in our disjointed conversation. At break time, I remain in my chair, but she makes a fleeting visit to the refreshments table and brings me a cup of apple juice and a mini pack of shortbread. Before I can thank her, she uses her chin to point to the table where our fellow pupils are congregated.

"You see the newbie?" she asks.

I scan the group and realize that she is correct, that there is a new face. A face with a pair of amber eyes, which appear to be jostling with Xavier's jaw for attention.

"Pervert or regular?" she asks.

"What? I… Well, he looks… I dunno, harmless?"

"Uh-huh. Maybe." She narrows her eyes.

"I'm Eve." I wait. She waits. I cave. "I said—"

"I heard you, lady. Luisa."

The class members begin moving back to their seats and we resume watching. Before he sits down, Amber Eyes glances at me and Luisa. She and I exchange looks.

"Pervert," she says, then puts in her earbuds. She is the personification of a full stop; when she is finished, so are you.

I move my pencil across the page. I can't quite get Sylvie's feet right. The arch, the delicacy of her toes. The way the pale spring sun struggles through the windows and hits her skin reminds me of *She* and *She* reminds me that my house, once a haven, now feels like a boxing ring. Aspen stealing inside and stealing my peace without ever having placed one toe over the threshold. I drag my pencil through Sylvie's feet. I do it again and again until they no longer exist.

Luisa finds me on the steps of the community center, where I sit gathering the strength to head to the tube station. She swings her bag over her shoulder and nods in my direction before descending the steps. At the bottom, I see her shoulders heave in a sigh. She turns, plucks out an earbud.

"You okay, lady?"

I blink back the tears that spring to my eyes. I have probably not yet managed to fully convince her that I am not a "weirdo." Weeping seemingly unprovoked will do nothing for my case. "Yeah," I sniff. "Just got a killer headache."

Luisa tilts her head. "Okay? You need something for that? Boots is right there."

"Can't. Pregnant."

"That's why you're running out of rooms and sitting on these steps like you're in a Britney Spears video?" She clicks her tongue. "You in a rush?"

"Not really. Home doesn't feel too much like home right now."

"Let's go."

She takes me to the Lyric Square street market, buys me arepas stuffed with beef and black beans and says "eat" with an authority that does not leave space for argument. The food is hot, flavorful, and the first bite reignites an appetite I assumed to be beyond resuscitation. "You're not having any?" I ask through a mouthful.

"Nah. Would just make me miss my abuela."

"Where is she?"

"Back home." I don't press her on it. She watches me until I finish. "Feel better?"

Surprisingly, I do. "Thank you."

"You need to start eating more. You either gotta be slower than blackstrap molasses or you're trying to do foolishness to that baby of yours. Which is it?"

"What? Neither. I'm just having a bit of a hard time right now."

She sucks her teeth. "You don't owe me no explanations, lady. But I doubt Xavier needs the drama of you keeling over in class. I know I don't." She shoulders her bag and leaves.

My engagement ring went back to Aspen via Henry Huntington after I convinced myself that it, having belonged to Aspen in any capacity at any point, was now tainted. Aspen, predictably, did not offer any thanks but pressed Henry to reiterate her desire to receive the remainder of her items.

Gloria's response to Henry arrives both in my email inbox and at the house in an official-looking envelope carried by Nate. When I ask him how he got it, he tells me that he was over at Gloria and Alex's, feeding Ellie and Ben their dinner alongside the nanny. It stings more than I have either the right or the words to express. I held one of Gloria's knees while she gave birth to Ellie. On the night Q died, she burst into the house and squeezed me so hard, some of his blood transferred to her party dress. We have never been this far apart. I have not stepped foot inside the Hampstead house since the day of the trust payment, my presence neither wanted nor required. That Nate still enjoys the freedom to go as he pleases, to negotiate the consumption of peas with our niece and nephew, to sit with our sister and brother-in-law under their abstract chandelier, and to act as messenger while I remain exiled smarts. Like something has crawled underneath my skin that I can't scratch out. My brother, the diplomat, passes on Alex's love along with two drawings from Ellie and Ben. We sit in the kitchen breakfast nook while Ma and Dad discuss the menu for another aunty's birthday next month. Dad, fresh off the successful completion of an aneurysm repair in a fourteen-year-old, is amenable to just about anything.

Gloria's response is succinct. She uses words such as *unfounded* and *malicious* but otherwise keeps it cute. Her letter can be summed up as saying "prove it" in legalese. I read it three times, the paper shaking in my hands.

"Glo is all over this," Nate soothes. "Calm down. Alex helped."

I picture Alex and Gloria exchanging notes, making amends, doing that corny yet adorable married couple high five they do whenever they execute something challenging, like getting Ben to remove his Spiderman costume after a week or, in this case, drafting an appropriate legal response to my poisonous mother-in-law. Alex flexed his legal muscles on behalf of Quentin once before, successfully demanding the removal of an unlicensed photograph from a magazine. It had taken a month and the magazine had to be pulled and reprinted, and a check cut to Q, who had used it to pay for a night at the Landmark hotel for Alex and Glo as a thank-you. I know he is doing this as much for Q as he is for me. I bite my lip and hang my head.

"What's wrong?" Nate lowers his phone.

"Glo still hates me."

He kisses his teeth. "She doesn't hate you. She's an over-worked mum of two. You know she can be moody."

"Exactly. I know that. I know her better than anyone. Which is how I know she definitely hates me."

Ma and Dad, trained to sniff out sadness, appear in the breakfast nook. "Eve thinks Gloria hates her," Nate snitches, eyes back on his phone.

"Ehn?" Ma asks. "Your sister does not know how to hate you. That sort of thing can't live inside her."

"You guys. Come on. I know you're giving her the benefit of the doubt, but she's barely here anymore. I can't go over there. Every time we speak, it's like pulling teeth. She's over it. She's over me. I get it."

Dad squeezes in next to Nate. "Eve, be reasonable. If she hated you, why would she spend her time doing all this work for you?"

"Have you met Glo?" I scoff. "When has she ever missed the opportunity to be the hero?" It is a spiteful thing to say, laced with bitterness and ingratitude. It is a statement borne of immeasurable grief and the pain of rejection. It is also true.

Ma frowns. "You should be thanking your sister. Every time you have needed her for anything, she has been there. You have never had to ask. Is that not what the eldest is meant to do?" She looks at Dad, gestures to me. "Gwa nwa gi nwanyi okwu."

I roll my eyes. Ma imploring Dad to talk sense into me has not been an uncommon occurrence in my time upon this floating rock.

"Chimerika shows her love by helping," Dad says.

"Yeah, but if it bothers her so much, she could just say no," Nate puts in. "Is it by force?"

"Nathaniel, would you also say no?" Ma is looking at us in shock.

"I'm just saying. Glo has a bit of a martyr complex. It is what it is. We don't love her no less."

Ma stands, shakes her head. "Someone who is protective of her family. The two of you could learn from her."

And she's right. Nate and I cultivated a selfishness that Glo never quite managed to adopt. She has always been fiercely protective of us, has always taken on the role of fixer without being asked. She has fallen on her sword for all her loved ones, and she wears that badge and wields that fact like heavy artillery. Any resentment she has is because she has chosen her role, and it is also because we have allowed her to choose it. Repeatedly.

I carry her letter to bed. I read it again. It provides little comfort. Aspen will find another way. There will always be another angle, a new expanse of flesh she can rip with her talons. I will be running from her for the rest of my life and tearing my relationships to shreds while I do so. She has, without even knowing, begun the process of ruination. Across the room, I glimpse Q's robe. A handmade number in rich navy. Gold embroidery at the cuffs and on the breast pocket. Aside from his camera equipment, this robe was his one luxury. He told me he bought a new one at eye-watering expense every three years. Since he died, this one has stayed draped over the chair in our bedroom, save for the handful of times I have wrapped myself in it. Now, looking at it makes my chest burn. I dive across the room and tear it from the chair. Later, I will visit the wheelie bin to retrieve it, my shame and regret resting heavily on my back. Even later, I will press my spine against the warmth of the radiator, the robe across my lap, asking *why* to an empty house for the millionth time. For now, it represents the armchair I had to sell, the click of the door on Christmas Day as he left to see his mother. It represents all the snide comments he pretended he couldn't hear, the arguments he refused to have with her but instead had with me. It represents my own unwillingness to serve him an ultimatum, too frightened to confront the possibility that I would lose. It represents my sister's cold shoulder, the one she is using to defend me, when it should have been him, when we should never have even reached this point. I can't look at it.

New Boy, aka Amber Eyes, is called Drew. Luisa and I find this out quite by accident. I arrive at the community center, hide in the toilets and make my way to class, slumping into my chair in a manner that I expect appears dramatic but is a result of a bone-deep fatigue that has been causing me to drag my body around as if it belongs to someone else. Sylvie has moved on to grace would-be artists somewhere else with the sight of her naked body, so today we are starting on still life. Xavier has arranged the predictable bowl of fruit on the plinth and is smoldering his way around the room, observing how we are faring with the task of drawing grapes and apples. Luisa waits until I arrange myself in my seat and wordlessly hands over a paper bag. This has become our routine. Luisa brings me a homemade snack, watching until I have eaten a lunch she deems satisfactory. Today's snack is a sandwich: shredded slow-cooked carnitas on a soft roll. I am about to thank her when we hear the pealing laughter of our classmate Siobhan. She has flushed a deep crimson at something New Boy has said to her and slaps his wrist with a high-pitched "Drew!" Luisa and I exchange glances. When our eyes return to the front of the room, "Drew" is peering at us with those eyes that would not look out of place in the face of a cat.

"Luisa," I whisper to her across the two empty seats she always ensures separate us. She never lets me see her art. *"Luisa!"*

"Jesus, lady, what is it now?" I like that she calls me "lady" despite knowing my name.

"You having trouble with the shadows under the oranges? I can't seem to get it right."

"And what does that have to do with me exactly?"

"Luisa. Please. I can beg if you want."

"Sure. I'd like to see that." She crosses her arms over her chest.

"Am I interrupting something?" We both turn to see New Boy standing in the row in front of us.

"You sure are," Luisa says at the same time I say, "Um, no." He grins. "Which is it?"

"You need something?" Luisa asks.

"Actually, I was thinking of relocating back here. With the cool kids."

"You shouldn't do that," Luisa says at the same time I say, "Uh, why?"

"This seems to be where all the action is. Whispers, illicit drug deals."

Luisa arches one eyebrow. "Drug what? Vete a la verga." One does not have to be a linguistic genius to understand that this is not a compliment.

"The paper bags, the furtive whispers." He's leaning on a vacant easel, staring at us over the top of it.

Luisa says nothing. "It's just food," I supply.

"Oh, I definitely need to be back here, then."

"And deprive Siobhan of your presence? Please don't." Luisa puts in her earbuds.

"Your friend is nice," he says, but he is smiling. He returns to his seat up front.

Luisa and I are making our way to the market after class when Luisa suddenly whirls around and steps in front of me, and Drew, whom I now realize was some way behind us, stumbles to a halt, immobilized by her glare.

"You're following us?" Luisa hisses. "You better fall back, or I will cut you."

"Well, this is awkward," Drew says, "seeing as this is the way to the station."

Faced with this response, I would have no choice but to melt into the concrete beneath me. Luisa, however, is incapable of experiencing embarrassment. Her arm, which was acting as a barrier, drops to her side. "Fine," she says.

Drew addresses me. "Is she always this pleasant?"

"She just really loves me," I tell him, earning a scowl from Luisa. We continue walking, Drew now in step with us. "Don't deny it, Luisa. This makes us friends."

Luisa looks at me. "You think so, huh?"

"You feed me. You protect me. These are not the actions of a person that doesn't want me around."

She squirms with discomfort. "I told you I have a devout abuela I'd have to answer to if anything happened to you."

"I mean yes, there's that. But there's also the fact that you like me. Admit it."

"Lady, don't flatter yourself," she says. But she is smiling. It suits her.

"You okay with me walking in the same direction as you?" Drew pipes up.

"Sure," Luisa says with all the enthusiasm of a teenage boy who has been given the choice between giving up masturbation or having his mother watch while he does it.

Luisa and I stop at the market and Drew walks on, holding up a palm to signal his departure.

"Interesting," I say.

"Mmm," Luisa replies. "What you wanna eat?"

Luisa and I arrive at the next class to find Drew in the back row. While I note that he has left our usual chairs free and has placed himself two seats to the left of me, all Luisa sees is an interloper.

"Dios mio," she says under her breath. She lowers herself into her chair and immediately plugs her ears.

To his credit, Drew remains silent for most of the class. This may be because he is hiding from Siobhan, who keeps throwing wounded looks at the back of the room, and it could also be because he is concentrating on drawing the worst interpretation of a bowl of fruit I have ever seen.

While he is visiting the refreshments table during break time, Luisa slides over the chairs separating us and hands me my paper bag. Small caramel-filled cookies.

"Alfajores," Luisa supplies, "with real dulce de leche."

"You're too good to me, Luisa." The buttery, gooey goodness melts against my tongue and I emit a sound that would not be out of place in an adult movie.

Drew chooses then to return. He is holding three plastic cups of orange juice, but when he spots the crumbs on my lips and the bag in my hand, his grin is back. He passes me a cup and offers one to Luisa, who looks at his outstretched hand for a long time before taking the cup from him.

"Don't drink it, lady," Luisa warns. "We don't know what he's put in here."

"Really? You think I carry around Rohypnol in my backpack?"

"That's a very specific drug of choice, pendejo asqueroso," Luisa replies.

Drew turns to me. "My motivations are pure. You, Mary, look like you need vitamin C. And you—" he leans forward to look at Luisa "—I'm just trying to bribe into giving me whatever is in the paper bag."

"Do you hear yourself talk? See, I told you he was off. Don't drink the juice, lady. Damn." Luisa snatches the cup from my hand.

"It's Eve. And have you ever heard of the saying 'You catch more flies with honey'?"

"You look like a Mary. And I don't know about flies. I just want something better than stale Oreos. Also, don't think I didn't feel your judgment hitting the side of my face. Need I remind you we are here to *learn*?"

My cheeks prickle. I am caught. "It's just…how do you manage to make apples look like tumors?"

"I'm new. Allow me."

"You should go back up front. Siobhan might kill us before you do." Luisa is already moving back to her chair.

"Spell out your problem."

"My problem is that I don't know you. You could be planning on disemboweling us with a rusty spoon."

"Any spoon would do. The rust is optional."

The look Luisa gives him could strip tar.

"You guys think murdering rapists come to life drawing classes proffering orange juice?"

I interject. "You see, we said nothing about rape. Nothing. You brought that up by yourself."

Drew laughs and once again Siobhan's eyes are on the three of us. "Tough fucking crowd back here. Alright. Cool, I'll be back."

Luisa's earbuds are back in, but when I look over a few minutes later, her plastic cup is empty.

"You okay, lady?" she asks me after class, after Drew is gone and we are shuffling down the corridor toward the door. "You know I don't like to pry—shut it up, I don't—and he was being annoying with the vitamin C thing, but you are looking kinda floppy."

I have come to a crossroads in my relationship with Luisa. I could fob her off with a lie, but Luisa has reluctantly gone out of her way to be someone to me and this is not a small thing. It does not count for nothing.

"My husband died. Before I found out about this." I point to my stomach. "If I look floppy, it's probably because I feel it."

She does not rip a string of revelations from me like a magician tugging at the ubiquitous knotted scarves. Instead, she says, "You're doing fine, lady."

Before my husband was my husband, and before he was even my boyfriend, he was the enigmatic tall dude on campus who carried a camera, kept to himself and was the unknowing recipient of longing for girls and guys alike. I was a girl too cowed by years of middling social success among her peers and too preoccupied with the threat of zero post-university job prospects to care too much about embracing my newfound independence. I treated my freedom the same way I treated the shared bathtubs in some of the halls: too frightened of infection to fully immerse myself. Therefore, Quentin noticed me before I did him, and by the time I did, he liked to tell me, he was too far gone. I didn't get it. I didn't know what he saw, and I spent a lot of time worrying about not fucking up. There were contenders waiting in the wings. I always considered us unevenly matched in the looks department. I didn't need to give him additional reasons to leave me. It's funny. You spend your time learning that you should not tie your happiness up in another person, that the love of another should only underpin your life instead of dominate it, that men are not the prize. You learn these things, but in the end you devote yourself to a man, because you are nineteen and he brings you books and is almost physically perfect to the point it hurts to look at him sometimes. Like staring into the sun.

Q's was the first birthday we celebrated together. He had made the requisite trip to Aspen's and spent a night there eating a cake ordered from a Michelin-starred pastry chef in

Mayfair and opening gifts wrapped in paper that cost more than my tuition fees. Now, he told me, on his return, he wanted to spend the actual day with me. I wondered how to celebrate. A party was out of the question—that wasn't his bag at all. He noticed me fretting and told me in a quiet voice that he wanted to spend the day in bed with me. He decided that his preferred bed was located inside The Savoy, so he booked a room because I did not have £700 to spend on a hotel room, and, he postured, if a man can't be decadent on the anniversary of his birth, when can he be? While I agonized over choosing grown-up underwear on the sale rack at M&S, I also convinced myself that finding the perfect gift was the only way to demonstrate to him that with me, he hadn't chosen poorly. When you are nineteen, the number of questionable thoughts you have far outweigh the prudent ones. I ended up borrowing money from Gloria so I could buy him two out-of-print photography books. One depicted Old New York from 1853–1901, and the other was a collection of Victorian portraiture.

He tried not to cry when he unwrapped his gifts behind the closed doors of the hotel room. His jaw tensed and he looked away, and I waited him out because he was embarrassed in the way twenty-year-old guys are when their emotions threaten to overflow. Later, after the sex and the room service, with his fingers tangled in my braids, and his heart beating a tattoo in my ear, he spoke about growing up with an absence of good people in his life. He was surrounded, as the rich and visible often are, by people who smiled and nodded, but who didn't care that he had recurring nightmares about his dad, which were followed by panic attacks because nothing around him seemed permanent. He explained in that precise way he had that he'd deliberated for a long time about approaching me at all, that he'd measured the likelihood of being rejected against the chance I might at least consent to being his friend. He decided heartbreak was a small price to pay for having me in his life in some way no matter how small. He admitted that he fell in love from a distance because he thought he observed the type of good in me that up until then he had considered a myth. He said it would be worth any disappointment if he got to spend time with me.

"I wasn't disappointed, though." He said it into the skin on my shoulder.

We spent a lazy evening and much of the next day in bed, and the next year we did it again. It became a tradition. White sheets. Discarded room service china. The sound of his laughter bouncing off the high ceilings. My heart full to the point of rupture.

He's gone. But he still has the indecency to have a birthday, which, for the first time in more than a decade, will not be celebrated under the recessed ceiling of a hotel room. You fool yourself into thinking it won't be that bad, that it's just another day where he is not there, another few inches in the ever widening gap that separates you, but you are unprepared for the pain. Pain you cannot even begin to explain to your family because all the things they are not saying about your husband speak volumes.

I am back in bed, pinioned here by a grief so sour I can taste it. Today would have been his thirty-fourth birthday and *fuck*; I can't get over the irony of it all. I spent so much time worrying about him leaving and now he's dead and I'm carrying the one thing that would have been almost guaranteed to keep him around. I would happily let him go if it meant he was still walking the earth, even if it was without me. It is like it was in the beginning, in the first days after he killed himself, like I am dying, too. I can't breathe. I can't move. My phone is off. The worst part? I woke up this morning and there was a second where I forgot it was his birthday. I forgot that today there will be no hotel, no laughter.

I am slipping away from him no matter how hard I try to stay in the excruciating present. I press my knuckles into my eyelids, where the tears are building up behind them. I am being pummeled anew with the truth that I will never see him again. There are to be no more birthdays. He is frozen in time, forever thirty-three.

Lifting my head from this pillow and doing anything other than lying here in a leaden haze of agony seems untenable, impossible. But I am pregnant. And while I do not want to negotiate with my unborn charge, I have no choice. The London day is trying to climb through the kitchen windows. The sun has the audacity to be shining, pouring its cheerfulness with great pomposity into my dark little world. I eat scrambled eggs. The plate I use is the one Q preferred when he brought me breakfast in bed. It slips from my hand and smashes against the tiles. I leave it there. In the living room, I am bludgeoned with the memory of him sprawled on the sofa, weakened so much by a case of flu he couldn't even make it upstairs. I'd kept vigil over him. Making him soup and forcing him to drink water. Kneeling by his side so I could kiss his fevered brow. There isn't a room in this house where I am safe, where I can be free of him. I make for the front door, stepping over a new letter from Aspen.

There is signal failure on the District line, which means that by the time I reach the community center, Life Drawing has all but finished and I have strained several muscles in my face keeping myself composed. Drew stands at the bottom of the steps, texting. I feel like if I can sneak past him, I might be able to make it into the Pistachio Room and put pencil to paper for a few minutes, draw myself out of the mire of memories if only temporarily. But I have been smacked with the stick of perpetual bad luck.

"What happened, Mary? You left me alone to be called a cabrón three times today."

Fashion connoisseur Drew is not, but he is always put together in that carefully casual way that fans of athleisure are. Today, however, his T-shirt looks slept in. There is stubble on his face.

"You forget how to iron?" I manage.

"No time," he says cryptically. "You good? I know we've all come to love your slightly homeless charm, but you're looking a bit…haunted today."

I know he is being kind, and given Drew's propensity for exasperating behavior, I should be grateful, but it is Q's birthday, and it is him I should be looking at. Drew, with his stubble and unironed shirt, is everything Q isn't. He is vital, able to breathe the uncharacteristically warm London air, able to slide his phone in his back pocket and tell a widow that she looks haunted. He is able to *be*. And that, today, is an affront to me. Looking at him turns my stomach. I turn to leave just as Luisa appears, trotting down the stairs and pointing a finger at Drew.

"I dunno what's going on between you and that Siobhan lady, cabrón, but if she asks me about you again, I'm slapping both of you." She sees me and her face softens just a fraction. "You okay, lady? Where were you today?"

I open my mouth. "I—"

"Whoa—" Drew holds his hands up "—nothing is going on. She's my kid's best friend's mother and she maybe isn't loving me turning her down when she made a move."

"Made a move? You saying she propositioned you or something?" Luisa scoffs.

"You're really having trouble with the fact that women are attracted to me, aren't you? Mary, you can see the appeal, right?"

"You have a kid?" Luisa asks.

"I know this destroys your theory that I'm some sort of incel, Luisa."

"Not really. Many women have a bad habit of settling."

"Can you believe this shit, Mary? All I wanted was to share the paper bag goodness, and even though you skipped class, I still got nothing but abuse."

Luisa moves to stand beside me. "Listen, shut up for one second, would you? Can't you see she's not talking? You okay?" She lowers her voice. "El bebé?"

"It's his birthday," I whisper. "I shouldn't be here."

Luisa nods. She takes my hand. She and Drew wait with me until my Uber arrives. As I climb inside, I hear them.

"She okay?" Drew asks Luisa.

"She don't need to be here right now. She—" But the door closes on Luisa's words.

The house may still be quiet when I close the front door, but Quentin's ghost is everywhere. During the drive home, I wept quietly into the sleeves of my hoodie until Selah, my driver, dug into his glove compartment and handed me an unopened pack of tissues. Aspen's letter has disappeared from the floor, and in the living room, there are bouquets. Sunflowers from Nate, peonies from Bee, a burst of orange lilies from Ma and Dad, and a box of those forever roses. I pick up the card.

*Thinking of you today and sending all our love. —Alex, Gloria, Ellie & Ben*

"I don't know how you children find such beautiful things," Ma says from behind me, and I gasp. I hadn't noticed her there on the sofa, her reading glasses in one hand, a folder of papers in the other. "Alex told me those flowers last for two years. Amazing."

"Hi, Ma. What are you doing here?"

"I told the others I would come. It's a hard day. Kedu?"

"You remembered?"

"Eve, come here. Sit down." Ma drops her folder of papers on the coffee table. "Mama said your phone was off when she tried to call you. I told her that today is difficult for you. I didn't think you would come back today. You are always somewhere else on this day."

I fall into her. I hadn't even considered that she might have first noted then remembered Q's birthday tradition. She had no guarantee I would be here today, that she would see me. But she is here regardless.

"Obim, how are you?" she asks.

And here in her arms, I feel safe enough for the first time to voice a little of everything I have been feeling—the rage, the guilt, the fear, the shame. All the ugliness of grief. I tell her that I'm triggered by so much, and I admit that carrying Q's baby is the biggest trigger of all, that I am scared of all the unknown ways I might both mess up and let down this child. And as I confess these things to my mother, I start to breathe a little easier. The constant tightness in my chest eases some.

Ma strokes my back, whispers first prayers and then the soothing Igbo refrain from our youths, when she dressed our scraped knees.

"Ndo," she says over and over. *Sorry* is a poor translation; it does not do the word justice. *I am feeling with you* is closer and far more meaningful. Ma holds me together as she always has. As she always will. When I find the strength to sit up, she still lifts the hem of her skirt and dries my face. She surprises me by fetching my wedding album, leafing to the pages of me in my traditional attire and reminding me through soft laughter of the saga that was transporting my coral beads from Onitsha to London. She traces the puzzled expression captured on

Q's face as he tried in vain to understand Dad's proclamations during the presentation of the kola nut.

"Such a handsome boy," Ma says. "We will always love him, Eve. You don't stop loving your family even when you don't agree with what they do. I am sorry for Quentin. We all are. I wish we knew he was hurting."

The bitter leaf from Grandma has arrived. In the kitchen, Ma boils the stockfish and shaki while I partially rehydrate the leaves. We sit together and mash the cocoyam. I ask her about the letter.

"It's not something I want you to worry about today," she says. "We will deal with it." There is no emphasis on *we*, but the word warms me.

"I'm really sorry that you've had to deal with her. With Aspen."

Ma grinds her cocoyam down to a paste, the way it is supposed to be done. "When she rang me today, she asked if 'my daughter' had received her letter. 'My daughter.' It's almost like she can't speak your name."

"She phoned you? Even though I'm back?"

Ma sees my expression and touches my hand. "She is a mother. Her child is gone and today must be the most painful reminder of that. Before Quentin was anything, he was her son. Losing a child is a parent's greatest fear." My mother, in all that she does and all that she is, reminds me why she is a better person than I could ever hope to be.

"Quentin always made sure he went to see her around his birthday. He always built her into his schedule." I don't mean for it to come out as it does, steeped in bitterness.

"That was good and proper for him to do," Ma says. "Quentin missed it at times, but his heart was a good heart."

I open my mouth to defend him, but I think of my ring

sitting in Aspen's house and close my mouth. "Do you remember when he asked Dad about marrying me?"

Ma laughs. "How can I forget? Didn't he tell your dad that he would 'allow' a 'religious' ceremony if it made him happy? I had to convince Nathaniel not to throw him out of the house."

I laugh along with her. It feels both refreshing and devastating to do so. "He was so nervous to meet you guys."

"Ah, that one I could tell. His hands shook when he tried to drink his tea. That is when I knew he was serious. That he loved you properly. I remember telling your dad, 'Ha hụrụ onwe ha n'anya.' Do you know what he said?" I shake my head. "He said, 'Is it love that will save my daughter?' He always worried about you and he didn't know Quentin then. But eventually he saw for himself that I was right."

I remember the day. After leaving my parents' house, Q was late to meet me, obviously, and I had already sent two texts and a brusque voice note when he turned up, triumph written all over his face. I wouldn't understand until later what made him so happy.

We add crayfish, stock cubes, pepper, the cocoyam paste and the bitter leaf to the pot and watch as the steam fogs up the windows. We eat in the living room, after Ma has successfully lit the fire. "You're welcome," she says to my stomach.

# 30

Having a spouse commit suicide reveals the less appealing side of the human condition. Death in general elicits questions, the most invasive of which is *how?* With suicide, it is all people can do to keep the question from forcing its way out. People want details. They want to know how it happened. Where. A play-by-play of the aftermath. They want to know the texture and hue of the guts spilled.

I slipped in Quentin's blood. There was so much of it. I was a couple of steps in before I realized what it was, what I was looking at. I wondered after the fact whether he kept trying, hacking away at himself until he reached the part of him he could cut out and finally be at peace. He was faceup. Pale. Blood pooling around him like a crimson halo. His lips were blue, his hair falling in his face like always. Habits die harder than we do, it seems. In the silent seconds before my world was changed, I held his hand, turned his wrist over and tugged his sleeve down over wounds of his own making. His eyes were closed, his thigh split open. I lay beside him because what else was there to do? I felt his blood turn my jeans then my skin wet. I phoned Dad. Shock took over and stole my voice. He said my name again and again until I could tell him what happened. There was a weapon. What there wasn't was an explanation.

Quentin was nothing if not dramatic. Some people coast through life barely causing a ripple, but Q was a tidal wave all his own. He was about big splashy gestures. He talked me into this big ramshackle house. When I landed my job at *Circle*, he had a hundred white roses sent to the office. Sometimes he tried to downplay that side of him, which I guess made it shine all the brighter, like trying to hide a fluorescent bulb under muslin. He was born after a fifty-three-hour labor that almost killed Aspen and ensured he'd be an only child. So, it made sense for him to go out the same way he arrived: with a bang that altered the course of more than one life.

Only those closest to me know the details of how he died. Journalists keen to draw parallels between Q's death and that of his eminent father tried their hardest, but it was kept out of the papers, gag orders swiftly imposed by Aspen and her underlings. Talking about it hasn't helped. Suicide doesn't work like terminal illness. You don't always get to prepare, to say your goodbyes. The end sometimes arrives without warning. It swings for you and all you can do is accept the beating. And like the breakup comparison, this is another lesson I never wanted to learn—not all losses are equal. Some feel bigger than others. Insurmountable.

There are still nights where sleep proves elusive. Those are the hardest. There is little to distract me from myself. I'm occupying the same space as every other parent-to-be, hoping against hope my child is born with ten fingers, ten toes and one pair of eyes. Praying, that since so many other things will fall outside of ordinary, that they will at least look normal.

I know normal is relative and beauty is fleeting, that we are nothing more than an assembly of cells and atoms, but given the road this child must walk, can I be blamed for temporarily clinging to vanity? I push back the duvet and head for the bathroom. I examine my own face. I pull the skin on my cheeks. I look down at my hands. I wonder what pieces of me this baby will take. Ben stole Alex's entire face. Ellie moves like Gloria in miniature. Ma gave me her eyes and Dad retaliated by completing my face with his nose and lips. What jigsaw of Q and me am I growing?

My phone pings with a text from Jackson. His pleas went unanswered and eventually stopped coming. I don't know how Jackson has been faring. I haven't cared. Grief makes you believe you are special, its one and only; like it is not careening around destroying millions of lives every day and is devoting all its unwanted attention on you. Glo's accusation of selfishness was on the mark. Powerless to control much else in my life, I have focused my anger on him. But my shoulders are tired of carrying this grudge. He wants to meet, and I hide my bump inside an oversize sweater and find him sitting at a pockmarked table in the Mexican café Q introduced to the two of us one blustery night after a pop-up Frank Ocean set in Shoreditch. We were all tipsy from cheap cocktails, good music and that short-lived carefreeness experienced on a Friday night, when the weekend stretches unspoiled before you. A lifetime ago.

Jackson stands when he sees me. It is an awkward reflex embedded in him by his upbringing, one for which I poked fun at him in the Before. Now his hands dangling by his sides, his eternally perfect posture, further loosen my resolve. I smile at him and his face floods with a relief so pure that when he hugs me, I squeeze him.

"Are you okay?" I ask him when we are seated.

"Why are you asking me? I should be asking you! I can't believe you're here. I was sure you'd tell me to bugger off."

"Don't think I didn't consider it. But it's you, Jack. And I should have reached out. I'm sorry."

"You had every right to cut me out. I shouldn't have opened my bloody mouth and said anything to Aspen. I didn't think. I haven't said a word about you to her since. I promise." He is speaking so fast, his words tumbling out as if I might leave midsentence.

"Hey, it's okay. Slow down," I laugh. "You look good, Jack."

He blushes. "Yeah, well. Getting shit-faced every day wasn't helping, so I went to Costa Rica. To dry out."

"Of course you did. And I am sure it's all documented on Instagram."

His cheeks flush again, he plays with the stack of napkins this place keeps on every table. "Almost fell off the wagon on his birthday, but I held it together. I'm sorry I didn't call that day—I just don't think I could have taken it if you didn't want to talk to me. I'm just... I'm really sorry, Eve."

"I didn't want to talk to anyone except my mum. I hope you weren't alone. I'm sorry, too. Yeah, I hate that you told Aspen, but I know you didn't mean any harm."

"No, I mean—" He inspects the scarred surface of our table for a moment. "He was my best friend. Every shitty thing that happened to me, he was there. And I thought I did the same for him, *was* the same for him. I should have realized he was...going through something. I didn't. I'm sorry. I let him down. I let you down."

I tuck a napkin into his palm and he smiles gratefully, wipes his face. "It's not your fault, Jack. I lived with him. He was my every day. I guess...well, maybe he just didn't want us to see. To spare us? I don't know. It's not your fault." I say these words and watch a bud of relief start to open up in Jackson. I have spent time agonizing over how I appear in the eyes of others, catastrophizing my own image, and Jack has been thinking of me and taking on the blame he was sure I had reserved for him. In telling him there is nothing to forgive, I have given him a gift I had no idea I possessed. One I might be able to give myself.

Jackson buys me a plate of tacos al pastor. I heap on the diced onion and pineapple and douse them in lime juice. The corn tortillas are fresh and hot. I accept a bite of Jackson's burrito, and we knock back Jarritos: pineapple for me, mandarin for him. He asks how I'm feeling, whether my ankles have started to swell, and shyly offers to buy me a deluxe pregnancy pillow when I grumble about the mild ache in my lower back. I accept his offer without hesitation and his smile blossoms, then fades.

"Did...did Quent know? About the baby, I mean?" he asks quietly.

"He didn't. Even *I* found out by accident. After he...he was already gone." I understand the core of Jack's question. It is not something either of us can answer. And perhaps it is better, in the luckless way of these things, that our child will never have to feel like they were not enough to make their father stay. That is something I will carry alone.

He's an excited boy filling me in on his trip, letting me scroll through his camera roll, grinning when I ask him about the blonde in the snake-print bikini. Time slips away from us and he insists on driving me to the community center so I'm not late. The last time I was in his car, he was aiding in my escape. He is, unknowingly, doing it again.

Drew has a companion today. She is immaculate in jeans, pristine Nikes and a purple cardigan. Her afro is plaited into braids at the front and left to froth out of the back of her head. She's pretty enough to make me pluck at my T-shirt and rake my hands through my own hair, awkwardly, like this is a competition. She is also about three feet tall.

"This is Zoe," Drew says. "Her mum had to work today, and she thought it might be fun to tag along to Dad's art class."

"I'm five," Zoe supplies. She sits beside Drew, her backpack at her feet, her colored pencils arranged in a tin beside her.

"Hi, Zoe. Here to outdraw your dad? Trust me, you can do it easy peasy. Piece of cake," I tell her.

Zoe giggles and Drew rolls his eyes. "Don't laugh at her, Judas. Mary is a hater."

"Judith?"

"Judas. Judas Iscariot was the man that betrayed Jesus."

Zoe looks at her father as if she wants to place a dunce cap on his head and point him to the nearest corner. "How can a chariot betray someone?"

"Alright, let's get you set up, smart mouth." Drew pulls Zoe's chair closer to the easel and then places a pair of giant JoJo Siwa–branded headphones over her ears. Seconds later, Zoe begins to sing under her breath.

"Okay, fess up," Luisa says, "whose is she? Really?"

"Are you trying to say you don't think I'm capable of bringing someone like her into the world? Luisa, you cut me deep."

"I sure can if that's a request." Luisa smirks.

"Her mum had to work?" I ask.

"Yeah. She's a nurse. Coparenting means handling stuff like this at short notice." Drew picks up his own pencil. "Just had to call Xavier and make sure my baby girl wasn't going to get here and see genitals. But we're cool. It's ceramics and shoes today."

My stomach gurgles. It has been less than cooperative since leaving the café. Wincing, I start to set up my own utensils while Luisa continues to needle Drew.

"So little mami here just wanted to 'tag along to Dad's art class'? That's what you're saying to us?"

"What's your issue, Luisa?"

"You could have come up with something believable, is

all. Who *wants* to hang out with you?" Luisa leans forward
to inspect her work.

"Anyone ever told you how charming you are?"

"Nena doesn't even look like you."

"Aw, c'mon, Luisa," I interject. "She's really gorgeous,
Drew. ọ mara mma nke ukwuu."

"That means 'beautiful,' right? You Nigerian, Mary?"
Drew asks.

"Ye—es." My stomach cramps again and cuts the word
in half.

"So's Zoe's mum. Edo, though." He screws up his face
when he addresses Luisa again. "What the f— What do you
mean she doesn't look like me? That girl is my clone."

Zoe's skin, like umber velvet, is much darker than Drew's.
Her eyes: obsidian to his amber. But the way they crinkle
when she smiles, the curve of her mouth and the spread of
her nose is all him. Their likeness does not hit you immediately, rather it reveals itself slowly. "Don't make me agree
with him out loud, Luisa," I plead.

"Hmm," she says.

"Baby girl likes to draw. Okay, and her presence here might
get both of you to calm down. Less likely to kidnap and
slaughter you if I've got my kid with me."

"So, you're using your daughter as some kind of decoy?
Clap for yourself," I say.

"Look at her." Drew reaches over and squeezes Zoe's
cheeks. She tolerates this with an eye roll and then brushes
him off. "How can you deny that face whatever you have in
the paper bag I know you've brought today?"

"You don't have no shame, do you?" Luisa says.

"Who has shame helped in this world?"

Still, when break time rolls around, I pass on Luisa's snack
of the day, queso pupusas, and divide my share between Drew,
who raises it in triumph before heading to the table to bring

us drinks, and Zoe, who asks Luisa to explain what she has been given. Only after she has answers to all her questions does she finish it in a few bites.

"What do you say, pixie?" Drew hands Zoe a cup of apple juice.

"Thank you, Luisa!"

Luisa smiles, powerless against Zoe's charms. "You're welcome, baby."

Zoe wants to know how I manage to draw things that look like they are supposed to. She tells me that sometimes she has a picture in her head, but when she puts crayon to paper, the result does not mirror her imagination. I tell her that practice helps, but when she looks crestfallen, I pull her chair closer and show her a couple of tricks I learned when I was younger. I teach her how to build on stick figures and how to add texture to trees. She hugs my arm, her excitement bubbling over. Headphones back over her ears, Zoe resumes her work with renewed confidence, and I breathe deeply as my stomach roils, then tightens.

"You good?" Drew asks.

I am not. I can't even pop an antacid for my woes. "I may or may not have had tacos on my way over here."

"And you didn't bring me any? See how Satan works?"

"Didn't you just inhale pupusas meant for me?"

"You really don't look good."

"Thanks, Drew. You always know what to say."

After class, Zoe weaves her way through the chairs and jumps into Siobhan's waiting arms. Not one to miss an opportunity to irk Drew, Luisa stands beside him and watches the scene unfold. "You're gonna have to go over there."

Drew picks up Zoe's discarded backpack. "I'm hoping she comes back."

"If she does, she's gonna come back with your girlfriend."

"She's not my girlfriend."

"Does she know that?" Before he can answer, Luisa nods at me. "You okay, lady?"

"Who knew tacos could cause this sort of pain? They're so delicious," I say miserably.

"You put chilies on those tacos?"

"Extra jalapeños," I confirm.

"So now you're experiencing chili feedback and we all have to hear about it. Come on, let's go get you a glass of milk."

I follow Luisa down the corridor.

Later, I will remember the sound of the air whistling in my ears on the way down, and how I thought, *Well, isn't this embarrassing?* As it happens, I think about how a fall from a bike led me to finding out about my pregnancy and how slipping down these steps might be how I find out that it is over. I hear Luisa's gasp and the sound of her bag hitting the floor as she reaches for me. After I hit the ground and Luisa has hurtled to my side, I try to laugh it off, because that's what you do, isn't it, when you fall in public—a ridiculous reflex. I try to tell her that I am fine and even raise a grazed palm to wave at Drew and Zoe, who have appeared at the top of the steps. But then Luisa places her hands on my knees and says, "Lady, you're bleeding," and I take in the blood spotting my pale gray joggers, then look at her face, searching for the calm I have become accustomed to finding there. It is gone.

Queen Charlotte's and Chelsea Hospital, I was told in the ambulance, is up there when it comes to both prenatal and maternal care. Otherwise comforting words that fell on ears deafened by shock and fear. Luisa, after unleashing a string of rapid-fire Spanish at the poor, unwitting paramedic who questions her presence in the ambulance, becomes my voice. She recounts the fall, provides an approximation of how far along I am and demands I be given another blanket. On the pavement, while I was being loaded into the ambulance, she tried to calm a sobbing Zoe, imploring Drew to take her home. She does all this without breaking a sweat. The terror I saw in her face turned out to be fleeting, and I can't be sure, but I feel like Luisa could bring about world peace if she got enough seats and enough tables.

"It's going to be okay, lady," she tells me in A&E, and I like this about Luisa, the way her timbre flexes as the situation warrants. Hers is not an expressive love. Everything she feels is communicated via the inflections in her voice. "Who do you want me to call?"

On the day I found out I was pregnant, Gloria sped through the hospital halls, arrived at my side breathless and slightly peeved, and while I was thankful, it was in that muted, lukewarm way where you assume things between you will never change, that your big sister will always love you in her imperfect yet constant way. You do not plan for when your obstinate bullishness will clash with her own and a lifetime of care becomes the casualty. I want Luisa to call my sister. I want Gloria to be here. I never thought a day would come when I would question whether she would agree. The person I need most is dead. The person I want has erected boundaries I fear cannot ever be taken down. I ask Luisa to call my parents.

Luisa makes enough noise to have herself cautioned by hospital staff. Her method is successful, and not too long after my arrival, a doctor pulls a curtain around us. Dr. Johnson, though not unkind, has dispensed with all but the most perfunctory pleasantries. She greets me but says nothing of the weather. She runs her eyes over the forms I was asked to fill. She is not, she tells me, an A&E doctor, but an obstetrician and gynecologist. She has chignoned braids and soft eyes and asks me questions that require answers; like why the dates of my last period escape me and when I had my last smear test. Again, she is not unkind. Her voice is level, devoid of exasperation, and her loafered foot is not tapping against the floor in agitation, but I cry anyway as the shock gives way to distress. Dr. Johnson does not balk. She exits our curtained cubicle and returns with a box of Kleenex, which she offers to me without comment. I explain that my husband died at the beginning of the year and this is the reason I don't remember things like the date of my period. She looks at my forms again, perhaps rereading my last name and putting two and two together. She makes a small note.

"Alright, then, Mrs. Ezenwa-Morrow. Let's take a look at you."

Ma arrives shortly after I hear the reassuring thud of my baby's heartbeat on the doppler, when I am a mess of tears and am trying to sift through the noise of jostling emotions. I hear first her voice outside the ultrasound room, then feel the cool softness of her palms on either side of my face. She bends to kiss my forehead. We watch as the grainy outline of my child forms on the screen and I think of Quentin's face, of the way wonder would spread across it like a sunrise. He missed this without knowing, and there is no way to gift it back to him in a mawkish retelling or through an ultrasound, the kind of photo even he couldn't take. Moments like these become part of you, are imprinted for the small eternity that you are. This, the doppler, the black-and-white soup of the screen, the cold gel against my skin, Ma's hushed exclamations of awe and the space where my husband should stand, will be knitted into me. There is too much. For only a second, there is too much. I hate him and love him in equal measure.

I seem fine, I am told, but they are going to keep me overnight for observation. I am transferred to a ward and Ma makes a list of items she knows will make the experience slightly less harrowing. She aways to bring me pajamas, the largest and silkiest of my sleep bonnets, slippers, a cardigan of Q's, and a few sticks of suya, freshly grilled that afternoon before she got the call and came to my side. I am left alone with the photo of Baby Ezenwa-Morrow. Luisa appears holding a plastic cup of tea, which she quickly discards.

"At last. Jeez, lady, you'd think you were Beyoncé the way these people were behaving. Like I'm not the one who brought you here. But then, they probably saw this one arrive, so precautions were necessary." She jabs her thumb over her shoulder at Drew, who is walking through the door as if his presence here is good and right, and the most natural thing in the world.

"Call me a concerned fucking citizen," Drew says. "How are you feeling, Mary?"

I show them the photo and watch their faces, relief blooming. "I'm okay. Luisa. You've been here the whole time?"

"I wasn't going nowhere until your people arrived and I knew you were alright."

"The next time I remind you how much you like me, what exactly are you going to say?"

"The same thing I been saying to you, lady. I have an abuela who would flay me if she knew I didn't help you."

"Okay, but you told your abuela about me." I smooth the blanket over my knees. "Sounds like love to me."

Luisa bestows one of her rare smiles on me. "You real annoying, you know that?"

I turn to Drew. "And how long have you been here?"

He drags a chair from across the room and falls into it, as if his body has been holding on for just this moment. "A few hours," he says, as if it is nothing. As if I am not a near stranger in his life. He sees my face. "Had to work out the logistics with the pixie and then I came right here."

"Zoe? She okay?"

"Yeah, she's cool. Or she was once I explained to her that you'd be fine and promised to report back when I confirmed."

"She was that worried about me?"

"She likes you. She's young. Her judgment isn't what it should be."

I laugh. Despite myself, I laugh. "Thanks."

"You mind if I bring her by tomorrow sometime? Tell me to back off if that's too much."

"Nah, it's not too much. I'd love to see her." It has been so long since I met and loved someone who has no connection to Q. Henrietta was my introduction to how this would feel, but these two, our friendship new and unmarred by time and circumstance, are walking me down this path. It is, I think, of note.

Drew stays long enough to charm a nurse into bringing me another blanket and adjusting the heating in the room, then takes his leave. He has a daughter to tuck in, one who is awaiting his status report on my well-being. "See you tomorrow," he says, and there is an alarming moment when I think he is going to hug me. Instead, he plumps the pillows behind my back and gives a mock salute. His ability to roam between serious and absurd is something to which I am not yet accustomed. You are never quite sure when you will be wrong-footed. I expect his romantic partners might find it exhilarating.

Luisa takes Drew's vacated seat.

"You really looked after me today, Luisa. Thank you."

She pats my hand. "Don't worry about it. Take it easy, okay? You just take it easy."

"You don't have to stay."

"I know I don't."

Silence settles between us, one neither of us feels the need to fill. I drift off for a few minutes, skating on the surface of sleep, and when I open my eyes, Luisa has a textbook in her lap and a fistful of highlighters.

*"Kaplan and Sadock's Synopsis of Psychiatry,"* I read, *"Behav-*

*ioral Sciences and Clinical Psychiatry* eleventh edition. Some light reading?"

"Some compulsory reading, lady. If you want a PhD."

"Excuse me?"

"What do you think I do all day besides feed you?" She shakes her head without looking up.

I am brought back to the inescapable fact that lives are lived outside of mine and people are not mere characters in my story but are stories all their own. My sphere is just that. And a small one, too, shockingly finite. Luisa exists outside of our shared experience, and I am ashamed to have forgotten this. "I don't know," I admit.

"I have a double degree in psychology and occupational health, a master's in child development, and now I got my eye on the prize—a doctorate in clinical psychology." Luisa registers my shock with a roll of her eyes. "Why do you think I come to art class? Sometimes I just want to look at pretty stuff and not talk."

"I guess I ruined that."

"You sure did." She marks a section of text. "But I forgive you."

Not for the last time, I think that Luisa is remarkable in a quiet, understated way; like picking away at the stitching on a charity shop coat to discover a Vivienne Westwood original underneath. "So, what's the end goal?"

She chews the top of her yellow highlighter. "Child psychology, I think."

The events of the day catch up with me and pull my eyelids closed. "Great. This kid's going to need you more than me."

A rustling of pages and then Luisa's hand on my leg through the extra blanket. "People are messy," she yawns. "Nobody expects you to be perfect, lady."

Sleep pulls me under, but before it does, I tell Luisa that expectations aside, I want to be.

She yawns again. "Yeah. But you're a drama queen."

★ ★ ★

Hospital bathrooms, from their sickly color palette to the flickering horror-movie lighting, are designed to encourage their users to accelerate their recovery. I turn away from my ghoulish reflection. Back on the ward, Nate is waiting, his fresh trim bathed in London sunlight.

"Hi, sis," he says.

"You're here."

He helps me back into bed, and though we do not voice it, we are both recalling the weeks where the setting was different but the action the same. "I'm here," he says. "Ma and Dad are just parking up, and Glo had to work, but she's called me twice already."

*But not me*, I think. "Dr. Johnson says I just need to be checked over one last time, then I'm good to go."

Nate turns my bonnet over in his hands. My little brother has the hands of a man now. They changed overnight and they still startle me. "So," Nate says, "a life drawing class, yeah?"

It arrives then, the moment of revelation, where my deception is laid bare, but when I meet my brother's eyes, there is none of the disappointment I expected; only puzzlement, and the patience of someone who has already forgiven you for the lie. "I tried. I swear I did, but I… I just couldn't, Nate. You were right. I didn't want to hear anyone say it was my fault. Maybe I'm not cut out for therapy."

Nate squeezes the bonnet into a tiny ball, then lets it burst from his fist, a silken flower. "Art is therapy, too, I guess. You used to do it all the time."

"How did you even find out?"

"Your friends. That dude. Drew…he's not…y'know… your…?"

"My what? God, NO. Nate, no. No. How could you even think that?"

"Just making sure, innit? I can't picture you with anyone but Q." His eyes are sad. I reach out and squeeze his fingers.

"Me neither."

"They're out there with Bee. You want to see them?"

"Yeah. Hey, Nate." I pass him the ultrasound photo.

Nate grips the photo in both hands. His smile is one that is built deep inside him. "The latest Ezenwa."

"Ezenwa-Morrow."

"That, too." He beams at me. "I'll tell them to come in."

Drew, Zoe and Luisa file in seconds after Nate leaves, and my ward mates raise eyebrows and harrumph into their pillows and bathrobes. There has not been this level of excitement for a long time, this number of visitors for a single person, and I find myself occupying the enviable but awkward epicenter of care. To be doted on in public is to surrender yourself to the opinions of strangers, and over the last few weeks my skin, previously thickened by grief, has started to thin out. Zoe has now been taken to the bathroom by a cherub-faced nurse, and Drew and Luisa are making the most of the temporary child-free zone to speak freely. Drew, evidently, has also discovered that an intellectual giant walks among us.

"Did you know," Drew asks, "that Luisa actually uses her brain for something other than cussing me?"

"La hostia. Stop making such a big deal. It's some books," Luisa growls. "Anyway, the more important thing is that I found out the origin story of Siobhan."

Drew sighs. "She's not an X-Man, Luisa."

"I thought she was just the mum of Zoe's best friend," I say.

"Sure, she is, but can you believe that Drew here modeled for the class?" Luisa grins so widely, I fear her cheeks may split in protest. "At least you look a little better, lady. You still look bad, but a bit better. Slightly less bad. But still bad."

"Thanks, Luisa. You did what?" I look at Drew, who is examining the corner of the blanket with an intensity reserved for the deeply embarrassed.

"Look. I was trying new things. It was once. And there was a strategically placed sheet."

"Obviously not strategic enough. Siobhan has been on his case since." Luisa is still smiling.

"I don't get it," I say. "How did this even happen?"

"Siobhan asked if I could help out her friend Xavier by modeling. What person doesn't get an ego boost from being asked to model?"

"Please. Don't think we don't know you got excited by the chance to show everyone your polla. I pegged you for a pervert the second you showed up in class."

"I didn't show my 'polla.' And like I said, it was once. And after that, I had to be talked into returning to class. As a pupil." Drew's discomfort pleases Luisa greatly.

"This is what you guys talk about when I'm not there?" I ask, laughing.

"Yes." Drew taps a fingertip on my knee. "And I know you're shocked that Luisa and I have conversations outside of our interactions with you."

"Yeah, but it's not like I enjoy them," Luisa mutters, eliciting a "fuck you" from Drew that is wrapped up in a chuckle.

Zoe chooses this moment to return. Her hair in two long braids on either side of her face. A picture of Garfield on her jumper. She approaches me shyly and offers me a drawing— trees using the technique I showed her and two stick people beneath them. She and I.

"This is brilliant, Zoe. Thank you so much." I smile down at her and she smiles back.

"We brought you a sandwich, too," she tells me and pokes her father in the leg until he locates the paper bag and hands it over.

"Luisa isn't the only one that can cook. This is my creation—meatball madness," Drew says.

"Meatballs are made from animals," Zoe points out.

"Aw, hell. C'mon, Zo, not this again."

"I don't eat animals anymore," Zoe insists. "It's murder."

"My child has decided yet again that she is a vegetarian. This is the third time in a month. I'm suspending playtime with Penny."

"Meat is animals, Dad."

"Baby girl, I support your choices. For dinner tonight, I'll make sure you get no meat and extra broccoli."

"Oh," Zoe says quietly. "I hadn't considered the broccoli."

"We can talk more about it later," Drew reassures her while Luisa shakes her head in disgust. "Okay, pixie. Give Mary here a hug and wait for me by the door so we can get you to Mum's."

Zoe smells of coconut and talcum powder. Her little arms encircle my neck and she whispers, "I know your real name is Eve. Sometimes my dad thinks he is funny," and then she is skipping toward the door. The three of us watch her go.

"Kudos to her mother," Luisa says. "She's raising an angel."

"One day, Luisa, you will give me the recognition I deserve. This sharp tongue of yours, have you ever considered that this is why you're single?" It is bold and extraordinarily rude. Classic Drew.

Luisa examines her nails. "Not all of us have to strip naked and pose in front of strangers to find love. You wanna tell us where your girlfriend is at?"

Checking that Zoe remains out of earshot, Drew leans forward to reply. "You women are crazy."

"Is that a fact?" says Luisa. "So, you don't like women, huh?"

"I get what you're insinuating, and while there is zero

problem with that, no. Unfortunately, I am still attracted to you people."

"So, if Eve here were to be overcome with lust and get naked right now, you'd hit that?"

"I am right here," I put in. "Like, less than a foot away from the two of you."

Drew clears his throat. "She's...not my type," he says carefully.

"The fuck you mean?" demands Luisa. "What's wrong with her?"

"She's kind of dramatic. I mean, throwing yourself down some community center steps for attention. No offence, Mary." He winks.

"That was an accident!" Luisa swings for Drew and makes contact with his arm.

"Jesus, Luisa, that might actually leave a bruise."

When they leave, the sound of their voices stays with me.

Before I am discharged, Dr. Johnson wants to examine me, and an argument flares up between Bee and Nate about who ought to accompany me. Bee, of course, announces that if it is going to be anyone, it is going to be her as Nate is unprepared to see my uterus in all of its splayed glory. Nate, who looks like he might regurgitate his half-eaten breakfast, says in a strained voice, "Surely it won't come to that," but Bee raises a knowing eyebrow and Nate retreats, defeated. Dr. Johnson watches the scene unfold with the measured patience of a woman who has seen and mitigated a thousand shit shows. She gives me the all clear and asks me to "take additional care when negotiating steps and stairs in the future."

Unsure what I expected, I exhale when I step into my bedroom and find it unchanged. I pin the ultrasound to the wall and plead with myself not to lose it. Motherhood was never a goal for me as it is for others. I was never a person who considered the childfree "less than." There is sometimes a haughtiness found in parents; knowing glances exchanged when you, unencumbered by teething tantrums and nappy changes, dare to express tiredness. I understood that families did not need children to be real. I scoffed at the idea that loving a child was somehow purer, more powerful than the love reserved for a sibling, a spouse or even a friend. I am unshaken in those views, but I am also tasting a new kind of fear, the kind that will underpin all my waking moments going forward and worm its way into my dreams. It is that which drove Ma to shout at Nate for coming home late and neglecting to call, that which brought Dad to the door of my nine-year-old classmate at midnight because I was frightened and the sleepover was ruined. It is what I see in Gloria's eyes when she scolds Ben for playing too close to the curb outside their house. It is the dread that comes from knowing that your child, even as they grow into their autonomy, can be snatched from you, that the world is littered with pitfalls and there is only so much you can do to keep them safe. You know that you will be irrational, and your fear is a product of love. In my case, on the worst nights, there will be nobody to turn to, nobody to yank me back from the edge. I will be partnerless in the singular madness that is parenthood. And there in my bedroom, months later, I understand that my questions for Quentin may never be answered, that closure is something I may never obtain.

# 31

Dr. Johnson comes to me in a series of dreams. She is somber as she confirms my worst fears—I have lost the baby, or, as I lie on the birthing table, that the baby is stillborn. Sometimes, she is wearing hospital scrubs as she details the adverse health effects for which my behavior is responsible. Others, she is in her white coat and loafers when she explains that developmental delay is almost certain. I am never happy to see her. My subconscious has now become a place I do the utmost to avoid. If it is not Quentin I find there, it is his mother. And now Dr. Johnson with her bad news and perfect Cupid's bow. When I wake, sweating, I must place my palm against the ultrasound photo until I can breathe again. And isn't it a markedly cruel irony that I still crave the thing responsible for my predicament? A pill, a mouthful of rum, Quentin. It doesn't matter.

I am under strict instructions to rest, to eat regular nutritious meals, which Ma is only too happy to provide, and to seek immediate medical attention if I so much as suspect anything could be amiss. The house once more becomes a revolving door for my family and for Bee, who brings me a collection of brand-new hoodie and jogger sets in extra large, and a book about what piece of fruit my unborn resembles at various stages. She helps me into a hoodie and asks if I may want to resurrect my Instagram page so I can document the remainder of my pregnancy. It is a question for a person whose mother-in-law is not moving mountains to inflict pain, not for someone who can only stare down at her stomach for seconds before guilt forces her gaze elsewhere. I shake my head and Bee does not press it. She kisses her fingertips and touches them first to my cheek and then to the ultrasound before she leaves. Nate is here to relieve her. I am not to be left alone. Especially in a place with an abundance of stairs.

In the living room, the bouquets have been cleared away, but I find a few sunflower petals hiding beside the hearth. They remind me of Henrietta and the rainbow of microfiber cloths she used to sanitize Room 111, the scene of so much joy and a wealth of despair. I wonder if she remembers me fondly or if I have become a cautionary or simply ludicrous tale, told over red wine and accompanied by guilty laughter. Of course, it is bold of me to assume I am remembered at all. In the kitchen, there are neatly stacked Tupperware containers of fried rice, yam pottage, stew and egusi soup. I make up a small plate for myself and another for Nate, who came directly from the gym. We sit in the breakfast nook and he watches me over his spoonful of rice.

"What is it, Junior?"

"What's what?"

"You're staring."

"I'm not."

I rest my own spoon against the side of my plate. "Nate."

"You don't say much," he says.

"About what?"

"What happened."

There are too many episodes of What Happened for me to pinpoint his exact gripe. "Can you be more specific?"

"You could have lost the baby. You don't say much about it."

"I... What is there to say?"

"I never know what's going on in your head anymore." It is not a complaint, but a statement planted by love and watered with worry.

"Trust me, you're not missing much."

He waits a beat, then swallows his mouthful. "We never used to lie to each other."

That I am the one Nate chose to be the audience for his occasional displays of emotion, his sounding board, the receptacle for his secrets, is not negligible. Our mutual trust, already damaged by my selfishness, is not inconsequential. He deserves better than what I have given him. When he collects our plates and heads for the sink, I remain in my chair and open my mouth. "You know how when someone's been sick for ages and they pass away, how everyone is like 'At least they aren't suffering anymore'?"

The clink of cutlery stops. "Yeah?"

"Well. I don't feel that way about Q. Every day I wish he was still here. He probably would have been in pain—I mean he had to be to have... But I still wish he was here." It is a relief to say it. Selfish of me to want him here struggling, suffering in silence. But I can own that selfishness because the alternative is and will always be worse. To me. I wait for Nate's judgment, the sword of Damocles I have avoided for too long.

"Yeah," he says, "me, too. Fucked-up, right?"

I twist to look at him, but my eyes only find his back. "Very fucked-up."

"I think Cleo probably thinks the total opposite for me. That girl wants me dead."

I laugh. "She told you that?"

"Not in so many words, but she left a couple of fun voice mails." Nate rinses his hands. "The weird thing about it is that they made me miss her a little."

"Are you sure you two can't salvage anything?"

It is only then my brother turns back to face me. "Whenever I used to talk to Q about Cleo, he'd say shit like 'If it ever stops making sense, you'll know.' It stopped making sense with Cleo."

I think again of Quentin's assessment of me, of my "goodness." He returned to it so often, like a refrain. He knew, he told me, that I would be good for him, but I wonder if he, like so many others, ever paused to consider whether he would be good for me. "I guess it stopped making sense for Q, too," I tell Nate.

When he crosses the kitchen and folds me up in his arms, I let myself droop into his chest. Here, listening to his heart beat, I can begin to admit to myself that something that was near broken is beginning to repair.

Shunted from a nap by something that disappears before I can name it, I find Gloria downstairs poring over her laptop, a mug of green tea at her side. I marvel and despair at how quickly it took for my own sister to become a stranger in my house; she is both out of place there on my sofa and completely at home, wreathed in the vulnerability that comes from not knowing that the thing you resent has entered the room. Her face is scrubbed of makeup, her socks, pink and patterned, her hair pulled back. In the relatively recent past, I would have jumped on the sofa with her and showered her face in kisses that she always pretended she hated but that would leave her eyes shining when I finally pulled back. Now it seems impolite to do anything other than clear my throat softly and pray she isn't startled.

She turns. "I thought you were sleeping."

"I was. I guess I woke up."

She turns back to her computer, one hand checking her hair, her toes curling in her socks. Gloria finds power in her workwear, and her suits have become her armor. We, her family, used to be the one place where that ceased to matter. Her discomfort makes my heart ache. "I was working from home today." As explanations go, it isn't loaded with detail, but it is enough.

I sit in an armchair. "How are Ellie and Ben?"

"Ellie's been chosen to play the lead butterfly in her year's Nature Play."

"Natural star quality, so of course she has."

"I've been instructed to make sure the costume doesn't 'embarrass me, Mummy.'"

"Can't have that."

We both laugh, then remember ourselves. Gloria's back straightens. "I'll maybe see if we can bring them by this week-end. They miss you."

"Do you?"

She sighs. "Eve. Don't."

"Because I miss you," I tell her.

"I don't have the luxury of missing you. I'm too busy sort-ing out your problems." And it might be true, but what Nate said also has a space in truth here. She could say no. She could refuse.

"You don't have to."

"What?"

"You don't have to sort out my problems. You could just, like, not do that. But then you wouldn't have a reason to hate me."

"Yeah." She looks at me with a blankness that chills my skin. "I suppose you have a point. Let me stop. Give me the name of your alternative counsel."

"Don't think I'm not grateful, Glo. I am. I really am. But I miss my sister. And if dropping all this stuff would, I dunno, make things better between us, then you can do it."

Gloria shuts her laptop with a snap. "I said I will. Just tell me who I should hand over to." She sees my face, shakes her head. "God, Eve. Someone else has always had to look after you. We do it because we love you."

"It's not by force, Glo," I say. My hands, I find, have squeezed themselves into balls.

"Perhaps not to you. It's just the way it is. You're our Eve and we have to take care of you."

"You don't have to," I insist, even as the truth of what she is saying is boring its way into me.

"I asked you to reason with Aspen. Didn't I? Didn't I ask you for that? When you ran off without thinking about any of us, wasn't it me who had to ask Bee to go and make sure you came home? We've asked, Eve. But you said no."

"I gave her back the ring! And I was scared! I'm still scared. I get that you're superhuman and don't experience that emotion, but you know my head was all over the place."

It is as if I have not spoken. "Remember when you were, like, seven and you came home from school that one time crying and told Ma and Dad it was because you were worried about some spelling test? Well, I knew it was actually because that girl with those stupid pigtails in your class was getting her little friends to pick on you, so the next day, I cornered her and told her that if she didn't stop, I was going to put her head down the toilet."

"You did what?"

"And when you were, like, four, you used to come back from nursery all the time feeling sad because some little shit had said something to you about your hair looking like a Brillo pad. That was when I knew I had to start looking after you. Fighting your battles. I've been doing it ever since. You learned how to do it for a while, but then you met Quentin and seemed to think there were no more battles to fight. You've been taking a back seat in your own life for the longest time. You're going to have a baby who is going to need you to be on top of your game. We've watched you give up all these past months and we've caught you because that's what we do, but that has got to be over at some point. You get that, right? You have to step up." I see tears in Gloria's eyes and everything inside me collapses.

"I'm sorry." It is the equivalent of slapping a Band-Aid on an open chest cavity, but if nothing else, Gloria deserves to hear it from me.

She takes a breath and reopens her laptop. "I have to finish this."

"I'll figure out what to do about Aspen, Glo. I don't know how yet, but I will." I move to the door. "Glo?"

"Yeah?"

"You threatened a *child* for me."

"I was also technically a child at the time, albeit an older one." She smiles. "I would do it again."

I am immobilized by Gloria's words even after she has gone home, relieved from Eve-watching duties by Ma and Dad. I retrieve *Sundown* and scrutinize the lines of Quentin's face. I examine his one visible eye and imagine I see something there other than the reflection of the window he faced. No wonder then, I reason, he couldn't share his anguish. I was not, for all his exhortations, his safe space. His struggle remained his own, and perhaps he felt he had to shield me from it. Perhaps he did not want to give me the burden of feeling I had to try and keep him alive when he was determined to die. It is impossible, after all, to reverse that which is terminal and maybe life was that for him—something he had decided he did not want to elongate. I will never know. And it is the not knowing that cuts the deepest. Leaving wounds I am unsure will ever heal.

* ★ ★

Both Luisa and Drew text and ask for my address, and three days later, a giant arrangement of white roses, baby's breath and freesia arrives at the house alongside a handmade card with a child's drawing on the front. Zoe's artistic license has led her to depict me with a swollen, transparent belly inside which a baby (complete with tiny hat and shoes?) jigs merrily. My phone buzzes as I place the bouquet on the mantel.

Zoe insisted on the see-through stomach. I tried.

Laughing, I fire a text back: Shoes on the baby?

She had a vision. Could not be swayed.

Thank you for the flowers. They're gorgeous. And thank Zoe for the card.

You doing okay, Mary?

Kind of.

Stop milking it and come back to class soon.

The doorbell rings and I drop my phone in my pocket and go to answer. At the door, Luisa and I blink at each other for a few seconds before she unwinds her scarf enough to snap, "Well, lady, you gonna invite me in or what?"

"Sorry! I'm just shocked to see you." I stand back and let her inside.

She pauses in the hall, her eyes swooping upward to take in the high ceilings. "Nice place." She follows me down the hall and into the living room. "And nice flowers."

"From Drew and Zoe."

"*He* sent them? Good for him." She is grudgingly impressed, and it dawns on me that I have missed Luisa and her curmudgeonly charm. I hug her, and after a "Whoa, take it easy, lady," she hugs me back.

"I can't believe you came all the way here to see me. And don't give me any rubbish about your abuela, Luisa. You love me. We're alone now. You can admit it."

"What I'll admit is that class ain't quite the same without you. And I'm making way too much food without you there to feed. Here." She gives me a cardboard cake box. "Tres leches cake."

"Luisa! Thank you so much. You spoil me. You want tea or anything?"

"I'm not staying, lady. I came to make sure you were following doctor's orders and to bring you that cake and this." Luisa thrusts a gift bag in my direction. Inside, there is a set of premium graphite and coloring pencils, a thick sketch pad. "Don't look at me like that. I just don't want you to forget that you can do this while you're sitting at home. You don't let a good thing die because of pain. No existe gran talento sin gran voluntad. That means there is no great talent without great will."

I clutch the bag to my chest. "I'm going to make you a cup of tea so I can cry without judgment."

"Jeez, lady, get a grip," Luisa says, but she pats my arm on my way out.

I bring her a mug and find her holding a framed photo of Q and me on our wedding day. A lifetime ago. When the world made sense in that most myopic of ways the young and unfettered have.

"Blanquito, huh?" Luisa says. "Handsome."

"Yeah. He was."

"You were happy." Not a question, but a statement. I nod. "You'll be happy again. He wasn't the author of that. It'll just be different."

I want to tell Luisa that it never occurred to me that I would have to learn to not want him, that this was going to be my life. I will sit before others and they will ask my story, and I will tell them my husband died, but this will become a footnote when right now it is the entire plot. Luisa doesn't touch her tea. I convince her to stay for an hour and she uses the time to study, occasionally looking up to check I am still there, drawing the bouquet on the mantel. She passes Bee on her way out and they greet each other in the cool noncommittal manner of two separates orbiting an entity that connects them. Bee takes in the bouquet, accepts a bite of tres leches cake, and because she is cold, we retire to my bed, where I turn on the electric blanket. When she tells me that she has been too busy with work to indulge in her usual self-care beauty routines, I scoot to the end of the bed, lift her feet into my lap and begin to paint her toenails. I listen to her speak about her day, talking through yawns, and I think about how in meeting Bee, another room inside of me was unlocked, just as it had been with Q. I am reminded of the envy I feel of the easy confidence that seems to come to others whereas I appear destined to stumble forward indefinitely, slowly developing until I reach my final form at some indeterminate time. Bee, always so sure of herself, is the anti-me. Gloria's words come back to me, and as Bee begins to drift, I apologize to her if she ever felt she had to prop me up, if our friendship was characterized by a one-sided duty of care.

Bee opens her eyes. "Was there a lost little girl quality about you? Yeah. Did that make me want to make sure nothing bad happened to you? Sure."

"I'm sorry."

Bee stretches and goes still. I gently lift her feet out of my lap and turn off the light. The moon tiptoes into the room and bathes her face in cool light. Just before I fall asleep, Bee slips an arm around me.

"You're forgetting the most important bit," she says, her voice thick with sleep. "You make everything worth it."

One of the more horrific conventions of grief is its sneakiness, its absolute refusal to be linear. You wake up and yes, you know he is not coming back—the half second you forgot already a memory—but you feel okay. You find the energy to open your curtains. You can even bathe without crying. You can eat breakfast and text your friends. Then something arrives to once again beat you to the floor. Something as inconsequential as hearing your dead husband's favorite song when Spotify shuffle cruelly presents it to your unsuspecting ear. Or something as momentous as the white of an envelope, menacing even from the top of the stairs, the contents of which inform you that your mother-in-law is suing you for your husband's ashes.

# 32

The last fight Quentin and I had was about communication. Although a fight suggests a mutual back-and-forth, and this was more of a sustained monologue. There was no real cause, simply an ongoing irritation that despite my years of badgering, Q couldn't seem to amend. I listed all the times he failed to call or text that I could remember, all the frantic voice mails I left, all the hours I spent looking for him. It was me fighting back tears while I surmised that he didn't respect me because why couldn't he just fucking *call* and tell me he would be late? It didn't matter that this was an integral part of who he was, scored into his DNA along with his aquamarine eyes and double joints. It also didn't matter that deep down I knew it was not done either with malice or deliberately. I roared my disappointment at him, and he sat there looking stricken, trying to fit in an apology between my outbursts, close to tears himself at the size and strength of my hurt. We made up afterward as couples do. I could never stay angry with Q for long.

But a few days later as I hacked an ice tray out of my freezer and left my third voice mail on his phone rehashing the argument, Quentin was bleeding to death, and to this day, I hope he never listened to what I said that night. I pray that his last thoughts of me were not accompanied by the sound of my voice delivering empty threats of divorce and calling him selfish. I never got the chance to tell him that his issues with communication aggravated the part of me that was convinced he would, at some point, stop choosing me. That night, he chose death. I turned out to be right. I thought I had more time. Because you never think your last fight is going to be your last. You think you will have forever to chastise your spouse, and you even look forward to the conclusion of the argument and to the reconciliation. The whispered apologies against your skin. Now, as I stare at the urn on the mantel he commissioned a stoneworker to carve from a block of limestone, there is little I would not sacrifice to have Q somewhere, alive, not calling me when he said he would, forgetting to text at the appropriate time. Instead, I get nothing but the prospect of having the last of him ripped away from me by his mother.

Henry Huntington seems almost apologetic in his letter. He understands, he states, that this has been a difficult time for all involved, that the courts do not generally like to wade into this sort of conflict, but he believes that the final resting place of one Quentin Christian Malcolm Morrow should be alongside his father and in the long-ready private cemeterial grounds of the Morrow estate. There is something about how family tradition was already flouted when I chose to have Quentin cremated and he uses words such as *farcical* and *bizarre* to describe the arrangements I made—Mrs. Bowes-Morrow's words, he points out, not his. The upshot is that despite repeated efforts to engage me in a civil and sensitive manner, my stubbornness and callous disregard of Aspen's efforts has left her with no choice. Each time I reread the letter, laughter always bursts unbidden out of me when I reach the words *civil* and *sensitive* being used to describe the woman who, days after Q died, told me that because of me, his life was a waste, that he never even got the opportunity to right the wrong of choosing me.

My days after the funeral were spent listening to the sound of footsteps from beneath the duvet, the smell of uneaten food and unwashed clothes lingering in the air. They were an increased dosage of pills, the clashing of tumblers against teeth, a life half lived in the merciful haze of sedatives and alcohol. Even then. Even though I shrank away from the touch of my family, even though I watched Q walk into our bedroom a hundred times before realizing I was too out of it to differentiate between the real and the imaginary, even though Aspen peppered me with accusations; despite all this, I arranged for Quentin's ashes to be split in two, and a second urn, bought at enormous expense, transported to his mother. Half of my husband lives under Aspen's roof and still this is not enough.

The letter has taken on a life of its own. I memorize its contents within the hour and various lines run through my head like the scrolling headlines at the bottom of a news channel. I lose my train of thought midsentence. Thrown off balance, I struggle through the most basic of conversations. Stepping outside of the house feels unfeasible; these rooms have now become a rampart. I relay the subject matter to my family, to Bee. I phone Jackson, who is in Turks and Caicos, and I ask him if he knew what she was planning, but his voice switches from sun-softened to alarmed and I know he is in the dark. He asks me what he can do, but what is there to say? His allegiance is not something easily drawn. It belonged to Q when he was alive, and now that he is gone, it is torn between the two women who loved him best. I leave him on the beach. I text my siblings and try to explain to them that I can no sooner leave this house than I can solve the Riemann hypothesis or bunny hop to the moon. My explanation is poor yet disturbing enough to bring both Nate and Gloria to my door that night after their workdays are over. Alex trudges in shortly afterward carrying a sleeping Ellie and Ben, whom he settles in the guest room. Bee, who arrives last, shakes rain out of her hair and wraps her arms around me. It is only when I go still that I realize I have been trembling. Ma and Dad, I note, have been given a reprieve. When the kids are down and the door to the guest room is closed, Alex pauses in the doorway and watches his wife. He crosses the room and squeezes both her shoulders from behind, slides his hands down her arms and kisses the top of her head. We witness the slackening of Gloria's body, Alex drawing out the tension with his affection. I think all of us, in our own ways, understand what it is to have a person whose touch is your solace. I look away.

Nate is full of questions. He asks Glo whether this is a legitimate threat. He wants to know the likelihood of Aspen's success. He demands to see the letter, and when Glo gives him her copy to read, he does so while uttering a series of whispered expletives. Bee rubs my back in slow circles. She offers nothing but the slight yet solid heft of her body next to mine. She asks why, a question up until now none of us have thought to.

"It's just unbelievably cruel," Glo says. Her feet shift, a prelude to more pacing, but Alex keeps her still. She reaches up and covers his hands with her own. "There's no reason for her to do this."

"Gloria says you divided Q's…you gave Quentin's mother some of his ashes already?" Alex asks.

I nod. "I did. I didn't want to. But it's the decent thing, isn't it? He's her son."

Nate's agitation pushes him to his feet. "Okay, so who among us knows someone we can pay to rush her?"

There is a brief moment of silence before the room thaws into frightened laughter shot through with a relief we all recognize as temporary. We sag against each other, composure gone.

"You're really asking if any of us can put a hit out on Eve's mother-in-law?" Bee wipes the tears from her eyes.

"Whoa," Nate says. "I said *rush her*, not kill her. I feel like the way she's moving warrants a slap at least."

"Hmm, advocating for violence against women, Natey. I'm not sure I like this." But Glo smiles as she says it.

"Tell me you don't want to deliver one hot slap. Just one," Nate challenges Gloria.

"Please. I've wanted to backhand that ezè amōosu for the last decade." Glo nods at Bee. "That means chief of witches." And we are all laughing for a second time.

"Is there any chance of her getting her way?" I refocus.

"If it was just this—just the ashes—I'd probably go with no. But good old Henry references the fact that she's been trying to contact you and that all her other efforts have been ignored—no, I get it, 'efforts' is the mother of euphemisms. He's going to use the fact that there was no written record of Q's wishes for when he died. It was left out of his will, so technically there is some legitimacy to Aspen's claim." Glo sighs.

"Legitimacy?" The word makes me want to drop to my knees. "I'm his wife."

"Eve, I know. I know."

Bee makes tea, fills small bowls with olives and kettle chips, which none of us touch. The facts sit alongside us, silent yet damning. Gloria is embroiled in a new high-profile case at work; her and Alex's caseloads now necessitate an increase in the working hours of Tess the nanny. There isn't time to tackle Henry Huntington. We sit here, yet another war council this time on the verge of subjugation, our collective resolve beginning to fray. We know there is little use in fighting, that Aspen may have found comfort in conflict but will find no closure in it.

Occasionally, one of us cleaves the silence with a curse. More than once, I glance at Q's urn and will myself to imagine an empty space where it sits. Fatigue settles over us like fine dust. Bee dozes off, Nate stretches, Alex and Gloria lean toward each other until their foreheads touch. I slip upstairs, and in the guest room, I smooth the covers back over Ben's leg where, like always, he has kicked them off during sleep. I untuck the collar of Ellie's pajamas where they have curled into the soft skin of her neck. I watch the rise and fall of their chests, the twitch of their muscles as they gambol through their dreams. I don't yet know what it is for my heart to fully live outside of me, but I am, day by day, growing closer to meeting that lesson. Gazing down at my niece and nephew in my guest bed, somewhere they have slept a hundred times, it suddenly seems ludicrous that they are here when they should be at home in their own beds, waking up to parents who do not have the added responsibility of me and my legal woes. My issues should never have been allowed to impact them. My guilt, I decide, will be exactly that. Mine.

The day it happens, I am nearing sixty hours without sleep. Henry's letter, whenever I close my eyes, flickers behind my eyelids, a weight about my ankles keeping me anchored in wakefulness. Exhaustion settles into my bones, and I begin to feel the light-headed drunkenness of too many nights wandering the house, driven from my bed by living ghosts. Ma cooks ayamase and monitors my efforts to eat it, and because too much of my recent life has been spent letting myself fall to pieces in front of the people who love me, I clean my plate and congratulate myself silently when she takes it to the sink. But as I leave the kitchen, Ma grabs my arm and she says, "Gloria is..." but she does not finish the sentence because we both know that Gloria is being pulled in a hundred different directions. So, we stand there in the kitchen, Ma's fingers tight on my arm, and we look at each other, searching for the faith and reassurance that has now, finally, run dry.

I pick my way to the armchair in our study and, with shaking hands, lift Luisa's gift into my lap, but the pencil will not move the way I need it to, and the lines do not connect where I want them to, and I feel I might drown in the depth of my powerlessness. And there is a scream building up inside me because I remember the blankness on Quentin's face when he broke up with me that one time in university, when he left me broken on the carpet of my room. I remember how he stopped for a second before he shut my door. I could only see his trainers from where I had crumpled to the floor, and I wanted to reach out and hold on to one of them and ask him to explain his "mistake." It is easy now to tell myself that he tried to save me from himself and it was love that brought him back, but there is no evidence to corroborate this, no confirmation of that which I use to try and comfort myself.

I lean back in the armchair and close my eyes, and this time it is not Henry I see but us, Q and me in this room. I was late to work, the gel on my edges already sweating out as I barreled from room to room searching for my other boot. He was in this chair, scrolling through a series of bookings on his website. He raised his eyes to me when I entered, asked if I was okay, and I, a tornado in miniature, peered under the desk knowing the boot was not there, feeling the heat of frustration bloom under my arms. He caught my hand before I walked out. And that was all it took, really. I was late, but I would be later still, and as soon as I felt his hands inch under my shirt and find flushed, dampening skin, my breath escaped my lungs a little easier. I kept the sole boot on even as I crawled onto him in that chair, and we laughed the low, incredulous laughs of two people who know better, and his laughter turned to a sigh when I leaned into him. Afterward, I made sounds about finding my other damn shoe, but he held me there and rested his head against my chest until I kissed the top of his head, then swatted him and left him in the chair. It was the last time, but I didn't know that, and perhaps he did. I went to work that day late but happy and now it strikes me how it is truly a privilege to move through life without worrying if happiness is short-lived, because you know you will, at some point, find it again. And it is only now that it seems so unlikely for me that the scream breaks free of me and fills the room, the house.

Maybe it is the unwillingness to accept that memories are all I have that pushes me to my feet and into my coat. Perhaps it is the lack of sleep, fatigue pairing with delirium and creating something new and terrible. I phone Jackson and he maneuvers around his jet lag and agrees to meet me.

When I looked for my husband's suicide note, I did so with the single-mindedness afforded by previously unknown agony. I was a woman on a mission. I tore up our house. I remember sitting in the kitchen, the contents of every ransacked drawer surrounding me, a few errant pieces of glass embedded in my foot from the tumblers I hurled to the floor in frustration. I remember going through the pockets of the empty clothes he'd never again wear, pain skewering every part of me. I recall pleading with the investigating officer—whose own calls I had been ignoring—to check the clothes he was wearing again. There had to be something, the belongings I was given held nothing. No answers. And afterward, post-hysterics, after screaming through the house like a monsoon, the destruction I left in my wake was quietly cleared, tidied away by those who could raise no objection. I rifled through his online life. Because we live in this "digital age" now where oversharing is mistaken for bravery and every part of our carefully curated lives is documented for consumption by the masses—equally thirsty for the validation of strangers. I combed through his Instagram page, searching for the coded message that spoke hidden volumes. But all I found were his perfect photos—mountains, lakes, crystal clear close-ups of the pain he was so adept at capturing in other people with no regard of that which he would create in me. His Twitter page was similarly fruitless, his last tweet so infuriatingly mundane I almost pulled out my hair. His email drafts were empty, his trash folder devoid of discarded attempts at an explanation or, failing that, an apology. But when I had searched his place of work, I did so in a state of shock. I groped under his still-warm body. I tracked blood across the floor so I could leaf through invoices, hoping for a scribbled explanation on the back of an outstanding bill. I thought he would know that I was gone, so I returned to where he lay, my knees giving way, my wrists twisting awkwardly as they hit the floor. A pain I would feel for weeks afterward. The unturned stones in Q's studio have brought me back here for the first time since he died.

I find Jackson on the pavement outside. I compliment him on his tan and he examines me, valiantly looking for a way to return the compliment. I wave away his attempt. I know what I look like. The key to the studio sits in my palm. We face the door, a heavy green tinted glass Q agonized over for close to a month before pulling the trigger. *QM Photography* is engraved into the glass. I chose the font.

"Why now?" Jackson asks, and to answer him would be to admit that the last stage of grief has stages of its own and I am cycling through various forms of acceptance, understanding you must allow the chips to fall where they may before rummaging through the debris and piecing together something that resembles a life. I want something in my hand to show my kid when I am asked what happened. And failing that, I want the strength to explain that it is okay that I don't know.

To Jackson, I say, "It's time."

There is one awful moment as the key turns in the lock that I almost turn and sprint down the street. This is the place, after all, where Q took his last breath. The place he chose to remove himself from me, from us. I do not know what I will find when I push the door open and the not knowing is something like a comfort. I could walk inside and find him sitting there waiting for me, that bemused expression on his face, as if I have no reason to be gutted. Anything seems possible when you are on the wrong side of a door. Beside me, Jackson begins to quake.

"I... I don't know if I can, Eve." His voice is not his. It belongs to a small, scared child.

"You don't have to, Jack." I have dragged too many into my spiral. I can give Jackson an out. I can give him that. It could be that this is the start. Where your love of something, of someone, dwarfs your own needs.

He steadies himself. Draws air in through clenched teeth. "I could really use a drink."

"You and me both," I tell him. We go inside.

The floor has been scrubbed clean. Of course it has. You do not leave a pool of blood on imported hardwood floors. There was, I believe someone mentioned to me what seems like several decades ago and also like yesterday, a professional crime scene cleanup squad who arrived on scene in hazmat suits like this was some sort of film, and removed every trace of Quentin's glorious and messy death. Still, I fancy that I can see a faint outline there on the floor, underneath the dust, undisturbed by neither client nor proprietor for months. Jackson and I stand side by side, the stillness of the air takes on an oppressive quality, and inside my head, I pray these walls hold secrets I will be fortunate enough to unearth.

We are methodical in our search, Jackson and I. We tackle the tiny back office first, trawling through ledgers, cracking open box files, bemoaning Quentin's abject lack of organizational skills. We find a Spode teacup with an unused tea bag still inside. We discover a small sack of fan mail and laugh humorlessly when Jack reads a couple of the more besotted notes. I turn on the computer and click through the inner workings of his business. I load his calendar. There are appointments and bookings littered across the page. There is a reminder about the photography retreat, which flashes plaintively at the bottom of the screen. Post December 31, there are entries, though sparser, and when I laugh at my foolishness, it sounds hollow. Jackson peers at the screen over my shoulder, looks down at me, puzzled.

"I dunno what the hell I thought. Was I expecting to see it scheduled in here or something? '8:30 p.m. Kill myself.' What a fucking idiot." I wipe my face furiously.

Jackson squeezes my shoulder. "Eve…"

"God," I say, standing up. "God. There's nothing here, is there?" And for the second time but definitely not the last, I come apart at the seams in Jackson's presence. He has to hold me up and I cling to him while the last of my guileless, idiotic hope dies. I keep thinking as I lose another bit of my mind that all that has gone before and everything that will come after this moment will pale in comparison to this excruciating truth: closure is not promised. It is a gift, and my husband chose to keep it from me.

Later, when I have convinced Jackson to go home and sleep off the rest of his jet lag, after I have made him promise to phone his sponsor and he in turn has made me promise to call him when I get home, after I have shut down Quentin's computer and tidied away his files and receipts, I sink against a wall, send a text and let the weariness of the last while finally drag me under. I am woken by the door of the studio closing, soft footsteps moving across the floor toward me. Luisa crouches before me, cups my face in her hands and absorbs the defeat that I suppose is leeching out of every pore in my body.

"Okay, lady," she says and sits beside me, pressing her back against the wall.

"I found these. In his darkroom." My voice has been made gravelly by sleep and sadness.

Luisa takes the photographs from my hand and goes through them slowly. The studio is bathed in the sickly glow of the streetlights outside. Enough to see each shot, all of them of me, all of them taken on my last birthday. He never asked me to pose for him that day. I didn't even register his camera. But there I am, laughing, hands in my hair pulling a face for Ben, enveloped in Dad's signature bear hug. *This isn't me*, I kept thinking under the red blush of the bulbs in the darkroom, but I forgot that trauma changes the landscape of your face, as if your features have moved slightly to the left.

"You look different. Happy," Luisa says, examining the photos. "It suits you."

More footsteps, then Bee stepping out of the shadow, head wrap secured, face bare. I blink up at her. "Did I text you?"

"No." She lowers herself onto the floor on the other side of me. "Luisa did. And I won't cuss you about that right now."

I look from Bee to Luisa. "You have Bee's number?"

"I made sure I took it back at the hospital. Wipe that look off your face, lady. I needed to make sure I had someone to let me know if you were acting crazy. I didn't know if I would need backup to get you home."

"Since when the fuck did *I* become *backup*?" Bee complains. She finds my hand. "Babe. Are you okay?"

Luisa passes the photographs over and Bee looks through them. She never releases my fingers.

"I dragged Jackson over here to help me look for a note. From Q." The admission hangs there in the semidarkness. I fill the silence with stifled, hiccup-y sobs, and both Luisa and Bee reach for me. They wrap me up in their arms and Bee wipes my face with the corner of her T-shirt. "There was no note. There is no note." I realize that I am clutching the front of Bee's shirt. I loosen my grip.

Bee brings my hand to her face. "I'm sorry, babe. I am. I'm sorry. I love you so much."

"Maybe," Luisa says, retrieving the pile of photos from Bee's lap, "maybe he didn't have the words." She hands me my favorite of the series: me with my head thrown back, eyes squeezed shut, afro escaping from the band into which I'd tucked it that morning. Look at the photo long enough and you might hear my laughter. "Maybe," Luisa says cautiously, "this was his goodbye."

Months spent castigating myself for what I didn't see, for what went unheard. Only now do I inch toward the prospect that this was by design. He had his reasons, and they were his to have, and my entitlement to them is something I must, in time, relinquish if I am ever to get to a place where moving forward does not feel like wading through mud. Where existing is not this great effort. There is little I can do to accelerate the process. But there is something.

"I have to speak to Aspen," I say into the navy velvet of twilight. Bee squeezes me a little tighter. The three of us sit there watching the London outside of Q's studio grind to a halt.

We agree to meet at Quentin's studio, after two days are wasted on tense email correspondence, I writing to the offices of Henry Huntington and Henry, on behalf of Aspen, informing me that she is amenable ("amenable"—laughable, isn't it?) to meeting with me as long as she sets the terms. I refuse to meet her at her home, in a private dining room at Alain Ducasse at the Dorchester or at Henry's office. Unwilling to be a participant in her zero-sum game battle of wits. The studio, a place I remember seeing her in only once, at the grand opening, where she stood in the corner sipping a flute of the champagne she had provided herself (what I chose was too pedestrian) and arranging her face into a practiced grin when someone of note made their way over to air-kiss and compliment her on her choice of outfit and on her brilliant son, is as close to neutral ground as it gets. It is the place where Quentin died. The scene of our mutual ruin.

My family predictably hides their surprise and focuses instead on protecting me, all of them including Bee insisting they be present. Ma, whose reaction is to call on God and check me for signs of fever, is the most vocal.

"Chineke Onye kasị ẹbelè! Màkà gịni?" She *can't* understand why, after all this time, it is now when I should be resting and concentrating on my pregnancy, I have decided to entertain Aspen.

"I should be there, Eve," Gloria says. Her brow furrows. "I can bet she's bringing her lawyers. She won't show up alone."

"Glo, you don't have time," I remind her gently. "And you've done enough for me. Way too much. She'll be alone. It was one of my stipulations."

Gloria, on Zoom because her office is currently her second home, leans back in her desk chair. "You have stipulations?"

"Has to be somewhere neutral, has to be just the two of us, one hour long."

"Na wa."

"I pay attention, Glo. You taught me well."

"Eve—" Glo leans into the camera on her laptop "—if you need me, I will move the earth to be there, okay?"

I can't remember the last time Gloria looked at me with anything other than weary exasperation, can't pinpoint the last time she pulled me in for hug. This gesture is not insignificant. If nothing else, meeting Aspen may bring me a step closer to my sister and that alone is worth it.

"I know you will. I love you, but I have to do this alone. I think you all know that."

"If she tries anything, I'll kill her." She hangs up. I believe her.

We meet on a Tuesday. It is such a non-day. Surely something this momentous should be heralded with some portent be it good or bad. I search the sky for a rainbow or a meteor, but the blank London sky stares back at me, belying nothing. The chill of the previous evening thawed into a warmth that tickled the soles of my feet this morning when I hustled to the bathroom and rubbed the body butter into my stomach, a tight little ball nestling beneath my ribs. Last night I made sure to dispatch my family to their various abodes, understanding myself enough to know that finding any one of them here this morning would shatter my already weakening conviction that this was a path I could walk on my own. At the front door, sweat lines my hairline like nature's own headband. My pulse quickens, my mouth is arid. The navy skirt is now an ankle-length knit dress in fawn that doesn't quite cover my growing bump, the braids now an afro, but I am nineteen again and Aspen's disapproval has morphed into something more sinister, leagues more insistent.

She looks the same. Blond hair perhaps a taste lighter than her usual ash, a small collection of the tiniest new lines around her eyes no doubt scheduled to disappear at the end of a needle in due course, but she is indisputably Aspen. In a turtleneck almost the same color as my dress, soft enough, I am sure, that my fingers would disappear into its folds were I to touch it. Diamond earrings that do not look a million miles away from the ones she accused me of harboring glint in the dim light of the studio. She does not look like a woman who has spent months trying to run me down. When she flicks her eyes in my direction, I see delicately tinted eyelashes but no remorse. We sit at opposite ends of the walnut table, Quentin's sole indulgence outside of his equipment. The air-conditioning is cranked even though the sun is still laid up, slumming it for late spring, as if summer is not but a hop, skip and jump away. She lifts a glass of water to her lips, presses her hand delicately to her throat like it is *me* coming for *her* neck and not vice versa. She looks remarkably out of place here, but then, so do I. When I crossed the room to open the door for her, we stood, each of us, on either side of the glass, separated once more by something solid yet breakable, and the monster in my head once again became flesh.

"You're pregnant," she says. Her voice can still cut glass.

"You knew that."

"I did. It's just so…visible."

A hundred retorts leap to my mouth. I purse my lips and thank myself for choosing a dress long enough to disguise my shaking knees. "Aspen, what do you want?"

Her lipstick is the palest, softest pink. A lifetime of loss has not robbed her of beauty, only humanity. If she is taken aback by my forthrightness, she tucks it behind her ears along with her hair. "You know what I want. His ashes. Our family be-longings." Her eyes drift to where the table dissects me. She stops short of voicing the rest.

"You have his ashes. Some of them. I made sure of it. I gave you the ring. I don't have the rest of your stuff, and I think you know that. What do you want?"

"You believe a mother deserves to have only half her son when he has been taken from her?"

"I'm his wife."

"You were. I am his mother, and I always will be. Let us hope, Eve, you never gain a better understanding of what it feels like to have your only child stolen from you." Her eyes drift and settle again. Her threat sits on the table between us. A monolith.

Underneath the table, I grip the edge of my chair. Panic rolls in. I close my eyes knowing that when I open them again, she will still be there. She is not something I can wish away. A bad dream to be chased by daybreak. "Aspen," I try again, praying my dented confidence holds, "blaming me isn't going to change the fact that he's gone." My voice catches on the last word.

She slips a handkerchief from her sleeve. "When Quentin's father died, do you think I had the luxury of coming apart? Do you think it would have been acceptable for me to commission comic caskets or run off somewhere, or ignore his mother? I had a child to raise. And I did my job, but you didn't let me finish it. Quentin's life was to be something remarkable."

On the wall behind Aspen's head is a six-foot print of one of Q's photos. Taken during a wedding in Lagos, it depicts a child, swathed in lace and Ankara, her neck draped with traditional coral beads. She laughs into the lens as the festivities spill out of the hall behind her and into the street. He won second place at the International Photo Awards, in the professional event category for traditions and cultures.

"Why can't you just let yourself see that he *was* remarkable. He was becoming everything he was meant to be." I have spent years trying to figure out what about me was so terrible she refused to be happy for her son because he was happy with me.

"After Malcolm died, I promised Quentin I wouldn't let anything happen to him. I made him that promise, and you made a liar out of me." Aspen's voice cracks. "I will do better this time. This is my second chance. This child will have everything Quentin was robbed of."

Aspen's picture in the newspaper on the day of her husband's funeral comes back to me. Q at her side, his face a mask of anguish. She is right. I do not know how her trauma has shaped her life. I only know Q would not allow it to shape his.

"You don't even know me," I tell her. "You never tried."

"I don't need to know you. I know that because of you, he never came home. Not completely. And now he never can." Her breeding and stiff upper lip are powerless against the raw weight of despair. I will be, possibly forever, the target of this misdirection. But grief does not always find its mark. It veers off course, wounds unintentionally, makes victims of us all. I signaled the end of Quentin Morrow and the beginning of Q. Q, a man who was looked at a million times. I was one of the only ones who ever really saw him. I could tell Aspen that he was terrified of flying but still sat through dozens of flights, sweating his way to new destinations for projects she can still see in magazines and on gallery walls today. I could tell her how he picked out all the red Starburst and set them aside for me. How he never learned how to properly mop a floor and sometimes broke with his newfound frugality and petitioned for us to hire a cleaner. How he cried more than I did. How he was married to his photography and I'm pretty sure I was his mistress. I could tell her there were times his anger blazed out of nowhere but fizzled out just as quickly. I could tell her I am sorry she is hurting so deeply. I don't. Aspen hoped for a better and shorter rebellion than me. When she found that there was nothing about me to hate, not really, she hated me all the more. I can't compete with that.

When she looks at me, it is with naked loathing. To her, I represent all she has lost. After Malcolm, Quentin was to be her salvation, but he chose himself, and because she could not hate him, I became the next best thing. Every year we remained together, an indictment of her plans. Every celebration, a betrayal. It was not enough that he never fully left her; she would never be content until he left me. In the end he left us both. I do not have the strength to hate her back. Death is the source of her spite, or simply the catalyst. I understand the cruelty of circumstance. I have been bolstered by the unremitting love of my family, my friends. Aspen has not had that. I feel sorry for her. She will never change. In a few years, she and I will meet at carefully chosen locations and speak through my child. The worst thing has already happened. The baby kicks. Something like joy blooms through me.

"I wish he'd left you a note," I say to her, meaning it. "You deserved that. We both did. But you're never going to take my kid from me. This isn't your second chance. It's mine."

I meet her gaze head-on. In it, I see there will be more letters from Henry, more calls in the wee hours from hidden numbers. I am one of the last links to her son. Her acceptance of this has not come easily and will continue to wound her in her lowest moments. It is easier to hate me than to hate herself for the things she also did not see.

"We loved each other," I tell her because the words need to exist as spoken by me. We did. Imperfectly. As all humans love.

The hour ends abruptly. Aspen turns from me, hiding her real tears. Her driver draws up to the curb and she gathers her things and sweeps out before the torrent can begin, pausing only to tell me in a destroyed voice that she will tell the world who I am.

"You act like who I am is something to be ashamed of." I stand up. "You know things didn't have to be this way, Aspen. Quentin could have done more to make us get along. I guess keeping us apart made it easier to hide everything he was going through. But you missed it, too, Aspen. We both did."

When the door closes behind her, I see she has left my engagement ring sitting on the table. I reach for it and thread it onto my necklace to sit beside Q's wedding ring.

I am still at the table when Drew calls me some twenty minutes later.

"Drew?"

"Are you okay? Did she try anything?"

"How did you know? I didn't tell you about this."

"Luisa said you really only told family."

"I told Luisa."

"Luisa also said you would not consider me family. Hurry up and have this kid, Mary, so you can beat her up for me."

I laugh, the adrenaline escaping me in a series of giggles I can't control. Tears threaten, but for once, they don't flow. "I'm fine," I tell him, and it is not a lie. "I'm okay."

Outside, as I lock the door, Gloria steps from a black cab. She moved the earth after all.

"Welcome back," she says.

I shake my head. "Premature."

"Perhaps. But I don't think so. Shall we go home?"

She slips her arm through mine.

# EPILOGUE

The morning after my daughter was born, I held on to one of her toes and hyperventilated as quietly as I could manage. This, like the ice cube tray on the night of her father's death, is important because for days after her arrival (almost four weeks early, water breaking during the celebration of Bee's birthday in a Michelin-starred restaurant to which we can never return), I was terrified of my own child. She was so small. There were a million ways to break her. I wet her baby curls with my tears. She has her dad's eyes, and when she turned them on me, it was like she was giving me a tacit nudge. *Get your shit together, Ma, we're in this together.*

To Quinn—that is her name—I am a soothing voice, a pair of lips against her temple. I am a heartbeat, a pair of wide, permanently moist eyes and a bush of uncombed hair. I am also her world. A lot of responsibility. But one I will savor before she grows up and I stop being the sun and just become her mother. Her middle name is Adanne, Igbo for "her mother's daughter." She is the two of us. I am cradling her in my lap, feet perched on the pouf Henrietta arranged to be brought into Room 111 when I told her of my impending return with a new companion, drinking in the tiny dimple Quentin left her, when Nate's head appears around the door.

"She asleep?" He steps into the room, sinks a hand into my hair.

"Trying to fight it."

"Luisa just checked in. I'm giving her and Bee half an hour of alone time, then we should get a move on."

One of the greatest and most surprising occurrences of the last few months has been watching my best friend and my new friend first befriend then fall for each other. Talking Bee down from the panic attack when she registered that the nights spent talking to Luisa had moved past their mutual need to care for me and were more about their inability to go too many hours without contact. Love reveals you, I should know, and loving Bee has softened Luisa's edges.

"Who knew," Bee said to me a month before Quinn was born, when she had practically moved in with me, which meant Luisa had also practically moved in with me, "that all I had to do was stop dating men to find something real?"

"Here," Nate says now, "give me Bug." He calls Quinn "Bug." Short for Ladybug. Every time he says it, my heart somersaults in my chest. His niece, at five months, is comfortable against his shoulder. He kisses her cheek and I melt a little inside. I marvel at how they have taken to each other.

It seemed right, fitting, to bring Quentin here for a last time. This island is where we lost ourselves in each other. It is where some of the most important decisions of my life have been made. He had no unhappy memories here. All he knew while he walked these shores and gazed at this same watercolor sky was love. A kind of impenetrable joy that made us, at least temporarily, invincible. He doesn't belong in white ceramic on his limestone mantelpiece. He doesn't need sad eyes resting on him, sometimes darting away with discomfort. He deserves to move with the sea breeze, to drift across oceans and sweep across the sand. He deserves the freedom he tasted and fought for so fervently when he was alive. I made the arrangements—Quinn's still too little for a flight, so we went the long way round—London to Liverpool to Heysham and then a four-hour ferry ride to the Isle of Man, split into manageable chunks with Nate and Bee by my side. Gloria, Alex and the kids arrived a day after we did. Jackson arrived a day later. On the day Drew flew in, he, Jack, Nate, Bee and I went to Port Jack Chippy. Drew looking absurdly adorable with Quinn strapped to his chest. We ate and spoke about Q. I apologized to Quinn because her father will come to her only through a series of stories and the photos he and others took. I nuzzled her baby cheeks. I sent a note to Aspen, asking if despite everything she wanted to be here today. Days passed with no response and then a professionally wrapped gift box arrived. Inside, the engraved rattle I was accused of taking. She declined to attend but wrote in her sweeping hand that she would be grateful for the opportunity to meet her grand-child whenever I return to London. She chose not to scatter her part of Q. She will keep him close forever.

Our group walks across the beach. The sun spears the clouds. Any words I have for Q have been said a thousand times already, so I recite the quote meant for his funeral ser-vice, when my tears did the talking instead. The quote is by Washington Irving. It goes:

*"There is a sacredness in tears. They are not the mark of weak-ness, but of power. They speak more eloquently than ten thousand tongues. They are the messengers of overwhelming grief, of deep con-trition, and of unspeakable love."*

I give Quentin to the wind, then I take our daughter home.

★ ★ ★ ★ ★

# DISCUSSION GUIDE

1. Eve and Quentin meet at ages nineteen and twenty. Do you think their age and lack of romantic experience has any bearing on their relationship dynamic? If so, in what ways?

2. The story begins after Quentin's death. Does knowing he is already gone and that he committed suicide shape the reading experience or color your perception of him in any way?

3. What significance, if any, do you believe Quentin's upbringing and background have on his relationship with Eve and her family, and his inability to voice his struggles?

4. How do you interpret the various manifestations of Eve's grief? When, if at all, do you feel the healing process begins for her?

5. Eve is from a Nigerian (Igbo) background. How do you think her culture influences how she and her family deal with Quentin's death and the grieving process?

6. Eve and Aspen have always had a contentious relationship. How do you feel Quentin's death impacted this? What do you think about the way Aspen and Eve behave in the aftermath?

7. Although Eve and Quentin were unsure about children, Eve learns she is pregnant quite by accident but ultimately decides to keep her baby. What do you think led to this decision? Do you think the same decision would have been made if Quentin was alive?

8. Eve becomes fixated on *She*. Why, out of all of Quentin's work, do you think this particular photograph resonates with her?

9. Despite her promise to Nate, Eve is unable to attend the support group and chooses a life drawing class instead. Why do you think she is so averse to joining the group or seeking out a therapist? Why does art appeal to Eve? Why does she choose to stay in the class?

10. What were your thoughts when it was revealed that Eve had given Aspen half of Quentin's ashes? Why do you think Aspen tried to get Eve to give her more—the ring, the rattle, possibly rights to the baby, etc.?

11. Why do you think Aspen did not acknowledge the happiness and creative achievements Quentin had in his life?

12. Eve meets Luisa and Drew during the life drawing class. What role do they play in Eve's post-Quentin life?

13. Eve and Gloria have always been close. Why do you think Gloria becomes so angry with Eve?

# ACKNOWLEDGMENTS

The ultimate thanks goes to God, who saw fit to bless both my pen and my path.

To my parents, who nurtured what they saw as a gift, thank you for speaking life into me, and affirming me from the very day I learned to hold a pencil (and then a scarf) and weave worlds from words.

To my siblings, Ngozi and Chuks, whose bafflement turned to gentle pressure and a soft yet straight spoken instruction to run after my dreams. Thank you for leading by example and letting me be the indulged baby sister for as long as you did.

To my sister-in-law, Charlene. Your enthusiasm surpasses mine and never ceases to lift me up. Thank you.

To my nephew, Elijah. Baby boy, you are part of the reason I tried so hard. You are worth it.

To Mrs. McHugh and Mrs. Robertson, the English teachers who took a painfully shy Jheri-curled girl and told her it was more than okay to find happiness on pages. I'm indebted to you.

To J. There aren't adequate words. This book exists because of you. Thank you.

To Farah, for cheerleading, pushing, shouting praise and

letting me doubt myself before sweeping the same doubt away. Thank you. Your encouragement lives forever in my heart.

To Satia, Jade and Isaac, who placed their feet on my neck. Thank you for dragging me to the finish line. Thank you for being so excited for me even as I was paralyzed with uncertainty and then shock.

To Troy, Eden, Aimee, Nanna, Nad, Alex, Teju, Amanda, Jon, Toyin, Precious, Eniola, Hani, Richie and all my friends who read, made suggestions, shouted louder than my fears and let me fall apart. I couldn't have done this without you.

To my legend of an agent, Amy. Thank you for believing in me and in Eve, and taking a chance on us. Thank you for holding my hand through every freak-out.

To Cat and Juliet, my editors. Thank you for seeing something in this story and for everything you have done to make sure it is the best it could be.

To everyone at Graydon House and Oneworld. These words would not be read without you. Thank you.

To every reader this work touches, thank you.

# AUTHOR NOTE

If you have been affected by the subject matter of this novel, or if you are struggling with suicidal ideation, please contact the following organizations:

**USA**

**National Suicide Prevention Lifeline:** available 24/7, 365 days a year. Dial 988 or 1-800-273-8255

**UK**

**Samaritans:** available 24/7, 365 days a year. Phone 116 123 (free from any phone)

**National Suicide Prevention Helpline UK:** available 24/7, 365 days a year. Phone 0800 689 5652

**You are important.**